THE LAST SWORD

The Ninth Century Book V

M J Porter

M J Publishing

CONTENTS

Title Page

Copyright

Map

Prologue   1

Chapter 1   9

Chapter 2   21

Chapter 3   28

Chapter 4   35

Chapter 5   45

Chapter 6   61

Chapter 7   70

Chapter 8   90

Chapter 9   106

Chapter 10   115

Chapter 11   129

Chapter 12   145

Chapter 13   156

Chapter 14   163

Chapter 15   172

Chapter 16   182

Chapter 17   191

Chapter 18   202
Chapter 19   210
Chapter 20   233
Chapter 21   242
Chapter 22   256
Chapter 23   265
Chapter 24   273
Chapter 25   280
Cast of Characters   285
Meet the author   290

MAP

PROLOGUE

B efore me, Icel is forced down on one knee, overextending his right arm, almost losing his balance on the slick surface. With him grounded, Jarl Halfdan darts forward over the grey and white ground ferociously stabbing downwards. I expect Icel to counter the attack with his bloodied seax or his sword. But he must carry a wound that bleeds copiously, draining strength from him. His movements are too slow, and Halfdan lifts a bloodied blade, a smile of pleasure on his ugly face at such an easy ending, the scar that mars his face showing between the hints of growing daylight and dancing flame.

"Don't you fucking dare," I bellow, my voice so loud it resounds like thunder, distracting Halfdan from the final cut, as intended, despite the battle that rages all around us.

With that respite, brief as it is, Icel has the time to recover himself, staggering upwards, while Halfdan faces me, a look of displeasure on his broad face. I can see his tactic now.

He means to deprive me of my warriors, one by one, isolating me, making me weak. It's good he started with Icel, a man who will never die easily.

Only, it seems he didn't.

Inserting myself between Icel and Halfdan, I realise that another warrior is sprawled on the snow drenched floor, the back of his head far too familiar to me. He better fucking live; that's all I have the time to think before Halfdan surges against me.

I thought him too craven to face me one to one once more. But that's not the case.

Halfdan's movements are supple and fluid, and he advances with the ease of a much younger man, but one assured of success.

He carries a seax and a war axe, although there's a sword available to him as well, the handle visible above his black helm, held tightly to his back. I thought my last kill had the eyes of death. Halfdan has the eyes of a confident warrior, knowing, watchful, eager. They promise death, and that's an entirely different proposition.

Hereman and Sæbald have helped Icel to either side, but he's not happy about it, even as he holds his hands against a weeping wound to the left of his body; the red-hue a dark stain that won't stop growing.

"He's mine, My Lord. He's fucking mine," he rants. It's not like Icel to be so bloody stubborn. He, of all my men, is more than aware when he's beaten.

Halfdan and I both menace with our seaxs. I feel the double eagle-head against the hardness of my gloves. His seax, I note, carries the emblem of the wolf, cold blue eyes peering from the handle, the disdain hard to ignore even from an immobile object.

And then we spring at one another, his seax goes high, mine low. Yet we both move aside, avoiding the cuts. For now.

I follow up with a similar swipe low with my weapon, and this time he goes low as well. Our seaxs clash, shimmering sunlight striking at just the right moment to make it appear as though sparks fly. I smell his rancid sweat, as close as we are, and I feel his strength. It matches mine. For now.

Face to face, I trace the line of his jaw, just visible beneath a yellow beard festooned with trinkets; so many of them they clack together as his head shudders with the effort of keeping me at bay. His scar is still there. It offers its own story.

In my other hand, I hold my war axe, and I'd like nothing more than to swing it at his head, but all of my strength centres on my seax. Whoever gives first will be the weaker of us. It's not going to be fucking me.

He's muttering to himself, his words unintelligible, either a chant or a similar refrain. Perhaps he calls on something otherworldly to beat me. I wouldn't be surprised. I trust in my skill, my strength, my ability, and if that's ever failed me, which it hasn't, I know my warriors will step in. They rescued me when I was outside Northampton. They saved me from the woodlands. They will always rescue me. I doubt Jarl Halfdan has the same assurance from his baying warriors.

The fighting all around us has ground to a stop, an uneasy truce. After all, why would men risk their lives when there might be no need to in but a few moments?

I eye his sword peering at me from over his shoulder. The leering wolf face, picked out in heavy silver, earns a grin from my straining face. I could take it right now. I could kill the fucker with that blade, end his life with the same item that has saved him on too many previous occasions.

I feel his stance start to falter, the tension on his face causing spittle to fly with his chanting, and I hold, press that little bit harder, aware I've not given everything, not yet.

And Halfdan breaks aside, panting heavily, his eyes showing fury as he skips backwards. I don't give him the time he needs to recover. He wouldn't offer me the same.

I launch myself at him, only realising by the flash of relief on his face that this is what he wants me to do. My war axe swings wide, and I thrust it to clash against his right side. His black leather byrnie holds, for now, but he loses balance. Halfdan might think to play with me, pretending to weakness when he's strong, but a particular blow will always show the truth of the matter.

Now that I've considered his enticing sword, I want it. I need to feel the weight in my hand and delight in slicing through his chest with it, or across his throat, or preferably, right through the fucker's skull, watching his bright eyes turn dull with the finality of it all.

His seax stabs out at me, and I force it aside with my war axe, swiping it across my body to do so. At the same time, I slash with my seax, first blood welling on part of his chin where his beard is shorn away by the stroke. A yelp of outrage disturbs his continual invocation, and again, he jumps away from me, feet light, even if he's using up all of his resources to stay alive.

Icel rants from behind me, his rumbles showing anger, rage, fury and impotence all at the same time.

"Take him, take him now, kill the fucker, use your seax, across his neck, don't just give the bastard a shave," and I roll my eyes at the instructions. Icel. Always so fucking helpful in such situations.

"Shut the fuck up," Edmund menaces, his words flecked with fury, but actually, Icel is doing some of the work for me, even while he struggles to catch his breath and regain his equilibrium. I can tell that Halfdan expects me to carry out Icel's instructions. It's evident in the way he moves to protect his neck, chin down. Better to lose his trinkets and beard than risk his neck. So, all I need to do is the opposite.

Icel, a canny bastard, even when he is being a bastard.

"His belly, slice open his belly." So I aim for Halfdan's seax arm, again, a welter of blood showing where he thinks to wear no protection but his wolf tattoos. I blind the beast—one less set of eyes to judge me silently.

"His thigh, stab into it." So I stab upwards, aiming for the area below his armpit, a notorious weakness that not even the toughest byrnie can protect. I miss it, but a flicker of consternation passes Halfdan's face. Will he be warier now?

"His neck," Icel screams; there's no other word for it.

"Shut the fuck up," Edmund bellows in response. The two will come to blows if I don't hurry up.

I slash down with my seax, cutting through the thick leather that protects my foe's calves, leaving part of it flapping free as he dances from my attack.

The Raiders are sullen in the encouragement of their jarl. Again, the words rumble from them, perhaps a battle chant, and I appreciate that they're creating a rhythm to guide Halfdan's blows.

He aims for my face, no doubt keen to repay the assault on his chin. I veer from the attack, offering my elbow as payment.

Halfdan's face is increasingly pinker, finally warming up after days of cold temperatures. His body is growing more limber, his actions more fluid. Yet, blood drips from his chin, landing on the churned snow, our passage back and forth, side to side, spreading it far and wide.

It looks as though I've slaughtered a pig and not just given someone an overly close shave.

"Take his right hand," Icel instructs, the fury still in his voice at being withheld from the attack, but I appreciate the lessening of tension. He knows exactly what's happening. Did he plan it, or have I taken it that he did, and now both of us will claim it as our victory?

Will this become one of Icel's oft recounted tales.

"In the reign of King Coelwulf?"

I slash at Halfdan's left leg, opening up a lesion above his knee. The blow doesn't quite strike true, or he'd be fighting with a broken knee.

Fuck.

While I'm low, his war axe passes over my head, a soft ding showing his aim was almost true, although my helm stays firm. I need to be careful. He might be growing weaker, but Halfdan is also starting to read the attack better.

I rush into him, war axe angled at his chest, his eyes reflecting rage, his chest rising and falling. He attempts to evade the action but tangles his legs before slipping in the growing mass of splattered blood decorating the ground. He bleeds from two places now. Neither a mortal wound, but I'm just fucking beginning.

And then his seax slicks into my lower arm, just above where I hold my war axe, and a hot spike surges up my arm. Now, he's drawn blood as well, although he doesn't know that because my glove absorbs the tell-tale sign. I don't react, even though a lesser man might.

But, Halfdan does sense something all the same because he comes at me, seax flashing, war axe looming, a flurry of strikes against me, although not one of them makes it beyond the guard of my seax and war axe.

Damn the fucker. He has the upper hand. For now.

I dodge and slash, turning, swirling, ducking low, rearing back, mindful of my steps on the slick ground, aware that Icel continues to holler but that I can't hear his words, not while my ears rush with the thrill of trying to evade my enemy. I've dreamt of killing Halfdan since the summer. This is my chance. I'm not going to fuck it up.

Seax arm up, war axe arm low, I keep up with his speeding attack. Then I get lucky, another slick on his chin, and more of the trinkets from his blond beard tumble to the ground, crushed beneath my advance. He bleeds more, this cut deeper, revealing the promise of bone beneath the flap of pale skin. I sense his fury and frustration, but most of all, his pain.

He can't hide it. Not as I am.

I follow up with a mighty blow against his right side with the war axe, but it only skitters over his byrnie. I'm forced to tense my arm to bring the action back under control.

Halfdan senses an opening, and he thrusts his war axe against my seax arm, and it hits home, my hand fleeing open because he's managed to hit, somehow, that part of my arm that tingles and brings about the uncontrollable response. My seax thumps to the floor, ringing too loudly of failure. I finally hear Icel's words, as opposed to just his noise.

"Shoulder, back, shoulder, neck," Icel's not the only one to be shouting. I detect Rudolf's higher tones, and I slash downwards, aiming for ankle and foot. Only Halfdan is too fast, and he jumps clear, turning the movement into an advance, his seax running down my bent back, even though it doesn't pierce the leather.

Instead of rushing to stand upright, I swing my war axe again, eyes focused on where my seax has surely tumbled into the churned and reddened snow. But I don't see it, although my axe digs into Halfdan's flesh once more. It's only a glancing blow. I'm starting to think he wears some sort of protective equipment designed to evade all but the most direct of blows.

When I stand upright, his seax is almost on my nose, and

he's standing too close as well. I'm thankful for my helm, then. I twist my neck, bring up my seaxless hand, and bang his seax aside with just my glove. The weapon cuts deeper this time, forcing the earlier cut deeper and wider, but the blood remains hidden.

"Bastard," I offer. Halfdan has two weapons, and I only have one.

"Hold," Icel calls. I take his advice, rushing Halfdan, war axe swirling, fist punching, landing on his chin wound so that my hand comes away bloodied this time, but at least it covers where he's drawn blood.

He howls, eyes glazed with pain, and I continue. Slashing, punching, threatening to head butt, and Halfdan steps back, once, twice, and then more and more, so that his warriors are forced to part ways as he all but runs away. Halfdan's almost back inside the ruin of the steading he sheltered within.

The chanting of his warriors intensifies, and while I think I've done a good job of revealing his weaknesses, he's suddenly running at me, weapons just on the verge of under his control. Slashing, hacking, and now I'm the one moving back to avoid the frenzy.

And my foot catches on something in the ground. I think it might be my damn seax. My arms spiralling, the air leaves my body. I'm down on the floor, the wet snow and warm blood seeping into my clothes, as my chin bounces on my chest, and for a frantic moment, I can see two of everything. Two of Halfdan, two of his seaxs, two of his war axes, and four of his arms.

I hear a collective gasp from my warriors, well, all apart from Icel.

"Get up, get up," he rails, and I think he's crazy this time, but I stay low, listening to Halfdan's cackle, his mouth wide open, his gaping wound a mockery of the same smile. He menaces me with wavering seaxs and war axes. He thinks his actions keep me on the ground, but they don't. I've seen what tripped me, and it was my damn seax, for two of them waver before me.

I reach for them both, eyes on Halfdan, not my blades, and

I crush it in my hand, unheeding that it's landed upside down, and blood pools between my fingers once more. The discomfort brings the moment back into sharp focus. Once more, I see only one of everything.

Halfdan aims a swipe at my head. I duck even lower, scurrying forwards in the snow so that I rear up behind him, fully armed once more, despite the injuries I now carry.

I bend my knees, mindful of the ache of cold and age, only to jump high, reach for the sword in its baldric with my seax hand. Just as my fingers brush the air above it, he turns, wrathful. The sword is loose, though. It tumbles to the floor, out of my reach, and more importantly, out of his.

His war axe looms at me, coming for my throat, my chest, my belly, each swipe just about missing me as I dodge, back and down, and then up and forward, trying to insert my war axe between his and mine. I release it in the air, catch it lower down the broad wooden handle, thrusting the bottom of the war axe into his bleeding face, his shorn beard and bloodied chin.

Halfdan's eyes blank, just for a moment. It's all I need. I'm rushing around him, eyes keen for the prize of his sword, half-buried in the snow. But before I can get my seax hand to it, I feel the unmissable ache of cold iron at my throat, and I still, hand extended, war axe facing down.

The bite of the iron comes ever closer, the reminder of my last injury making it difficult to swallow or breathe or consider moving.

Fuck, the bastard has me. He'll kill me, here and now, even though I'm fully armed, and his sword is almost within reach.

Silence reverberates, not even Icel offering his advice. I close my eyes, picture my stern Aunt's look of horror, the glimmer of anger on Edmund's face, and the dismay that Pybba will wear.

This is it.

I thought to die before, protecting my warriors, protecting Mercia. But now it seems Jarl Halfdan is to have the last bastard word after all.

CHAPTER 1

Two weeks earlier

I grit my teeth, try not to glare at the shit storm taking place in front of me.

I wish I could dance and generally make a complete arse of myself like the rest of my men. But I can't. Not now. And it's beginning to feel as though I might never again.

"Leave it alone." A sharp slap on my hand forces my fingers away from the hot and itching wound that almost decapitated me.

"It," and I pause, silently say the word that should come next, instead. "Itches," I finish. My Aunt turns her steel eyes toward me. She's dressed as every inch the aunt of the king. Her clothing is immaculate, her nails clean, her hair neatly braided and held beneath a small wimple that speaks of practicality, not wealth in its simplicity.

"I precisely know what it does and doesn't do. I also know what you can and can't do. Now, leave it alone, or it'll become infected, and then they might as well have taken your head off and had done with it, there and then. Much better than listening to all this continual complaining." Although a faint smile touches her lips as she watches the rest of my men, her voice is sour. I don't miss that her eyes linger on Edmund's back.

I should be with them. But I'm not. No, she's made me sit at a table, as though I'm a lord or some such, and all I can do is watch. It's not the way I usually celebrate the feast of Christ's birth. I might not drink, but I would usually be in the heart of the conversation, tears rolling down my face at whatever antics Edmund or Hereman were performing because they'd taken their fill. But not today.

I don't know what fucking irritates me more; the damn hot skin that rims my neck or just how ineffectual I feel.

I've been weak as a mewling child, more unsteady on my feet than a newborn foal, and angrier than a boar in flight. I don't know, from one day to another, and sometimes, from one meal to the next, how I'm going to feel or what I'm going to feel. The pain has rumbled on, occasionally agony, but generally just infuriating, every movement, no matter how small, setting off yet another avalanche of strange sensations prickling over my body.

"Here, drink this," and she offers me her beaker. I sniff it unhappily as I palm it into my hand.

"It's fresh, cold water, nothing else," her nose high in the air, pretending to offence. I know her better than that.

I eagerly swill it, all the same, the sharp bite of water that's no doubt been cracked clear from the water barrels, restoring the alertness of my senses that I've been missing.

"Better?" she demands to know, deigning to speak to me, although I've offended her. To the far side of her sits one of the monks from Gloucester. I don't know why we need such a figure here in Northampton, but my Aunt insisted on having the man dragged here for the Yule feast. His facial expression fluctuates between horror and understanding, revulsion and a fierce desire to be involved, as he watches the Mercians and my warriors cavorting around the hall.

We've eaten well, and now they drink too well. I can do nothing but watch and feel excluded. I never believed myself capable of such pettiness.

From outside, there's no sound. None at all. Well, not that I can bloody hear. A thousand men could assault the walls of Northampton, but I'd not hear. No. Outside it snows, the white stuff coating the landscape, muffling all sound, obscuring all but the largest objects. If I were known for having deep thoughts, I'd almost think it held the promise of a fresh start. But I know fucking better. When the thaw comes, and the water pools in any and every crevice, pit and puddle, the mud coming slick off my boots, threatening to topple me at any moment, I know it'll just be the same old shit, just that much more unpleasant, stinking of damp and cold and, well, shit.

"Grrr," I growl low in my throat. I feel enclosed. I feel hobbled. I feel as frustrated as Haden in the stables. It's a fucking Yule-time miracle that I can't hear him kicking the wooden walls from here.

I want to be gone from here, and it's more than just the snow, lying as tall as a small child's waist, that keeps me trapped.

"You must calm yourself," my Aunt offers, but it's half-hearted. She might be able to prevent me from scratching and pulling at my neck wound when she sits beside me, but she can't tell me what to do or how to do it.

Furious, I push myself up from the table, determined to do something. Anything.

"Bring me my cloak," I demand from Hiltiberht, who's scrambled to my side, his eyes never far from ensuring I have all I need. I wish Rudolf had been this bloody attentive when he was my squire. But then, Rudolf had other skills.

"My Lord," a quick bow and he's already back, as I weave an unsteady path between the detritus of the feast, ensuring I don't tumble over discarded stools or slip in the slime of spilt ale. My aunt sips her wine. I can feel her gaze at my back, but wisely, her tongue is still.

I could almost weep for that small piece of understanding.

"Here you go," and Hiltiberht offers the warm cloak. The fur collar, I know already, will bedevil me, but at least outside, I'll be cool, if not downright frozen. My neck will stop itching so that I can think clearly for longer than a heartbeat.

"Shall I come with you?" he asks, voice both hopeful and filled with resentment at being pulled away from the feast. I wish I had the skill to be so expressive with just five words.

I force a smile, aware it almost cuts me deeper than a knife.

"No, stay here. I'm just going to check on Haden."

"I can do that," he offers brightly, perhaps trying to be helpful.

"No, no, stay here, enjoy the singing and dancing. The scop is yet to perform." I see the excitement in his body then. He's desperate to hear the scop, as is Rudolf and the other youngsters. I don't even know where Edmund managed to procure the man's services.

Tatberht eyes me from his post at the door. He asked for it. No, he demanded it. It seems he didn't want to get involved in the reckless behaviour either.

"Damn fools," he spits, forcing the door open, mindful of any snow that might tumble from above his head with the movement. We need to be careful not to get snowed inside the hall.

"You sure you're alright to go alone," Tatberht checks, perhaps one of the few who'll question me. I nod, immediately regretting the action as yet another shard of pain shudders from my neck wound.

"I know, I know. You just need some air. Watch where you go. It's deep in places you might not expect," he continues. Again, I'm fucking thankful that he doesn't say anything further.

"Thank you. You should have a drink."

"I should, but I ain't going to. Too old for my head to ache for days afterwards." He grins with the words to take the sting from them.

Outside, the snow reflects brightly under the crisp, clear sky. There'll be no more snow tonight, I notice, to my surprise. It's been snowing all bastard day. But, it'll be cold, the stars winking overhead as though priceless gems, worth more than I could ever imagine, and I'm the damn king. I shiver into my cloak, forcing it tightly around my body, wishing it wasn't necessary, but appreciating that if I don't control my ill-humour, there might well be blood shed this night.

I don't fucking want that.

There are a few braziers, bravely battling against the wind

that seems to cut with a knife, but it's the moon and the snow that makes it possible for me to see my way to the stables. A wry smirk touches my cheeks, which have grown too used to looking glum in recent weeks. I can hear that brute, even from here. His hooves sporadically kick against the stable door. He wants out. I want out. Fuck it, we probably all want out.

A semblance of a path has been forced through the thick snow to allow easy passage from one place to another. I eye it warily, noting the shimmer of water that speaks of icy patches, and press on, not towards the stables, but rather towards the rear of Northampton. I have a mind to climb the ramparts, look out over all I can survey, assure myself that the entire landscape is covered in snow, and not just Northampton itself. This weather isn't a punishment, even if it feels like fucking one.

The cold tugs at my throat, and I wrap my cloak around it ever tighter, even if it now risks overheating. Stepping carefully, the sound of good cheer dogging my unsteady shuffle, I make it to the stairs that lead to the rampart. There's a light up there, just one, the flames beckoning me, even as I eye the steps warily. I don't need to slip and injure myself further. I don't need to fall, knock myself backwards, jolt my barely healed wound, and be forced to start all over again.

But fuck it, I need to see more than just the interior of Northampton. The craving burns my skin, even as I shiver against the cold.

"Hail," I try and call, hoping to garner some advice from the men on guard duty. But my voice is thin and reedy, speaking of frailty and broken promises.

Fuck it. With one hand on the wall, brushing the icy surface, I place my first foot on the step. I pause then. Expecting some sort of outcry, but there's nothing. A tight smile touches my cold face. I anticipated the voice of my Aunt, recalling me to the reality of my situation, but she's in the hall. She's warm and amused and no doubt listening to the scop. Although, perhaps not yet. I can still just about hear Hereman's bellow as he laughs and jokes.

They'll all make damn fools of themselves tonight. But, while they're doing that, they can't watch what I'm about to attempt.

My left foot lifts from the ground, and then I'm committed. I either go back to the floor or continue upwards. I know what I should be doing, but bollocks to that. I need to see.

With shaking knees, cursing my enforced weakness, I gingerly make my way upwards. They're slippery, I can't deny that, but they've been cleared of snow. Care's been taken to ensure that they're not as slick as they could be. It's a job with no great sense of accomplishment. No sooner have they been made passable than the snow falls once more.

My breath is harsh in my ears, a great pluming cloud before me, temporarily blinding me. The men on watch duty will see my expelled breath first, and then only me, emerging from behind it.

And then my left foot slips, completely missing the next step, and I reach towards the expanse of uneven wall with both hands. If I fall now, it'll surely be to my death. I've no idea what lies beneath me, but I doubt it's enough snow to cushion a fall from such a height.

Not that the vertical surface is much help. My left leg wavers, my right forced to take all of my weight. My heart hammers in my chest, my legs weak. Fuck.

"Who's that?" The words are fraught with terror, but I'm scrambling to maintain my balance, desperate not to be found in a heap at the bottom of the steps.

"Here, you daft bastard," and I feel hands on my arse from behind me.

"What you doing coming up here?" There's outrage in the words, but they stabilise me, just as much as the hands, and then I'm heaving air into my chest, unaware I've even been holding it.

"It's the bloody king," this comes from above me. I stare into perplexed eyes and a wrinkled forehead.

"I must see beyond the fortifications," I state, trying to infuse my voice with some sort of menace, but it's impossible. I've scared myself, and now my legs feel weak, my voice even frailer than when I started.

"Well, it's a bloody good job that Beornfyhrt was there to catch you," is the slightly mollified response.

"There's a knack to it. See, you have to place your feet close to the wall. That's the part that's easiest to keep clear of the snow and ice. Now, come on, up you come. You can't bloody go back down, not in the state you're in."

With Heahstan before me and Beornfyhrt behind me, I stagger up the remaining half of the steps. I feel sick, the cold cloying at my skin, even while it burns. Each step upwards, I expect to feel once more my traitorous foot slip.

"Closer to the wall," Heahstan urges me, every second step, and I shuffle to do his bidding, aware that behind me, Beornfyhrt has removed his hands from my back but no doubt waits to offer his support once more.

I pity the fuckers, stuck out here while everyone else is ripe with ale and good food.

"There you go, safely does it, at last," Heahstan states, moving into the light from the brazier so that I can finally see the strain on his face. There are two pink spots on his white cheeks, no doubt caused by my actions, and I bow my head to them both.

"My thanks."

"Well, don't thank us yet. You've got to get the fuck down later. It's a bastard. I can assure you," Beornfyhrt, his hood covering all but his nose, speaks as though from beyond the grave. There's no understanding to be found in his words. But why should there be? No doubt, he'd be content if he was confined to the hall, as I was.

"Well, there's your view," Heahstan sounds more conciliatory, as he indicates the vast area beyond the fortifications.

"My thanks, again." I feel more in control, more assured of myself now that I'm so close to achieving my intention.

"Just thank us by watching where you're fucking going, and let us know before you attempt to leave. We'll help you."

A brief wash of heat touches my clammy skin from the brazier that keeps the guard men on duty warm, and I consider huddling beside it. But no, I didn't come here to feel warm.

Then, I step toward the wall, the view over the fortifications slowly coming into focus—the crisp whiteness of the landscape flickering beneath the bright moon, massive in the sky. The bite of cold is more severe. I welcome it as it dries my frightened sweat, my heart slowing in my chest.

Beyond the walls of Northampton, the landscape stretches far into the distance, untouched by any but the occasional hooting owl and the pitter-patter of animals about their business. They should be in their dens, shielding from the snow.

Certainly, there's nothing to show what happened here so recently. Yes, the remains of the Raider camp can be determined as a jagged assortment of lumps and bumps beneath the white, easier to decipher from the shadows than the snow, but there's nothing to speak of the men I ordered slaughtered, by spear or by arrow, when I first recovered.

I didn't come to the rampart for forgiveness. I don't seek some God-given right to have killed my enemy. No, I came here to check, to see with my eyes that the fuckers haven't thought to return using the snowstorm to cover their actions.

The view comforts me, even as it worries me. If they're not here, those that still lived, then where the fuck are they? Are they, as I hope, nursing their wounds in Grantabridge? Are they, as I suspect, perhaps considering a return to their northern kingdoms. I fucking hope so. But I know I won't get my wish. I never do.

A sudden shudder runs through me, and I shelter deep inside my cloak once more, the sheen of sweat gone, the wound at my neck pulsing, as though it has a life of its own.

That's why I came here.

I feel weak. I feel useless. I feel fucking lucky to be alive, and I've never lived by luck. Did my skill desert me in the woodlands? Did I nearly die because I put the life of one of my warriors before mine? Did I care more for him than for Mercia?

These thoughts have plagued me, even while my Aunt has nursed me, an accepting look on her face. It seems she knows me better than I know myself.

So lost in my ruminations, I startle when a gust of air close to me informs me that I'm no longer alone.

"It makes you contemplate your life like you never have before," Pybba speaks softly, his words a counterpart to my thoughts. Is this what this is about? Am I contemplating my mortality when I never have before?

"Some fuckers have no understanding of what it's like to see your life flash before your eyes." I hold my tongue, keep my eyes firmly forward. I'll not give him the satisfaction of watching me wince at the harsh rebuttal of the way I treated him. He bloody needed it. I won't apologise for that. He thought to curl into a ball and die just because a Raider took his hand.

"The wounds we carry mark us just as much as every life we take to protect Mercia. We never lose them. They're just more obvious reminders of the burdens we carry." Pybba speaks with his years of wisdom, and I should probably thank him for following me from the hall and up to the blast of cold air that shudders over the parapet. But I'm not feeling thankful for his words. They're harsh. And they fucking hurt.

I believed myself impervious to blades and axes. But I wasn't. And I nearly died for an arrogance I would never have claimed to own. Is that how Pybba felt when he lost his hand? I don't want to ask.

"All we do, is vow to take the life of the warrior that did this to us." Fuck, I startle. I've certainly not heard Edmund arrive. His voice is bitter with resolve. I always thought he coped well with the loss of his eye. But I never asked. I just assumed. "Add another to the list of those who've fallen beneath our blade. They take our blood and some part of us, but never all of us. We can't be broken. Not like fucking that."

I feel Edmund step to the right of me, Pybba already to the left. What a sight we must make. Pybba, missing his right hand, Edmund, missing his left eye, and me, with my neck slit as though I could have been decapitated with just a bit more effort; if the blade had just been a little bit wider.

"For every fucking ache and night of pain, I vow to kill

another of the bastards," Hereman's heavier tread beside his brother's, is somehow, only to be expected. The wounds he gained were multiple and painful. They've taken a long time to heal. All I need now is for Icel to join us.

"In the reign of King Wiglaf," Icel's rumble begins, and I groan, I can't help it. I peer along my row of warriors, noting the gloomy expressions on them all, the spark of amusement in Rudolf's bright eyes.

"When did you fucking get here?" I ask, cutting off Icel, not that he seems to notice.

"I took a wound that festered and took half a year to heal, here, on my belly," and Icel points to where he must have been injured. "I see that scar every time I remove my tunic. It reminds me of why I do this. Of why we do this." His tone brokers no argument, and still Rudolf smirks, a glint in his eyes, the moon catching the brightness as though a summer's day.

I nod at him, aware my cheeks begin to tug in amusement. I feel like I've not smiled for days, too caught up in my misery. I really should have been less self-centred.

"Why aren't you listening to the fucking scop?" I demand to know. None of my warriors turns to me with surprise. They know to whom my question is directed.

"Boring old fart, drawling in his ale. Anyway, he won't share his new 'finest work' until the Lord King is there to listen to the tale being woven for him, and even Lady Cyneswith refuses to order you back to the hall."

"What?" the news unsettles me, and the little fucker grins. He still takes great pride in knowing everything.

"Lady Cyneswith gave him the task, as did Ealdorman Ælhun," he continues.

"Did you know about this?" I demand of Edmund, turning slightly, so they know who I ask.

"Aye, My Lord," it's Pybba who answers mournfully.

"I've heard him practising," Edmund admits, and there's no indication of what he thinks about the scop from such a bland statement. "Muttering phrases beneath his breath. I hope his performance is worthier than what I've heard." I consider complaining. Edmund's the one who's always wanted a damn scop. But I don't.

A companionable silence falls between us, little more than the sizzle of the fire in the brazier and the crack of water freezing hard, reaching my ears, just audible beneath our breathing.

Before me, I see the battles I've fought since the summer, the ones outside Northampton coming clearest to mind, but all of them there, hovering. A feeling from one, a remembered action from another; my emotions from them all.

"You'll recover yourself," Pybba speaks once more, despite no one asking. "You'll recover, and the rage will return, and if it teaches you to take a little more care, then that's all to the good. Sure as anything, you won't fucking take that risk again."

Now my smile broadens. Fuck it. I should have convened this meeting before now. I should have realised how well they knew me. I've not become any less in their eyes, just because of my injury. And why would I have done so? I've never thought that of them before; one-eyed, one-handed, shredded down half their body, cut around the throat; it's always been evident to me that they were still lethal bastards just as I am.

"Right, can we go the fuck inside now?" Rudolf breaks the companionable accord that's settled over us.

I'm almost about to say yes when Edmund startles beside me.

"What the fuck is that?" He points, not out on the battlefield behind us, but rather behind us. No doubt he'd already been turning to climb down the stairs when he glimpsed whatever disturbs him.

"What?" I demand to know, but before the word's out of my mouth, I've seen it too.

"Well, that's not a good sign," Rudolf offers, the joy drained from his voice, once more the serious warrior he's become of late.

There's a spark of light out there, just erupting from behind the shadowy woodland to the other side of the Nene. I can't determine how fast it's moving, but I think it's quick.

"A rider," Edmund complains, mouth downcast.

"It's got to be bloody urgent to be out in this foul weather," Hereman concurs.

I want to rant and rave. I want to stab at them with my words, explain it's this ill-feeling of unease that's been adding to my frustration and apprehension about my wound. But it's none of those things. I knew peace wouldn't last.

I did think it might make it beyond the Yule feast.

But apparently fucking not.

CHAPTER 2

They all make it to the gateway before I do. In fact, it if weren't for Heahstan and Beornfyhrt's assistance, I'd probably still be stranded on the bloody rampart.

Any sense of serenity from our impromptu meeting has erupted long before I can see the rider being allowed access to the inner workings of Northampton. Brands have been lit, more braziers as well, and yet the snow remains deep enough to flounder in, and of course, I fucking do.

I don't recognise the voice of the man as he disappears inside the hall, Hiltiberht scampering to take care of his tired horse, head hanging, chest heaving. There's a sense of anticipation that all but erupts as I stride into the sweltering heat of the hall once more, trying not to show my fury at being abandoned.

Rudolf casts me a long look, a hint of apology in his keen eyes. I don't get the same from the others, as they crowd around the hearth, my Aunt with them, Ealdorman Ælhun as well, none of them noticing that me, their king, isn't with them. Damn fuckers.

Only then, the rider, shrugging free from his snow and ice-encrusted cloak, so it looks as though he's clothed in the pristine night sky, spots me, and takes to his knee.

"My Lord King." I watch, almost amused, as realisation dawns on the face of Edmund and Hereman, Pybba as well, although Icel doesn't seem to be concerned either way.

"Stand, man, stand. Take your cloak from your shoulders and

warm yourself before the hearth."

I can see the affronted expression on the face of the scop. He's been upended from his spot beside the hearth, shoved to the side, and he's none too pleased about it. I almost pity him. He thinks he's found himself good food, a warm hearth and a captive audience to get himself through the dark months.

He might still have. But probably not while I'm in residence. Not if the expression is anything to go by on the rider's face. I'm impressed he can convey so much emotion with his eyebrows frozen, eyelashes glinting wetly, and his nose brighter even than the fire, where it burns red at the edges.

"Ealdorman Aldred sent me, My Lord King. From Gainsborough. My name's Æthelgar."

I'd quite like to know what Ealdorman Aldred is doing at Gainsborough, but I don't ask. There'll be time for recriminations when I know what's happening.

"Tell me," I demand.

"Ships, My Lord King, on the Humber Estuary. A force, massing North of the Humber, under Jarl Halfdan."

The name brings a genuine smile to my face. I thought he'd fucked off to Northumbria, and I'd never see him again because the king of Mercia can't ride into another man's kingdom.

"In this weather?" It's Edmund who asks, his eyes high in his hairline, disgust in those words. He's never been one to enjoy the cold.

"Aye, My Lord." Æthelgar directs his words to Edmund, opting for the address because he's not sure of the correct title to use. I notice that Edmund doesn't deny the title. Interesting.

"The snow's deeper in Gainsborough. I've only made my way here by staying on the Foss Way and never veering far from the drainage ditches."

"A cold ride then. And when did you leave?"

"Four days ago, My Lord King. And the Raiders were noticed a week ago now. It took two days to return to Gainsborough because of a blizzard."

"At least the Raiders can't move in this weather either," my

Aunt thinks to interject, but I shake my head. Nothing dissuades the Raiders. Not fire, or ice, flood or tempest. The only thing that deters them is my warriors and me.

"Did you see any ships on the way here?" The Foss Way doesn't run all the way to Northampton along a river, but it might have been visible in places.

"None, no. I don't think they'd risk it. Not at the moment."

"And what does Ealdorman Aldred expect me to do? What were your orders?"

A flicker of uncertainty on Æthelgar's chapped face, and I can imagine the scene all too well.

"To inform you and ask for instructions as to what to do."

"I understand. My thanks. Tell me, how many were seen?"

"At least ten ships. It was impossible to be more specific from such a distance."

"Eat, drink, get warm. We'll care for your horse. I'm not sending you out in this weather anytime soon."

I can feel eyes on me, some nervous, others assured, and then the scowl of the scop as well. He's fiercer than my Aunt with his silent protest.

"Now, I believe the scop will entertain us," I stride back to my place on the dais, aware that everyone follows my movements in that hall. My warriors, those I've not been with outside, have fallen silent, all apart from Wulfhere, slumped over the table, snoring loudly, the sound reaching my ears despite the mass of bodies in the hall.

I consider smiling as I settle myself, discarding my cloak with a flourish. I also consider growling at them. But neither response is the correct one.

No, I need to listen to the scop. Hear his song, see if it genuinely honours me or not, and then, well then, it seems I need to decide whether I'm going to fucking war again. Just the thought makes me shudder with cold.

"You're going nowhere," my Aunt hisses at me as she reclaims her seat beside me, head bowed as she fusses with her skirts to hide the words. "You can't risk your wound in this weather, and you can't risk your neck with that wound." I nod and offer nothing else. I haven't considered all of my options yet. They're more varied than they might have been this time last year and equally narrower as well.

I swallow my cold water, enjoy the sharp, clean taste, and then the scop, centred once more around the hearth, bows to me, his hand above well-covered head, twirling end over end, in an elaborate gesture that makes me squirm. It reminds me of who I am far more than the pulsing cut at my throat ever could.

I catch sight of Hiltiberht slipping back into the hall, Tatberht speaking with him, no doubt ensuring all is well before dismissing him back to the others. I glance at Tatberht. He meets my gaze evenly, impossible to decipher his true thoughts. Then the scop opens his mouth, and from his miserable-looking mouth emerges a voice rich with flavour and warmth, with honeyed tones to entice fair maidens to their bed, despite their desire for innocence. And I confess, my mouth drops open in shock.

I hear a dry chuckle from my Aunt.

"He might look like he slept in a hedge, has never seen a comb in his life, and chews his nails to satisfy his hunger, but he is quite skilled."

I focus on his words then, trying not to fidget.

"We tell you tales of Coelwulf, king.

Man of Mercia, honourable above all other.

A hero of our times. A hero for all times.

He slays Raiders, sends empty ships home;

Nothing but creaking wood, and the silence of the grave,

To women and kings, none shall return from Mercian shores.

Mead cups overfloweth, for lack of drinkers."

"Did you make him say those things?" As transfixed as I am, I can't help but offer the aside to my Aunt, being careful to lift my hand so that none can read my lips.

"There's no need for me to tell anyone anything. Your antics speak for themselves."

I note the use of the word 'antics' considering that she means to belittle me, but her vivid eyes assure me she's only too well aware of how she speaks.

Damn the woman.

Rudolf sits, eyes alive with the tale, Hiltiberht beside him, while Edmund is still, only Icel showing his amusement at the way the scop speaks of a man they've watched vomit on their shoes and shit on a molehill. A man who almost died on the blade of someone who wasn't even trying to kill him.

"What will you do about Jarl Halfdan?" My Aunt uses the distraction of the scop to demand an answer.

"I'll have to send someone north. I can't go myself; I accept that. But, there are many men I can rely on now. Proven men."

"There are, yes. But what of Jarl Halfdan himself? I know you crave his blood."

"I'm not alone in that," I mutter, not wanting the scop to realise that my attention has waned. Not because he's unskilled, but because this is altogether too much to be subjected to for one man. I would wish he'd turn to my warriors. No man acts alone. No man saves a kingdom without the aid of others.

I marvel at the scop's leathery face, the way his hands beat time on the drum, the inkings that cover his long arms before the skin is covered by a tunic, purposefully cut short, just over the shoulders. It would do him no good on a day like today. No wonder he needs a warm hearth and someone willing to feed him. His hair is a wealth of bright curls, his eyes half-closed so that I can see more inkings on his eyelids. I can only imagine how much that fucking hurt.

"Kyred. Send Kyred," my Aunt instructs me. I want to tell her to stop her discussion, remind her of who's king here, but I intended to send Kyred anyway. This way, she'll believe a victory has been scored against me.

"I'll not send men into this weather. I'll dispatch him, but not yet. Only when the thaw comes."

"And what if Jarl Halfdan has had his triumph by then."

"I doubt he'll have been able to crack the ice over his water butt. I'll trust that there's time, yet."

Her grumble of disquiet is lost beneath the scop's soaring

voice.

The scop spellbinds every man, woman, and the few children within Northampton. He paints a story of someone, not me, who knows no defeat, only success, who quakes at nothing, has no fear, believes only in his actions' righteousness.

I feel like halting him, pointing out the jagged scar on my neck, the healed wound down my neck, the cut on my leg from where Hereman almost hobbled me. But I don't. Instead, I listen, intently, swept along in the battles he brings to life, the tale of the way I tricked the Raiders, the story of how I killed so many of my enemy, defeated the jarls, even when they thought they'd won. I appreciate the scop and his power in a way that Edmund has been desperate to impress upon me for many years.

I might just send the scop with Kyred.

But no, that would be cruel. Maybe there's another way, though.

I've fought, and killed, and bled and wept for Mercia. Now, I have the means to ensure others know that truth. Now, I just need to find a suitable candidate for my purpose.

Will I truly rip apart my family of warriors and send one of the youngsters into the bitter north winds, where the enemy waits to take their next strike? Perhaps I won't, after all. Neither will I send Edmund, although, no doubt, he'd like to know the tricks the scop employs to keep his audience's attention.

"In Repton, Coelwulf king, tricked the men of the North.

He went before them, bound and gagged.

And then he bathed our church in their blood.

In Repton, our king slays all Raiders,

Even a man twelve feet tall."

He was not, I believe, twelve feet tall, but the tale seems to grow with the telling. I roll my eyes at the exaggeration, at the omission of those who helped me kill the bastard.

I focus on the fire, memories of the battle clear before my eyes, seen in the collapsing logs, burning to ash, in the fiery flames, leaping over and above the fuel. A slither of satisfaction enters my heart, but I throw water onto it.

The deed is far from done, as my messenger has just shown me.

I can't take pride in an unfinished job.

I vowed to protect Mercia, as the great scop is telling all who will listen.

My vow is not yet complete. For less than a heartbeat, I allow the devious thought that it might never be, and then I dash it out with the depth of fallen snow, watching the smoke of the flames as it ebbs away.

I'll not doubt myself. I'll not allow the worry of my most recent wound to hamper my actions.

I've always fought. I've always risked my death. Stepping that little bit closer to it has merely firmed my resolve that I'll risk all for my kingdom. If I must die for Mercia to be free from the Raiders, then I'll happily do so.

But not fucking today or tomorrow. Or anytime soon. Not while it snows. Jarl Halfdan will have to fucking wait.

CHAPTER 3

"**S**teady there, My Lord. I fear your head might not fit through this door." Edmund's voice is laced with derision. It seems he's not happy with the scop's work.

I roll my eyes at him.

"You should have regaled him with less fantastical tales if you didn't wish to hear them embellished beyond all reason and practicality."

"Fuck," Edmund mutters, turning his flushed face away from me. It seems I wasn't to know of Edmund's involvement in the elongated scop's praise-song from the previous night.

It's bitterly cold outside. I've only rushed out to empty my stream into the pit, and Edmund has caught me on the way back inside.

Outside it's icy, everywhere. Even the snow cleared paths are slippery, and I'm not the only one to have nearly slid into the cesspit. It'll not be a pleasant way to die beneath the yellowed ice that's formed over it. The smell has been just about extinguished in the deathly temperatures. I'm sure the same can't be said beneath the ice.

"I found it a pleasant listen," I jibe, determined to have my fun with him. The more furious he looks, the more I smile. It seems my humour has been restored to me.

Yes, my neck itches beneath the cloak and the skin is puckered and tight, but I already feel more confident. The truth of my survival seems only to add to the legend growing around me. I don't much want the legend, but last night, I learned a valuable lesson. That legend will do me far more good than harm. It might make young boys piss themselves with fear if it leaks beyond Mercia's myriad borders. It'll certainly ensure those who wish to claim my kingdom will do so with more wariness than ever before. Like fear, wariness is an insidious thing, undermining confidence and making men weak when they should be strong.

"Then my work is accomplished," Edmund mocks.

"No, not yet," I caution. "But it is begun." Edmund fixes his perplexed eye on me, and I shrug. All will become clear in time.

"Bollocks, it's cold," Hereman's words are too loud, echoing in the enclosed space. Overhead, the sun is a watery brightness. We've been slow to rise this day. It's a day for feasting, and drinking, if so inclined. But, I have much to consider. I seek out Kyred amongst those men who've decided the only way to cure their pounding heads caused by drinking too much ale is to strip to their skin and face one another in the confines of the dubious shelter provided by the stables. The occasional whinny speaks of unhappy horses. No doubt, they wish they could do the same. Anything is to be preferred to being trapped, not by the walls, but by the weather.

"You've got cold bollocks?" I direct to Hereman. He grins at me, running his hand through his rough hair.

"I've got a fucking cold everything," he retorts. He, too, has stripped to his waist, and I can see the jagged scars of his wounds. Some might look away from them, but as Pybba said on the ramparts, these scars tell the story of our lives. We should never dismiss them.

I lost sight of him last night as the scop regaled the hall with the stories of how the greatest king Mercia has ever claimed held back the Raiders. I confess, I felt some pride and then quickly chased it away. I can only hold such acclamations when the job is complete. And right now, it isn't.

"Where's Kyred?"

"Vomiting all over himself in the corner," there's no sympathy in Hereman's words as he points to where he means. "He took a mighty blow to his belly. Poor fucker's can't stop being sick."

"Who did that to him?" Kyred is a mean fighter. I wouldn't expect anyone to get the better of him.

"Heahstan. Foul bastard took the punch when Kyred was distracted by Haden trying to eat his hair." Hereman's chuckle assures me that I've missed a great deal of hilarity.

"Thanks," and I make my way to Kyred. He's wedged against the wooden wall, and it looks like if he tries to stand, he'll tumble over. Hiltiberht hovers close to him, as do others of his men. But, the conversation is light-hearted.

"Kyred."

"My Lord King," his bleached face startles at my words, and I wrinkle my nose at the sour odour of ale brought back up.

"Are you well enough to speak, or shall we talk later, when you're fully recovered?"

"No, no, now is fine," there's a flicker of understanding on his face. I imagine he's already deciphered what my next words will be. He's no fool.

"Help me," and two hands clasp his forearms. With only so much shuffling, he's on his unsteady feet, a brief flicker of pain on his face attesting to his injury. He takes the jug of water Hiltiberht holds and throws it over his head, shaking his hair from side to side as though he's a dog. I step back, and I'm not alone.

"Fuck's sake," I complain while Kyred's eyes wobble in his head. Not the wisest of moves, but I appreciate the desire to seem keen.

Kyred grabs his tunic from one of his men, a cloak from the other. It makes sense now why the men have stripped to the waist. Better that than have nothing clean to wear. Who in their right mind wants to be cleaning clothes on the banks of the Nene when it's so damn icy?

While Hereman battles one of Ealdorman Ælhun's men, the rise and fall of cheers making it unnecessary to watch the battle, helped by Icel's vocal commentary, we make our way outside. A gust of wet wind covers my head, no doubt sheeting the stuff from one of the roofs overhead. I'm pleased my cloak covers my head.

Together, we walk in companionable silence to the gateway that leads to the bridge that once crossed the Nene. The bridge remains in pieces. Those who wish to enter must first wait for the wooden planks stored on this bank to be shoved into place. But it does mean that the gate can be kept open, only two guards on duty, for now, and even then, their eyes peer towards the raucous noise coming from the stables.

"I can't go North. Not at the moment, and no matter how much it pains me."

"Aye, My Lord King. I appreciate it as much. My men and I can leave before nightfall."

"No one can leave until the thaw begins. I'll not risk losing men in the snow and blizzards which might yet rage."

Kyred's lips pull down at my words. I detect the hint of a scar on the left side of his face, only visible with such a movement. I imagine it's a childhood injury. It's too small to have been inflicted with an adult-sized weapon. Or, he was just a lucky sod to miss a larger wound.

"But Jarl Halfdan might take advantage of the weather."

"He might, yes, but I'd rather a contingent of warriors able to meet him in battle than the straggling remains of such a group, battered by the cold, snow and ice. It's the wrong time of year to be laying a siege, for spilling blood, for trying to traverse the Humber and the Trent. But, Ealdorman Aldred doesn't have our experience. I'll provide him with the support he needs, but he'll have to wait for now."

"Perhaps," Kyred admits, but I see the tension in his hands, visible beneath his cloak. He wants to be gone, now that I've given the order.

"And don't think of leaving without my permission. There's a time for fucking heroics, and it's not in the midst of the worst snow I've seen for years." I pitch my voice, infuse it with just enough menace that Kyred bows his head, capitulating to his king. It's a feat I can only accomplish with those who aren't my particular warriors. Edmund, Icel and Pybba would ignore my words and risk it all anyway. Rudolf wouldn't even think he should obey my order.

That's why I've chosen Kyred.

That, and it'll stop any disagreements forming between Edmund and Icel. The two still need their heads banging together on occasion to remind them of just who is fucking king and who isn't.

"When you get to Gainsborough, you'll have the command of the warriors, not the ealdorman. You'll decide what needs to be done and if you need reinforcements. Don't stand alone against Jarl Halfdan. A mean bastard like that can scent an easy victory."

"Aye, My Lord King. I know what to do," and Kyred bows smartly, inclining his head towards me. My gaze settles on the water beneath us. The surface is frozen in places, but not everywhere. The water in the centre of the river continues to flow if slowly, trying to forge a wider path, sheer the ice away, make its course that much easier. I know how it feels.

"So, what did you think of the scop?" I hardly notice Kyred bowing his way from my presence, his face shimmering with the sweat of unease. Rudolf's voice fills the space he's left behind.

"You tell me?" I ask, almost pleased to be distracted from my darker thoughts.

"Well, I mean, he described me just about fine, but you, well, I don't know who's been telling him such stories."

I grin. I can't help it. Damn the fucker.

"It seems I have a reputation to live up to, that's for sure, and you need to build one yet."

"Well now, My Lord, I'm not sure about that. I think I sounded pretty good. Certainly, some of the women have been eyeing me this morning and last night."

"No doubt wondering if you've got the stones to live up to your reputation."

"I assure you, My Lord, that I certainly do." His voice is dark with menace, an illusion spoiled by his delighted chuckle at the end of it.

"Let's hope it stops Edmund's bloody moaning," and then he too leaves my side. I remain a while longer. The cold bite is a welcome change to the smoky heat of the hall. There are too many of us inside Northampton for it to be truly comfortable. Anyone walking into the hall at night would find it difficult to find somewhere to place their little toe, let alone their whole body. Still, we're getting by, somehow. And food is in plentiful supply. I suppose I should thank the Raiders for that, but I won't.

Finally, I realise I'm shivering and turn to head back inside. The stables remain a writhing mass of shouting men, and I avoid it, mindful that my Aunt stands on the extremities, waging her bets with Edmund. I don't want to intrude on whatever that is.

It does mean that the hall is nearly deserted. Gardulf lingers by the fire. His eyes are hollows. The wounds he took have taken too long to heal. If my Aunt hadn't been at Northampton, I don't know what would have become of him. Well, I do. I don't like to think about it.

"My Lord," he bows his head low, and I walk to his side. I've put this conversation off for long enough already.

"Gardulf. How do you fare?"

He looks surprised by my question.

"About as well as you," is his reply, and in that, I realise he understands better than others might think.

"The wounds we carry mark us as the men we are," I state flatly, recycling the words once more.

"Then I must learn to welcome less of them. I'm fucking fed up of feeling like this." I nod, a knowing smile on my lips.

"They tell me it won't last, but they're not the ones who feel sluggish and feeble."

A companionable silence falls between us.

"I suppose I should say thank you for supporting me against my father."

"There's no need. Edmund is a pig-headed bastard. Anyone would do the same."

"They might, yes," he admits with a slither of amusement in his voice. "But, you're the only one to whom he'd ever actually listen."

"Just do me a favour, and try and avoid those blades, as you say. I don't want to have to answer for any other wounds you might take."

"Will you go north?" he asks then, no doubt thinking that he'll miss another battle.

"No, Kyred and his men will. It seems I'll be staying here for a while longer yet." The thought unsettles me more than it should.

CHAPTER 4

"**M**y Lord?"

The insistent voice rouses me from sleep. I turn aside, try and find the peace of sleeping once more.

"Get up, you lazy fucker," of course, it's Edmund who speaks to me with the respect he shows the latrine ditch.

"What?" There's little light in the hall, and Edmund leers so closely that I can smell his breath. I choke, bat him away and struggle upright, careful not to knock my healing wound.

"There's another fucking messenger from the south this time?"

"What?" My mind is too sleep-sodden to function. Kyred and his men only left yesterday, as did Ealdorman Ælhun, both parties taking advantage of the sudden thaw to escape the confines of Northampton. I don't envy Kyred. The Nene runs too full, and I know there'll be water lying in any dip or hollow as he travels north. He and his warriors are in for a wet ride to Gainsborough.

"There's a messenger from Bishop Smithwulf. You'll want to hear what he has to say."

"Pestilent fucker," but I'm becoming more and more alert, able to make out the shape of the messenger as he huddles close to the fire. I can hear the steady stream of rain from outside, drumming onto the roof, accompanied by the steady trickle of water falling somewhere. I hope it's off the roof, and outside the hall, and not in a puddle somewhere.

"Hand me my tunic," I demand of Edmund. He's dressed and shaved. I'd ask him what he's been up to, but it's not necessary. I don't want to know the details of what happens behind the door in the room my Aunt has taken as her own, into which Edmund is an almost exclusive visitor. I don't even want to ask why he's taken to shaving.

"What the fuck does Bishop Smithwulf want."

"Come and listen. I'm not going to face your wrath." The words are far from comforting. What have the Raiders done now? I thought I'd driven them back from Mercia's borders for the comfort of a warm winter indoors. I couldn't have been more wrong.

"Good man," the messenger is thin-faced, hands busy as he spoons pottage into his mouth. Long hair snakes down his back, a thin beard and moustache, thick eyebrows as well, meaning there's almost no skin to see on his face. But that there is blacker than the night, teeth flashing starkly in a mobile face. His eyes are intelligent if shadowed. For a moment, I think he must be one of Bishop Smithwulf's monks, but his hands are far too rough to do nothing but pray.

"My Lord King, my name is Gregory. Bishop Smithwulf sent me to inform you of developments in London. He begs me to remind you of the words you spoke at your coronation and to advise you that he recalls your first meeting after all and all its unfortunate consequences." His words carry a hard-edge, and I know he speaks another tongue with more ease than mine.

"The Raiders?" I demand to know, face already downcast, trying not to wince at the memory of that meeting with Smithwulf. It was almost good that he didn't recall it, for him as well as for me.

Gregory's hesitation in replying speaks of something else.

"King Alfred of Wessex and the Raiders," he responds eventually.

"King Alfred? What does he have to do with fucking London? London is Mercian."

"I know, My Lord King, but the Raiders threaten the safety

and security of London, and King Alfred has approached Bishop Smithwulf, offering to keep her safe because the Mercian king is incapable of doing as much."

I know now why Edmund didn't speak these words to me. It's all I can do to hide my temper before this stranger. But I do. Alfred can speak. He's hardly a warrior of great renown.

"How many Raiders?"

"Seven ships. King Alfred faced them in Wessex, and they've retreated to London. Only, he's followed them."

This is hardly devastating news—seven ships, against the might of Mercia. But Alfred's intentions are unsettling. Does he mean to take advantage of Mercia's plight to his advantage? Damn the bastard. And, has he followed them or chased them? I'd like clarity on that point.

It's not the first time the Wessex kings have shown an interest in London. It's a valuable possession. I'm sure they'd profit from it, but it's Mercian and will remain so for all time.

"Bishop Smithwulf isn't inclined to make any agreement with King Alfred, but he does beg your assistance."

I'm sure he does, I think ruefully, entirely awake now, mind busy considering the best course of action.

"I confess, My Lord King, that I've been delayed on my journey here. The snow, as I'm sure you can imagine, blocked the way for six days, and I've rushed here with the thaw." He doesn't need to mention the rain. We can all hear it.

"Then it's urgent that I make a decision now?"

"Not urgent, My Lord King, no, but perhaps, lingering would not be beneficial." His words are enough of a warning.

"My thanks. Eat, drink, rest. You've arrived early?"

"I travelled all night, My Lord King. Better to get here before the next snow falls if we're to have more snow. The bishop is convinced it'll be a harsh winter, with an early summer. I hope he's right. This cold gets into my bones. I'd sooner feel the sun on them."

"Then sleep as well. I'll have a response for you when you wake."

I turn aside, aware that my Aunt has overheard much of what's been said, although most people still sleep. It's far too early to be thinking such thoughts.

Icel joins our small group beside the hearth while Gregory gratefully finds a corner to spread his cloak and sleep. I note how he moves far from earshot. He won't hear what we're saying and won't be forced to relay our words to Bishop Smithwulf or even King Alfred of Wessex.

For a moment, I consider what I'd like to say to Alfred if I ever met him. All these years, his family have been undermining Mercia, ensuring the Raiders never went further than the Mercian kingdom when they were evicted from Wessex. The news that he chases a group of only seven ships from Wessex to London is no great accomplishment. His sister escaped to Rome with her husband, King Burgred of Mercia. For a moment, I consider that Alfred means to fill that void left by Burgred. I'd like to see him fucking try.

Or, perhaps that's not the point.

"Explain King Alfred's motives?" I demand of my Aunt. She has more experience in politics than I do.

"He's as ambitious as the rest of his family." Her voice is filled with disdain. I almost smirk at her hatred of the House of Wessex. "But ambition doesn't always transfer into skill." Perhaps, if I do ever meet Alfred, I'll take my Aunt with me. That'll make him reconsider his actions without having to open my mouth.

"Perhaps," and Pybba speaks. I've not even realised he'd joined the group. "He wishes to become an ally, as in the past."

Icel spits into the hearth at the words. His drawl adding a menacing sound to the comfort of the crackling logs. We all know what he thinks of that idea.

"Has he even heard of you?" Edmund demands to know, and I snap down on my sarcastic response. After the scop's words, it seems to me that everyone in Mercia and Wessex must have heard of the great King Coelwulf of Mercia, but perhaps not.

"I imagine King Alfred believes Mercia has no true king and is instead under the command of the jarls." My Aunt speaks with consideration. I can listen to her without interrupting, although I have to caution Rudolf with my eyes to prevent him from flapping his mouth. Who the fuck woke him? I have no idea.

"And so he's as rapacious as the Raiders? Seeking to profit at the expense of Mercian men and women."

"I would imagine so, yes. As you say, the Wessex kings have long coveted London. His father was the same, his older brothers as well. After all, Æthelwulf married his daughter to Burgred. That spoke of his intentions towards Mercia's most profitable port."

"And he'd sooner allow the rest of Mercia to fall under Raider control than keep his bloody thieving little fingers from it."

My Aunt's steely eyes hold my gaze. Perhaps I spoke with too much fury, but it boils me. I can't deny it. A fine form of repayment. I've spent six months fighting off the Raiders, and now fucking King Alfred moves to make a pact with Bishop Smithwulf to protect London from such a small force.

London will hardly be threatened by it. It's not as if it's the three hundred and fifty craft that tried to take London over twenty years ago. I still remember the repercussions of such an attack. They'd been felt, even by my father, as estranged as he'd been from King Berhtwulf's court; even by me, as removed as I'd been by anything to do with politics.

Mercia and Wessex had worked together then. It didn't appear that Alfred would welcome such close assistance this time.

"We don't know his intentions." Pybba offers, but his heart's not in it.

"Oh, but I think we do," I reply heatedly, and he dunks his head. Not an apology, but an admission that I'm probably right.

"You can't go to London. If you sent Kyred to face Jarl Halfdan, then you can't travel to London to counter King Alfred." I glare at my Aunt. She's both right and also wrong.

"The weather will be worse in the North. It means we have time yet."

"But the same can't be said of London?" She taunts me.

"The same can't be said of King Alfred. I'll not have it. I'll not bloody have it at all." I weigh my words, hoping she'll understand.

"And who'll hold Northampton in your absence? Ealdorman Ælhun has gone."

"You will," I make the decision without thinking it through but immediately know it's the right one. Who better than my Aunt? Should the whipped Raiders decide to make a return to Northampton's walls, she'll spare no thought for their health. In fact, she might well step outside and slay them herself, and not necessarily with a weapon. Her tongue will be just as fierce.

But Edmund's eyes bore into mine, even as my Aunt glows with triumph.

Great, I've pissed off Edmund, even as I've won my Aunt's agreement for a journey to London.

"Tomorrow," I announce, refusing the opportunity to change my mind. "Provided it's not pissing it down like this," and I indicate the roof around us, and the sound of the rain almost drowning out all sound, "we travel to London. We'll deal with King Alfred or the seven ship-loads of Raiders and then make our way to Gainsborough. I can't fight on two fronts."

Pybba grunts with acceptance; even Icel seems mollified. Rudolf is almost skipping from foot to foot. Perhaps I'm not the only one struggling with the confines of this bloody weather.

But Edmund doesn't step aside, even as my Aunt lays a warning hand on his shoulder, before stealing away.

"What? I can't make every decision based on whether it's going to piss you off or not." I wait until we're alone to respond to him.

"No, you can't, but I can't protect your back and hers at the same time. I'll remain in Northampton. You can face the Raiders or King Alfred without me. And don't try and convince me otherwise."

"I wouldn't bloody dream of it."

"And Gardulf remains behind as well."

"I think you should ask him before you make such a demand. He won't appreciate it. Not now he's recovered from his wounds."

"I'm his father," is his hot reply.

"And I'm his king, and he serves me, not you. And while you might not realise that, he certainly does."

I stalk from his side then, outside, into the darkness that assures me I've been woken far too early, and there's an entire day to get through until I can legitimately reclaim my bed.

"Fuck," I complain, wrapping my cloak around me as I make my way to the stables. I've been trying to avoid Haden, and he knows it, just as surely as I do.

"Hail," I call softly. With the hall as full as it is, there are some, not many, who've taken to eschewing the heat of the hearth in favour of some privacy. It seems they'd rather share their night time excursions with the knowing eyes and snorts of horses than with the men and women of Northampton. I would envy them because it's warm inside the stables, the press of so many bodies ensuring that despite there being no hearth, it's still almost pleasant, but the smell sets my eyes watering. So much horse shit, in one place. It could kill a man or a woman.

No one responds to my call, apart from one sharp kick on a wooden door.

"Morning," I make my way to Haden's side. His black and white head is hanging over the stable door, intelligent brown eyes watching my approach, the sign of reproach evident in how his head is held away from my questing hand.

"Suit yourself then, you grumpy git," I retort, shoving my hand back inside my cloak, unsurprised when his nose immediately tries to follow it. He thinks I bring him a tasty morsel, and I do, but it's old and so wrinkled, I can't think it'll taste pleasant. But he takes the apple, if you can still call it that, all the same. A flicker of satisfaction assures me that we're allies once more.

I open the stable door, slink beside him, reaching for the brush that's kept there for my use. Or rather, it's replaced there whenever anyone else borrows it. It's not entirely mine. But it almost is.

I consider it, pulling the few stray brown horse hairs from it, almost smirking to realise how much care has been taken to en-sure I don't know it's been borrowed.

"Tomorrow," I start conversationally, and Haden's nose whips up, almost colliding with mine. "We're going for a pleasant little ride," I assure him, knowing it'll be far from pleasant. I should have used a better word.

"London," I inform him, although he has no idea what the word means. He just watches me as though we might be about to leave, now. "To visit the bishop, and perhaps, find ourselves some Raiders to slay." Now he settles. Maybe Haden does under-stand the word Raider. Maybe he thirsts for blood, just as I do.

"We'll travel along Watling Street," I continue, the words more for my benefit than his. "And when we get to London, we'll have decisions to make." I hear a rustling from somewhere and realise that others might find my conversation amusing or worrying. Should a king converse with his horse?

I lower my voice.

"It'll be wet and horrible, and we'll have to cross the river at Passenham again." Perhaps, I should order a bridge built there. It would certainly keep my feet drier.

"Hopefully, you won't have to swim it." Ah, so Edmund seeks me out once more. No doubt he's been sent here by my Aunt.

"Fuck off, Edmund." I don't wish to continue our earlier argu-ment.

"She said that's what you'd say."

"Then she knows me better than you. And she wouldn't have said 'fuck,' she never does."

"What she does and doesn't say behind closed doors might surprise you."

I feel my face wrinkle in disgust. It's as though he speaks of my parents, enjoying one another in the comfort of their bed. I don't need that image in my mind.

"What do you want?" I resolve to be more conciliatory, just to prove my Aunt wrong.

"Gardulf wishes to accompany you."

"As I said."

"I've forbidden it, so obviously, he'll come regardless." Edmund's voice is bleak.

I hold my tongue. I'll make no promise to keep Gardulf safe.

"Penda will remain behind as well. He wishes to learn from the scop."

"I have no argument with that." Such news will thrill Tatberht. And speaking of him.

"Tatberht will accompany you. He's made that clear, in no uncertain words."

"I'll be pleased to have him." And then there's silence between us. The matter of Hereman hovers there. But I won't prompt him. He can tell me in his own sweet time. I run the brush over Haden's flanks, finding comfort in the regular movement, in the feeling of being useful, even as my wound not so much aches, as tears. Every so often, I'm forced to touch it, check the skin is still tightly sealed because it doesn't feel like it is. There have even been instances when I've been convinced blood floods down my chest.

I wish the sensation would go away. It wakes me in the night. Other times, my neck is so hot and sweaty, I feel as though I bleed again.

I should be grateful to be alive. I should revel in knowing that I'm healing. But it's taking too long, and I know I've lost strength while I've been unable to practise and exercise with my men. I might blame the weather, but that's not the only part of my disgruntlement.

"If Kyred returns in your absence or sends for more men, what should I do?"

"I'll send word to Ealdorman Ælhun. Tell him we need Wulfsige, either way."

Edmund's face twists at the news.

"He's becoming more tolerable by the day," I chide him, almost enjoying the immediate means of revenge for remaining in Northampton.

"And what of Grantabridge?"

"If we see those fuckers this side of midsummer, I'll be

amazed. Just keep the gate shut, and don't repair the bridge. You'll be safe." I order, and he nods. I don't want to leave him behind, but he's made the decision. It seems he cares for my Aunt more than me.

That should probably annoy the fuck out of me.

But I'll ensure we part as friends, not enemies. He protects my Aunt. That should please me.

I reach across Haden's back, hand extended, and he grips it, a faintly embarrassed expression on his face. His grip is firm, reminding me of my frailty. But I keep a grin on my face. I'll not have him see me weak. Never that. Or rather, never again.

CHAPTER 5

"**F**uck this weather," Sæbald stares mournfully from the stable door. It's not raining. It really can't be called that. It's more as though someone throws bucket after bucket of water from the glowering skies overhead.

"At least the snow's melted," is Gyrth's less than helpful reply, even if it's cheerfully stated.

I share Sæbald's dejection. Yesterday, it was impossible to stay upright, the temperature plummeting overnight and freezing all the water. I didn't want to risk the horses. Now, if I mean to leave, I'm going to be subjecting every one of us to the deluge. Can I truly be arsed? Is London that important? But I know it is. So does Sæbald.

"Well, the sooner we leave, the sooner we'll get there,' Rudolf chirps, and I'm not the only one to groan. Pybba seems shrunken beneath a billowing cloak, the edges treated with fat to ensure the water slicks easily from the edges. He stinks. Well, his cloak does. But we all stink. My Aunt set the youngsters to treating the cloaks yesterday, hardly seeming to notice the task's rankness.

Those poor youths. They won't get rid of the smell for days, if not weeks, no matter how much they wash and scrub at their hands. Still, it might make them less attractive to one another, which would put paid to the frequent fistfights between the women, not the men. Rudolf has learned to keep himself to himself. Hiltiberht hasn't yet, and because of his closeness to me, and not, I think because of his good looks, he's become the lad they all want.

Even that can become too much for one lad. I remember the experience well. Much easier to keep himself to himself. He doesn't want a litter of children claiming him as their father in every settlement throughout Mercia.

"Really, My Lord, in this?" Pybba's voice reflects his dismay, his missing stump of a hand wrapped tightly in sheets of the cured fabric. At least he'll only have one drenched hand, not like the rest of us. But that's not the point. I'd sooner he had the two about which to complain.

"Aye, London beckons us, and we can't shy away from the contrary bitch."

With that, and despite my misgivings, I encourage Haden out of the stable. His enthusiasm has long since waned, and I've still got to get him over the makeshift bridge that crosses the Nene.

Edmund waves to me from where he shelters in the doorway of the great hall, my Aunt beside him, Penda as well. They look a motley group, but they're warm and dry, the overhang of the thatched roof ensuring the only danger of getting wet is from a stray drop of rain making its way through the matted mass.

"Come on, you stubborn git. You'll enjoy it. In time."

"My Lord," Pybba persists in arguing. "Will we even make it over the ford at Passenham?"

I almost stop then, the perfect excuse to delay once more, nicely presented to me. But, well, I can't stand another day playing games and listening to the scop. There's only so many times I can hear my praises sung without wanting to throttle the man. I'd be surprised if he even knew one end of a sword from the other.

"Come on." I urge Haden, hiding from view the wrinkled apple I carry to tempt him. Haden whiffles into my hand. He knows what I'm about. It remains to be seen whether he accepts my bribery or not. I don't even think he's decided. Not yet.

One hoof at a time, Haden emerges into the torrent. I'm already standing in it, the heavy thud of rain threatening to drive my hood back from my face, to allow water to pool down the back of my neck. I feel sweat forming around my covered wound. My Aunt has wrapped it, warning me not to expose it, not yet. Her words weren't a comfort.

"If one of the Raiders sees that, they'll simply work to slice it open once more. This time, I've no idea how it'll heal if it does heal. Keep it covered, even from your allies, in London."

Her dark tone spoke of Bishop Smithwulf. I thought she admired the man, but evidently not now he's paying homage to King Alfred of Wessex. She hates the Wessex ruling family, always has.

And then Haden stops, his front hooves in the wet, his black and white head there as well, and his brown eyes glare at me with disgust.

"An apple for your pains," I try again. The bastard nips my fingers as he takes it, and I know he does so purposefully.

"Well, let's be having you then," and he stalks into the rain. He's covered in a cloak as well, treated with the same fat so that he smells of both burned flesh and the stables. It's disconcerting, and I spit aside my distaste.

Behind Haden trail the others. Samson dips his head low, accepting the benediction of the rain, Dever's sigh reaches my ears, but I turn my back firmly on the stables. I can't have Raiders at both the north and south of Mercia. I'll have to contend with those in the south. As well as with King Alfred.

Perhaps I should have gone north, in place of Kyred. I'm sure Kyred would have the slick manners to counter King Alfred's pretensions. When Alfred faces me, I've not yet decided how to approach him. I'd like nothing more than to wipe the confidence from his smug face. The fucking bastard.

And, in the North, I'd have the long-overdue opportunity to kill Jarl Halfdan. I'd like that. He owes me a debt. But I didn't know about Alfred when I sent Kyred. I wish I had.

At the gateway, four drenched Mercians wait to assist us across the divide of the river. There are another four men on the far side, just in case any Raider attacks while the horses are led across the stick-thin bridge that we've constructed for such an occasion. I hope we don't have to make an abrupt return to Northampton. It won't end well. Not without a permanent bridge in place.

Already, it's impossible to see much beyond my nose. I do consider turning back. But no. My intentions have already been delayed by a day. I won't allow any further postponement.

I expect Haden to refuse the bridge, and indeed, he stops, stamps his front hoof, covering my legs in a thick brown sludge that speaks more of the latrine pit than a ploughed field. But then he sniffs the air and confidently places a hoof on the wooden bridge, and then another. I lead him onwards, proud of him, despite it all.

"My thanks," I incline my head to the Mercians. They're not just saturated; they look more fluid than flesh. But they'll be inside soon enough. Unlike me.

One of the men grins; another grimaces. And the third mumbles something unintelligible beneath the thud of the rain. A host of fifty Raiders could appear right now, and I'd not hear them.

I mount Haden, grimacing at the wetness between my legs, despite the leather that coats my trews. I encourage him away from the bridge, eyes peering into the woodlands, noting the stream of smoke billowing from the great hall behind me, waiting for the rest of my men.

It doesn't take long for every one of them to cross the bridge. I pause, just to ensure the Mercian guards make it safely back, the bridge dismantled once more. Only then do I head towards the road. If we can find it, that more than any great skill, will guide our steps to London, well, to Passenham. What we find there might put an end to this ludicrous quest.

Gregory leads the way, coming from behind my warriors to direct Haden's steps. I allow it. It's better than having to try and decipher where we are. Well, I'll allow it until we reach Watling Street. Once there, I'll decide on my next action.

If it weren't raining, we could make it to London in little more than a day. But it's not just raining; it's a biblical deluge. If I questioned a priest, no doubt, they'd inform me that this was God's way of keeping the Raiders at bay. I'd set him straight on a few things. How the fuck can we counter the Raiders while it rains like this?

But, once we make it to the old roadway, it does become a little easier. Not that the rain eases, far from it. Instead, the road still carries its drainage ditches, and not all of them are clogged with filth from the winter storms we've endured. It makes it slightly easier going, the puddles less than I expected.

I lift my head, try and gaze around me, but it's impossible to determine where the sky ends, and the landscape begins. Everything is wet, a few stubborn patches of snow visible on the few peaks, but it's as though the blizzard that coated the land was nothing but an illusion.

I hunch inside my cloak. Haden's breath puffs in the air before us, but he's keen enough to canter alongside Gregory's horse, a long-limbed dappled animal. I don't miss that Gregory allows his horse to go where he wants. It might be a competition, but of course, Haden and I are above such things.

Instead, I settle into the misery of the journey. I can't hear the complaints of my warriors. Thankfully. Not that I would disagree with them. But, at least they have someone against whom they can direct their vitriol. I have only myself to blame. Well, apart from the fucking Raiders and bloody King Alfred.

I'm trying to get all the facts ordered in my mind. It seems to me that the Wessex king has fought no more than three hundred and fifty Raiders; perhaps, if I'm feeling generous, I might increase that to four hundred.

What have I faced since the summer? Not just hundreds of the fuckers, but thousands of them. Thousands upon thousands of them. Speaking of biblical, they're like a plague on this land. They seem to live only to die on the blades of my warriors. If that's what they desire more than anything in this life, then so be it. I'm happy to oblige.

But the Wessex king has allowed them to escape him and travel to London. I confess I have my suspicions about King Alfred. Has he done this on purpose? Has he joined forces with the Raiders in an attempt to steal London from beneath my nose? If he has, how does he mean to hold it? London is on the northern side of the Thames River. Yes, there's a wooden bridge to the southern bank, but it's certainly not how I'd think to hold a trading site of such size. Has he then managed to turn Bishop Smithwulf? Has he used the archbishop of Canterbury's power over the diocese of London to bring Smithwulf to his side?

I bark a laugh then. When the fuck did I learn about diocese and archbishops? My Aunt's endeavours to make me more civilised might just be working. Damn her. And damn Edmund. I need him here with me, not in Northampton.

"'Ware," the cry comes from behind me, and I swivel my head, peering into the greyness, hand already inside my cloak and reaching for my seax. Perhaps that's what I need. A bloody good fight! Maybe then the slither of worry I carry will dissipate.

But I can see nothing. Although, I can't see Sæbald either, and he's the one that shouts the warning from the line of men that disappears into the gloom behind me. Fuck, it's a grim day. I can hear the jangle of the horses' harness and the soggy impact of hooves on the stone-lined road, but little else.

"What is it?" I demand to know, coughing away the silence of our journey. Only, I get no response. None at all. Frustrated, I bring Haden to a stop, turn him and make my way back along the line. Pybba looks miserable, his reddened nose peeking from beneath his cloak. He makes no move to follow me as I try to find the source of the disturbance. Rudolf, of course, encourages Dever as an escort, and so too does Hereman with Billy.

But that's about the extent of support I receive from my grumpy looking warriors. I'm almost tempted to reprimand them, but I don't. I'm drenched, even beneath my cloak, and that of a drying horse can only best the scent of a wet horse. I pity the stable hands when we arrive where we're going. If we ever arrive.

"What is it?" I demand to know, riding through what can only be described as a low-lying cloud. I finally catch sight of Sæbald. He's left the safety of the road, so too has Gyrth, and now they peer upwards, and I swallow bile.

"Poor fucker," Wulfred mutters, and now we all look upwards. There's a body there, dangling from the end of a rope as though little more than a leaf clinging to the branches of the tree. But this corpse has long since breathed its last.

"Bloody bollocks." It's impossible to see much of the body. Water runs over it, distorting the shape of what remains of the face and lank hair, and I turn and spit.

"We'll have to get the fucker down," I acknowledge, although Sæbald has already moved to examine the creaking and twisted rope that holds the body upwards. It's tied tightly to a lower branch in the tree, the rope fraying.

"They'll be down soon enough if we just leave them."

"No, I need to see whether it's a Raider or a Mercian." I'm already angry. We're too close to Northampton. This body might have been here for some time, but if it's a Mercian, it could mean that there are Raiders somewhere close. That's not what I want to discover, not when I'm riding away.

"Well, stand back," Sæbald calls, and with a sickening noise of cracking bones and oozing mud, the body lands before me.

Haden shies away, rearing from the unexpected appearance of the dead person.

"Fuck's sake," I rebuke Sæbald, even as I turn Haden, battling with him to prevent him from landing, front hooves first, onto the desiccated remains.

"Sorry, boy," Sæbald calls, appearing from behind the tree. I suppose it's my fault, really. I shouldn't have taken Haden so close.

"Who is it?" I call over my shoulder, bringing Haden under my control with my knees, ignoring the jolt of pain and the ripping sensation that emanates from my neck wound, my healed leg wound making itself felt because of the cold and the damp. I wanted a battle, not a reminder of my frailties.

"It's impossible to tell." Rudolf, never one to be offended by gore and defilement, has slipped from Dever's back and crouched down close to the broken body. His voice filled with interest, and

I find myself shaking my head at his insatiable curiosity.

"The eyes have been pecked away, the lips as well. I can't even tell if it was a man or a woman. There's no beard, but it might just be someone who didn't grow one or someone too young to have one." He meets my gaze evenly.

"There are no weapons. I can't even say whether they died on the noose or some other way. There's too much skin missing. It's bloody grim."

"What about their clothes?"

"I'm not putting my hands in them. There are all sorts of wild-life inside the carcase. We should just bury the poor fucker and move on."

It's not the answer I want to hear. I make as though to dismount only for Rudolf to caution me.

"It's not worth it, My Lord. There's nothing to see here. Nothing. It's just decomposing flesh, and quite frankly, I can't tell one body part from another. It was far from a gentle landing."

"Sorry," Sæbald offers once more, a smirk on his face for the devastation he's caused belying those words.

"We can't dig in this. Hunt around, find some stones or something to cover the body. Poor bastard."

Rudolf is quick to leap into the shadows of the tree line from which the body had been suspended. I startle as he disappears into the darkness, peering all around me, trying to determine why this place would have been chosen for such a gruesome scene.

"Watch Rudolf," I instruct Hereman and Sæbald when no one jumps to assist him. I stay on Haden, but turn him and direct him along the treeline, first to the north and then to the south. I gaze into the undergrowth, my senses alert to anything unusual.

Haden is jaunty beneath me, a sign of his unease. But I see nothing.

"It's done, My Lord," Hereman's voice reaches me just as I'm about to turn back.

"We'll catch up with the others," I order, still waiting, tense. This seems so wrong, and yet, whatever happened here was months ago, certainly long enough for the body to be unrecognisable. Could it have been one of the Raiders we fought, or was this before that? Perhaps this was even someone who was murdered by the jarls in Grantabridge before I came to stand against them.

I swallow, meeting the eyes of Rudolf. He's running grimy hands down his cloak, the green lichen from the meagre collection of stones he's found, evident in the streaks that stain his garment.

"Thanks for your bloody help," Rudolf calls to the others with wounded pride.

"Coelwulf, I found this just now." I go to his side and take hold of whatever it is. I squint at the shimmering object; my heckles thoroughly roused now.

An owl is depicted in the delicate silver wire.

"A Raider then, or killed by one of the fuckers?"

"Aye, that's what I think," he confirms. It's not enough of an answer, but it'll have to do, especially as at that moment, the rain begins to fall even faster. The drum of it sounds all around, making it impossible to hear anything, not even my breathing.

"I think we should be building a fucking ark, not travelling to London."

"If only we had that fucking option," I retort to Rudolf's comment, and then, we're back on the road once more. He's been speaking to my Aunt's monk. I'm sure of it.

I risk lifting my head, scenting the air, looking for even the slightest break in the impenetrable grey that surrounds us.

There's nothing. It's going to be a long fucking journey.

But, at some point in the late afternoon, the sky finally wrings itself out, and a thin wedge of blue sky appears, far overhead, in the direction we're travelling. Of course, it's all too fucking late by then.

"How much further?" Pybba grumbles to me as he brings Brimman alongside Haden. The two horses ignore one another, although I notice that Haden begins to increase his pace, just enough to stay in front of the white horse. Not even the foul conditions can thwart his need to be first.

"I recognise this place, I think. Not much further to Passenham."

"And then what?"

"We'll find somewhere to dry out and begin again tomorrow."

"Couldn't we have waited until tomorrow?" His petulance is starting to frustrate me.

"No, we fucking couldn't," I cut off his complaints as Gregory hails me from the front of the line of mounted warriors.

"Passenham, My Lord King."

My face falls. I knew the river would be in flood. I hadn't thought it would be this full. The river not so much runs its natural course but spills out all over the lower-lying landscape surrounding it. The river is at least three times as wide as the last time Edmund and I traversed it.

"Great," Pybba turns Brimman aside, his fury evident in the hunching of shoulders and the way he seems to disappear beneath his cloak.

"Was it like this when you came this way two days ago?"

"No, My Lord King, it wasn't. Although, well, I confess, they did warn me this was likely to happen."

"Fucking wonderful." I allow the words to settle. I can see the light that spills from beneath the closed doors of the houses in the settlement, some of it visible in the imperfections in the wattle and daub smeared wooden beams.

"There's another way. Well, a narrower stretch. They told me to use it if the rain didn't let up." This cheers me as Gregory moves his horse around the growing patch of boggy ground, heading to the higher-lying ground.

"Come on, follow Gregory," I order the rest, and to the loud objections of everyone there, they slowly obey me. I don't take the comments to heart. I feel the same way. Perhaps it would have been better to build an ark, or certainly, to bring a damn ship to London. But no, it would have taken too long to traverse East Anglia.

I raise my hand, hail the one interested face that peers from the doorway of one of the homes. I recognise the man I spoke to when Edmund accompanied me. It's evident he knows who I am because he directs me to where Gregory is already going. This, then, must be a common problem for the people of Passenham. I spare a hope that none of their homes flood. But, they're built above the rush of the water, on the far side, unlike here, where the cultivated land is much flatter. I catch sight of a school of fish, swimming where the wheat should grow, and I grin.

Darkness is upon us by the time Gregory encourages his horse down a steep embankment. I can see why the river doesn't flood here, but equally, I can hear the rush of water. It's going to be deep, even if it's a short journey.

"Here it is," but Gregory's voice is no longer confident.

"See," Rudolf has noticed first. "There's pieces of rope across the water. They must use this all the time."

Rudolf, of course, is correct. Three lines are running into the churning water, held on either side around the trunks of sturdy-looking trees. The lines flap wetly in the force caused by the water.

"Bloody bollocks." I knew we were wet. Now, we're likely to be drenched.

Hereman, with his usual confident swagger, approaches the ropes first, Billy stepping carefully. It's as though there are steps cut into the river bank, only these are much longer than usual steps, rather small platforms, stretching out.

"How deep do you think? Feet or thighs or arse?"

"Fucking arse," Pybba mutters sourly.

"Feet," Icel confidently states as though he knows that for a fact.

"Thighs," Rudolf suggests. As Hereman plunges into the water, it becomes apparent that they're all wrong.

"Fucking bollocks," Hereman gasps as the water reaches up to his chest but then stops.

"There's flat stone beneath the water," he calls as Billy erupts from the far side, water streaming from his sides. I hardly dare watch, and already my thoughts turn to Dever. How will the old boy get across this raging torrent? It might cover his head, and I certainly don't think he'll be able to swim against the current.

And then a flaming brand appears from behind Hereman, the light settling over his drenched face. He's dropped from Billy, and they both shake themselves as though dogs. I can't see that it'll do them any good. Not when they're as wet as they are.

"Do you need some help? Not the best time for such a crossing, as I told him, yonder." The man juts his chin towards Gregory as he calls to me, his words loud and well-practised. I nod.

"Aye, it's not, but we're needed in London."

"Then we'd best get you across," is the resolute response.

Another two brands emerge from the gathering gloom, and I become aware of men, and women, shouting, one to another. Their movements are well practised.

I watch, surprised, as more ropes are laced through the ones already in place, others wrapped around trunks, and flames leap from what must have been a waiting pile of logs. It warms me, even from this side of the riverbank.

"Come on, let's be having you."

I knee Haden forwards. Billy might have gone first, risking it all without the aid of the people from the settlement, but I go next. I want to show the others how much easier it's become now we have help.

A man stands in the water, back to where the river tumbles toward Passenham, wedged in place between two ropes, his eyes watching me. It seems he's there to catch hold of any wayward people, horses or animals. I can't think that he stands there un-aided. There must be something to assist him. Perhaps his feet are held in place by some pieces of stone; no doubt placed there when the river is barely a trickle above the rock.

Haden falters when he realises I intend to cross the fast-flow-ing water, only for Billy to whinny. Before I can prepare myself, water is making its way up my legs, and then continuing, higher and higher, the icy cold driving the air from my lungs. Fuck, it's cold.

But Haden's steps are firm, as I hold tight to the ropes to either side, arms outstretched, ready to release myself from the stirrups if I must. Not that I'll abandon Haden. The deepest part of the river is only narrow, and in no time at all, water sloughs away from me, and hands are there to help Haden as he struggles up the slick bank. I can see that some steps have been cut into the fluid-looking bank, but they're waterlogged now and no use to anyone, even with the wood chips placed upon them.

"My thanks," I call to those at the waterside, but my words are lost as the next horse makes his way to the water. For a moment, Rudolf meets my gaze, and I almost caution him against coming any further, but I strangle my worry, watching instead.

Dever is the smallest of the horses. He might even be the oldest. Not that he'd ever allow that as an excuse.

"Come on, lad," the man in the water encourages. Dever takes the final step down to impact the flat stone of the river bed. Immediately, I tense. This whole thing is too reminiscent of when we had to get Rudolf across the Trent. I fear to look, even as I jump from Haden's back, preparing to dash to their aid if need be.

"Stay back," one of the villagers cautions me harshly. "We know what to do. It's better if you don't even try to help." I feel stung by the words; even as I vow I'll not heed them.

But then Dever is beside me, Rudolf's teeth chattering, one of the women coming towards him with a beaker that gently steams.

"Here, drink this. It'll drive the cold from your innards. Mind, it's fiery." She hands the same to me, even as others move, hands filled with straw, to wipe the water from our horses. It's an impressive arrangement.

I swig the fluid, not even thinking what it might be.

And then I choke as Hereman's gurgle of delight rumbles all around me.

"Puts hair on your chest," the woman laughs, and I glare. They could have warned me. Still, the resultant fire in my belly is appreciated, as I warm my backside close to the fire, Haden being offered tasty morsels as well.

"Does this happen a lot?" I ask the woman who nurses the cauldron embedded into the heart of the flames.

"More than you'd think. We need a damn bridge, but, well, it's also a fierce deterrent for those we'd rather not allow any further into or out of Mercia." She chuckles while filling another beaker, this one-handed to Icel. I notice then how the surface of the substance bubbles violently.

"What's in it?"

"Ah, old family recipe. I'm allowed to tell no one but my son or daughter as I lie dying. Always been that way."

Icel sniffs his beaker carefully, and I fully anticipate him reeling off the ingredients, but he doesn't. Instead, a pleased expression touches his cheeks, and he offers a bow to the woman. She curtsies, giggling, only then there's a roar of outrage from the river, and I rush back to it.

"Fuck."

Wærwulf has come off the saddle, Cinder struggling to stay upright, and I don't want to look and yet can't tear my eyes away.

"Come on, you daft beastie," the man in the water grabs a fistful of harness, and muscles straining, holds on to the flailing horse.

Wærwulf has wedged himself between the two ropes, walking one hand over another as he makes his way slowly, but surely, to the far riverbank. But it's Cinder that concerns me. I see his nose go under the water, and my legs are already moving, even as the men, in some well-practised movement, beat me to it. One of them flings a rope toward the man in the water. Quickly, he lopes the reigns through it, and then a chain of men and women, all straining on the rope, begin to pull Cinder to safety.

If I weren't witnessing it, I wouldn't believe it possible. But first Wærwulf, and then Cinder stagger up the riverbank, Cinder sheepishly, Wærwulf with fury.

"Fucking beastie, get yourself here," he orders, and Cinder does as instructed, eyes filled with reproach.

"How did you do that?" I demand of no one.

"As long as you have the reins, it's quite easy. It's when we lose the reins that we struggle." Satisfaction laces the voice, and I nod, all but speechless, as Sæbald is the next to make the crossing.

Before the moon has fully risen, all of the horses are on the river's far bank. The villagers have ensured we're all revived, providing warm drinks and hunks of cheese, even as others slick the backsides of our animals clear of the water.

"I can't thank you enough," I state when the final person, the man from the river itself, has made his way back to dry land.

"It's what we do," he offers, with a slight tremor, as I notice the blueness of his face and hands.

"Here, bring a drink," but there's already one waiting, and a colossal cloak covers him, all at the same time.

"I'll reward you," I announce, already thinking to reach for my coin bag.

"Aye, and who are you, the bloody king of Mercia?" Only the laughter dies as he looks at me, contrition already showing on his face.

"Sorry, My Lord King. No disrespect intended."

"None was taken. But yes, I am the bloody king of Mercia, and I'll reward you if I want."

"Then, I'll not turn you down, not for the good of the village."

He rallies quickly, and I admire him.

"Tell me, do you help everyone without first knowing who they are?"

He shakes his head; hands clamped around the steaming beaker he holds.

"No, but we recognised the bishop's messenger, so assumed you had to be someone important. Didn't think it'd be the bloody king himself."

"Then, I've had the last laugh. I have news the Raiders are in London. Don't let them cross the river if you can do so without injury."

"We wouldn't help them. We're more likely to put the river between ourselves and their sort. You need not worry. But you won't make it to London tonight. Not in this bastard weather."

"We have to try, all the same."

"There's a settlement, about halfway between here and Icknield Way. They'll give you the use of a barn for some sleep."

I nod. Edmund and I must have missed such a place on our journey back from Grantabridge.

"Hopefully, it'll be drier when we come back this way. I'll speak to you about a bridge then."

"As you will, My Lord King. Travel safe and kill the bastards, whoever they turn out to be."

Somehow, even though I've been in a river, I feel drier now than at any time since we set out. Two lads run ahead of my reconstructed warband, lighting the way back to the stone road. Voices call from the houses when we approach, and one of the youths shouts back, ensuring all is well.

"My thanks," I offer, once more, and then turn Haden back towards London. We've still got a long way to go.

CHAPTER 6

Eventually, I have to call a halt to our headlong dash along Watling Street. The horses are tired, and we're tired. More than once, I've had to jolt Rudolf awake in Dever's saddle.

Gregory spies the next settlement easily enough, flame light piercing the night. It's a relief to step under the roof, the constant drumming moving from on top of my head to further away. It didn't stop raining for long. And it's colder than a day old corpse. I shake myself, hastily remove Haden's saddle, and then find him water to drink and oats to eat. He seems content enough, and with everyone pressed together, it almost feels warm.

The morning dawns, watery, and with the threat of rain, but no actual rain falls from the sky.

"Come on, mount up quickly. We might yet avoid the worst of this fucking weather." The thought is surprisingly cheery, and the distance is quickly covered by horses eager to enjoy their freedom, even though it's bastard cold.

I'd almost sooner the rain.

By the time the sun is beginning to set, the clouds have turned the forbidding shade of grey and pink that can mean only one thing—more bloody snow.

"We'll have to press on," Gregory insists. I agree. I don't want to be caught in a snowstorm.

"But what of the Raiders?"

"They weren't within London when I left. They shouldn't be now."

"Where were they then?"

"To the west. They'd made themselves comfortable. The ships had been brought ashore, wooden tents erected. Hardly a pleasant way to spend the winter."

"But to the north of the Thames?"

"Yes, to the north."

"Take me there, not to Bishop Smithwulf."

Confusion forms on Gregory's thin lips, and I can sense he's going to argue with me. But I'm his king.

"Very well, My Lord King. To the Raider site."

"What do you plan?" Icel questions me.

"Kill 'em and do it quickly. Then bloody King Alfred can sod off back to Winchester, and the problem of London and whether it's threatened or not will be solved. Then we can turn our thought to bloody Jarl Halfdan."

"A passing good idea," Pybba announces, as though he's thought of it himself.

"Warn us when we're just close enough not to be seen," I demand of Gregory. Again, he merely nods, perhaps voicing his objections in his mind rather than out loud. I find I like him more and more.

My air puffs before me as we work our way westwards, the scent of London reaching my nostrils, the promise of heat and warmth, quickly lost as we skirt the broken-down walls of the place before moving on, to the market site, from Londinium to Lundenwic; my Aunt knows the history. It's just easier to call it bloody London. Only the most pompous will correct the mistake.

Someone should really think about rebuilding those broken defences. Fuck, I realise that 'someone' should be me.

And then the snow begins to fall, and the landscape transforms before my eyes.

This isn't one of my crowning glories. But, when are my decisions ever the right fucking ones?

"Stay wary," I encourage my men. We've been cold, and wet, and very, very cold, and now we must face an enemy while the world becomes black and white. Mostly fucking white.

My blood pulses with heat, the promise of the coming battle restoring me. I know I'm not alone.

"There, My Lord King," Gregory's voice fills with foreboding as he brings his horse up short, his breath wreathing him. I've already smelt the wood smoke from the campsite.

"Return to Bishop Smithwulf," I instruct Gregory. "You've done what must be done. Inform him that I've arrived. I'll be with him within a day or two, all being well."

"But, My Lord King, there are seven ships." Incredulity laces his words.

"It doesn't matter how many there are," Rudolf's confident words make good listening. "There could be thousands of the bastards, and we'd still finish them all."

"Won't you wait?" it seems Gregory isn't to be told, his face pale beneath the cloak over his head.

"It's not what we fucking do," Icel offers the only explanation.

"Now, be off with you," Hereman's words are the very opposite of a gentle caress and both Gregory and his mount startle and are heading back the way we've just come, without even realising.

I watch his departure as he rides towards the light and uncertain shelter of London's broken walls.

"It's no better than a bloody pig's sty," Hereman mouths, his nose wrinkled against the smell, which is pervasive, despite the blanket of snow covering up even the most unsightly of scenes.

"I've never much liked the fucking place," I confirm. We were here, not many years ago, fighting for King Burgred. It could have gone better, that's a certainty.

"So, we're taking them all on?" Rudolf's voice is resolved.

"Yes, we will, but first, we'll have some fucking fun. Over there, beneath the trees."

By chance, an area of woodland has risen before us, visible as a mass of black against the white.

"I'm surprised they've not chopped it all down to burn or

build houses."

"Let's just be grateful they bloody haven't," I mutter, shaking my head at Icel's dour words.

It's impossible to stay hidden from even a cursory examination on the snowy landscape. All the same, I feel better beneath the reaching branches of the pine trees. The wind has dropped away. Now it snows, obscuring the view before me, but not before I've decided what we'll do.

"Burn the ships?" Icel demands to know.

"Scuttle the ships?" Rudolf asks, and I glance at him, perplexed.

"Where have you been learning such fucking words? Surely, you should have just said 'ground them.'"

"Been gathering some knowledge," Rudolf retorts. "Nothing wrong with learning stuff you don't already know."

"Of course there isn't," I feel stung into replying, but a smile plays around my lips. I should send him to a monastery. Have the monks teach him to read and write. He'd be a natural. But then, he'd have to hang up his sword, and I don't believe that's likely.

"Slit their throats while they sleep?" Pybba seems to approve of that tactic.

"A combination of all three, I think," I grin at them. "Why choose only one way of killing them when the options can be so fucking varied."

"Provided you organise it in the correct bloody order, that is?" Wærwulf chuckles darkly.

'Well, obviously,' I expel. It doesn't dissuade him. He just grins all the wider.

"So, My Lord, what is the correct bloody order?"

"We'll just find that out as we go, won't we," I laugh, eyebrows high, swigging from my water bottle—the joy of what must be done coursing through my body.

"But tonight?" Pybba prompts me. There's no forgiveness for making him ride in these conditions, but the thought of a fight has perked the grumpy sod up.

"No time like fucking now. The snow will both hide us and

make it easier, all at the same time. It'll be brighter than day, and they won't be expecting us. And therefore, we can take as many as we can before they're half-awake."

"So, we kill 'em while they sleep and then fire their ships, or scuttle them, was that the word?" Icel directs this to Rudolf.

"Yep, we scuttle them."

I'm standing in the snow, the horses sheltering under the trees, chewing on whatever lichen they can find. I've left no one to watch them. I can't leave a single warrior behind. Not if this is to succeed.

I know my Aunt would criticise me for such ill-thought-out action. Equally, Edmund would complain. But Icel, Pybba, Hereman and Rudolf, don't seem to mind. It might be bloody reckless. It might also be the most inspired thing I've ever done. I'll know soon enough. And so will my warriors.

I can see the collection of poorly constructed steadings that the Raiders have decided to call theirs in front of me. I'm sure they're on a farm site, and I spare a thought for those who must have been killed. Bishop Smithwulf didn't fucking mention this. Either that, or they've found some ancient ruins, those that litter the landscape, as though die cast upon a board; without reason, or not that I've ever been able to determine.

Some say that the rivers move their course, that farming land might once have been little more than a bog, that bogs might have once been dry. That the sea might have been closer, that the coastlands, wider. Such words make my head itch. They make little sense to me. Rivers can't move, neither can roads. Although, well, perhaps that's not true of roads. I've seen steadings built across abandoned tracks, and equally, steadings moved to make way for them.

There's a sturdy building at the heart of the site, but it's not large enough for them all. Not even by half. Light spills beneath the spaces in the stonework, through the pieces of wood that have been used to try and fill the gaps, to make the building tall enough to carry a roof. And with the light comes noise and laughter, some bad singing, and a sense that these warriors have nothing to fear, even here, in Mercia.

It fucking boils me.

Some of the Raiders even seem to have upended the ships they brought with them and turned them into shelters. It makes my task easier. They'll not be going back into the Thames anytime soon. There'll be no escape for these bastards.

Sæbald and Gyrth are down at the water's edge, ready to spark a flame and set those ships that are adjacent to the water aflame. Rudolf won't be getting his wish because all of the boats are close to the river, not in it. Cocky bastards have decided this ramshackle arrangement will ensure their safety. Only then do I consider how long they've been here and why this is the first I've heard of yet another invasion on my kingdom.

The weather turned bad even before the Yule feast, rain falling for days without ceasing. It's been no better since my men and I fought on into the worsening conditions until all of our foes were dead or fled. Dead would have been more rewarding. I imagine these Norsemen have done the same. I'm grateful for Northampton's protection and sturdiness then. These Raiders have little more than a canvas above their head, and the fires that pollute my breath are poor things, the wood damp, hardly burning at all. I imagine they'll be pleased to bleed for me. At least they'll be warm for the first time in weeks, if only for a moment or two.

But my wound plagues me as I turn to survey my warriors, all of them eager to begin the slaughter-work. It itches and works at my resolve, trying to undermine me even before I've taken the first attacking blow. Will it burst open? Will it be my blood that warms the enemy? It better fucking not be.

I think of my Aunt's dire warning. I consider Edmund, no doubt warming her bed and thinking of nothing but heat and fire.

Fuck him. He's abandoned me when I probably need him most. I won't let that stop me. I'll have this victory without him, and he'll be excluded from the scop's next song or verse.

And then Wærwulf sidles to my side.

"I've heard them speaking," he whispers. We're all aware that sound strangely travels when snow coats the land. I could hear a conversation taking place from London itself and think it was coming from just in front of me.

"What did they say?" From his tone, I know it's not good.

"King Alfred of Wessex, it seems, has broken his agreement with them. He promised riches and winter in London itself, waited upon by servants and slaves, where food would never be in short supply."

I nod.

"Fucking bastard."

The kings of Wessex are only too keen to prostitute Mercia, provided their precious kingdom remains free from attack.

"They speak of Jarl Halfdan and the other jarls as well. They know of you but don't fear you. They also say that they'll first join Halfdan, as soon as the weather allows them safe passage by river and sea, and then they mean to take their revenge on King Alfred."

Such information makes me pause.

Is Bishop Smithwulf aware of this deception? Is he willing to allow Alfred into London? I know the Raiders attacked London recently. Has Bishop Smithwulf been susceptible to them ever since? I have no way of knowing.

Equally, the thought of these Raiders returning to harass Wessex is fucking appealing; I can't deny it. Sooner they were there than here. Rather they were keeping Alfred's eyes from Mercia. But, of course, Wærwulf has heard mention of Jarl Halfdan, and that involves travelling to the Humber, and I can't have them doing that.

"We attack them all the same," I confirm, and Wærwulf grunts. He didn't expect anything else.

"There are few enough guards. Some by the river, a few outside the steading. But nowhere else."

"Take Icel and Hereman, and direct your attention at the steading. I'll have Rudolf and Pybba take the men by the river, and then they can order Sæbald and Gyrth to fire the ships."

"If they burn."

"Yes, if they bloody burn," I admit. It's not ideal, but when is it ever? At Repton, the land steamed with heat; Torksey was no better. Outside Northampton, it rained as though it might never cease, and now we have snow. Let's see what advantage snow can give us.

"And be warned, there's some sort of ditch, or perhaps an old, ruined wall, running around the camp. It's low in most places but might deceive beneath the snow."

"My thanks, inform the others."

There are whispered conversations taking place around me while I eyeball the campsite. Perhaps, I should take more care, learn the landscape better before attacking. But no. My blood runs too hot, and the only way to escape the strange sensations fizzing through my skin is to slay these foes.

I'll just have to fucking get on with it.

Ordheah and Ingwald stand to either side of me, eyes straining through the swirling snow. Around them, the remainder of my men stretches to either side.

We have shield, seaxs, axes and spears to hand, although not all in one hand, while Icel, Hereman and Wærwulf scurry through the campsite, their intent to tackle the steading at its heart. I don't know how many Raiders shelter within it. It doesn't matter. They'll all be fucking dead soon enough.

A soft shush, and although I can't see, I appreciate that Rudolf and Pybba have already killed the ill-attentive guards. Now, in a strange reversal of what happened outside Northampton's walls, we need to do the same.

The sound of snores and farts fills the cooling air. I don't blame them. The only way to pass the time when the weather is like this is to sleep.

I reach the first shelter, the canvas sagging beneath the gathering snow. I could leave, and they might just suffocate when the material collapses. But no. There is to be no chance.

The waft of warm air burns my face as I pull the entrance

aside, moving inside quickly, and stabbing down on the man who sleeps there, his beard hoar-frosted. My seax is in and out without thought, and blood wells quickly along his chest as his breath chokes and then ceases.

Too fucking easy. They won't all be like that.

Outside once more, my warriors are doing the same. They dip in and out of the shelters, some inside for longer than others, and then because even fools might sometimes be lucky, a cry warbles through the deadened air, the howls of outrage, and the familiar sound of iron claimed from weapons belts fills the air.

It'll be a bloody battle then, and not just a fucking execution.

CHAPTER 7

The structures before me seem to erupt as though deer fleeing before my arrows.

Moments ago, it was an almost silent advance against our foe. Now I face leering faces, red with fury, white with cold. These fuckers are angry, and that makes this all the more enjoyable.

"*Angreb*," the word trembles through me, but my eyes are already on the Raider before me. He's naked to the waist, the inkings that mark his pale skin, impossible to ignore; his beard rich with trinkets, his dark hair, because I can only see in the shadows and light of the snow and the moon, tightly braided so that a vivid red scar that runs across his forehead is visible.

No doubt he means to terrify with his bulk and menacing face, but I've fucking seen it all before.

He rushes me, and then I realise he's not had the time to put his boots on. A reckless error. A fatal one as well.

My foe leaves marks behind him on the white surface as he rears towards me. I hold my seax steady. This has been close work so far. Those who've died have been as sleeping babes content at their mother's breast. Not so anymore. We've roused hornets by killing their queen, and they come for us.

A sharp glance to left and right shows me two things. Firstly, my men are with me. Secondly, we're fucking outnumbered, massively.

"*Skiderik*," my opponent spits at me, considering where to aim his attack. I have no such great thoughts. Instead, my seax stabs cleanly into his armpit, the blood warming and melting the reddened snow, even as I follow up with my forehead smashed against his nose.

He might not have felt the blow that'll drain him dry, but he sure as fuck felt the broken nose, the wet sound bringing a smirk to my face.

I leave him, writhing in the snow, his weapon waving feebly in his hand.

He should have put his fucking boots on. No man should fight with cold feet.

I feel my body thrum with the satisfaction of a good kill. This is what I've been missing. Without this, I've felt weak and feeble. I've not fucking enjoyed it. Not at all.

Next, three Raiders sneer towards me. They've taken the time to dress, or perhaps were already dressed. The shriek of a woman rushing to the dying man assures me I've interrupted him. Poor fucker. Dying with his seed unspent.

I don't mean to kill the woman, but she runs at me and then startles, her breast bloodied.

"Fucking bollocks," and I wrench my seax free and slice her neck wide-open. It'll be a quicker death. That's all I can offer her surprised eyes.

My three foe-men look from the woman to my seax. A look passes between them. I imagine it's an outrage that I've killed the whore. I can't see it being in compensation for their dead comrade—just one less to vie for her services.

Two of the men are tall, bristling with rage as well as weapons. The other is a full head shorter, but far from being a child, with his grey-flecked beard, snow slowly melting amongst the stiff bristles.

His nose is far from straight, his head entirely devoid of hair, although I detect something inked onto it. That must have fucking hurt. But not as much as what I'm about to do to him.

They think me alone, only for Ordheah and Ingwald to materialise at my shoulders. A more equal battle then.

The shorter man comes first, his pronounced steps, forced to lift his feet high above the rapidly growing snow, slow and steady. His intentions to aim for the right side of my neck are broadcast far and wide, his sword stabbing upwards. I don't know if his movements are so slow or my senses stretched too tight. A fresh well of blood from his chest, where I've decided to throw my seax at him, watching it fly straight over such a short distance, assures me he's dead.

He falls backwards, and I rush to grab my double-eagle headed seax, my hand bereft without its steadying presence.

The larger man to my right might have some skill, as he and Ingwald clash, sword against sword, while Ordheah's foe is already silent in the snow.

A temporary grave of snow will hide his bulging eyes quickly enough, no doubt, the stench of opened bowels as well. It'll be best if a thaw never reaches this bloodied place.

Behind my enemy, I catch sight of Icel, Hereman and Wærwulf. They wipe blades in the snow, the flicker of advancing flames capturing them so that they cast a haloed glow that speaks of death and destruction. Flames begin to lick their way along the sodden roof of the building. It'll burn the wood and saturated thatch if we're lucky, but the stones will no doubt remain standing.

Between the three of them, they drag a giant piece of loose stonework, flickering grey and menacing, and wedge it against the door.

The scent of burning flesh tickles my nostrils. The collapsing roof should do the same.

My neck wound twinges, but I ignore it, taking a desultory swipe at Ingwald's enemy. The two are evenly matched. I don't have the time to fucking waste.

Our foe clutches his throat where my seax pierces it, Ingwald's face sheeted in the man's blood.

"My apologies," I offer. He grunts with thanks, his eyes too shadowed to see his true thoughts.

And then I turn because something's happening, and it's not

to do with those trapped in the steading. No. Someone has taken command, and a fierce line of men face mine, shields clutched in blue hands, and I think we might be about to have a real battle.

"Shields," I bark roughly, Ingwald taking up my cry, even Icel turning from his place at the sealed door to see what's happening.

I see him shake his head as my warriors rush to me, Pybba and Rudolf amongst them. Down by the sluggish river, I can see flames beginning to lick over the boat timbers. It's not bloody quick, and it's not fucking spectacular, and I fear a heavy flurry of snow might extinguish the orange sparks, but enough damage should have been done. I hope.

"To me," I bellow, to the comforting and familiar huffs and groans of my men. Once more, I realise this is what I've missed.

I've felt excluded, too weak to get involved in their mock battles and playful banter, my Aunt watching me with her sternest gaze. I shouldn't have allowed myself to be cowed. It was just a cut. It's healed. It will heal. In time, my Aunt advises it might not even be visible, not beneath the lines of my neck. It doesn't feel like that, red, raw and puckered as it is. But it's covered by a neck guard. Not one of my foes knows it's there. Not with Jarl Olafr dead and buried before he could tell of his brief triumph. The bastard.

Certainly, it's not affected my arms and hand. I've killed. I've left a trail of blazing red in the snow.

"Prepare to attack," I bellow, licking the pure, white snow from my lips, enjoying its freshness.

But the Raiders have learned that surprise is the best form of attack. They rush at my shield wall, even before our shields snap together, one next to another, to another, the sound reassuring, practise making it effortless.

"Brace," and my order ripples away, even though it's heard in the stillness. All around us sleeps. But not here. Here we fight for our lives. Here we fight for Mercia. Only our enemy isn't just the Raiders; no, it's Alfred of Wessex. He might not be armed and coming against me, but I can smell his stink on this fuck-up.

The thud of our opponents forward momentum forces us all back a step or two, the snow offering too little to brace against before we recover.

Now, sweat beads my lips, not snow, the air before me, super-heated. I can feel the breathing of my enemy. I can smell their sour sweat and rank, sleep-muddled breath. I can detect the trembling of arms. They seem formidable, but they're not. Why I consider, didn't King Alfred of Wessex just kill the fuckers and have done with it?

"*Angreb*," we all know what that means. It's no surprise as shields are slightly lowered, and blades snake towards us. I knock the barbed point of a spear aside with my seax, wishing I could sever the edge, but I don't have the time. I feel another blade at my feet, and I lift one foot, and then another, and then stamp hard. But it's gone before I can pin it in place. And then the fucking spear is back once more.

My neck aches with the sharp response, the movement like a tear, even though I know my wound won't have opened, even if it feels like it has.

I try and move aside to avoid the spear but can't relinquish my position, not while we're all being ferociously attacked.

"Fucker," I expel, considering what I should do. There's no one behind me to take my place, should I step aside. The shield wall is more prone to shattering than an icicle falling from the eaves of a roof. I won't allow all my warriors to perish because I fear the slice of cold iron through my flesh.

But, the decision is taken from me, as enemy shields seem to vibrate and the spear is snatched back. Something's happening, but I can't see what it is. I know what it is, all the fucking same. Somewhere along the line, one of the Raiders has fallen aside, their place hastily taken by those next to them, so that the gap need never have appeared, but it's given me the chance I need.

I slide my seax around my shield, above the man who tries to kill me, and then I reverse my grip and stab down with all the force available. I whisper a hope that he's not wearing a helm, and then I hear a shriek of horror, even as my blade slides forwards, before continuing its downwards journey.

I don't know what I've impaled, as I wrench it back, but my opponent stumbles. I rush forwards, driving Ingwald and Ordheah with me, even as blood drips onto my exposed hand. I think it's snow, but the smell tells me differently.

Hastily, I turn aside, batter my seax against the shield there. I've forged a path, but not for long. Not if the number of Raiders rushing toward me is to be believed. Behind the Raiders shield wall, the fire has caught on the building's roof, while Icel and Hereman move to spread it as far as possible. Wærwulf is engaged in a battle against two Raiders, his movements concise and placed with care. He'll triumph. It's just a matter of time.

A sudden tempest sees the fire spread evenly over the roof, the screams of those trapped within, causing more than one of those rushing to the shield wall to reconsider their actions. They could help their allies. If they fucking wanted to. It would aid me if they did, but then it might imperil Icel, Hereman and Wærwulf. The three stand together now, blocking both the entrance to the steading and access to the rock that keeps the door shut. I can see where the wood of the door bows. There are desperate people in there. I spit aside my distaste. They should have stayed at bloody home.

Not that the fire on the steading burns alone. The one from the ships is starting to drive back the falling snow. It falls in patches now, making it more difficult to see. I imagine Sæbald and Gyrth are already rushing to assist the rest of us.

I brace myself for the warrior careering towards me. Only his steps falter, his head turning, no doubt called to aid those who've decided they might benefit from rescuing those in the burning steading—my face twists with consternation. I hope Icel, Hereman and Wærwulf will know to do the right thing now because I can't shout to them. The instructions are too long and complex. They'd be lost in the gusting flames.

The black smoke threatens to choke me as the wind stirs it. I expect to taste only smoke, not ash, and I'm forced to bend double, hack up whatever I've inhaled. My old wound screams in agony.

"Fucking stand up," Rudolf's voice is rough with fury, the clang of metal on metal, assuring me that I might just have to thank him for saving me. I spit aside the ash, inhale sharp, clean snow, raising my seax to counter the next attack.

Pybba has joined Rudolf, as have Ingwald and Ordheah. The five of us fight all-comers, those who still rush to join the battle, and those members of the shield wall who surely feel it faltering.

A wide-eyed blond-haired warrior screams his rage at me. His byrnie is speckled with snow, the leather flashing blackly against the leaping flames. He carries not one but two war axes in his hands, one much larger than the other. I grip my shield, pressing it forward as I rush him. The blows send shockwaves along my left arm, while with my right, I stab and slash with ferocity, mouth shut, careful not to inhale more of the acrid smoke.

It smells like pork, and I know it's fucking not, even as my belly rumbles.

A tumbling piece of ash settles onto the head of my enemy, but he doesn't notice, even as I watch the flames flicker along the edges of his hair, no doubt dried and cracked. I wait for his scream of agony, even as I hope the snow doesn't quench it. I stab with my seax and my shield.

Blow after blow connects, his axe on my shield, his other axe trying to stop my seax, but the movement of swinging and aiming is much slower than that of stabbing. Blood erupts from between my gloved fingers as I finally land a blow on his exposed forearm, the force pinning it to the side of his body.

Fuck, that must hurt. And now, of course, he's aware that his hair is wreathed in a halo of heavenly fire.

His eyes reflect the fire of the ships; his lips opened in a shriek of agony. I wrench back my seax before he runs screaming into the snow, tripping headfirst into a pile of the stuff.

He sizzles. I watch him, knowing it would be easy to kill him now, to drive my seax through the back of his neck, his weapons lying to either side of him. For a moment, just a moment, I think I might let him live.

"Ah, fuck that," and Rudolf drives his sword through my foe's back.

"Get on with it," he growls, and my eyebrows rise into my hair while Pybba cackles evilly.

"You let loose a real tyrant," Pybba continues before he lays into his next target, a tall, wiry man with black rims for eyes.

I spare a glance for what's happening around me, but all is chaos. The twin shield walls have long since collapsed. There's no order to this battle. But then, there rarely is when it comes down to it. We all fight for a cause but not one of us wants to fucking die in the stinking mire of piss and blood, gobs of flesh and cracked bone.

A sudden whoosh of hot air and the roof on the steading collapses in on itself, to yet more cries of rage and wrath, more than one of them cut off mid-air. Poor bastards. Still, they'll have known what it was like to be too hot, even if only for a heartbeat or two. The entire battle pauses, every single attack, eyes riveted on the scene. I shudder at the furtive hands trying to find the means to escape.

One person, hair aflame like the holy men in the illustrated gospels I've seen, makes it all the way up one of the stone walls, dragging himself upright, before collapsing in a sputtering heap into the snow that's quickly becoming thick enough to cushion his fall.

Behind, more reaching hands can be seen, but they're weak, feeble. They won't survive.

With quick steps, I'm in front of one of the fresher foe-men, hand on his weapons belt. It gets no further because he's tumbling to his knees, his belly sliced open, bleeding into the snow too fast for that which falls to cover the outrage.

His enraged cry recalls everyone to the task at hand. I face two Raiders now, one tall and wide, one short and slender. I could aim for the neck on the shorter and hit the groin of the other.

The shorter warrior grins at me as though appreciating my dilemma. But it's not a dilemma. A blow to the neck and groin will kill an enemy just as fucking quickly.

But before I can aim my seax at his neck, the largest man swings a huge sword toward me. It must be as long as the shorter of the men, the blade far from sharp.

"What the fuck do you mean to fell with that? A bloody lion?" I've heard of such creatures, fierce killers. I'd like to meet one if it was inclined not to kill me.

Garbled laughter spills from his toothless maw, and I grin at him, enjoying this respite.

Daft fucker. Does he have the mind of a child, or is this just his way? I'm wary of the shorter man. I know how effective two working as one can be. I need only glance to where Pybba and Rudolf attack one warrior. With concise cuts wielded by Rudolf, the man doesn't know what to counter, even as Pybba slices beneath his armpit, liquid pooling down Pybba's hand as though it were honey from an upturned pot.

I keep the shorter man in my sight as the sword weaves before me. It's almost hypnotic, but when the shorter man rushes me, my seax is level with my thigh, aiming for his belly. He focuses his energy on landing a blow with his shorter weapon. I'm sure such a tactic has worked before, but not tonight.

His steps slowly falter as he runs himself onto my seax. The weight is uncomfortable, realisation slow in coming. I thrust my shield upwards, ramming the sword. Only it's not enough. I'm forced to drop my seax, the man with it, and the tall man's eyes flick from me to his ally. Comprehension is much faster, and his sword whirls through the air again, the aim uncanny as he reaches for my neck. I can't duck away in time, the dying man coming for me with one bloodied hand and his short sword still outstretched.

"Fuck," I'm trapped between the two, even though the one is dying.

"You didn't bloody think that out, did you," Rudolf's jibe isn't wrong, but it's far from helpful. And then he spins into the taller man, Pybba rushing to knock the long sword aside with his shield.

It almost saves me, but the tall man's face has twisted. He has revenge on his mind. Pybba's shield may as well be a feather as he batters it aside. Equally, Rudolf is dismissed with a jab of his fist to slip into the snow.

I consider my sword but know it's no good against my foe. It won't be long enough. I have my shield.

Only then, the shorter man trying to kill me shudders, his last breath erupting with a bubble of blood. I know what to do.

I wrestle the sword from lifeless fingers, even while holding my shield against the coming attack. I drive the blade at the taller man's neck. If he sees the projectile, there's no indication. He abruptly convulses to the ground in a surprisingly compact way, the sword tip just about touching my boot.

I suck in a much-needed breath and bend to assist Pybba and Rudolf to their feet.

The cockiness has been knocked from Rudolf while Pybba flexes his arm, a glimmer of frustration on his face.

For a moment, the battle rages around us without including us.

"Bastard," Rudolf kicks the dead man in the arm, and his hand releases the sword in reaction. It settles softly in the snow, disappearing and leaving only an imprint behind.

"My thanks," I mock gently, wishing only to restore Rudolf's good spirits.

"Well, we fucking distracted him for you," Pybba answers darkly. He's clenching and unclenching his hand, weapon held to his body by the elbow of his handless arm.

"Can you fight?"

"If I fucking have to, I'll use my teeth," Pybba rages, no doubt, directed at himself as well as the Raiders.

"Why do we bloody do this?' he asks next. My eyes swivel to meet his, my mouth opens in shock so that snow settles within it. Does he genuinely mean to question me, here and now?

"I don't mean this," and he points to the chaos around us, his eyes alight with mischief. "I mean this," and he points between us.

"Makes the time pass more quickly," I retort over my shoulder.

I've seen the next problem.

Icel and Hereman are surrounded, Wærwulf trying to fight his way back to them, alongside seven Raiders.

"Come with me," I order, and Rudolf rushes to do as I ask, but Pybba remains, his gaze on something else. And I see the problem. With the shield wall gone, there are patches of fighting. In some of them, my warriors are triumphing, but in others, they're hounded by our foe. Sæbald and Gyrth are as stranded as Icel, Hereman and Wærwulf, where they battle, backlit by the orange glow of the burning ships.

"Go with Pybba," I order Rudolf. His mouth opens and then snaps shut. "Gather others as you go." He doesn't argue. For once. A fucking miracle.

This might be about to become a stand-off, two smaller fronts raging against one another. I'm starting to realise that while there might be seven ships, there certainly aren't warriors to crew those seven ships. Not here. Has this just been another of the lies that trip from the mouth of men who should be my allies? Or are they elsewhere, doing who knows what?

I'll consider that later.

"Ælfgar, Gardulf, with me," I bellow their names, rushing to assist my warriors. They've successfully beaten back those who tried to kill them. Gardulf, with practised ease, is checking the dead, his seax offering final cuts where they're needed. His father would be proud had he been there to see it. Perhaps that was why he didn't come and nothing to do with my Aunt. Maybe it's easier to hear of such exploits after they're accomplished rather than witness them first hand.

I'm not a father. I'll never know. Although, well, my eyes betray me as they flicker to Rudolf, making his way to the others.

No, I'd always rather be there, just in case.

I genuinely wish I knew who Gardulf's mother was, but it seems I'm never to be offered that information.

"Aye, My Lord," Ælfgar responds, and I know they'll follow on behind, Gardulf straightening, his face shadowed by flames and snow. A dazzling combination.

For now, my focus is on the man encouraging the other Raiders. He stands slightly back from the coming altercation, a fine weapon in his right hand, the iron glinting with the promise of death. Thankfully the screams of terror from inside the broken building have stopped. There's no one alive in there to rescue, but that's not stopping the Raiders from battling against Icel and Hereman.

The seven men hounding my two warriors are all dressed. I notice that first. They wear leather byrnie and weapons belt. Perhaps, they were guarding another entranceway, or, and I think I'm probably right, they've just returned from elsewhere. Have they been trading, or most likely, stealing from a local settlement? They wear dark cloaks laden with snow, swept aside to allow access to weapons on belts. They couldn't be more visible unless they set their hair on fire, as so many others have.

Including the commander of this group, there are eight Raiders. I should like to know his name if only so I can make some mention of it next time Icel decides to share stories of long-ago battles. Perhaps, Edmund might even sing of my triumph over him. But no, I've had enough of such fucking tales of my exploits.

"Wærwulf," I recall him to my side. Now there are four of us, against the other eight.

"Bastard," Wærwulf grumbles. His chin is awash with blood, and when he spits it aside, a thin stream of pink steams from the settling snow. It's a more violent act than decapitation.

"We rush them," I pant, ensuring the three hear me. "We rush them, and then we try and separate them, and that way, we'll release Hereman and Icel. I'll concentrate on the fucker there," and I nod toward the commander once more. His stance, and actions, speak of an arrogant bastard who thinks himself above actually wielding his weapons.

Warriors like that disgust me. Have they forgotten how much such tossers frustrated them when they were merely ships men? How quickly the mighty forget from where they've come.

My eyes sweep the battlefield. Pybba and Rudolf are already

battling to aid Sæbald and Gyrth. Lyfing and Ingwald are beating four men into submission, as though the snow is eating their foe. Wulfred, Osbert, and Ordheah are fighting for their lives, just like Sæbald and Gyrth, their grunts reaching me after I've watched their action. But Goda is alert to what's happening, so too is Siric.

Content that all is as well as it can be, I seek out the commander once more. I hunger for his death. Cocky fucker.

Gardulf moves with the ease of the young, loping through the snow. I envy him, but then I have no time for that because the commander has realised his mistake.

While Gardulf attacks the back of the first man, unbalancing him so that he falls face first in the snow, and it's nothing to stab into his back, the commander leers at me.

His white teeth shimmer with leaping flames from his shadowed face, the rest of him black as night. He appears etched with snow. I can't imagine he appreciates the cold, but what do I know of these Norseman and those with whom they ally?

I spare a glance for his weapons, noting the curved blade he brings to hand and allow myself to grin.

This might be more fucking fun than I thought.

He inclines his head toward me, an offer, or a greeting, I hardly know.

Words stream from his mouth. I don't understand their lyrical quality, although those he orders have no problem. Not that they turn aside from their endeavours. If anything, they redouble their efforts.

I kick snow aside, wincing as the movement jars my neck. I might typically crack my neck from side to side, but that's currently unimaginable.

"Come on then, show me what you've fucking got?" I taunt. Whether he understands or not, and I imagine he does, how else would he have survived in Wessex this year? He leaps forward.

He moves like lightning, one moment before me, the next almost upon me. I'm ready all the same. Shield raised, it absorbs the blow easily enough, even if the weapon is curved. I'd already noticed that my foe must use both hands to direct the blade, so while he's trying to regain control of it, snatch it back from my shield's weight, I slash cross ways, and then upwards with my seax.

The impact isn't as significant as I planned, and no blood slicks my gloves. The weight of my shield drags at me as well, pulling at my neck wound. I'm almost pleased when he's once more free from its clutches.

"That went bloody well, didn't it?" I mock, but the warrior's eyes remain focused. He doesn't even glance to see how his men fare. I do, and I'm pleased. Wærwulf has taken one of the other foe-men with a slicing blow that's severed his nose. Blood stains the spot, a desecration, even while the man tries to fight. I don't think he'll stand for much longer.

My opponent hesitates this time. He's tried speed. Perhaps now he'll attempt to fool me by hardly moving at all.

I eye him, searching for a weakness, but there doesn't seem to be one. His hands are clasped, one above the other on the handle of his sword, as he sways softly. I remain still. I'm not going to offer a tell as to my next action. He'll just have to wait.

Only then, a crash fills the air, not one of a falling building but something else.

Fuck, some of these men are mounted.

A screaming horse rushes, riderless, from the depths of the darkness, legs driving into the snow, eyes wide with fear. It's all I can do to evade around its wild hooves, and of course, my foe-man is there to take advantage of my distraction.

I hear the blade whipping through the air. I jab upwards with my shield, bending my knees, ensuring I'm beneath the protection of the linden-board.

The blade hits at an odd-angle, knocking against my knuckles painfully, while my arse dips into the snow, my legs apart but rock-solid beneath me. Gritting my teeth, I erupt from the camouflage as though a whale from the green waves, in the stories the scops tell, my shield arm fully outstretched.

My opponent has his curved sword in the snow, dropping low,

balancing only on one foot, although he faces me. Or rather, he faces my shield, and it whacks into his open mouth with a ringing sound louder than dropped iron on one of the ancient tiled floors, the colours lost to the passage of too many feet, and the open-air above it.

He buckles, head thrown backwards, falling, falling into the snow, his sword swallowed by the weight still falling from the sky as though ash from the funeral pyre.

But it's not done yet, even as I drop my shield to loom over him. His hand is busy around his waist, but again, it's a distraction. A shimmering blade abruptly appears in his other hand, no doubt from some hidden place up his sleeve. He explodes from the snow in a fluid movement that doesn't require knees, and the blade is before my nose.

He licks his lip, no doubt thinking my death imminent, but I've fucking had enough of this.

I dodge the knife, slipping to the left and beneath it, stabbing backwards as I go. I feel my seax cut fabric, and then deeper, the warm scent almost choking me.

A garbled roar and my opponent slumps into the snow. I'm panting, eyes busy, even as I watch him. He's not done yet.

Or maybe he is.

One of the fighting men thrusts Wærwulf aside contemptuously and rushes to face me. I see few enough details, but I notice he shares the same weapon as my struggling opponent.

I think to finish the man before he can grip hold of the flapping skin that threatens to spill his innards to the outside, but a slither of iron, sparkling in the snow and flames, catches my eye. I move aside, just in time, almost colliding with Wærwulf, who doesn't mean to let his opponent slip away so easily.

I grin at him, and Wærwulf chuckles low in his throat, seemingly unaware of the deep gash on his nose.

"Fucking fuckers," he offers, as though we talk of horses or dogs. "You finish off yours," he continues. "This little fucker is all mine. Damn bastard."

The original opponent has made his way to his knees. His lips are turning pale, his eyes red-rimmed, and yet he's not about to give up. That much is evident from the way he tries to stand, one hand hidden by the snow, the other beneath his cloak.

"Fine. But mine's already half-dead, so get on with yours, or I'm bloody taking him." Aware of a diverse collection of bruises, and perhaps, some cuts as well, as the wind changes direction, swirling flakes of snow that land wetly on any exposed flesh, I step carefully, one leg lifted high and then the next. Already, the depth of snow reaches my calf.

"Please," the bleeding man says to me, the word etched with pain, even as Wærwulf and the other man clash once more in a welter of grunts and crashing iron. A crunch of snow accompanies each step.

His eyes are only half focused on me. He staggers, trying to retrace our footsteps from earlier. I know what he wants. But fuck it. I don't know where it is. He'll just have to die without it. I'm surprised he shares the religion of the Raiders.

Seeing my resolve, as my hand settles on my seax, shield only loosely held now that he's all but dead, he surges forward, arm outstretched in the snow, moving from side to side. He'd do better if he were a hound and had a damn nose to sniff it out.

I jab down, through his neck, with only a passing thought for my injury. He collapses into the snow, warm wine melting it so that it runs red all around him. I half notice that his fingers twitch just on the weapon's handle as I turn aside.

Wærwulf's opponent is bleeding as well, pain-hazed eyes seeking out his commander. He opens his mouth, sucks in a deep breath, as though to shout for aid, as Wærwulf stabs into the gaping maw. Teeth shatter, blood erupts, and then the two are finally still.

"Stupid fuckers," Wærwulf spits, kicking the body for good measure. His shoulders move up and down. I appreciate how physical our opponents have been. Other Raiders are less supple. If they could all move with the same elegance as these two, we might need to shift some weight from our bodies and equipment.

I notice then that Icel and Hereman have won free with the aid of Gardulf and move toward me. The steading is little more than a concertina of flames and lost hopes and wishes.

Icel's chest heaves, and he hawks into the snow.

"It's too bloody cold for this," he complains, perhaps, like me, feeling the bite of the air inside his body every time he breathes. We should be before a hearth, not forging one in the heart of a blizzard.

"Where did that horse go?" A slither of worry has wormed its way into me. I wish we'd not left the horses. Not when there are such desperate warriors. I'm pleased there was only one horse and not the mounted host, I'd assumed at first.

Pybba, Rudolf, Sæbald and Gyrth can be seen, clashing with a handful of the enemy, but not huge numbers. Sæbald and Ingwald are bending to run snow over their weapons, keen to clean away the stickiness of death.

It seems the battle is almost won. And yet, I feel uneasy.

This has been too effortless. Where are the rest of the bastards?

"There, the horse is down by the river. No doubt it was thirsty. Why else would it have been in such a hurry?" Hereman comments, his voice drips with scorn. He's heaving great gulps of air into his chest. He coughs, spits as well, and I spare a thought for them, trapped between the burning building and a line of the enemy. They've inhaled far more of the smoke and ash than I'd have liked. I try not to consider that the ash could have come from those trapped by the fire.

I've never been one to relish the thought of consuming another.

The moment extends between us, and then as one, we turn one to another.

"That was Cinder," I explode, peering into the darkness as though I can see the horses from here.

"Wærwulf," I shout, entirely unsure of what to do. This battle is nearly at an end, that much is clear, but what of our mounts?

Rudolf hears my words, even from such a distance, as they

echo in the air. He takes much less time to make the connection between the stray horse and our mounts and flees through the snow, his long legs perfect for skipping over the increasing layer of fallen snow. Hereman meets my eye.

"Go back. Check on the horses. Icel, accompany him, Wulfred as well. If those bastards have stolen our horses." The threat hangs between us, and I try not to consider how ineffectual it sounds.

What will I do if my horse is gone? I know. I think everyone there does.

Furious, I stalk through the detritus of the battle, bending when I hear gargled air to cut short any suffering.

"Sæbald, get your arse over here," I bellow when I'm sure everyone has survived, even if some of them limp or bend to tie another's wound with a piece of ripped cloth from one of the bodies.

Sæbald arrives, Gyrth as well, and behind them, I can see that Rudolf is rushing Wærwulf to Cinder's side. Between them, they're calming the horse, even as she dances before the fires. I wince, noticing the rein that trails on the floor. I hope she doesn't stumble on it. I'm not in the mood to kill a horse for one of my fucking stupid mistakes.

"What is it?" Sæbald huffs, tone resentful. He's not realised what's happening.

"Go with Gyrth to the horses. Hereman and Icel have already gone to check on them."

"What?" This isn't a usual request, yet Gyrth touches Sæbald's arm, indicating Cinder. I turn aside, so I don't have to witness the disbelief in Sæbald's eyes.

I just need to gather my warriors together. Then we'll all be off to ensure the horses are well, but Cinder still needs to be brought under control. I march down the slope, careful where I place my feet, imagining at least ten different scenarios. None of them has a pleasant ending for my foes who've stolen my horses.

A cry wrenches through the air. I'm running even before I realise it. I know I won't get there in time, but all the same, I'm going to try.

My body feels too slow, my legs slow to pump, my arms flailing uselessly at my side, while before me, Cinder rears. The flames have crept too close to her, Wærwulf and Rudolf unable to calm her enough to move away from the carcase of the ships, slowly collapsing in on themselves, one and then another, as though some strange presentation; as though arranged and not some chance.

And Rudolf is on the floor. He's slipped in the snow and muck from the foreshore of the river, just as Cinder has reared again.

I can hear her cry of terror as though a wail from a distant shore.

"Get her down," I'm gasping.

"Now, girl. Come down. Come down," Wærwulf is reaching for her reins, Rudolf scrambling on his back, but it's all just too slow.

Panic beats in my chest. I move faster, faster, as though I'm a kestrel on the hunt, diving from a great height to pluck the tiniest field mouse from a field of barley.

And then I'm between Rudolf and Cinder's front hooves, but it's too late now. I can't escape myself.

"Down girl, down," once more, my voice snaps through the air, so authoritative, it seems to command the snow to cease. Everything around me slows down. I can see the pattern on the snow, winking in the firelight. And then a hoof touches my chest, pain exploding from beneath my byrnie and I'm flailing, head thrown back, hands reaching behind me to ensure I don't land on Rudolf. At the same time, my left leg tries to absorb the blow, stretching out, lowering my centre of mass, desperate to stay upright, even as my right seems to crumble beneath me.

Wærwulf's words are a shriek I can't decipher. I'm on the ground, the snow a strange comfort, the chill of the blizzard making it impossible to feel everything.

Cinder is level now. One hoof to either side of me. A long horse's tongue reaches down, a whiffle of hay and fear reminding me of the stable, and not this bloody field of slaughter, where the snow has become the sword on which a silversmith might hawk his wares.

"Fuck."

"Are you alright?" Rudolf offers me his hand, even as I stroke Cinder's nose, assuring her there are no hard feelings, well, other than the persistent ache in my chest.

"Maybe." I expel, taking his hand, pushing Cinder aside, Wærwulf with a firm hold on her reins.

I go to stand, breath catching at the shriek from my neck wound and the piercing ache of a rib, broken, no doubt.

"My Lord," Icel's voice is filled with menace, and I know what he's going to say, even before the words leave his mouth.

"The horses are gone." There's fury in the statement, impotent rage, boiling anger, and worse of all, absolutely no condemnation, even though I know it can only be my fucking fault.

CHAPTER 8

"**F**uck," I explode. I'm running through the rapidly building snow. Well, if you can call it running. I look like a young child on unsteady legs. I might topple at any moment. And fuck, my chest hurts.

I've abandoned the battle site. I'm not alone. All of my warriors rush back the way we've come. Only Wærwulf is mounted, and he walks Cinder close beside me, not risking her by asking for a canter or even a trot. All the same, I know what we're going to find when we get there. Icel wouldn't lie.

Hereman has remained behind, Wulfred beside him. Only Icel rushed back with the terrible news.

"Some fucker's stolen my bastard horse," I mutter to myself. I could scream with rage. Bellow with it, as well. It's not just that it's snowing faster and harder than ever before. They've taken my horse. My friend. And it's all my fucking fault.

My arrogance astounds me, as does the presumption of those bastard scum.

But more than anything, they've taken my friend.

I can't imagine that Haden made it very easy. Not at all. Yet, I fear that they'll have injured him trying to assert their dominance. I'll bloody kill all of them if those wounds are mortal. I'll send them to their deaths, and I'll fucking enjoy it.

"Coelwulf," Hereman's snapped words emerge from before the flying snow. It almost blinds me as it gusts into my face. I have to find Hereman by sound, not by sight.

"Be fucking careful," he growls, holding me back with an outstretched hand that trembles as I finally find him.

"What?"

But I can already see why the caution's needed.

"They lead that way," Hereman indicates the marks in the snow. I can't orientate myself enough to see which way he points, whether it's towards the battle site or the river. There's snow festooning his beard, and eyes pierce me. He wants answers as much as I do.

"Are they all gone?"

"Yes, all of them." And then he pauses, and I wait. Whatever he's about to say won't make easy listening.

"There's a trail of blood."

"Bastards," Wulfred explodes, beating me to it. The comfort of the forest beckons to me, promising shelter from the intensifying blizzard. But if we don't follow the impressions in the snow, I might never see Haden again. I know what needs to be done.

"I'm going after them," I call to my warriors trailing behind. We've left a fiery and bloody mess behind us, but it's invisible from here. Sæbald has thought to bring a flaming piece of wood with him, the cloth from one of the dead men, wrapped around it. I can just about make him out as he's rimmed in an orange bright enough to blind me.

"I'm fucking coming."

"Me too."

"Don't even think about saying bloody no," I expect the response from them all.

"Is anyone injured?" I growl. "Does anyone have a wound that will hinder us? If they do, speak now. We need to move fast, or we'll lose them forever." I hold my silence about my potentially broken rib. I'll pretend it's that which makes my chest ache.

"My Lord." It's Tatberht who speaks, emerging from the curtain of white, his face paler than the gleaming snow. "I need to remain behind." I can see how he's hunched against a wound. I don't want to leave him, though. Not if he's going to die. I couldn't. I bloody won't.

"Sæbald, get a fire going. Rudolf, quick, find some twigs and branches, help Sæbald. Ælfgar," but he's already moving to Tatberht's side.

"I'll stay with him," he grunts. I'm grateful I don't have to ask.

"Here," and I'm surprised when Wærwulf lands in the snow. "Keep Cinder with you. In the morning, go to London. There'll be a healer there." I'm amazed by Wærwulf's offer, and I think Tatberht will argue against the necessity. But something passes between the two men, a lingering look before Tatberht limps beneath the branches, Cinder, head trailing, following meekly behind. All traces of the terrified horse have gone, but I can see where she bleeds from a wound on her belly.

I understand then that Wærwulf concern is for his horse, as well as his comrade. Both Cinder and Tatberht need help that we can't provide. Not here, in the freezing conditions, the snow seems to grow taller between one breath and the next.

The scent of pine needles catching alight makes me wish for heat and a hearth, but I'm not going to abandon my friend or any of the other horses. We need to get them back, and we need to get moving. Now.

"Eat the food, drink the water," Wærwulf commands. "There's some moss as well. Use it for Tatberht's wound."

Rudolf erupts from the woodlands, his arms loaded with decent sized branches. There might be enough to keep them warm during the night.

"There's blankets as well. Perhaps a spare cloak," Wærwulf is fumbling in the saddlebags.

"We'll find it, thank you," Ælfgar announces firmly, a hand on Wærwulf's shoulder. "I'll ensure she's well," he continues. "Go now, before you lose the trail."

I meet Ælfgar's pained eyes, Tatberht already slumped beneath the sheltering branches of a pine tree, hidden from view, even the fire obscured.

"We'll find you in London," I confirm, and it's a threat, not a promise.

He grins and turns aside. Only then do I realise he holds his left hand in his right. Ælfgar must carry a wound as well.

I almost reconsider. The lives of my men are too important to me. But, Ælfgar and Tatberht are hardy fuckers. If they've realised they can't keep up with us, then they're perfectly capable of ensuring one another stays alive. I'll have to trust them to do so.

"Aye, My Lord," Tatberht's words emerge from beneath the bowed branches. "You're not getting rid of me that bloody easily. You know it. I know it. Now, go and find Haden before he eats one of the Raiders and Wombel before he does something fucking stupid." The words are meant to cheer.

"Stay alive," and I firmly turn my back on them, heading back into the raging storm.

"We need to stay close together," I throw my words to my warriors. "Make sure you always know who's beside you. If we leave anyone behind, or someone falls back, they'll be dead before we can find them, if we can bloody find them."

It's as though snow bears face me, not men, the creatures appearing before me as though from a story the Norsemen tell. Cloaks are enclosed in white, fat snowflakes dancing between us, and every single face is set in a grimace beneath helms and hoods.

"We know what to fucking do," Pybba announces, daring me to argue with him.

"You bloody better," and I turn to follow Hereman.

He's been growing increasingly impatient, and I understand his fear. The tracks are already starting to disappear. Only, between the translucent snow, and the light from the increased number of brands, we can see the trail of bright maroon.

My eyes fix on it, a hundred different scenarios in my mind. I allow my ire to drive my feet in and out of the piling snow. It's hard going, and sweat beads down my back, even before we've moved beyond the trees, my breath trying to melt the snow before it can land on the ground or me. Fuck, my chest hurts.

The line of hooves continues in a reasonably straight line close to the tree line, although I detect that our mounts didn't neatly follow one another. In the strange glow from the snow-laden clouds, I can almost see how difficult Haden and Billy would have made it. Samson and Dever as well. I can't see that any of them would have been easy to quell. That only makes me worry about the blood. Not that the line grows any wider. But it's persistent, long, and without any breaks.

I hope it's from one of the fucking Raiders. Not one of the horses.

"Where the fuck are they going?" Hereman's huffs over my shoulder. I don't waste the breath to answer. They could travel to Frankia, and we'd still have to follow on behind. Although, I understand why he's uneasy. Now that I've worked out which way's which, I can't help thinking that we might be following our horses back towards Grantabridge. It would be fucking typical.

Gregory implied that these Raiders, known to King Alfred, were an entirely separate group from the jarls at Grantabridge. Perhaps he was unaware they knew one another. But I don't fucking think so. What other tricks has the crafty and deceitful Alfred of Wessex tried to present as fact?

Beneath my feet, I feel the ground begin to climb, steeper and steeper. My steps falter, and I've no idea how much time has passed. We could have been walking for half the night or only a matter of steps. The blizzard is disorientating. I walk through a tunnel, and there's no hope of ever reaching its end.

And I'm beginning to be weighed down as well. I've not appreciated just how heavy snow can be. I remember then some half-heard story of sheep caught out in the snow on the hills surrounding Hereford during a late winter storm. The animals, protecting their young, were entirely covered by the snow and unable to escape its confines when the storm ended because of its weight. I'm beginning to see how easily that could happen.

And then Hereman stops in front of me. I don't even notice, barrelling into him slowly. I reach for Hereman, keen to pull him backwards, only to fall back myself.

"Bollocks," I complain, my arms disappearing into the thick snow that ends just below my shoulders, my breath ragged, my chest agony.

"Shhh," is Hereman's cantankerous reply. He doesn't help me up. I consider staying there. How much easier would it be just to lie down, allow the snow to cover me, the cold to warm me, or so they say? I could be just like those damn sheep. Just as stupid as them.

"Get the fuck up," Rudolf's words are tight with anger, his hand waving in front of my face, even as Icel ignores me to stand beside Hereman.

"Is it stopping?" I ask, but Rudolf shakes his head, dislodging snow from his shoulders in the process.

"I don't think it's ever going to fucking stop," he grumbles. I haul on his arm, considering just for a moment, pulling him down as well, but there's no need for us both to be wet and cold.

When I'm back on my feet, I'm facing the wrong way. I pick out the exhausted faces of my warriors. Some offer me a grin, but most are head down, chastised like a hound caught chewing the deer instead of returning them to their master.

I would shout some encouragement, but again, Hereman demands silence.

"What is it?" I whisper, using Icel's tracks to join the two of them.

"Over there. I can see something."

I look where Hereman indicates but can detect nothing but the continuing blizzard. I shudder, the sweat already cooling on my body. I need to get moving again and quickly.

"A building or horses?" I ask with frustration, only for Hereman to round on me.

"If you shut the fuck up, I might be able to work out what's happening." His words are as sharp as the jagged wind that's compounding my misery. I bite my tongue rather than tell him what I think of him—damn bastard.

"The blood has stopped," Rudolf points out. He's not wrong.

"And where are the tracks?" I've been following blindly behind Hereman.

"They stopped back there, but the blood continued." That

makes no sense, although perhaps it does. Lyfing appears with his brand. We've all been picking up whatever we can find and setting the scraps aflame. We've been travelling for far longer than I thought we would.

"See, the hoofprints have been filled in, only the blood's survived, and then, only when the snow's scraped away."

"So, where are they?"

"Over there, perhaps," Hereman admits. He doesn't look happy about it, well, on what I can see of his face. His beard is entirely frosted, his nostrils rimmed with white, his lips pressed so tightly together, I wouldn't be at all surprised if he told me they were stuck together.

"Or, we've lost the path," Icel rumbles. Lyfing is busy with his brand, and I know what he's doing. While I breathe heavily, each gasp agony, I wait for his cry of discovery, hoping it won't come. It better fucking not come.

"There's nothing here, as far as I can tell." No one corrects him. He's hunting in the snow; we all know that.

"Then, we'll go that way. It's as good as any other," I announce. We're exhausted, pushed to our limits and then beyond. Yet, if I call a halt, no one will follow those orders. We're hunting for our horses. We won't stop until we find them.

I raise my voice above the rasp of the wind. "Check your weapons. Make sure they run clear of scabbards and weapons belts. You'll be fuck all use to me if your seax is stuck solid." I'm working my weapon lose, hoping not to be the arsehole who failed to wipe the gore from their blade after killing the fuckers by the river.

Rudolf struggles. One hand on his seax, the other on his weapons belt.

"Fucking no," he's chanting, and I reach across.

"Put both hands on your weapons belt, and I'll pull." He nods, snow dislodging with the movement. I try my luck, but it isn't moving.

"Bastards had sticky blood," Rudolf huffs, but I'm not giving up. With my arm trembling from the effort, it finally begins to move. I expect the seax to come loose with a sudden sundering, but it does the opposite, painfully emerging bit by bit until I'm holding a sharpened blade, darkened by blood and filth.

"Clean it," I instruct tersely, not wishing to compound the problem by berating him.

"You'd have looked a right bloody fool if that had happened in a battle," Pybba offers darkly, the hint of reproach impossible to ignore. Rudolf wisely holds his peace, although his eyes are furious and blazing. He's angry at himself. Not at me.

"Is the snow stopping," I ask again, convinced that it's not falling as heavily as it was.

"Maybe, certainly, it must be close to sunrise," Hereman states, brokering no argument. The pink clouds have turned a menacing brown colour. If it doesn't stop snowing soon, I fear it'll be set for the entire day. Getting to this spot was hard enough. Getting back will be impossible. Not that we're going back without Haden.

"Lead on," I call then, my words muffled, and it takes Hereman longer than I expect to take the first step. Maybe he didn't hear me. Or perhaps he was just orientating himself towards whatever caught his eye.

We're turned so that rather than facing the snow, it comes at us from our left-hand side. It could make the going easier, but it doesn't, not now we're shuffling up a steep slope as well. It was hard enough to judge how deep my feet went without the hill. Now each step jars, the ground beneath my feet closer than I think it'll be.

I glance upwards, hopeful of finding an end to the torment that's seen me slick with sweat and shivering with cold, my neck itching and growing too hot. My chest aches, although perhaps it isn't broken because I shouldn't have been able to walk this far. Only then do I realise what's stopped Hereman.

There's something there, hinted at in the darker shadows that give way to driving snow at the two edges. I don't know what it is, maybe a steading or a barn. But, there's nothing else. No hint of pale flames, such as I see when I look back along my line of men following behind. There's no promise of warmth.

Hereman pushes on in front. I struggle to keep pace with him and Icel. The pair power through the snow and the storm as though it's little more than a summer shower of rain, bringing the promise of renewal without the deluge of winter.

I grit my teeth. I came to London to beat back our enemy, not hike through a bloody blizzard searching for my stolen horse.

As we near the top of the hill, I begin to make out the building's shape because it's certainly no longer snowing as thickly as before. Not that the building is complete, far from it. I harbour a thought it's little more than an ancient hill fort, perhaps pressed back into use by the thieving bastards who've stolen our horses.

The layer of snow thins closer to the summit, although I can't see any grass or rocks. I grunt with the knowledge that I've just waded through the stuff that's sloughed from here, driven downwards by the fierce wind. But it reveals something we've been missing. A selection of hoof-shaped impressions appear. Our horses are here.

A shouted voice, the words unintelligible, sounds close. I'm crouching low, desperate not to be seen before we've had the opportunity to plan our attack. We're facing the remains of a rampart, forged from the earth by the labour of many men, speckled with snow, as though an owl caught in flight. I suspect a ditch is hidden beneath the snow, as does Hereman, it seems. He and Icel move forward slowly, carefully, not wishing to disturb any stray rocks when we're so close, using their swords and spears in a way that was never intended.

I can't see over the white rampart, but I reach for my seax, sliding it free of its sheath, just to be sure it'll come away when required. I might have kept my fury from showing when Rudolf encountered the problem, but it's a serious matter. It slides easily into my hand while my eyes, rimmed with ice, stare at where Icel and Hereman labour before me.

A rush of wind brings the unmistakable scent of horse manure my way, my heart thudding in my chest. Haden is just over that rampart, as are the other horses. I've never been happier to smell horse shit in my life.

"Watch it," Icel's whisper is not quiet. I would hush him, but at least we've all seen what he's found. There's the ditch, but it's not a deep one. Hereman's spear meets the snow before the deadly glinting blade at its end.

He moves to the left and then the right, continuing the action. The ditch is complete, as far as it's possible to tell. I gaze along the rim of the rampart, and it's visible, just perceptibly, where the growing sunlight touches the snow, as a dip.

"How are we going to do this?" Pybba has made his way to my side. Lyfing, Sæbald and Gyrth have gone in the opposite direction. They're crouched low, their cloaks so covered in snow that if I didn't know they were there, I'd hardly see the movement. The rest of my men are close, huddled low, preparing themselves.

Another voice drifts towards us. I hold myself tight, not wishing to give away even the smallest of movements, head lowered, cloak over my body. The unique sound of boots walking through snow grows louder, the unmistakable crack and crunch. Will we be seen? Will our presence be detected before we can plan our attack? I know what'll happen if that's the case. Perhaps it would be better.

A shouted instruction echoes from behind the barricade, and the footsteps pause and then begin to turn aside again.

I wait, all the same, until I can't hear the brittle sound, and only then lift my head. Icel's eyes meet mine.

"They're preparing to leave." The words fall heavily into the chill air.

Quickly, I assess the situation. I know so little about this place, and yet does it truly matter? I've attacked other unknowns in the past. I did so yesterday.

"Beornstan, Siric and Oda, follow the others and attack when we do."

"Aye, My Lord," Siric states flatly, Beornstan nodding, while Oda doesn't meet my eyes but rather checks his weapons belt before moving to follow the indentations in the snow.

"Icel, Rudolf, Pybba, Osbert, Leonath and Ingwald, circle in the opposite direction to Sæbald. Again, attack when you hear us." It's not the greatest of plans, but it'll work. It always has in the past. Not, I appreciate, that we usually have horses to bloody rescue.

"Hereman, you and I will go first. Wulfhere and Gardulf follow on behind, while Wulfred and Goda are to follow them. The rest of you," and I wish there were more than the six remaining men to act as reserves, "get to the horses. Take them away from here, if it gets fucking nasty. The way to London is that way," and I point back the way we've come, "but anywhere there are no Raiders is fucking good for me."

Resolved faces meet my look. I don't have to tell anyone how important it is that none of the horses is injured. At least, I hope it's not.

The snow sparkles before me as though precious gems, but beneath it all, the same old muck and filth lie hidden. I find a grin for my frozen face, eyes feeling as though they're held open by the cold. I rush forward, leap across the ditch, and I'm scurrying up the exposed mud rampart before I can consider another way of doing this, banishing all my aches and pains, the thrill of what's to come overriding everything else.

Hereman is quickly at my side. I catch sight of Icel and Rudolf, Sæbald and Lyfing doing the same.

My eyes are everywhere, trying to find the horses, to determine what we face. There are the smouldering remains of a fire, the ground almost free of snow around it, and the backs of at least twenty-five warriors greet me.

I growl low in my throat.

Our horses are there. Heads hang low, exhaustion in their stances, while these bastards pilfer the saddlebags and stuff items back into them. They've spent a reasonably comfortable night thanks to our provisions.

I scan the animals, seeking out Haden, but the quick sweep shows me Billy, Stilton, Keira and Dever's similar black and white markings, but not his height. Of Haden, there's no sight. Not yet.

The snow reveals lumps and mounds, perhaps fragments of quarried away walls, the stones put to use elsewhere. There even seems to be a level area, maybe a road of some sort, and it's along that part of the structure that Sæbald is loping along, his movements steady. The rest of my warriors follow him.

I rush to catch up before Sæbald meets our foes.

For now, the men seem unaware that they're not alone. But the horses aren't.

Dever picks up his hanging head, eyes fixing on Rudolf, with a look that borders on the calm acceptance that he'd come, mixed with slight dejection that it's taken so long. He lifts his right foot, and almost languorously, stamps down on the foot of the Raider, trying to adjust the saddle so that he can mount.

The man's howl of pain covers the sound of our advance, and even better, draws the eye of every single Raider to their comrade, derisive cries filling the air.

I smirk. It seems even the damn horses have learned the art of distraction.

Sprinting through the snow, legs held high, until I reach the clear area, my seax twirls into my hand. I've already chosen my first target.

Once more, blood stains the snow. I consider the pleasure I take in such a sight.

There's nothing more satisfying than seeing my enemy's body fluid slowly draining through the crusted layer of snow. If I were a scop, I'd have the words to describe the interplay of the wine-hued substance, through the crystalline structure, all infused with the glowing sunlight. But I'm fucking not. It looks like what it is, red on white. I've never seen a better sight.

The Raider slumps to the ground, head impacting the snow with a satisfying crisp snap. Billy all but winks at me; only I know that horses can do no such thing.

I run my hand along Billy's nose, appreciating his warmth. I twist his reins around the saddle and then slap him aside on the rump. He goes keenly. He's free. He needs to remain so, and that's the position I've entrusted to Wærwulf and the others. Yet, I hear him falter and Hereman's soft murmur. It seems I'm not the only one to have missed their mount.

All eyes remain on the wounded man, so it's easy to free Stilton, another of the Raiders taking a sharp stab through his neck. Only, he wavers, refusing to fall, almost coming to rest against Stilton's back. I'm forced to shove him aside so that he more thuds to the snowy ground than collapses into it, even with my one hand holding him tightly. This time, I know the Raiders will realise they've been found.

Stilton rushes free, eager to join Billy without any further encouragement. They're not the only horses to have been freed from their captivity because there's no other word for it. Keira is free, Kermit too. Added to which the party led by Icel and that by Sæbald have our foes just about encircled. They could escape, to the north, but only if they're fucking quick.

Hereman lopes beside me, a grin on his face because Billy's been retrieved. But the rest isn't going to be so easy. The Raiders know they've been found.

The words of one of the warriors, face dark behind a hastily donned helm, snap through the sharp air. The Raiders reach for weapons and helms immediately, but not shields because we carry our shields. The horses didn't have them when they were taken.

"They mean to protect the horses," Wærwulf calls, his words reaching everyone. I can see the eager look on Rudolf's face. The warrior, still hopping in pain, thwacks his long sword against Dever's side, not to hurt him, but certainly a threat.

"Rudolf, no," my words echo louder than Wærwulf's and are matched by Pybba. We both see the danger.

Haunted eyes in a greyed face glare at me with fury, and I think he'll disobey. Rudolf surprises me.

"I'm coming, Dever. Don't worry. I'll kill the bastard in good time."

Laughter rings through the air. It draws my eye, and I'm not alone. Only Hereman seems immune as he swings his axe at the man who stands between him and the rest of the animals. That sound restores us all to the task ahead. Our foe might laugh at us for rescuing our mounts, but he's the daft bastard who'll be bleeding his last into the powdery substance.

So we fight. Hereman's warrior puts up a good enough defence, but he has no shield. Hands can only resist a war axe for so long. I take the next man. Hereman's movements are enormous, leaving me little room to use my shield, but I have my seax, and that's all I need to slice the reddened nose from the face of the bulbous man who thinks to ride Chocolate.

Yet, the squat warrior isn't without skill. As my seax flashes in the growing daylight, his sword counters the movements. Each and every one of them. I feel my arms growing heavier and heavier. I've walked all night in my byrnie, carrying my weapons and my shield. My stomach growls, and my throat is dry, but I know where my succour is if the stealing swine haven't feasted on it already.

The ground before us rapidly clears of snow beneath the heat of our movements. I'm just about to make a killing blow when the man stops, pinned, blood pooling and dripping onto the layer of grass and stones revealed beneath the snow.

"Stop fucking around," Hereman instructs, surveying the dead man, pinioned by the spear that ended our altercation. I shut my mouth tightly. Better that than tell him what I honestly think of his unwanted interference.

Gardulf's foe also stumbles in the snow, blood welling from his foot. My forehead wrinkles.

"How the fuck did that happen?" I bark, but Gardulf is too busy beating back the Raider to answer my question. Hereman's too eager to smack the horses' backsides and have them escape their captivity, even if it means coming through me.

Fusty breath engulfs me, the horses' acknowledgement of their rescue, and I run my hand along nose after nose. It's as though we've broken the shield wall, and in doing so, gained allies.

As the horses stream free, I check for Haden but don't see him, even as I rush inside the circle and begin to attack our enemy from behind. Those who face Icel and Sæbald expect only a horse at their back, not a reaching blade.

And then, all the Raiders are dead or dying, and all the horses are free.

"Where's Haden?" Rudolf calls harshly. I peer into the herd of mounts, all claimed by one of my warriors, well, all apart from Billy, because Hereman, and his spear, are busy ensuring all the bastards are truly dead. He's so powerful; the spear passes in and out of their bodies without seeming to encounter any resistance.

"Isn't he there?" I demand to know, worry making my words sharp.

"No, no, he's not," Rudolf shouts, the words spoken in panic.

"But all the others are?"

"Yes, I've accounted for them all," Wærwulf assures me of that. I turn, peering all around me, making use of the growing daylight, wondering where my damn horse is. Has he run off? Has he been injured? My thoughts return to the trail of blood that's brought us here. Was it from my Haden? My chest aches once more. Fuck.

"Hereman, stop," my hand is on his arm as his fierce eyes greet mine. Beneath him, one of the Raiders is writhing in agony, his hand on his belly, bright blood flowing from it.

"Where is the black and white horse? The big horse?" I demand to know, my eyes trying to hold his against the oncoming blankness of death.

I get no response. My hands are abruptly around his neck, shaking him, repeating the question, only Wærwulf has appeared as well.

He asks the question in Danish, and there's recognition in those eyes and a quirk to the moustached mouth that speaks of amusement. For a moment, I think there'll be no answer, especially as the prone man chokes on blood, barely able to breathe at all.

But then he garbles something, rich with derision. I turn to Wærwulf. But there's no need to ask for a translation, not when Wærwulf reaches forward, grabs the man's cheeks, between one hand and forces the lips together, trapping the tongue. Wærwulf severs the tongue in a neat movement, the pink flesh landing on the choking man's chest, and then he's still. Everything's still, and I breathe deeply, fear threatening to undo me.

"He said the big horse had the heart of a mouse. He said the big horse was no use to anyone. He said," and Wærwulf hesitates, no doubt judging me, ensuring I can take the news. "He said the big horse is over there, in the far corner."

Wærwulf stands as he speaks, pointing to where he means, to where the dying man's hand is pointing.

"No, he's not," I begin, only then I understand.

Fatigue forgotten about, I leap through the snow and exposed stonework, my eyes raking the area before me, looking for my beloved horse because he's not standing, not in the far corner.

And if he's not standing, that can mean only one of two things, and it better be the fucking second of those.

CHAPTER 9

Rudolf hurries to follow me as I career onwards, others not far behind. Here, the snow lies deeper, the hilltop lower than the more exposed area where we've just battled against the Raiders.

The light shimmers so brightly now, my eyes water from the reflection of the snow, the water freezing as it falls down my cheeks.

"Haden," I suck in air to call his name, time and time again, but there's no reply.

"Haden, where are you, you damn brute?" I'm not ashamed to own the desperation in my voice as I reach the extent of the enclosed area without finding him.

"How fucking hard can it be to find a massive bloody horse?" I'm babbling; I know I am. Fear, panic, the edges of my grief, all about to explode from me if I don't find my horse alive and breathing. The longer it takes to find him, the more convinced I am that it'll all be too late.

Belatedly, I notice something I've not seen before; the trail of blood glinting beneath the topmost layer of snow.

"Follow it," I urge Rudolf, Icel and Wærwulf, who help me.

"How bloody big is this place?" I get no answer, nothing but the harshness of my breath, the fear constricting my chest, and all for a damn horse, that's left me one too many time to face my death, alone.

I race ahead of the others towards an area where the snow lies more thickly. Already I'm in it up to my knees, my trews growing dark as the snow melts on meeting the heat of my body. And still, the thread of red continues.

Until it doesn't.

"No," I'm moaning, the sound low in my chest, a sound I've only ever heard from mother's whose babes are born dead. "No," but my hands are scrabbling, up to my elbows, and then up to my shoulders and only then do they touch something solid and marbled, even through the leather of my gloves.

"No," I cry again, using my hands to dig into the snow, ignoring the shriek of my neck wound, the ache in my chest. Rudolf joins me, Icel too, the big man shifting twice as much snow as I do, while Rudolf thrusts it behind him through his legs as though he's a hound digging for a bone.

"No, no, no," I can't stop myself, even when I try and clamp my mouth shut, stop the words from coming forth, impossible to know whether they're spoken aloud or inside my mind.

Something moves beneath us, the cleared snow falling back into the hole I've been digging, covering whatever it is I've found before I can uncover it. A soft sound reaches my wind-scoured ears.

"Did you fucking hear that?" Rudolf asks desperately, his frantic eyes meeting mine across the disturbed snow.

"I did, did you?"

"Yes," he confirms, and Hereman joins me, axe in his hands and raised above his head.

"No, no," I cry, only thinking that he means to cleave my mount in half even while he lies beneath the snow.

"This'll be quicker, you damn fool," and somehow, he's scooping the snow clear, using the axe head as though it's a spade.

And the snow moves and settles once more.

"Haden," I call, and this time everything in front of me moves. The snow rearing up, as though the waves swallowing a stricken ship. I'm blinded once more, snow covering me, so I may as well be the one covered, but I've heard a sound that makes my heart soar.

I batter the snow aside, and there, standing before me as though born himself from the snow, is my horse.

Staggering forward, I aim to fling my arms around his neck, only to trip on whatever it was I found buried in the snow. I fall, at Haden's hooves, the thud of my landing, on ground clear of almost all snow, sending shock waves of agony through my neck, hands and knees. I whimper once more and then startle aside, face to face with the blued face of a Raider abandoned by his allies, with my horse as well.

Silence greets my actions. I shuffle backwards, but Haden's lips rest on my head, and I wait, just a moment longer, taking his benediction.

"Stop fucking around," Hereman's words are laced with worry and frustration combined. Wrapping my hands around Haden's nose, finding my feet once more, I understand how cold he is. And how bloody weak.

Rudolf is already worrying about something on his back leg.

"Here, get his saddle off him, and then we'll warm him up." Pybba's practical words restore me to myself. I can hear Rudolf talking to Haden as he examines him. I want to look, but right now, the best I can do for him is to remove the saddle.

Only, the catches are twisted, caught up between the matted hair of his white and black underbelly, run through, here and there, with streaks of red.

"Is it his blood, or that bastard's?" I spit from beneath his legs. I'm forced to my knees, fingers grown numb from all the digging, unable to loosen the catches and buckles that hold the saddle and sodden under-blanket.

"A mix, I think," Rudolf almost reassures, and finally, the straps spring apart, and the saddle thuds to the ground in a jangle of clashing buckles and the thud of a snowy landing.

Blanket after blanket covers Haden's back as soon I reappear, but I've seen what concerns Rudolf.

"How the fuck did this happen?" The skin over Haden's upper rear leg is torn, a jagged gash almost all the way to his knee. It's that which bleeds, and no doubt, what led to him being left to die with the blue Raider.

"What did you fucking do?" I direct my question to Haden. He turns his head slightly as he chews contentedly on a handful of oats offered by Pybba.

"I think he fought the bastards and then killed this fucker here," Wulfred appears his words a welcome summation of what's been happening.

"Are the other horses injured?"

"Not as badly as Haden. They'll be fine."

I scurry for my saddle, remembering all the items stored in my saddlebags, hoping they're still there.

"We need to stitch it," Rudolf's voice is filled with gloom. "If we don't, it'll just keep weeping, and he'll get weaker and weaker, especially out here."

My mouth hangs open in shock at the words.

"How would we do that? Who would do that?"

"I can do it," Rudolf confirms, nodding firmly to convince himself that he can. "I just need something to use as a thread."

"And a needle," I half-taunt.

"I have a needle," he immediately replies. "You can't be a lord's squire without knowing how to repair his oft torn trews," Rudolf's eyes blaze into mine. "But my thread won't hold. Not against his movements."

Rudolf grips a handful of snow, clearing away the dried and crusted gore from the black part of Haden's leg.

"Would this work?" Wulfred has returned to his mount, and now he stamps back through the snow, gripping a ball of something in his fist.

"I use it for fishing. Well, I would if I ever had the fucking chance." I laugh, the sound bubbling from my throat in relief and disbelief that Wulfred might ever have the fucking patience to tickle a fish from the river.

Rudolf takes the twine eagerly, stretching it between his two hands. I've not noticed, but Pybba has been away and returned as well. He holds Rudolf's saddlebag, and he's pouring through the contents.

"What else do you have in there that I know nothing about?" I ask, aware I'm on the cusp of either laughing or sobbing. Haden's flesh is cold beneath my hands. Too cold, even with the blankets from the other horses, and they'll be getting cold as well.

"Where the fuck are we?" I ask, apropos of nothing. No one answers.

"Hold him steady," Rudolf barks. I move to Haden's head. Wise eyes greet mine, a promise in them that I'll hold the fucker too.

"I've no idea how much this will hurt," Rudolf mutters to himself. "Everyone stand clear or remain alert. I don't want anyone knocked out by a stray hoof if he rears."

"Haden, Rudolf will help you," I find myself talking to him, suddenly self-conscious because others listen.

"Ah, you can do fuckin' better than that," Wulfred complains. "It's not like we don't all talk to our mounts. Call yourself a fuckin' king." He spits into the snow, staining it with his foul breath, but I appreciate his words, all the same.

"Haden," I feel his entire body flinch, and although I can't see what Rudolf's doing, I have to assume he's begun. "You have to let Rudolf work on your wound. Stay still, and don't," but my words are cut off as he whinnies shrilly, trying to escape me, backing away from my scrutiny.

"Hold him fucking still," Pybba speaks for Rudolf, annoyance in his voice. "He nearly stabbed himself. Bloody horse," but Rudolf doesn't complain, so I take that to mean he's okay.

"Don't do that again," I caution Haden, infusing my voice with iron. I can hardly keep track of who I am and what I'm doing, relief making me giddy and foolish, but I know Haden isn't safe, not yet.

"I believe," Sæbald speaks from behind me. "That we're not that far from the woodlands of last night, and therefore from London. Although, everything's relevant. There's snow up to our armpits in places. We might as well be in Hereford for the amount of time it might take us to reach London."

"Will it be quicker to return to Northampton?"

"No. Look, the snow hasn't just fallen here," and Sæbald has taken the time to assess our situation, and he's right. From our position on top of this hill, we can see far into the distance, the clear, bright day, offering unparalleled views of the vista of purest white, the welcoming sight of the sullen Thames in front of us.

Haden huffs into my face, his eye pain-hazed and uncomprehending. He's weak; that much is evident. I need to get him somewhere warm. I can only imagine how long he's been under the snow before we found him, too exhausted to remain standing against the onslaught of the weather. I don't allow myself to consider that he'd given up on his life; given up on being protected; given up on me.

"We need to go back the way we came," Icel rumbles. It's impossible to tell which parts of his beard are rimmed with snow and which with grey. But his eyes pierce me. They thrum with the desire for revenge. Surely, I think, we've done enough in killing all of the fuckers, but perhaps not.

They came to Mercia, they took command of the farmhouse steading, and then they stole our fucking horses and wounded my men. I know we've not killed enough of them to account for the seven shiploads we were led to believe were here.

Hereman's crouched in the snow before Haden, more trusting than I would be in his current state of mind. But Hereman's pushing aside the snow from the body I found. Some of the others, Gardulf leading them, assured their horses are well, have returned to the slashes of glistening red in the disturbed snow, picking their way through the bodies. There's no way to bury them, not with the ground covered as it is, and not when the exposed soil is mainly rocks.

"Who are you, you fucker," Hereman mutters to himself.

My arms are starting to shake from holding Haden so still. I also detect a tremble in his legs. Fuck, why did it have to snow so much? I don't know how I'm going to get him to safety. Rudolf might be able to stitch up his weeping wound, but how will Haden cope with the snow, with having to constantly lift his leg, when he's already so damn weak? The poor bastard.

"I think they tried to slap him on the leg with their sword, and the fucker turned it edge-on, evil cocks." Pybba speaks conversationally, no doubt using his experience to ground Rudolf and me in what needs to be done instead of the worry of what'll happen if it all goes wrong. "It's a deep wound, but not overly long."

"Then what's taking so much fucking time," I growl softly enough that no one but Haden hears. His breath huffs on my hand, and I know he's thinking the same.

"Here. What do you make of this?" Hereman holds up his hand, something glistens wetly in it, and I grimace.

"Did you pull that from his finger?"

"No, I chopped his fucking finger off. He does not need it now," Hereman's words ring with amusement. He has a good point.

"It's a bloody ring," I retort, not wishing to take my eyes from Haden. I purposely adopt Pybba's soft tone, not wanting to alert Haden or Rudolf.

"I fucking know that you arse," Hereman's reply ripples with frustration. "Look at the design on it."

I don't want to, but there's something there that catches my eyes. It's not a small item, far from it. Some might even determine it's gaudy.

"Is that a bastard dragon?" I exhale, trying to keep the fury from my words.

"Aye, My Lord King, that there is a bastard dragon."

Icel holds out his hand to examine the piece. For a moment, we can hear nothing but the pull of the needle through Haden's flesh, a sound that makes me tense my arse and grit my teeth, and then Icel speaks.

"I've seen this before," his words are ominous, with no thought to maintain the lighter tone of the conversation. "This is the Wessex Wyvern, and that means, My Lord King, that these fuckers either stole it from them or, and I think it much more likely, they've been paid off by King Alfred of Wessex or paid to do something."

"Attack Mercia?" I menace.

"More than likely," Icel confirms. His lips are tight, his shoulders tense, and then he thrusts the ring back toward Hereman and stalks away. I turn and watch him discreetly. His shoulders are tense, rising and falling too rapidly as he tries to bring himself under control.

"Would King Alfred do that?" I ask of no one, but Pybba replies all the same.

"Would you, My Lord? If it was the only option."

The words reverberate in the still air, muffled by the snow, and yet flung far and wide by the clear sky, all the same.

"I would never have it as my only option," I snarl low in my throat. "I wouldn't sacrifice another just to save myself."

"Then, My Lord," and Pybba speaks with certainty. "You're a better man than all the others, far better, but then, you have no problem in being up to your armpits in the entrails of another. I don't believe that's King Alfred's way. Not at all."

I nod, thinking of Icel as he tries to control himself.

If I think I've been fighting for Mercia all of my life, then Icel has been doing so for even longer, and not just against the Raiders. He's had to fight the fucking Wessex warriors as well. If that ring's presence is anything to go by, it's beginning to look as though we might have to do the same.

"Fucking bollocks," Hereman has uncovered more of the body, and now he steps back, revulsion on his face.

"What?" I demand to know, eyes still on Haden, urging him to remain still and calm.

"All done," Rudolf calls, the stress in his voice impossible to ignore. This means a lot to him, and he wants it to work. So do I. But, it does mean that I can step back from Haden, release him from my hold, and look at what's forced Hereman to scurry backwards in the snow, away from the body.

"What?" I ask, but Hereman can only point.

I glance into the cleared pit. It should be nothing but snow and rocks and frozen grass, with a body nestled there, as well.

"Bloody bollocks," I expel, words almost beyond me, and I just happen to glance upwards, meet Haden's eyes. They speak of triumph. And I laugh.

"What the fuck did you do to him, Haden?" I call, as his front hoof paws in the snow.

"Well, it looks to me like he aimed one hoof through his skull, and one through his chest," Pybba speaks with the cold detachment of someone who's managed to dismiss the object before us as ever having breathed and lived; as ever having fucked and swined; feasted and drunk.

"Well done, boy," Pybba speaks with pride in his voice, and I laugh, the sound too high, too filled with emotion, but I'm not alone. Rudolf joins me, the worry on his face evaporating insight of what Haden has achieved.

"Looks like you won the fight, boy," and then he collapses to his haunches, and I go to him, place my hand on his shaking shoulder, and just hold it there. I need his strength just as much as he needs mine. And this is far from fucking done.

CHAPTER 10

"How will we fucking do this?" I'm asking the question, gazing at the assorted bodies before me, even though I'm the one who's supposed to know everything.

Rudolf hasn't joined Gardulf and the others in pilfering the dead, but all the same, there's a small pile of baubles before him, coins showing the faces of kings I've never heard of, let alone where they rule. It seems Rudolf's been paid a tribute for tending to Haden. Not that Haden is entirely free from danger. Far from it.

My horse shakes beneath the furs, his brown eyes pain-hazed, and I know we need to get going as soon as possible. We need to get him out of the frozen air and somewhere warm. But it's not going to be easy, far from it. And first, we need to contend with the dead.

"Burn them," I decide. "I'm not leaving them, and neither can we take the time to bury them. It's too fucking cold for that shit."

"There's nothing to fuel the fire," Hereman grumbles.

"Their clothes will have to bloody do."

I could send men to the far distant treeline for branches and dried pine needles, but I'm not going to do that, not for our enemy. Not when it's so fucking cold, and Haden's life is far from assured.

"Pile them all together. As long as one of the Raiders burns, the others will catch as well, soon enough. There's enough fucking hair for them to go up quickly, and they hardly lack meat and fat."

No one argues with me. It's always the worst part of any battle, deciding what to do with the dead.

Pybba thrusts a piece of torn tunic into the embers of one of the fires the men kept the previous night. The promise of warmth almost undoes me, but I'm not staying here, roasting myself on the pyre of my enemies.

We're all surprised when the fabric ignites, flames greedily licking over its surface. Hereman thrusts his spear into its heart and rushes to where the majority of the Raiders fell. Behind us, one or two of the horses gives a startled whinny, the scent too reminiscent, no doubt, of the previous night.

"This fat fucker will be perfect," Hereman huffs to himself. He jabs his spear into the blue-veined flesh of an exposed belly, whiter than the snow. I grimace at the wet sound and sizzle of hair leading beneath his trews. I'd turn aside, but I want to watch these bastards burn.

They took my horse, they wounded him, and while Haden might have had his revenge, I haven't.

As soon as the man is ablaze, we move as one to bring the other bodies closer, lie them one atop the other, in a loose but tighter circle to the one they fell within when they tried to protect their stolen mounts.

The flesh of the dead is little colder than the icy wind blowing up the hillside. We need to be gone from here, and not just because I risk Haden with every breath that I linger.

Not that I can ride him. No, that would injure him further and risk undoing the neat stitches that Rudolf has used to draw his severed flesh together.

"Bring me Wombel. I'll ride him." With Tatberht left behind in the woodlands, Wombel is riderless. Not that Haden will like it, not one bit.

"We'll walk down the hill, aiming back the way we've come." Our footprints are easy enough to find as we crest the embankment, mindful of the deep ditch. Their presence allows us to retrace our steps. And I don't think there's any chance of the snow thawing. Not for a long time. There might even be the promise of more snow to come in the pink haze that hovers, far to the east, from where the bastard wind blows.

I'm leading Wombel, with Haden walking at my side, head down, movements far from flowing. Ælfgar's mount, Poppy, has the added weight of Haden's abandoned saddle added to her own, but she doesn't seem to mind, as Rudolf guides her alongside Dever. The two horses resemble old men, drinking their mead and putting the world to rights. Every so often, their noses touch in camaraderie.

Not that we're first, far from it. Icel and Samson lead the way, Icel able to ride because it's almost as though no snow has fallen beneath Samson's long legs. Hereman and Billy follow on behind, although Hereman walks beside his horse, as do most of us. We're not taking the risk, not now we've been reunited.

From the top of the hill, the smell of roasting flesh pollutes the clear, bright day. I don't look back. We've done what we can for the dead. If they don't burn to ashes, aside from the missed pieces of metal on their bodies and the odd bit of bone that doesn't quite catch, then the starving animals will be able to feast; the birds as well as the wolves and other residents of the woodlands.

It's a fitting end for the bastards.

"But there were only twenty-five of them," Rudolf seems to have returned to his favoured past-time of counting the dead.

"Yes, there were," I confirm. I find I might not mind his attempt to distract.

"So, how many did we encounter at the riverside?"

"No more than forty, maybe fifty." Icel's voice rumbles from in front, our voices audible above the crunch of the snow and the jangle of harness.

"So where the fuck's everyone else? They'd have needed to be pretty handy with an oar to manage seven ships with so few of them." I'd been thinking the same, and evidently, I'm not alone.

"These bastards might not even have been with the ship-warriors," Wulfred's words are a truth I don't need to hear.

"If that's the case, there was no more than a ship-worth of Raiders at the steading. And there were seven ships, weren't there?" This Rudolf directs to Sæbald. After all, Sæbald would know. He ensured they all burned.

"Just the seven, but not all of them were water-tight. I'm sure of that."

"So seven ships, and, depending on their size, we can account for no more than one, at best two, of the contingent of ship-warriors. Then where the fuck have they gone?" Rudolf's words are muffled. He's finally stopping Dever, and mounting up now we're down the hill and free from the accumulation of snow at the base. I cast a baleful look at Haden, unsure how he'll respond to what I'm about to do.

"It's for the best, lad," I offer, mounting Wombel from the wrong side, for me, just to ensure Haden can't interfere. I've not missed that his gait is laboured, his nose flecked with sweat, and we've only just started. All the same, I don't think he'll like it.

As soon as I'm upright, I risk looking at Haden. His eyes are filled with remorse and defiance, a heady combination if ever I've seen one. I'm almost grateful then that the snow makes it difficult for him to walk. If it didn't, I would bet my seax on the little fucker skipping out of my reach, determined to prove he's quite capable, despite his wound.

But, all of the horses are tired. We rode with haste from Northampton for two days, and we didn't stop until we found the enemy. And then they were forced to ride all night again, through the growing level of snow, and under the instructions of men they didn't or want to know. And now, there's no choice but to retrace our steps. I'm tired, and so are the horses, even if they much prefer the gentler hands of their warriors.

At least the sun is warm on our faces. While it might not be hot, every so often, some heat works its way into my cold face. I could eat. I really could. And nothing small and delicate; maybe an entire hide of venison or boar. I don't think I'd be that picky.

"Maybe they're in London with Bishop Smithwulf or Wessex

with King Alfred," Hereman's words drip with scorn. But, it's something we need to consider. Have we been lied to, or are the fuckers close to London, on Mercian land?

"They could have made their way to Grantabridge," Lyfing states, his words easily reaching me, even though he rides at the rear. "There are any number of roads, and trackways, if they'd had a guide."

"But, wouldn't they have taken their ships?" Rudolf's question is almost a jibe.

"Not if the bloody things had massive holes in them and couldn't be risked along the Thames or the open sea. Even staying close to the coast, I imagine a holey ship wouldn't last that long, and some of them were more holes than ships." Lyfing tempers the words with just the right amount of humour. But they rouse me from my stupor, lolling on top of Wombel. His gait is smooth enough, but I'm not used to him. It's uncomfortable to ride a different horse.

"So, the others might be hiding elsewhere," I state, the idea forming in my mind as we get closer and closer to the tree line where we left Tatberht and Ælfgar last night. "They could be anywhere, seeking shelter, but maybe, using the trees for cover." Only Lyfing and Sæbald are working themselves into an argument.

"And what the fuck do you know about ships?" Lyfing directs at Sæbald. The words are so loud, I'd be amazed if they didn't hear them in London.

"More than you, you daft bastard," the words bely the affection they're spoken with, and of course, Lyfing completely misses it in his rage.

"Shut up the pair of you," I call, but the words falter. I cough and begin again.

"Shut up, all of you. Listen to what Rudolf's telling us. If we didn't kill them all at the ships, and we didn't kill them all up that damn hill, then where are they? Might they, perhaps, be hiding in the fucking woods, where we left two of our men last night?"

My words crack with thunder. Immediately comprehension dawns on Sæbald's face, the bright light highlighting the scar on his shaved chin, despite the bristles covering it. His eyes flick towards the trees, rising from the ground before us as silent sentinels, the only element in the distance that isn't shrouded in white.

"Fuck," he complains. I can see where exhaustion rims his eyes. I imagine I look little better, but this probably isn't over, far from it.

"We concentrate on finding Ælfgar and Tatberht. If they've gone on before us, then we do the same. I'd rather stay and kill 'em all, but not in our current state. With rested horses and some decent food, we might be able to return. Even better if the snow thaws." Of course, the Raiders who stole our horses did the same with the bounty of food they found. Perhaps I shouldn't object to them enjoying their last feast before they died. But I'm hungry. So are my men. We can't eat the oats meant for the horses.

"We'll know where they are," Icel calls from the front. "Our path is well marked, even now." I can't truly see it, not from my position behind him. By the time Wombel paces the place Samson has already traipsed through, the snow is so disturbed, it's impossible to tell whether we stick to the same route or not.

I can't even see the river, not from where I am. There are the trees, growing larger and larger, and the hill, which still burns behind us. If there are Raiders out there deciding when to attack us, we're not exactly making it difficult for them to find us, far from it.

"I imagine the Raiders are keeping themselves warm at King Alfred's hearth. The Wessex royal family always knows when to fight and when to use words and treasure to ensure they win." Icel's words are filled with disdain. I'm already more than half-convinced of the truth in that statement. Not that I've ever met King Alfred, or in fact, any of his brothers. But sometimes, there's just no need. His actions, and those of his brothers, and his bastard father, speak for the sort of individuals they are. I wouldn't trust him. I don't trust the Raiders. They're probably perfect allies.

"So why would the ships be by the Thames?" Rudolf presses. Some of my warriors slump in their saddles, sleep taking them because we move so slowly through the snow, the horses unable to do more than copy the actions of the mount in front of them. In effect, only Icel needs to be awake to ensure that Samson doesn't diverge from the path. We know there are no impediments to our passage, provided we remain as we are.

"As Lyfing said, they were hardly ships at all. They were leaky barrels, meant to give the illusion that there were more Raiders there. It'll be a trick. Or, and we can always think the Wessex warriors capable of killing so many of them, they're somewhere else."

Again, my tired eyes glance toward the trees. Are we being watched? Do I feel the heat of another's gaze on my back? I'm not convinced, but neither do I dismiss it out of hand.

"How many oars were there?" I ask, and then when I realise how quickly the words emerge, I raise my voice. "How many oars were there."

"We didn't count the oars, Coelwulf. There were some. That's all I can honestly say. And, if there were more, wouldn't they have kept them somewhere out of the elements? You can't get far with a warped oar. Or a leaky ship," he adds as an afterthought, causing Sæbald's head to whip up from where he must have been sleeping. Damn the fuckers, is there nothing about which they won't argue?

"Then, we won't know. Not until we either get set upon by the Raiders, or we reach London, and Bishop Smithwulf can tell us all where they are."

Rudolf nods at my words, but his eyes are on Haden's wound. I catch his eye, wrinkling my forehead, a question there. I don't want to make a fuss. Rudolf tries to smile, offering reassurance, but the worry fails to lift from his young face. His cheeks are glowing pink, no doubt from a combination of windburn and the heat of the sun on them. If anything, it only serves to remind me of how young he is.

Rudolf is the youngest of us all. Yet I'm relying on him to keep Haden alive. It's too much of a burden for him. I doubt he'd have it any other way.

And then the forward momentum of our journey comes to an abrupt halt.

"What is it?" I call to Icel, unsure why our slow enough progress has come to a stop.

"This is it?" And he's already dropping into the snow, tangling Samson's reins on the saddle to prevent him tripping.

"What are you doing?" I caution as Icel moves towards the trees. "We need to get to London."

"That's as might be," Icel confirms, "but no one's left this spot this morning. It seems to me we might need to check that Ælfgar and Tatberht have managed to leave."

"Fuck," I'm already dismounting, looping both Haden and Wombel's reins together, cursing as I do so. I don't want either of them wandering off while I'm beneath the trees.

My back flames with agony, my feet as well, my chest a persistent ache. I'm not used to such a long walk over treacherous terrain. Gardulf hastens to join us, even quicker than Rudolf.

"Check on Haden for me, Rudolf," I call to remove the sting of the betrayal. Then I'm bending, allowing the low hanging pine branches to brush against my back. I grunt at this fresh outrage but hurry to keep up with Icel. If he's walking into a shit storm, I'll be with him.

"Tatberht," I call, my words a harsh whisper. "Ælfgar, where the fuck are you?" But there's no response. Beneath the branches, it's a whole new world, and I have to blink to clear the reflection of the snow from my eyes so that I can see.

All sound is muted. It wouldn't help if I roared for my missing men. I doubt they'd be able to hear me.

"Where the fuck are they?" I hiss to Icel instead. He doesn't reply. I grit my teeth. I know how valuable Icel is to me, especially after I thought him dead, but fuck, he's an annoying old bastard.

We move from below the branches of another tree, the ground

beneath it, deep with discarded pine needles, and the general softness of a forest floor. There could be bodies buried here for all I know. Not even the smell would appear wrong to my senses. Of course, I hope there aren't bodies here, well, nothing more than the small animals that have breathed their last.

I'm abruptly too warm and wish I'd thought to discard my rigid cloak, but I can't, not now. It's difficult even to stand upright.

When Icel stops in front of me, I almost walk into him.

"What the," but my words tail off. Icel has found our warriors.

I step around Icel. The first thing I notice is the stillness of Ælfgar and Tatberht. In the half-light, I can't tell whether they live or not, but sure as anything, the Raider lying on the floor before them, not one, but two swords, in his back, pinioning him to the ground, is about as dead as it's possible to be.

"Bloody bollocks," Gardulf's words are shrill. I turn, hand already on my seax, but he's pointing his weapon at another body, further out, almost where the branches finally touch the ground. And it's not the only body there, looking more carefully, as I do now.

"What the fuck happened here?"

"The bastards came for us," Ælfgar speaks, his words old and tired. "But we killed 'em all. Cheeky young bucks," he continues, as though talking of weapons practise and not life and death. I rush to him, crouching down, a grunt escaping me as all sorts of fresh hell burns down my back. Wulfhere has hurried to his grandfather's side.

"We were ambushed during the night. We killed those we could. Luckily, the rest of them ran off. I," but Ælfgar doesn't need to say anything else because Tatberht's eyes have fluttered painfully open at Wulfhere's insistence. I can see where blood has seeped through his bandage.

"We need to get you out of here."

"He can't be moved," Ælfgar interrupts me. "Why else would we still be here?"

"Why can't you move?" His face is a welter of bruises. I don't know how they managed to kill their attackers, not with Tatberht so injured.

"Even breathing makes blood pour from the wound," Ælfgar moves away from where I realise he's keeping Tatberht upright. The older man wilts on himself while Ælfgar climbs to his feet and stretches his back, as much as he can, beneath the low hanging branches. Wulfhere takes his place.

Both of them are blue with cold. I can see where the fire has been dragged across the ground.

"We need to camp here tonight," I state, brokering no argument.

"But what of Haden?"

"What about Haden?" Tatberht's words are sharp at the mention of my horse, even struggling to sit.

"He's wounded. Like you are. We'll have to get him in here. Start a fire for everyone. We all need to sleep."

"What about the other Raiders? What about London?" I sigh heavily. Icel is right to remind me of these problems; even it is bloody unwelcome.

"All of us together, even nursing Tatberht and Haden, will be more than a match for the fuckers, if they try their luck again. None of us has slept."

"And none of us has food," Gardulf reminds me, a growl from his belly reinforcing the point.

"We'll have to hunt if we want to eat. Before we can hunt, we need to be warm and get some sleep." And then I pause. "Where did your dead come from?"

"Behind us, we think, in the heart of the woodlands." It's not the answer I want to hear, but it's to be expected.

"Gardulf, tell the others to get in here. Bring the horses as well. We're stopping for some rest and to help Tatberht. We'll be on our way tomorrow." He nods and backs out from the tight space, but I know he's unhappy. I'm sure Pybba will relay Gardulf's interpretation of the orders to me later.

"Icel, help me move the dead, and then we can find some wood." Ælfgar makes to stand as though to help us, but I shake my head.

"Stay with Tatberht. Keep him warm until the fire can." I've noticed Ælfgar's wound on his left arm, well, really on his wrist. I shouldn't have left them. I should have realised they'd be easy prey. But then, I hadn't truly appreciated how small the numbers we followed were. I believed it to be the rest of the ship-men, and that was patently not the case.

I grab the hands of the first dead Raider, surprised to find they hold some residual heat. I would have expected the body to be frozen in death, as well as from the cold, but they've been under shelter since they breathed their last.

"Where are we putting them?" Icel grumbles. He has the feet of another Raider in his hands, backing away from Ælfgar and Tatberht.

"As far as we can get them toward the edge of the trees. Sooner they were buried under the snow than here. At least they won't smell, not for a while yet."

By the time we return to Ælfgar, Tatberht and Wulfhere, half of my warriors have arrived, Pybba taking some control, sending Leonath and Siric to hunt for wood. At the same time, Rudolf bends to examine Tatberht's wound, Hereman hauling the remaining body over his shoulder.

He grins at me, the ice from his beard and moustache already starting to melt.

"I prefer it when I have to kill the fucker's first. This is all too easy," he grins. It's impossible to dampen Hereman's enthusiasm, even now and even here. The sight of his dripping moustache reassures me that I'm not risking a cold death for everyone in staying here. It's far, far warmer away from the open expanse. The trees provide shelter, while the snow, far up the branches, acts to warm rather than chill.

Not, of course, that Haden seems to approve.

His shrill whinny reaches me. I know there's no choice but to retrieve him myself.

"I'll be back," I fling over my shoulder, bending low and wishing Haden, for once, could just do what needs to be bloody done.

"Come here, you daft sod," Oda's holding tight to Haden's reins; Oda beneath the trees, while Haden remains on the snow, front legs apart, all of his weight on them, head down.

"I'll get him, Oda. You go inside." Behind Oda, Sæbald waits patiently, his mount calm, for all the wind is picking up. I can see where the snow has been moved, peaks and troughs forming, as though the sea itself has frozen in place.

"Right, get your arse in here," I order, with no hint of apology in my voice. "In here, or out there, on your own, because I'm going to be warming myself before the heat of the fire."

His eyes glower at me, his front hoof raised as though to stamp down on my foot.

"You can just fucking try it," I muse, walking away, looping his harness around his head first. He can't trip, and I leave it to him whether he follows or not. For a moment, I think he's more stubborn than I am, and then I hear the sound of hooves impacting the spongy ground.

Not that it's easy going for him. I have to stop and hold branches above his head, Sæbald helping from the rear before we make it to the makeshift camp. The horses have been given space beneath the lower hanging branches, and the majority of them have happily slumped to the ground, legs beneath them. They remind me of hounds, not horses. But then, we're all fucking knackered.

Leonath and Siric have excelled themselves. Two fires are merrily burning away, stones forming a circle around the burning wood to stop the flames from spreading over the dry pine needles. My tired warriors are drooped, some almost asleep already. I don't have the heart to send anyone on guard duty, and yet, I can't allow us to remain unprotected.

"I'll keep a watch," Wulfstan offers, coming to my side and speaking out of the side of his mouth. "Have someone come and relieve me before darkness falls." He carries his fur in his hands, no doubt to keep his legs warm while he stands or sits, fighting his exhaustion.

"If you find anything to eat, save me some," is his parting shot as he bends and then disappears beneath the low-lying branches. I'm unsurprised when Ordlaf follows him, a tired grin on his face.

"Don't bloody forget about us," he calls before vanishing.

Now all I need is someone to guard against whatever might be in the interior of the woodlands. Three Raiders won't have come alone.

Eahric finds me next. His cheeks are already suffused with a healthier pink, and his brown eyes wink at me.

"Eadulf and I will mount the first watch. I confess I slept nearly all the way here from the hilltop. We'll keep each other awake with tales of the women we've bedded and those we wish we had."

"Aye, well, the women I've bedded," Eadulf comments sourly. "And the ones you wish you had." I roll my eyes at them, but at least I don't need to send a more unwilling member of my warband to complete the task.

Haden has already settled, his eyes closing drowsily. I can see his wound in the glow from the fire. It looks angry and tight. Yet, nothing leaks from it. I don't know if that's a good indicator or not. I'd ask Rudolf, but he's asleep, propped up against Dever, his left hand over his head, his feet angled towards the first of the two fires. Once more, I'm reminded of his youth.

Tatberht sleeps as well. He's been rolled onto his side, and a clean bandage applied to his wound. I think of Eowa, in the forest close to Warwick, and my Aunt. If either of them were here, I wouldn't worry for Tatberht or Haden, but they're far away, and all we have are our rudimentary skills.

"Right, Ælfgar, you know what needs to be done." Ælfgar looks unhappy but painfully scrambles to his feet. The wound high on his left wrist, leaking afresh.

"Can't we stitch it?" he asks, and he does have a point.

"We could, but Rudolf is asleep, and if it's seared, then the wound-rot won't take your arm."

"Well, get on with it then. I warn you, I'll scream like a woman in childbirth when you apply the heat." I shake my head.

"I'm sure you won't," I try to console, but then he shows me the extent of his wound. While I rip the torn cloth aside, I heat my knife in the fire. I should really get another one. It's supposed to be for eating, not for closing wounds, the similarities merging in my mind, and bringing bile to my throat.

"Hold steady," I instruct Ælfgar. Almost everyone is asleep, every horse as well, but Icel watches me, Pybba too, from his place close to the second hearth.

"Right, I'm doing it," but Ælfgar's shriek is just as loud as he warned me it would be, even though I apply it before I say I will. I hold my knife over the hand-sized wound, gritting my teeth against the sizzle that makes my stomach rumble. When I pull it aside, he collapses to the ground, silent but breathing heavily, sweat beading his face.

"Thank fuck for that," Lyfing calls sleepily from beside the first fire as I return my knife to the fire for cleansing. I spit out my unease.

What the fuck is happening within Mercia? I wish I knew.

CHAPTER 11

When I wake, I can't remember where I am. Above my head, the bough of the pine tree is dark. Only the smell reminds me that I'm outside and not beside the hearth at Northampton, or preferably, Kingsholm. I think of my home. I'm there so rarely; is it truly my home?

The space we're sheltered within is warm, despite the fact I know snow lies deeply all around, and there's even the smell of meat roasting to rouse me fully.

Not that I'm alone in sleeping. Other than Hereman and Ælf-gar, almost everyone still sleeps. Beornstan grins at me when he sees me sit upright.

"Poor bloody thing ran in here looking for somewhere warm for the night, and I caught him and slit his throat before he could do anything about it."

My mouth falls open in shock. Are we so lacking in menace that the hare had no problem in trying to find a bed beside us? It's doesn't reflect well on the mass of iron with which we adorn ourselves.

But, Beornstan's grin speaks of his triumph, so I hold back my sarcastic response.

"Hardly enough for everyone," Hereman's face is downcast. I can hear his stomach growling from here.

"No, but a fair start, and better than fuck all," I retort. Hereman's strained grin is all I need to see to know he's starving.

"The fuckers died full and sated. What good has it done

them?"

I amble to my feet, feeling every ache and twinge, tears in my eyes for the savage pain that starts at my toes and makes its way to the top of my head. I peer all around me, eyes seeking out Haden, who still sleeps, and then Tatberht.

"Everyone seems well," Hereman states flatly, although Ælfgar's face is sheeted and sweating still.

"Just the pain or a fever?" I demand to know.

"The fucking pain," and he grits his teeth, unsuccessfully trying to get comfortable.

"He needs wine or ale or a smack around the face to make him worry about something else." Hereman. As fucking sympathetic as ever.

"I'll check on the others," I stand as tall as I can, feeling every ache and creak in my body. My thighs burn, my arse as well. Hereman nods.

"Walking through the snow'll do that to you. Uses all sorts of body parts you didn't realise you even fucking had." Ah, the compassion slips from his tongue like honey from an oatcake.

I cast him a frustrated look. He smirks, enjoying himself.

"I notice you're not on your feet."

"No, I tried that. My back aches like a bastard, my thighs as well. This body ain't made for trudging through snow. Or for surviving on a handful of berries. We need water," he cautions as I turn my back on him.

"I'll just go and find some then, Your Grace," I consider sweeping a bow but know it'll hurt more than the satisfaction I'll get from taunting the bastard.

I find Eadulf and Eahric sitting together, just where the snow starts to lie on the ground, finding its way through the thick tree cover. They're both huddled under their furs but have alert enough eyes.

"Anything?" I ask.

"Nothing but a few hares and the odd robin, come to try their luck. I'm so fucking hungry; I could have pecked him, and not vice versa," Eahric chuckles. I notice then that his lips are jagged from lack of water.

"I'll get someone to relieve you and find water," I promise, standing clear of the trees, boots wedged in the snow, just gazing around me. Nothing's changed since we came beneath the tree line. The snow is just as thick, the wind just as cold, and the sun is all but set, lending the view a strange texture, more pink than brown. The sun might be about to disappear for the day, but the snow will light our path if we have need of it.

Ordlaf and Wulfstan aren't together when I hunt for them. I come across Ordlaf first, his eyes fluttering in sleep.

"Go and get Hereman," I order him, but not unkindly. "He's awake and can take your place. He can moan to himself rather than to Ælfgar, poor fucker."

"Are they cooking something?" Ordlaf asks hopefully.

"Yes, a hare. Beornstan caught the poor bastard. There might be enough for everyone to have a mouthful."

"Ah well, better than nothing," Ordlaf springs to his feet and immediately regrets it, his eyes closing in pain.

"Walking in the snow," I offer, as though I realised the cause of the problem first.

"There's a brook down there," and he points. "The water is clear, if fucking cold," and he's gone. I remain behind, guarding the position until Hereman comes crashing through the under-growth. He's happily chewing on one of the cooked legs, and I roll my eyes at him.

"Fucking hungry," he explains again, not bothering to move the bone from his mouth to inform me.

"There's water down there when you need to swill your mouth." This seems to delight Hereman more than the food.

"I'm going to find Wulfstan. Keep alert."

"Aye, aye, your grace," and I chuckle at his more cheerful tone. As long as he's not hungry or thirsty, Hereman can endure almost anything. All of my warriors can.

I stoop to quench my thirst in the brook, the sharp coldness of the water bringing me to full alertness in a way reminiscent of a sword or spear levelled at my throat. I hurry on, seeking out Wulfstan. He's not where I expect him to be. I turn, looking all around me, but the visibility is poor. There are low hanging branches everywhere.

"Here," a sharp hiss reaches my ears, and I swivel. Wulfstan furiously beckons me to his side. I go hand already on my seax. What has he discovered now?

I expect it to be Raiders, or hopefully, the bodies of Raiders, but it's neither of those things. As I rush to his side, I quickly appreciate what's caught his attention.

Somehow, in this great vast woodland, we've sheltered within, we've managed to strike our camp within spitting distance of a wolf's den. From inside the den, and entirely out of season, are the gentle nips and barks of puppies.

Wulfstan wears a daft smile, even as I grip my seax tighter. Where there are pups, there's sure to be a dame, and probably not a very happy one, with us close.

But Wulfstan shakes his head, reaching out to knock my hand aside.

"She's seen me, been all through the camp while you lazy sods slept. She has no problems with us, although I think she's a bit annoyed that someone else caught her hare."

My forehead furrows in shock. Wulfstan chuckles.

"We're not all bloody-minded murderers," he states. "And make sure you keep the other fuckers away from here. She's been kind enough to leave us be; we can do the same for her. Poor bitch, trying to keep the pups alive during the winter. She must have caught late in the season."

I confess I'm speechless.

"Tell 'em yourself," I eventually splutter. I've taken enough ridicule from my men recently. Wulfstan can handle them himself.

"Aye, well. I'll tell you what, take yourself away from here, and then no one will even know where they are, other than the two of us."

"Fine, but if someone gets attacked by her, I won't call them back."

"What, and leave her puppies to die? I never took you to be such a cruel old bastard." But he's laughing as he walks away, a last lingering glance showing me that he's enjoyed his time out here far more than he should have done.

In the sudden silence, I march steadfastly back towards the brook, pausing to empty my stream close to another tree. Above my head, the canopy sways slowly, rhythmically, and I can't see the sky. I feel enclosed and perversely safe from harm, as though the trees want to protect me, just as much as they do the family of wolves.

Perhaps I could bring every man, woman and child to live here, allow the Raiders to run riot over Mercia, rely on this natural protection.

"Coelwulf," Sæbald's words break my reverie, and I nod to him.

"You got some sleep?" I demand.

"Aye, I did, and Wulfstan told me to watch out for his wolves. Daft sod's getting soft, but I'll not kill 'em. Pybba's on his way as well. He and Lyfing are going to hunt for mushrooms and berries. Sounds bloody delicious." His face turns sour at the thought. I smirk and slap his back, and he winces.

"We'll get some proper food soon. It's just lucky that they didn't eat the oats for the horses, or we'd have no choice but to press on in this crap weather."

"Make sure they don't forget me if they do return with anything edible," Sæbald calls after me, and I raise my hand, eyes rolling. Damn fool. Complaining about the food and then demanding not to be forgotten.

Maybe, the wolf will bring more hares or squirrels or any other creatures that live within the forest.

It would certainly be welcome.

Back with the rest of my men, I check on those who are awake and Tatberht and Haden. They both seem well, but of course, they don't need to move a great deal. It won't be like that when we make our way to London. Perhaps I should leave them both here, but then I'd have to split my force. Still not knowing where the remainder of the ship-men from the boats are, I don't want to take the risk.

I'll have to be patient. It sits ill with me, not helped by my griping belly.

I slump back to the floor, face towards the fire. At least I'm warm. That's something about which I can be grateful.

Rudolf still sleeps. My warriors purposefully don't disturb him, keeping themselves occupied with trips to the stream, trips to relieve themselves, only then turning to weapons, and the horses' saddles and reins. I watch Oda through sleepy eyes as he runs his hands along the leather and ropes, ensuring all are supple and free from ice and water. I think I should probably do the same, but I'm too fucking sleepy.

Next time I wake, the flames from the fires leap ever upwards, the scent of something that might be pleasant emanating from beside the hearthstones. Pybba is smiling, Lyfing as well, while Rudolf looks as though he might eat Pybba's remaining hand if he doesn't hurry the fuck up.

"If you eat it before it's ready, it'll do you more harm than good," Pybba berates Rudolf.

"If I don't eat something, I'll do you more harm than good," Rudolf retorts. His cheeks are flushed with heat. Pybba slaps his questing hand back, time and time again.

"Will the meat ever be cooked?" Rudolf asks of Wulfstan. It seems the wolf has brought us our supper once more.

"It'll be ready when it's ready," Wulfstan's words hold the same edge of irritation as Pybba's. This conversation isn't a new one.

"How's Tatberht?" I ask, sitting upright and brushing stray pine needles from my shoulders and back, wincing. Sleeping off my aches and pains isn't working.

"Sleeping," Rudolf announces, his eyes remaining on the cooking meat.

"And Haden?"

"Not asleep," is his less than helpful reply. Wulfstan meets my gaze, a smirk on his face, as I wrestle to my feet, trying not to cry out with pain when my muscles object.

"Has everyone on guard duty been relieved?"

I can't see Sæbald, or Eadulf and Eahric.

"Yes, some time ago," Pybba confirms, once more slapping Rudolf's hand aside. "Ordheah, Siric, and Wærwulf are there now. Ordlaf has just gone back. He begged for the duty, something about it stinking of farts and horse shit in here." I grunt, wrinkle my nose, and immediately regret the action.

"He's got a bloody good point. I'll go check on them all."

"There's no need," Icel responds. "I just went, and they're all fine. They've had some berries, and they know there'll be food waiting for them when they get back. I even think we might be able to catch some fish from the brook if any of us can walk beside it without sounding like a hundred warriors."

"I might just go and try my luck," I begin. Icel nods sagely. He knows me too well to try and prevent me from doing something twice.

Haden is standing now, and I call him. He strides towards me, almost managing to avoid everyone else, and then comes to a standstill.

I run my hand along his nose, meeting his eyes and only then cast my eye toward his wound. To my eye, it still looks red and sore, but the stitches that Rudolf made are holding. For now.

"He's been trying to lick it," Rudolf lifts his voice to complain. "I've told him to leave it alone, but he's having none of it. It probably itches and feels tight and uncomfortable, but better that than a ragged great big wound." His petulance brings a smile to my face.

"How does it feel to have someone who won't do the right thing, even when it's for their own good."

"I don't know what you mean, you old git," but Pybba grins into his chest, and Hereman mutters something beneath his breath. I laugh.

"Come on, old man. Let's get you some water."

I lead Haden through the branches, having to hold them high to allow passage. It's an effort, but I can see where the other horses have gone because of the marks in the rich loam. No doubt, Haden has been this way already, but he's my horse and responsibility.

Ordlaf nods as I appear. He's sitting on the ground, running his blades through a mass of tufted grasses taken from the brook.

"Could hear you two coming from London," he states quickly, no doubt wanting to explain why he's not standing, threatening to slice my throat open.

"And have you heard anything else?"

"Nothing but the occasional scurry of some creature going about their business. There's no one here but us. Well, not now there isn't."

"Have we scared them away?"

"Doubt it. They've just gone elsewhere."

The words aren't the comfort they should be.

"They might come back?"

"Maybe, but we'll hear them if they do."

Haden has taken steps down to the flowing water. Now he drinks quickly, his entire body quivering with the movement. I wince at the flash of reddened flesh high on his leg.

"A nasty cut," Ordlaf confirms, nodding his head at Haden.

"Maybe he'll grow his hair long to cover it," I offer, eyebrows high.

He nods and grins. That's what the vainer of us do if we take a slice to the face.

"Well, not everyone likes to see something as ugly as this," and he lifts the hair running down the back of his neck to reveal the angry skin.

"It probably doesn't much help that you have to tell everyone how you got it."

"Well, no, it's not the most inspiring of stories. Falling over in the stables and impaling myself on the fork used to clear the filth from the horses bedding was not my finest hour."

I laugh then, and so does he. It's not a fine story.

"But then, that's not what I tell the women who ask." He's beaming, a devious glint in his eye.

"I imagine it's not," and we're both laughing, even as Haden lifts his head, glaring at us with affront. We laugh all the harder.

And then I hear a crack of a broken twig, my hand on my seax, even as Ordlaf leaps to his feet, all humour drained from our faces.

I risk looking at Haden, his front hooves in the trickle of water. I have to hope I'll keep him from further injury because from nowhere, two Raiders appear, leering faces, looking from Ordlaf to me, to Haden. They wear thick cloaks flung over their arms, revealing the rippling muscles they lay claim to and the array of weapons around their waists.

I find a leer sliding onto my face.

Two of them, against all of my warriors. I hardly think so.

"It seems that you might have something of ours?" I'm not surprised he speaks my tongue. At some point, it was bound to happen to all the Raiders. Jarl Halfdan speaks my language. The bastard.

"And what might that be?" I ask out of mild curiosity.

"That horse. He's ours. He ran loose last night. We'll just take him now."

I hear the rustle of Haden's interest.

"Then tell me, what's his name?"

"We don't name our animals. There's no point. They're merely weapons."

"Ah, but you name your weapons. I know you do."

A flicker of unease belies the man's ignorance, but the smirk is back quickly enough.

"He's called '*Skiderik*.' See, I'll call him. And he'll come to me."

"Why would you call him a bastard?" I ask.

The crafty look in the warrior's eye falters, but he presses on all the same. So, he thinks to shock me by understanding my language, but I'm to be ignorant of his.

"You speak my tongue?"

"Of course, I do. Better to know your enemy."

The man turns to the other, a string of words fleeing from his mouth. His fellow warrior chuckles at something the man says, and I regret my hasty and cocky reply. It's not as if I know more than a handful of words.

"I wouldn't do that," I'm beyond relieved to hear Wærwulf's bluff retort. Not that I have a problem with being caught in a lie, just not immediately.

"I think, if you were to attempt it, you'd be dead before you got any closer."

Wærwulf stands to my right, hand on the seax handle at his waist, the other resting on the sword pommel slung over his shoulder.

Now, there's more panic on the man's broad face, and it only intensifies as first Hereman and then Icel joins the small collection of warriors.

We outnumber them, and yet, I can't help thinking that two men such as this wouldn't be alone in the forest. There must be more of them. Perhaps, they'll appear from behind a tree, just like Wærwulf, Hereman and Icel. Any moment now, I expect Pybba and Rudolf to arrive as well.

The fact that Siric and Ordheah haven't joined our group assures me that there aren't Raiders trying to attack from the snowy plain beside the woodlands. No, despite Ordlaf's words, these bastards have been hiding in the trees, just as we have.

The moment stretches before us. I think the Raiders might just make a run for it; try their luck with getting lost beneath the trees. But, of course, they don't. Instead, another eight Raiders coalesce before me.

They all look as though they've been fed well and recently. They glow with health and vibrancy, which is wrong when the weather's as grim as this. These must be some of the missing ship-men.

"There's no way to escape. The ships are all burnt; even if it hadn't snowed so much, you wouldn't be able to find them."

"They're not our ships," the first man states confidently. "Not that you could call them ships. They were barely able to stay afloat even in that shit-pit known as the Thames."

I can't tell whether he's bluffing.

"Now, just give us the horse, and we'll be gone. Well, we'll go when we have a horse each. It's not the weather to be travelling on foot." His renewed confidence speaks of something about which I'm ignorant. It could unsettle me, but I can't see that they have enough men to counter my warriors. I'm sure by now, all of my men are preparing to defend us. I just hope someone realises they need to stay with the horses.

I'm not about to let more of the Raider bastards steal our mounts. Again.

"He's not your horse," I smile as I speak, summoning Haden to my side. He comes immediately, not even looking at the other man. "I think, you know, that he might just be my fucking horse," my cheeks break into a cheery grin. "I think I might have been there when he was foaled. Fancy that, you fuckers. I can tell you about his dam and his sire."

My opponent sighs heavily, a look of regret on his face, although it's trickery.

"I chose my words poorly. He *will* be my horse. Now, hand him over, and we won't have to attack."

"You won't be getting your hands on my horse without shedding my blood." I've caught sight of Rudolf beneath the branches, Pybba as well. I want Haden to go to Rudolf, but of course, he glares at the enemy, not at his friend. Could he make it any more challenging to keep him safe?

"I have no problem with that bargain," the warrior announces expansively, sliding his seax clear from his weapons belt. It glistens with menace, the iron bright in the gloom. But it's nothing I've not seen before. All that remains to be seen is who will make the first move.

The other leading Raider licks his lips, his black beard wobbling with the action, his tongue little more than a flicker of pink. He looks keen for a fight, his war axe steady in his hand. Rings glint from his fingers, and I look forward to slicing the fingers to get at his prizes. Rudolf will be delighted with such precious gems to add to his store.

I step forward, making way for Haden to walk behind me,

but of course, he doesn't. I don't want to give away my intentions, but it would be easier if Haden were out of harm's way. He stamps his hoof into the soft ground, the sound far less menacing than he might hope on the spongy texture. It seems Haden wants to fight all the same.

"Go on then," I murmur.

Haden has bunched his long legs beneath himself and launched at the Raiders between one heartbeat and the next.

The gap between us is small, and yet Haden still manages to reach a gallop, stopping with perfect precision, just before the two front warriors. He rears, one hoof impacting the first man, the second smashing into the raised arms of the other, who's had the speedy reactions to try and stop his nose from being broken.

The crack of both impacts echoes louder than iron on iron, and then all hell breaks loose.

I rush forward, determined to complete the attack that Haden's begun, Rudolf dashing to do the same, Icel's heavier tread just behind me.

Pybba calls for Haden, his voice shrill with the order. I don't think Haden will obey. I slap his wound, hating myself for the action, but knowing I only do it to protect him. He doesn't wear his saddle or any of the accoutrements of battle. It would be too easy for one of our opponents to wound him once more.

Haden whinnies with pain, plunging towards Pybba. I only hope Pybba can bring the brute under control before he tears his stitches. But then I think only of my foe-men.

The man who spoke with such confidence is on the ground, his nose broken, possibly his jaw as well, blood pooling all around him. He shrieks, hands going to his face while his legs kick out.

"Shut the fuck up," and I stab down, eager to silence him. All around me, I can hear the winged denizens of the woodlands taking to the air. The cry of an animal in distress, even a man, making it imperative they all escape with cracking wings, powering against the icy chill of the air.

Ordlaf takes the other warrior, and then we all gather to face the remaining Raiders.

I've not studied them, partially obscured as they are by the first two men, but they're equally as well provisioned.

My seax slicks out, a feint towards the first man's throat. He steps backwards, ducking as he does so, and encounters my fist. The force of the blow almost knocks me to the floor, and he buckles, gasping for air, hand clutching at his throat. He's only winded, for now. A single stab and his heart is forever still.

Icel barrels one of our opponents to the ground with a sweep of his massive hand, following it with a lethal cut to the Raiders exposed neck. Blood arcs into the air, but he's already focused on the next enemy.

Hereman is dismissive of this new attack. His spear flies through the air, his aim never in doubt, and now one of the enemies is suspended in mid-air, his legs flailing beneath him, pinioned to the thick tree trunk.

His shrieks are feral, ringing louder than a church bell.

"Fuck's sake," I hear Hereman complain, but my eyes are on my next opponent.

He has shifty eyes, busy behind me, as though waiting for someone to come to his aid. But what he doesn't know is that if there are more of his comrades out there, then my other men will have ended their lives. There's no hope for him.

His belly is huge, straining the byrnie that covers him. I imagine how easy it would be to slit that open, his entrails following quickly. It's as though he reads my mind, stepping backwards, not forwards. I tilt my head to one side. I might be a frightening proposition, but fuck me, he's supposed to be Raider scum. Does he genuinely mean to bolt?

Rudolf's shriek from behind me, 'to get fucking down,' brings a grin to my face once more. Daft fucker.

All the same, I do as he asks, feeling the weight of his foot on my back, and then he's in the air. My warrior has frozen in terror. I wince as Rudolf's seax embeds itself into his exposed skull with a satisfyingly grating sound. The man drops, Rudolf scampering to stay upright.

"A little showy," I call, ensuring I'm there to sweep aside the seax of the man to his right, who thinks to make a strike from behind.

"You were too fucking slow," Rudolf calls, voice high with exuberance, sword now in hand, as he battles another of the Raiders. The man behind him is moaning on the floor, his hands already covered in the slickness of his innards as I catch sight of Hereman finally silencing the shrieks of his impaled victim.

Ordlaf is busy beside me, his sword in one hand, seax in the other, as he counters the attack of one of the Raiders. He's of middling height, his helm in place, black leather byrnie impervious to Ordlaf's attack, although I know it's just a matter of time.

"And you were too damn impetuous."

"I thought we should get it done with before it gets dark," Rudolf still argues, even as he elbows the warrior in the nose and then uses such distraction to jab the sword hilt into the man's throat. I skip across, wincing at the motion, use my seax to slick open his throat. Only then do I turn, force Rudolf's seax free from the dead man.

"Here, you left this," I offer him, blood and gore dripping to the floor.

Rudolf screws his face up at the sight.

"You could fucking clean it."

"I," and I thrust it at him. "Didn't make it dirty," but I'm laughing as I speak.

The enemy is all dead, bar one—Icel toys with him.

"Are there more of you?" I shout, even though I doubt the man will hear me. Icel swivels at my words.

"Are we after a nice chat, or am I fucking killing him?" His words are slow, laced with a strange combination of amusement and frustration.

Behind him, the warrior looks from Icel to me, his lips curled, plotting his escape.

"You could ask him before you killed him?" I hedge.

Icel swirls his sword, the blade coming to rest on his opponent's bulging throat.

"Answer the man." Confusion, wars with malice.

"How many of you are there?" But still, there's no reply.

Wærwulf lifts his head from where he's stripping a corpse and mumbles the question in Danish.

A single word is muttered in response.

"There are more," Wærwulf confirms, swishing his hand as though giving permission for Icel to continue.

"How many more?" I ask quickly, eyes rolling, frustrated that I have to be so specific with my question.

Icel's huge body sighs once more as Wærwulf asks this new question.

"*Tredive.*"

"*Tredive?*" Wærwulf questions, but the man is vehemently shaking his head.

"Thirty," he flings back to me.

"Thirty? Well, where the fuck are they?"

Once more, Wærwulf makes his demand, but I don't need a translator to understand the response. Icel's foe clamps his lips tightly together, the universal indicator for saying nothing further.

Now I sigh, peering into the gloom around me.

"Hurry up, and fucking finish him off," I inform Icel, turning aside. If there are more of the bastards out there, I want to know where they are.

The sound of a blade slicing into flesh assures me the last of this small group of warriors is dead.

"Haden is with the other horses," Pybba informs me, coming to a sudden stop in front of me, hand on his weapons belt.

"Oh, I see you did not need me."

"I do, don't fear. There are more of the fuckers to kill. Somewhere." I'm determining where they'll be. I'm sure they must be beneath the trees. No fool will be out in the snow. But should I check?

Only then, a new sound splits the air, and I turn to my warriors, a smile on my face.

"I do believe that the wolf might require some assistance."

"What wolf?" Rudolf demands, a lingering look at the treasures he's yet to take from the bodies.

"The ones that Wulfstan found, over there." I point, but there's no real need. The yapping of the wolves is only just heard over the shouting of yet more Raiders.

"We need to help Wulfstan," I advise, looking to Ordlaf, but he shrugs his shoulders. He knows to remain behind.

"Come on then," and I surge through the trees, eyes firmly on the floor. I don't want to trip on a tree root or discarded branch from the winter storms. In the near distance, the unmistakable sound of iron on iron rings through the cold air. My breath plumes before me, but there's joy on my face.

The Raiders might have stolen my horse, wounded him even, but I'm going to make the fuckers pay. All the fuckers.

CHAPTER 12

I hear Wulfstan before I see him.

"Fuck, he's roaring like an old boar," Rudolf mutters, breath huffing beside me.

"He was adamant the creatures weren't to be fucking harmed."

"He should 'ave told the other bastards that," Rudolf exclaims as we emerge onto a scene of total devastation.

Here, there's a small space between the close-packed trees. Just enough for a force of, say, about thirty Raiders, as the dead man told us, to assemble.

But they're already on the defensive. Any chance of taking us by surprise has long since evaporated. Not, it seems, because of their incompetence, but because of something else.

A man howls beneath the boughs of a tree. His shrieks are the loudest I've ever heard. He flails, one hand trying to drag himself back towards his allies, dug into the thick forest floor, one foot trying to beat against the ground, his other hand flailing for a seax that's just out of reach.

The mother wolf has him, and she's fucking pissed.

Her growls rumble with the menace of a hundred of the fuckers. Behind her, I can hear the weak and pitiful cries of her pups. Wulfstan is there as well, rage evident in the way he holds his body, weapon ready. He's become their unlikely protector once again.

Lyfing has my warriors in a tight formation, shield against

shield, spears prominent where they poke above shields or beneath it.

The Raiders are entirely screwed.

Wulfstan and the wolf to one side. My other warriors to the other. And now those who fought beside me have erupted onto the scene as well.

"Shut him the fuck up," I bellow, startling everyone there. Perhaps, at last, I've learned to step with more ease. Or maybe, the growls of the mother wolf, the howls of the wounded man, and the jaunting calls of my warriors have merely overlain everything else.

"I'm bloody trying," Wulfstan grumbles, stabbing down once more and missing the man by a small distance, where he dances, prone, on the floor. Blood covers him. He's less man than a piece of raw meat, pink, grey and white adding to the scene. And the wolf isn't letting up. She's trying to pull him away from her cubs, teeth flashing pinkly, her head shaking from side to side where it has hold of the remaining limb.

I wince, feel a moment of pity for the dying man, which evaporates when I spy close by the too-still form of one of the pups. It seems he deserves his death after all. Bastard.

The Raiders have only one path to escape that I can see, and it's not climbing the trees, although they might well do that shortly. Perhaps one of their Gods will swoop down and rescue them.

"Rudolf, Pybba and Icel, go and shore up that gap." It's tiny; it really is. This open space has been formed because one of the trees has seemingly moved aside. My fanciful thoughts make me believe it picked up its roots and moved there to avoid the worst of the fighting, not wanting to risk its precious limbs. Either way, it blocks much of the path. My three warriors will hold it easily, even if all thirty of the Raider scum attempt to make their escape.

And still, the man on the floor screams. It is the most unholy of sounds. They'll hear him coming if he does make it to Valhalla, that's for sure. And if he's a Christian, then I imagine our caring God might well kick him out for spoiling the tranquillity of the bloody place.

Goda's voice encourages my warriors. I'm keen to get involved, Hereman and Wærwulf at my side.

My warriors move forwards, one step, and then two. Then they're running. I like this line of attack.

"Get ready for the arseholes to make a run for it," I thunder.

Fucking cocks. I hate the Raider bastards. I detest them even more when they underestimate my warriors and me.

I reach for a handful of old grasses, run the blade of my seax through them before discarding them to the ground. They're tinged with the red of my kills, and it feels sacrilegious in this beautiful place. But we're only just getting going.

Goda and Lyfing urge my warriors onwards. The two sounds clash, the sound shaking the trees, causing any of the hardier birds who've thought to remain behind to squawk with indignation and scurry into the sky.

And then the weaker of the Raiders panic.

The first to rush towards me, eyes wild beneath the dull-iron helm, is all legs and arms. He more stumbles than runs, and as though he doesn't see me, or Hereman, or Wærwulf, he just keeps coming.

It's too easy to halt his headlong dash, to raise my seax and stab upwards into his exposed jaw. His pulse thunders in his neck, and then it's all over, and I don't think he's even opened his screwed-up eyes.

Fine Raider fodder, that one.

But, there are determined bastards still fighting in the group that faces my men. Sæbald lashes out with his war axe, thudding it into the skull of a Raider who battles against Goda. Our foe tumbles to the floor, stunned or dead. I don't know. The Raider behind him doesn't care either, stumbling over his twitching body to take his place.

Hereman takes the life of the next Raider, who thinks to escape. I can hear more weapons at work, no doubt Icel, Pybba and Rudolf about the same task. And still that damn man screams, the cries of the wolf pups growing in intensity. They're not scared. Not anymore. I imagine the little brutes are hungry, and there's some fine meat on display here. The smell of rust must be driving them mad.

I wish one of them would eat the fucker's tongue.

Wærwulf thrusts his elbow into the face of the next rapidly departing Raider, and he plummets backwards, head impacting an unfortunately placed stone. He doesn't even twitch in death.

"Shit," Wærwulf mutters, a bereft look on his face.

"Dead is dead," I mollify, and he shrugs his shoulders, dismissing the matter.

By now, at least a third of the foe-men are down. The moans of the wolf-eaten man joined by the rest of the sacks of shit who can't defeat my warriors. I'm not surprised. My men are keen, eager, to finish the task of ending the lives of these insolent ship-men. They're on Mercian land. They should have remained in fucking Wessex with their new ally, Alfred the weak.

But the fight is far from done.

Now, some of our opponents begin to notice how fucked they are. The chances of escaping are growing smaller by the sword swing. Do they want to die here? I doubt it. Craven bastards.

The eyes of two ship-men meet over the heads of the others. I know what they're thinking. I don't need Wærwulf to shout the warning at the gabbled conversation they roar to one another.

"Rudolf, 'ware," I bellow, hoping my harsh cry reaches his youthful ears above the rest of the unholy racket. He hears everything else he shouldn't. This better be one of those occasions when he listens to the parts he needs to know.

I can't see him, or Icel, or Pybba, but I have sight of our opponents. Muscles bunched, I surge through the rest of the enemy. There are enough of my warriors to finish them. But Rudolf is about to be faced with desperate men. And desperate men never fight fair, or well, or even with the skills they've honed throughout their years of fighting. But sometimes, they can be fucking lucky.

I won't allow luck to win this day. Not when skill should be the only answer to these fuckers.

Easily, I push aside any knife, blade, or axe that comes close to me, almost as though I'm immune to the attack. I focus only on the two Raiders, both tall men, both well provisioned, both determined to live through this. They couldn't be more wrong.

They collide with Rudolf and Pybba with a din that almost blocks out the shrieks of the wolf-eaten man. Almost. Rudolf heard me, which gives me some respite, as does Icel's square face, knowing and determined, standing behind Pybba and Rudolf. He'll step in to assist them once and if he's needed.

Leather byrnies greet me, arms raised, helms slightly askew. Were they ready for this attack or not? I really can't tell.

The first man thrusts towards Rudolf, perhaps expecting it to be easy. Rudolf's seax flies through the air, countering every attack, almost at the point of anticipating every move before it can be made. Fuck, Rudolf is a good warrior. Wiry, strong, light on his feet. I remember being like him.

The other warrior hesitates for just a moment, noticing Pybba's missing hand, no doubt thinking it'll be easy. How he fails to note the hulking shape of Icel behind Pybba, I've no idea. I don't have selective eyesight. I don't allow myself only to see what I want to see.

Not that I need worry. This second warrior is slow, his movements laboured. I suspect he already bleeds. Pybba anticipates his first blow, easily parrying it with his sword. While Rudolf and his warrior trade strikes with lightning speed, Pybba and his opponent are precisely the opposite. While Rudolf blocks his foes movements, Pybba becomes the one to lead the way. I pause, my bloodied hand aiming towards the ground, eyes noticing what Pybba won't be able to see.

His opponent leaks from a wound on the back of his arm. Where there should be a continuous line of inkings, blue or black, impossible to tell in the muted light, there's a river of maroon, even the flash of pink and white. This man is dead. He just hasn't realised yet.

Over the heads of my labouring warriors, I meet the eyes of Icel. He meets my gaze and nods. We both know what needs to happen.

A roar distracts me, and I turn, eyes wide.

"Fuck."

The wolf-eaten man still squeals, the howls of the pups, the growling of the mother, more menacing than a hundred Raiders. Yet, I've become the focus of the attention of the fifteen or so ship-men who still fight for their lives. While half their number counter my alert warriors, Lyfing and Sæbald refusing to back down, encouraging the rest of my warriors, seven men eye me up. They carry cuts; some look deep and painful. Two men have lost their helms. Another has only a shield with which to fight, his weapons lost. Three others leer at me: nasty looking bastards, the lot of them.

What they do have, is the determination to live.

What they don't have, is the ability to make sure that happens.

And I'm quite happy to kill every last fucking one of them.

My seax counters the most desperate of them, the man with just the shield. The wood splinters, leaving my seax no more than a finger's breadth from his nose. It would be cruel to prolong his agony. I loosen my grip, thrust the seax upwards, only to catch it, my grip reversed, allowing the blade to stab into his nose, and through it, into the softness of the mass behind.

He doesn't even blink in the time it takes me to end his life.

"Which of you arseholes is next?" I huff.

A moment of indecision and one of the helmless men is before me, although his face, scratched and torn open, especially down his right cheek, tells me he'd sooner any of the others stood in his place.

His brown eyes, and darker skin, shaved head, and beardless chin, make him look no older than Rudolf. But his build speaks of an older man. Still, old men can know fear, and he shows it. I don't need to look down to know he's pissed himself.

Yet, he's not given up.

"*Skiderik*," he spits into my face.

"Pleasure to meet you," I growl as he counters my attack with a slash of his war axe. Hair and blood glisten on its edges. He's struck one of my men, and that fills me with cold rage.

With my seax, I knock aside his war axe, the impact of the two weapons jarring my right arm, even as my left elbow snakes up and jabs him in the throat. He gags. Face already purple, as he staggers, trying to keep upright, war axe flailing ineffectually, eyes losing focus, even as his chest heaves, only no air is going in.

"Fucks sake," I mutter, and my seax slicks open his throat. Sooner it was over than I have to watch this performance. I jump back, avoiding the warm fountain, as he tumbles to his knees, and then to the ground.

I'm no longer alone, no longer wedged between my men and the Raiders trying to escape, while the rest fight against my men.

Pybba is sprightly beside me, Rudolf's breath more laboured. Icel has done fuck all but watch so far. No doubt he'll still have some shit story to regale me with later.

"In the reign of king shit-for-brains, I stood and watched while fifty opponents were killed," I can hear it now.

Then Icel surges forward, perhaps able to hear my thoughts after all. With a single backswing of his giant sword, one of the three men is all but cut in half.

"Bloody bollocks," Rudolf complains. I catch sight of him trying to avoid a wet severed ear from landing on his leg.

I chuckle. Icel is a mean bastard when he puts his mind to it.

Pybba launches himself at the next helm-less foe. The man has mean, crazed eyes, ungainly, curly hair moving under some hidden gust of wind, revealing the long scar that runs along his forehead. A nasty wound. I imagine he nearly died from it. I could commiserate with the poor fucker, but he eagerly meets Pybba's attack, again seeing weakness where there is none. Pybba fights with more than just his seax.

Just before the blades should meet, Pybba almost skips, thrusting up one foot and then the other, taking the man in the nose, blinding him so that it's easy to stab upwards into his exposed underarm. A howl of agony fills the air.

Will that wolf-eaten man not simply fucking die? Only now, the wolf no longer growls, but instead, I can hear the snapping of those mighty jaws from here. I swallow my revulsion. I would sooner the wolves ate something else, but it's the winter, and meat is meat. Sooner she eats a dead Raider than one of my men.

The foe-men who were still battling the remainder of my men are all but dead. I watch as Rudolf sizes up his next opponent, Lyfing behind him, keen to take the kill as well. I never thought I'd see the day my men would be forced to squabble over who gets to take a life.

I step back, Icel with me. The Raiders are entirely outnumbered, two patches of fierce fighting all that's left of the initial force. I rush around the action that's all but done, watching where I place my feet. It's not that easy with splayed body parts everywhere.

I catch sight of Wulfstan. He watches the wolf-bitch with dazed fascination on his face as she rips chunks of flesh from the dead man's upper leg and middle. The pups have tumbled from their den, the scent of fresh meat too much to keep them away.

The injured pup lies beside the man, his cries piteous. I confess I feel more grief for the animal than I do the dead man. Because, thank fuck, he *is* finally dead. The terror on his face is impossible to look away from, but Hereman has done the right thing. The Raider has a spear thrust deep into his chest, stilling his heart.

"What about the pup?" I demand to know, half an ear cocked to the attack still taking place behind me.

"I can't get close enough to check," Wulfstan worries. Yes, worries. His face is drained of all colour, and he seems uncertain.

"Will she not let you?" and I stride toward the body and the pup, but her contented chewing and ripping cuts off. I've never had such fierce eyes settle on me or heard such a menacing growl.

I hold my hands out to either side, slowly retracing my steps, never breaking our locked gaze.

I swallow, tasting more fear than I have for years.

"See what I mean?" Wulfstan huffs.

"I do, yes, but still, we could help the little shit if she'd just let us."

"I know that," it's almost a howl of outrage, and then Rudolf is beside me. His breath is rough, his chest heaving, but of course, he grins, despite the slither of blood on his lips, which he licks and then spits away.

"Fucking hate the smell of Raider bastards." His words are far too loud, drawing the attention of the she-wolf. I stick out my hand, keen to stay his forward movement. But when did Rudolf ever heed my bloody words?

He bends forward, hand extended, as though no more than a tame wolf-hound to be petted, and fuck me, the she-wolf pays him no attention.

I don't look at Wulfstan. I can feel the outrage from here. I softly chuckle as Rudolf runs a gentle finger along the wounded wolf-pup. The animal's cries are pitiful, and the she-wolf ceases her chewing. I hold my breath, but she does nothing but tears flesh for the three other wobbling balls of fluff. They chew eagerly.

"What's the matter with it?" Wulfstan calls to Rudolf. Rudolf, on both knees now, has gentle hands cupping the pup, and he earns himself a lick from a small, pink tongue.

He giggles, yes, giggles. My young squire, become a warrior in the last six months, garnished with the accoutrements of war, with many kills to his name just from the morning's work, giggles at a soft tongue on his gloveless hand.

I watch, open-mouthed, as he manipulates legs and paws, grinning at me.

"A broken rear leg. We can set it, and it'll heal."

"Right, so what, we've become nurses to sick animals now?" My words are scathing, and Rudolf's not the only one to howl. Wulfstan joins him, and they both turn appalled eyes my way.

"Fine, fine, do what you can for the little shit. His mother helped us out, alerted us to the rest of the Raiders. You can do what needs to be done."

I turn aside, wipe my hands of the matter. They'll do it whether I say they can or not. Better to give my half-hearted assent.

"Are they all dead?" I call to Lyfing.

"Aye, My Lord, all of the fuckers have breathed their last. Are we going to leave the feast for the wolves?" He demands to know. There's not as much disgust in his voice as I think there should be.

I feel the heat of many gazes on me. Beornstan sports a wicked cut down the side of his nose, oozing into his mouth, the ragged edges no doubt in need of stitching together. Oda is on the ground, knees drawn up to his chest, hand on the back of his head. It comes away reddened as I watch him. He must feel my gaze because he lifts his other hand in acknowledgement, although his eyes are unfocused, and he sways even on the floor.

"Anyone else hurt?" I ask, buying myself some time to decide what to do with the dead.

It's not like we can leave them here to burn or bury them; that would be a monumental task when we have so little food to aid us in the endeavour. I want to be going, on my way to London. But, can I leave these men as food for the denizens of the woodlands?

I shrug. I probably fucking can, in all honesty.

A chorus of denials reach my ear, and I nod.

"You fought well, men. More of the Raider filth lies dead before us. Now, enjoy the pillaging. I'd get on with it while Rudolf's so distracted." The comment brings a cry of outrage from Rudolf and dark chuckles from those already busy at the task. Rudolf always gets the best results. Always.

But, with the aid of Pybba, Wulfstan and Rudolf are earnestly discussing how to help the wolf pup that started so much of this shit show.

"You could just make yourself a new rug," Icel rumbles, but his words are edged with humour. And then I hear the whinny of Haden and turn aside. Where is my daft horse?

With Goda at my side, I bend low and work my way back to the camp. Ælfgar and Tatberht are sitting upright, weapons in hands, only relaxing when they catch sight of me.

"Sorry we missed it," Tatberht winks, but it ends with a groan.

"Well, sometimes you just have to leave it to the youngsters," I retort, not liking the look of either of my wounded warriors.

"Where's Haden?" I ask, squinting into the pack of horses. They, too, seem to take my arrival as a sign of victory and begin to spread out once more.

"Over there," Ælfgar informs me, nudging his chin into the darker reaches of the hanging branches. "He's in a funny mood."

That doesn't surprise me. I'm pleased that my subsequent actions will only be witnessed by a few of my warriors.

"Come here, you daft sod," I beckon him, standing two horse-lengths away from him. Haden's brown eyes are more than reproachful. I can see where a slither of blood escapes his stitches.

"Really, you think you could have done more?" I demand from him. Yes, my answer is silence, but there's a lessening in the tension of his head.

"Come here, and I'll ensure all is well," I ask, my tone softer than the words. "Or, I'll just leave you." I half-turn, aware he'll come then. A rough nudge and I run my hands along his black and white neck, working them towards the site of his original wound.

"There you go, and you have my thanks," I mutter, pleased to note the stitches are still tight and clean, with no sign of inflammation. He might have hurt himself with his antics, and I might have reminded him of the wound with my slap, but no further damage has been caused.

He nickers softly, the sound as much of an apology as I ever get from him, as he lets me lead him back to the rest of the horses. Billy watches him with a hint of interest, Dever walking to greet him, and then everything is over and forgiven.

I stride back towards my warriors, refusing to take note of the smirks on their faces. I've seen them with their damn mounts. I'm not the only man made a fool of by these contrary animals. After all, we all braved a bloody blizzard to get them back.

CHAPTER 13

We leave the bodies where they are, naked, of course. We don't want to make it too hard for the woodland inhabitants to eat their fill.

I'll send someone back when the snow clears, and the weather warms, but until then, the meat may as well not go to waste. It's not my way. It has never been, but I'm assured from the meaningful glances coming my way that not one of my warriors wants to dig a grave beneath the spreading boughs and into the thickly matted loam. And we sure as fuck can't shovel the snow aside and then force the frozen soil to one side.

The weather might have warmed overnight, but it'll still take days. I need to get to London. I want to see what else King Alfred of Wessex has been up to, the weasel. And, of course, I have wounded men and wounded horses. I need to consider the living, not the dead.

A parting glance at the pile of greying corpses, the she-wolf contentedly chewing away on a meaty piece of belly while her pups romp in the dark blood assures me that all is as best it can be. Even the wounded one, with a splint, cleverly worked into place using nothing but torn pieces of cloth that should be easy enough to chew through is involved. So, I lead Haden back to where we entered the woodlands.

We have two wounded horses, four wounded men, two of them badly injured, and while the trickle of water is all around us, the expanse of snow hasn't moved. Yes, it's become darker, more watery, but we could do without the impediment. I can be grateful that the wind has dropped, that the sun does feel warm on my face, but against all that, my belly rumbles and I could eat until I was sick.

My legs continue to ache, my back as well. My feet hurt in odd places. I don't want to complain, but I quickly realise I'm not alone. None of us moves speedily or easily, the march in the snow robbing us of our fluidity. We forgot about it in the heat of battle, but without our battle-rage, every ache and pain has re-asserted itself.

I pause and gaze out towards the Thames. I can see it, a gleam of silvery thread through the white landscape, and from there, I seek out the blackened ruin of the fire. Not that it's easily visible. The snow has obscured everything, even the burnt-out wrecks of the ships and the single steading.

I risk a glance behind me, thinking to see the hill we fought upon, but it's too far away. We must have walked a good distance that night, or so I tell myself as my thighs twinge, my knees as well. Even with the rest we've had, this will be a long and un-comfortable journey to London. Perhaps we should wait, but no, I have wounded and injured men and beasts. I could wish my Aunt was here to help, but she's in Northampton, safe behind high walls, or so I hope.

Haden's head hangs down, even though I don't even attempt to mount him. Tatberht has been reunited with Wombel, his face as pale as the corpses, worrying me no matter his loud exclam-ations that he's bloody capable of riding, Wærwulf with Cinder. Cinder is subdued. Oda remains unsteady on his feet, Jaspar more in charge than Oda. He's complained of a headache, to be expected, and we've all done our best to keep him alert and talk-ing during daylight hours. The last thing we want is for Oda to close his eyes and never wake. Head wounds can be strange like that. I've seen enough of them to know that.

It's bastard slow going. I know we followed a road to this place, but I can't determine where it lies. All hoofsteps and foot-prints have been obscured, only the odd scampering of animals and birds around to assure us that we're not alone in this bleak landscape.

My belly rumbles angrily.

"So how many did we kill this time?" Of course, it's Rudolf who asks the question. He's none the worse for wear despite the three battles we've fought in as many days.

"Not enough," is Icel's less than helpful reply, for all his voice thrums with amusement, not frustration.

"Not enough to account for all those ships," Pybba confirms.

"But I didn't think the ships fully crewed?" Rudolf retorts.

"We have only the words of our enemy to tell us that. They were no doubt talking horse shit."

"So, a number then?" Rudolf presses.

"Thirty in the woodlands, plus the five you lot faced off against, and the men that Tatberht and Ælfgar killed." Hereman joins the conversation.

"There was a man for every horse up on the ridge, so that makes twenty-seven."

"So about sixty so far, or one ship's worth."

"And however many there were down by the river."

"How many? At least fifty?"

"More like seventy," Hereman argues.

"I would say eighty-nine," Pybba interjects, a grin on his old face. Pedantic old fucker.

"Not bad, I suppose," Rudolf's words are far from filled with satisfaction. "About a hundred and fifty then, so between two and three ships full."

The knowledge brings an unhappy grin to my face. It might mean there are a lot more of the fuckers out there. Let's hope the weather has them trapped, or better yet, has frozen them to death. Not a nice way to die, but dead is dead. I scan the sky, noting the white fluffy clouds, looking for some indication from the birds that they might be feasting elsewhere.

Of course, there's nothing to be seen. Not here.

The Thames estuary slowly comes into clearer sight. I glower at the outline of land to the far side. Wessex, or rather Kent, a kingdom to which Alfred lays claim. He's as bad as the fucking Raiders. Can no one keep their eyes inside their own possessions?

My mood sours. If I could get all of my adversaries together in one room, I could end all this now, but of course, that's never going to happen.

And then I trip over something lying hidden in the snow.

I land, face averted from the wet slush, arms disappearing up to my elbows, while Rudolf cackles behind me. Little shit.

"Wait," I sit back on my knees, unheeding of the dampness oozing into my trews. I'll regret it, but for now, there's something more intriguing that concerns me.

I push the snow to one side, eager to know what's felled me. I'm not as surprised as I might be when a marbled body emerges from the snow.

"Urgh," Rudolf has joined me, his humour gone, tongue sticking out between his lips.

"Raider or Mercian?"

"I don't know, not yet." I lift my head. "Does anyone have a body?"

I hear the sound of boots in the snow, the white blanket turning translucent with each step; damp, not dry anymore.

"Here." It's Siric who calls in the affirmative.

"Frozen solid, poor fucker," I'm on my feet now, wincing as the cold of the water touches my knees when I walk. I mean, I could hurt more and be more uncomfortable, but I'm not sure fucking how. Not at the moment. I consider my men who carry wounds as well. This is a miserable experience all around. Damn the bastards for thinking to fight through the winter months.

Passing Haden's reins to Rudolf, I slither my way to Siric. He's further down the line of miserable men and horses. If the Raiders attacked us now, they wouldn't know what hit them. So much fury would be unleashed upon them, caused not by their appearance but by the damn weather.

"Urgh," the sound leaves my lips unbidden. "You could have fucking warned me."

Siric shrugs. "Which bit of 'frozen solid, poor fucker,' didn't you understand?" His words are acerbic.

"Well, the staring eyed bit. The blue eyes glaring into my very soul bit." It's not easy to explain what unsettles me so much.

"Raider or Mercian."

"Raider, look at his arms," and I do, noting how the inkings, normally so fearful in life, seem to sag along his unmoving arms. It's as though, while he's frozen solid, they've become deflated.

"You'll never get his rings from those fingers, not unless you chop them off." It's Gardulf who offers the words, leaning from the back of his mount. He looks altogether too cheerful.

I dig down with my foot, a cry of triumph when I hit something solid.

"The road," I explain, as Siric's brows furrow in surprise.

"Makes sense," is his grudging reply. "Still, I'd asked how they got here and where the rest of them are." That's always the problem. We can find them in one place at a set time, but without knowing exact numbers, we can never be sure that we've tracked them all down, offered a sacrifice of their blood into Mercia's soil.

"Are you going to?' Gardulf asks.

"Going to what?"

"Slice his fingers. Those rings look like they might be worth quite a bit." The gems flash with more life than the body. I appreciate the pull of them.

"No, help yourself. Cold little sausage fingers, not my idea of fun," and I make my way back to Haden. Pybba has been digging through the snow as well.

"The road is here too." That makes sense. It ran close to the river, but not too close. It's never good to advertise the proximity of a road that'll lead somewhere affluent when there are Raiders on the hunt.

I stride back to Haden, closing my ears to the sawing action from behind. I'm not a squeamish man, but I don't fancy what Gardulf's doing. Even Rudolf has left the body I found alone.

"I can't imagine there were only two of them," I call over my shoulder, refusing to turn and look. The wet sound is enough to know that Gardulf has retrieved one of the fingers.

And so it proves. There's a patch on that road, about twenty horse-lengths in total, where Raiders have frozen to death in the snow. I would expect them to have more sense, coming as they do, from somewhere much colder than Mercia. Damn arseholes.

We walk on, the occasional strike of a hoof on the stone road assuring me that we follow the route back to London. I'm more than half curious to see what we discover there. Will London be under attack? It wouldn't be the first time. The Raiders came to London five years ago, when King Burgred was Mercia's king. Ineffectual fucker. He should have killed them all then, but of course, he didn't.

I won't be making that mistake.

I hope we'll make good time, but of course, we don't. The wet slush makes the road both slippery and challenging to cross. There are entire patches clear of snow, melted away under the feeble heat from the sun. They lull me into believing the way will become easier, but it doesn't. It's trickier. I slip more than once, relying on Haden to keep me upright. I'm sweating and cold, and then hot, and damn, my thighs and feet hurt. I don't even want to talk about my knees.

And then the sun begins to sink, disappearing in a cool haze of mauves and crimsons, the promise of a cold night ahead. I've had enough.

"We need somewhere to spend the night," I call over my shoulders, hoping someone sees something that I don't. If there were a hall or a settlement close by, it's no doubt been overrun by Raiders. No, what we need is more woodland, or a cave, or just for fucking London to appear on the skyline.

None of those things happens.

My men grow sullen, the horses cantankerous. Haden nips at my ear, making it bleed. Bastard horse.

"It's not my damn fault," I just about explode. "Can you smell smoke in the air? Can you see lights in the distance? Can you so much as see a strand of trees as opposed to an individual one that'll offer no protection from the plunging temperatures?" Just to add to my misery, the wind has returned. It's not quite a blast of frozen pebbles on my face, but it's not far from it.

If the hedges demarcating land and territory were in full bloom, they would assist us, but they're more skeletal than a corpse left to rot from a noose throughout the winter.

I resign myself to a long, cold and miserable night plunging through the snow. At least the moon is bright enough by which to see—a small mercy.

No one speaks, and yet, I'm sure we're all alert. My legs are cold, my knees even colder, my neck wound aching.

"What the fuck is all this shit?" Hereman roars, coming to me despite the gusting wind. He must have shouted those words. I find a smirk touching my ice-rimmed lips. It must be bad if Hereman is moaning.

And then I see it, thank fuck. London.

"Nearly there, boys," I call over my shoulder, grinning and then regretting it as my teeth ache when I open my mouth, the deathly cold flooding in. There better be a fucking fire waiting for us in London. A fucking massive fire and a feast to fill my hollow belly, or, fuck it; I might just set the fire myself. If London burns, then King Alfred will have nothing to claim.

The thought warms me through the remainder of the journey, a wolf grin on my rictus face.

CHAPTER 14

Not that I get a chance to fucking enjoy being behind the dubious shelter of London's crumbling walls.

The gates might well have been pulled open once I'd proved I was the king of the damn place, but news of my arrival preceded me.

I'd no sooner led Haden to a warm shelter, hay and water hastily provided by an innkeeper with a broad grin on his face at the size of the ruby on the ring I pressed into his hands than I have not one but two unwelcome visitors.

"My Lord King," the innkeeper, a thin man with a long face and even longer beard and hair, neatly tied back from his face, almost hits his nose on the floor he bows so low.

"What?" I'm eating, savouring the warmth if not the texture or the taste of the bowl of pottage laden with a whole single piece of wrinkled and indeterminate meat.

"There's someone here to see you."

"Edmund!" I'm on my feet before I even think. His familiar face is as weather-worn as mine. It seems he's been caught out in the bitter weather as well. But he wears no smile, not even the hint of one.

"Tell me," I demand to know, dragging his arm so that he'll follow me to somewhere with more solitude. Only Bishop Smithwulf is there as well. His face is just as twisted as Edmund's and far from as welcome.

"Wait," and I hold up my hand as the cleric opens his mouth to greet me.

While Rudolf goggles, his hand spooning the mixture so quickly I swear that boy doesn't even chew, I take Edmund away from the rest of my warriors.

"What?" I insist this time. I think Edmund will um and ah, beat around the bush, tell me anything rather than get to the point. I'm grateful when he doesn't.

"Your Aunt is well. Northampton is secure. Kyred isn't, and neither is northern Mercia."

"Fucking cocks," I explode. Those bastard Raiders, will they not give me a moment's peace?

"You need to return to Northampton and then ride north, or you risk losing everything we regained last year."

"Jarl Halfdan?" I ask, just to be sure. Edmund nods. He looks decidedly unhappy. I'm not surprised.

"The news came in only two days after you left. You can't imagine how pissed off I was when the bishop had no idea where you were upon my arrival."

"I've been burning ships and killing Raiders. As usual."

"Well, I hope they're all fucking dead because you can't linger here, no matter what Bishop Smithwulf says to you," and that's all the warning I get before Smithwulf, a thick cloak around his shoulders, interrupts our conversation.

"My Lord King, where have you been? There's much that needs to be done here. Surely my rider, Gregory, warned you of the problems."

"What do you think I've been doing, Bishop Smithwulf?" I find I have no patience for the man with his broad face and long body, piercing eyes and petulant mouth. Already I'm considering what we need to do, how quickly we can get to the north, whether Haden is well enough for the journey. Certainly, Tatberht will need to remain here. I can't risk him. But, I could return him to Northampton. He won't like being left behind. Fuck, fuck, fuck. Too many problems and too little time.

My heart thuds in my chest. The thought of good food and sleep fleeing through my mind, only to be dismissed just as quickly. I need to get north. If there's a chance to kill that snivelling little shit once and for all, then I must take it. No matter what. I'll not eat for a week if I can face him in open combat once more. I'll block the river. I'll have all the ships from Torksey laid across the expanse of the Trent. Then, no one will be coming to rescue Jarl Halfdan before I can slice his throat open. I grin, despite myself. It might be a significant problem just to get to the north, but I'll do it. No matter what.

"My Lord King?" a flicker of unease on Smithwulf's face assures me that he has no idea what I've been doing.

"The Raiders, threatening London. The seven ships filled with Raiders. I've been off killing them, burning their poor excuses for a ship, and ensuring London is safe."

"But, but," he blinks, once, twice, three times, words beyond him. Edmund has manoeuvred so that he's standing beside Bishop Smithwulf. His remaining eye rolls. I try not to glare furiously at him. Surely, he could have ensured Smithwulf didn't know where to find me when I arrived.

"What of King Alfred of Wessex?" Bishop Smithwulf's voice holds too much reverence when he speaks of Alfred.

"What of him? We do not need to do anything but berate him for encouraging the fucking bastards onto Mercian land. He should have killed them all. It's not that hard. Slash their throats open, drown them in a river, cleave in their skulls with a war axe, run them through with a bloody spear. Or, and I quite like this one, get the fucking horses to do it on your behalf. They don't like bastard Raiders any more than I do."

Bishop Smithwulf looks as though he might be sick on his expensive cloak; his face drained of all colour. I could have been less graphic, I suppose. But, I catch sight of Rudolf watching me with a cheeky grin on his face, Pybba shaking his head although he doesn't look that angry, while Icel nods along sagely and Hereman grins. Every single one of my men, apart from Tatberht, who's been tucked up in one of the innkeeper's few good cot beds, has observed my conversation with the bishop.

"King Alfred, he's coming to London to forge a treaty with

Mercia."

"There's no need for a treaty. Mercia's no longer threatened in the south. The Raiders are in the north, and King Alfred isn't about to get his arse up to the Trent, is he?" I expel my breath slowly, aware I've let my frustration show but equally conscious that the bloody bishop of London seems to doubt my abilities. What has he done? Well, he's evidently had a nice bloody chat with King Alfred, without my permission, I might add. Smithwulf better have stepped foot in Wessex rather than Alfred in Mercia.

"Remember, Bishop Smithwulf, if King Alfred had truly meant to assist Mercia, then our dear king and predecessor, King Burgred, need never have given Mercia to the Raiders in the first place. Wessex gave up on Mercia, and now Mercia doesn't need Wessex, other than for Wessex to kill every last one of the bastard Raiders that sets foot on this island."

"But My Lord King, I've assured King Alfred of your attendance. A place has been agreed, mutually agreeable, in Southwark." Now my eyes narrow, even as Edmund nods, showing that the bishop has indeed done all this. At least it's on the far side of the Thames, in Wessex.

"On whose authority did you arrange this? It certainly wasn't mine. Was it?" I fix the bishop with my gaze. I could draw my seax here and now, and I think he'd be less sure of my suppressed fury and disapproval.

"Ah, My Lord King," and I've got to admire the shovel of horse shit for his persistence, "I did it for the benefit of all of Mercia."

"No, you did it so you wouldn't have to fight for the men and women of London so that you could pretend to be more important than you truly are. I warn you, Bishop Smithwulf, I have no argument with the church, but you'll not take instructions from Canterbury in Kent, rather than your God-given and anointed king, in Mercia." Well, I never thought I'd use that argument against anyone, and yet it has some effect. I might remember that next time my Aunt tries to make me feel like a ten-year-old child.

Bishop Smithwulf visibly deflates, Edmund there with a lone stool for Smithwulf to sink onto without thought. It would have been better if he'd just fallen on the floor. Rudolf has returned to his pottage, Icel as well, although Pybba continues to watch me. I have no idea what he's thinking. Does he want me to forge an alliance with King Alfred? I can't see it, but I've been wrong before.

Certainly, Icel will think any treaty with Wessex a waste of time and effort. But then, he's fought the Wessex warriors before. They've always been greedy bastards. But ineffectual. Always ineffectual.

"What will I say to King Alfred?"

"Of Wessex," I finish when he seems not to realise the implication in his words.

"Yes, yes, King Alfred of Wessex."

"Thank him for his offer of assistance, but tell him it's not needed. Advise him that concentrating on killing our mutual enemies will be most beneficial. If he doesn't, then Mercia will ensure any of the bastards who yet live know that Wessex is a green and pleasant land, with far better vineries than can be found in Mercia."

The innkeeper, caught between his king and his bishop, has fallen into what he knows best. He hands a wooden tankard filled to the brim into the bishop's lifeless hand and hovers with a bowl of pottage as well. I smirk despite it all. I can't see the bishop accepting what is, essentially, warriors fare. Bishop Smithwulf will be used to a table of more refinement.

I dismiss Smithwulf from my thoughts and question Edmund.

"Tell me what you know?"

"Kyred sent word as soon as he could that the rumours are true. Halfdan means to try and retake Mercia. He has allies from Northumbria. They're massing on the far side of the Humber, and they outnumber all of the ealdorman's forces, Kyred's as well. And they have ships. How else would they get across the Humber?" Edmund shrugs with the words. While Bishop Smithwulf absently sips his ale and even takes the offered bowl of pottage, I return to my warriors.

Weary eyes greet mine, rims of blue still evident on nose tips and ears. It's been fucking cold. We've been stuck in a blizzard, we've had our horses taken from us and fought to get them back, we've been hungry and cold, if not thirsty, and yet every eye there shows the eagerness of men who anticipate a much bigger fight yet.

"Fuck it," I exclaim. "Eat, drink, sleep, in the morning we're heading to Northampton, and then, onwards. It seems we have an old enemy to kill, once and for all."

Not that I sleep. I stay awake, peering into the depths of the fire. The innkeeper has happily piled it high with wood and charcoal, eager to show my warriors all the hospitality he can. He's fed us well, even it was far from appetising, but my thoughts are on what I'll find in the north.

That bastard Jarl Halfdan.

He once taunted me. I thought he'd killed my friend, Icel, and under his auspices, he sent Raiders to hunt me down, right into the heart of my land, around Gloucester, even before I was proclaimed king. He's hunted me, and I've stalked him back. I thought I'd never have the opportunity to face him again, but like a boil that must be scratched, it seems he's as desperate as I am to try his luck one more time.

"So, Jarl Halfdan has cast aside his previous allies?"

"Yes, there's no mention of Jarls Anwend, Oscetel or Guthrum."

"Wonderful," I huff with annoyance. And yet, can I be angered by that? Maybe Halfdan has been turned down by the Grantabridge jarls? Perhaps he wanted them, and they told him where to go. I just hope Halfdan hasn't found allies who are stronger than the Grantabridge jarls. Or even, weaker than they, resolved only to take commands from Halfdan. If the Raiders ever learn to work together, to unite in any way more than with half-arsed oaths and alliances, broken with some perceived slight, Mercia might genuinely be in trouble.

"Are any other names mentioned?"

"Not in the message received in Northampton."

"And we can believe the message? It's not some sort of trap?"

"No, I knew the rider, so too did Wulfsige, returned from Warwick. It's no trap."

"Any idea of numbers?"

"It's impossible to know from such a distance. Kyred rode out and looked. He doesn't believe as many as were at Repton, but he can't be sure of that."

"Fuck. I'll need to gather the ealdormen then and their warriors."

"So it seems," there's no enthusiasm for such a task from Edmund or me.

"We have the men under Turhtredus and the warriors who protected Northampton. Won't that be enough?" I shrug at the suggestion. I don't know the answer to that.

If there's to be a pitched battle, then the more warriors I can call to arms, the better. But if this is to be sneaking assault, more undertaken by stealth than outright defiance, I would be better with men who've fought with me since Repton. Those who know what to do without running to me for instructions all the time.

"Bishop Deorlaf will send those he can, as will Bishop Ceobred of Leicester, and of course, Burgheard of Lindsey will be praying for your arrival."

I nod, agreeing with those statements.

"But, I don't have the time to go and petition them."

Edmund looks at me, a perplexed expression on his face, both eyebrows high, for all only one eye peers back at me.

"You've just told the old wind-bag that you're Mercia's anointed, God-given king. Why the fuck do you need to petition anyone? Send out your orders, summon the warriors you need. There's nothing to be gained by delaying or by seeking a conference about it all. Every ealdorman, and bishop, acknowledged who you are, giving you an oath."

"Have you discussed this with my Aunt?" I ask darkly. Edmund sounds so like her.

"Perhaps," he counters, already defensive. I change the subject.

"Gardulf fought as a warrior. Be proud of him. Tell him you're proud of him." My father didn't live long enough to tell me anything like that. Admittedly, I wasn't an honourable man when he died, so he could hardly have done so. All the same, I still feel the ache of that loss. Edmund's lips clamp shut.

"You're a daft shit, most of the time," I inform him. I don't have my Aunt's eloquence. Perhaps, I'll repay his devious ways and tell my Aunt that Edmund is lacking with regards to his son. She'll certainly not allow him to get away with it. The thought makes me smirk.

"Why are you smiling?" Edmund is right to be suspicious. I merely shake my head.

"You had to be there," I evade, and we're at a stalemate.

Bishop Smithwulf has been escorted back to his home. I'm pleased he's gone. I'm half-minded to leave Edmund behind to make sure Smithwulf does as I've commanded, but no, I need all of my warriors.

"Did you kill all the Raiders?" Edmund asks, his words soft, as he leans forward on his knees, eyes gazing into the glowing embers, just as I do. Damn the fucker. He gives me the opportunity to be less than accurate with the truth, and yet I don't take it.

"We killed the ones we saw, we killed the ones who stole the horses, and we killed the ones that tried to overpower us in the woodlands. The weather killed yet more. Those who we spoke to assured us that there were never seven shiploads of Raiders. I can say no more than that."

I notice that he nods at my words as though I've merely confirmed what he suspected.

"What if there are more, and they come for London?"

"Then Bishop Smithwulf can crow about it all he wants, but if he makes a treaty with King Alfred, I'll personally shove his golden cross up his arsehole."

"So, you'd leave London defenceless rather than admit to

Bishop Smithwulf that the Raiders might not all be dead."

"The Raiders are all dead," I say with certainty. I hope that I'm right.

Edmund says nothing in return. He doesn't even turn to look at me to judge the truth for himself.

I can't leave anyone in London. I need them all to defeat Jarl Halfdan. If I'm lucky, and I don't like to rely on that, then the Grantabridge jarls will stay before their fires, while the London Raiders are all solid on the frozen ground.

If not, well, I can't be in two places at once, and Halfdan is the priority. London is a crumbling ruin the Raiders have already defeated once. Twice won't do much more fucking damage.

CHAPTER 15

We leave with the light. It's a thin and reedy thing, more hinted at than anything else, but I'm not the only one awake and ready to go.

We've eaten, we've slept, we've drunk, and we're warm. What else do we need?

Well, I need a horse. I'm still not prepared to risk Haden, and Cinder needs to be allowed to travel alone as well.

But it seems there's an easy answer to that. Edmund hasn't travelled to London alone, but in the company of a handful of Ealdorman Ælhun's men, well, Wulfsige is their commander, apparently on the orders of my Aunt. I'd taunt him for that, but I don't want a black eye to go with all my other aches and pains.

We take two of the mounts, the Mercians eager to assist their king. I smirk at them, clasp their forearms, and then abandon them to the innkeeper and Bishop Smithwulf. I'm sure by the end of the day, they'll have sourced horses with which to return to Northampton. Fuck, I would.

My mount is an energetic creature who immediately earns Haden's enmity in allowing me to saddle and mount her without any fuss at all. I don't grin at Haden. Now isn't the time for one of my lessons. All the same, he nips my ear when I get too close to him—damn brute.

Tatberht insists on travelling with us, as does Oda, somewhat restored to his usual self with thanks to some decent food and ale. The ale helped more than the food.

Outside the crumbling gate, I hesitate and turn back to glance at London. It's not a magnificent place. I'm not entirely sure why the Raiders and King Alfred, and the Wessex scum who ruled before him, are so enamoured of the place. But it's part of my kingdom. I need to have defences built. I won't deny that. Once I've dealt with Jarl Halfdan, London and Bishop Smithwulf will require my attention.

I can hardly fucking wait.

Edmund rides beside me, Jethson his usual arrogant self. Despite the layer of watery snow that remains, hiding the damp patches, he steps high, swishing his long tail. Haden plods beside me, the weak sunlight flashing on his wound. Even to my eye, it looks much better than when we arrived in London.

I reach out, attempting to pat his neck, an apology in the action, but he moves aside. I hear Rudolf laugh at the sight. I'm not surprised when Haden allows Dever close to him. I roll my eyes, and Rudolf merely laughs harder. But, it just reinforces the fact that Haden is slow with his wound. Dever has never been the fastest of mounts.

And that brings me to my next problem. I want to travel quickly, almost too quickly to the north. I know how fast we could get there, but I have slow horses, wounded horses even. Do I risk Haden? Do I risk Dever? Do I risk any of the other horses? It's not that they wouldn't strive to do what I commanded. It's just whether they would survive it. I have no problem ending the lives of the Raiders, but with horses, I'm not such a callous bastard.

It would be quicker, perhaps, to surge along Ermine Street to the Humber, but I'm not going that way as it would mean by-passing Northampton. Instead, we head north along Watling Street. We'll travel along Watling Street from Northampton until it meets the Foss Way and until the Foss Way joins Ermine Street. It won't be much further, so I reassure myself.

The day is cold but clear. I push onwards, half an eye to my compromised mounts, the other half on the terrible condition of the roadway. The snow has melted in most places or turned to ice, indistinguishable from the wet patches. The fact no one else travels the road assures me that it's not the weather to be out and about.

I spare a thought for the river at Passenham, hoping that the initial surge from the snowmelt has subsided or not appeared yet. I don't fancy another wet crossing with injured mounts.

We stop around midday, the sun as warm as it's going to get on our faces. It feels pleasant, fuck, it almost feels as though it burns my skin after the cold conditions of a few days ago. I chew contentedly on the cheese and bread offered by the innkeeper as I walk amongst my men.

"Tatberht," his face is bleached, but he grins at me.

"I'm fine, My Lord. Not much further now," there's more than hope in his voice.

"Aye, we'll get you tucked up in a nice warm bed soon enough. My Aunt will see to your wound."

His cut has been variously cleaned and packed with moss and honey. He smells well, perhaps a strange observation to make, but a much-needed one all the same.

"That'll be pleasant," he offers, trying to smile. He's stayed on his horse, easier that than dismounting and trying to get on once more. It's an effort with his wound. But he's a stubborn bastard. Nothing will stop him.

"How is she?" I demand of Wærwulf. He's riding a dun-coloured horse while he leads Cinder. Cinder has none of the reproaches of Haden.

"Better than I expected, to be honest."

"That's good, but we've got a way to go yet."

"We certainly do," Wærwulf confirms. I'm distracted by Oda. He's swaying as he empties his stream into the undergrowth. I try not to notice the shocking yellow colour of his piss, but it's hard as it splashes into a pile of snow.

"Here," I thrust my water bottle at him. "Drink this. You need more water and less ale."

"The ale helps me see straight," he tries to joke but grips the water bottle eagerly enough.

"How's your head?"

"It jolts with every missed step by my horse, but I can live with it, for now."

"Be wary. Head wounds are nasty, and you don't always know what damage has been done."

"Thank you, boss," he grunts, and I slap his back and turn aside.

I can tell that my men are eager to be on their way, but I hold them until even I'm desperate to feel the distance disappear beneath the hooves of my horse. My thoughts are of Jarl Halfdan. King Alfred of Wessex owes Halfdan a debt. I'd never encroach on land that belongs to Wessex, but I'd certainly be preparing to act against his pretensions.

London will never belong to Wessex. He needs to fucking realise that.

Northampton appears out of the gloom the following day. We rode as far as we could yesterday, but, in the end, our excursions from the previous few days were too much. I made them sleep in the same barn we used on the way to London. My warriors didn't argue half as much as I thought they might.

My Aunt greets me in the courtyard. There's a flurry of activity from the returning riders, and yet we're strangely isolated from it all, even where we stand in the middle of it.

"King Alfred is a weasel," I begin. She nods, her keen eyes already noting the wounded animals and men in that order. Fuck, she's a woman after my own heart.

I know she has no love for Wessex.

"He's just like his brothers and father before them. They're all unpleasant men." She confirms, the tone of voice betraying her hatred of the Wessex scum.

"Bishop Smithwulf thinks altogether too much of King Alfred."

Her lips purse, hand clasped before her.

"I'll have Bishop Wærferth bring him into line. Bishop Smithwulf thinks himself only a step from becoming an archbishop, just like at Canterbury and York, but Mercia's archbishopric has always been Lichfield, not London. The pope saw to that many years ago."

I bat aside her words about bishops and bishoprics. I don't care. I'm not religious, I just like believing, and that's an entirely different concept. I know that the bishops would share my thoughts. They're not half as pious as they think themselves to be.

"What will you do about Haden?"

"I can't leave him," I assert.

"Then I have tonight to heal him," and she doesn't even ask me about Jarl Halfdan. I'm pleased about that. I imagine she hates the bastard as much as I do. After all, it was on Halfdan's orders that Edmund was injured, and Icel thought lost. But it'll be Edmund that infuriates her, I would imagine.

Tatberht has finally managed to dismount, and he walks gingerly towards the hall.

"What of Tatberht?" I ask, but she shakes her head. She's not even examined him, and yet she seems adamant.

"And Cinder?"

"She'll be well, like Haden." I don't watch her worm a path through the men and horses. Instead, I focus on Ealdorman Ælhun, returned from Warwick, no doubt on my Aunt's instructions.

"Walk with me," I ask him, making my way through the cleared pathway. Snow still lies in some places, but it's mostly water now. I don't speak to him until I've mounted the walkway, trying not to groan because my legs ache, my arse as well. My substitute horse wasn't Haden. I've spent some time deciphering whether the beast was too narrow or too wide, and I still don't know. I sat as I always do, and yet my thighs ache, my feet as well.

I'll be pleased to have Haden back.

"Tell me?" Of course, Ealdorman Ælhun will know more than Edmund's informed me, I'm sure of it.

"There's little else, other than what Edmund knew. A messenger arrived yesterday, more urgency than substance to his message. Kyred is fearful of Jarl Halfdan, but only because Ealdorman Aldred is pissing himself in fright."

"So there was no more information about numbers or intentions?"

"Not about the numbers, no," Ealdorman Ælhun admits. His face is filled with tension. "I hardly need to expand on his intentions. He wants Mercia. The damn bastard." Rage floods the ealdorman's voice. It doesn't surprise me, but his language makes me appreciate he's spent far too much time with my men and me.

"I'll need you to leave Northampton again." Ealdorman Ælhun nods as I speak.

"I'd expected as much. Do you want me in Warwick or Repton?"

Again, these words show just how far our relationship has come since the first time we met. I'm glad to have Ælhun as such a steadfast ally and proponent of my rule.

"Repton. If Jarl Halfdan slips beyond our reach, he'll want Repton back. He ran from there with his trews around his ankles. He'll want to forget that humiliation."

"You can rely on my warriors to do what must be done. Sooner death than being ruled by a Raider. But what of Northampton? Surely the jarls from Grantabridge will take advantage if we abandon it?"

"Northampton is strong and secure. The walls and rampart will protect her."

"And your Aunt?"

And here is my worry. Will she leave Northampton? Will she want to return to Kingsholm? Where will she be safest?

"I'll speak with her. She must remain either in Northampton or make her way west."

"And London?" I sigh at the reminder of the place.

"Bishop Smithwulf would rather have King Alfred of Wessex as his king than I. But, we've hunted down the Raiders. Killed them all. London is safe while we look north. Right now, the biggest threat comes from King Alfred of Wessex, not the Raiders."

A flicker of emotions over Ealdorman Ælhun's face, causing the frost of his beard to twitch, and I don't know what he truly thinks of Alfred. He better share my feelings towards Alfred. I should hate us to come to blows about the Wessex king when our thoughts are so aligned with regard to Mercia itself.

I reach out, gripping his forearm, feel the iron of his muscles, even though I once thought he was no warrior.

"We'll beat the fuckers," I reiterate, perhaps because I need to hear the words, but really because there needs to be an acceptance that we face almost insurmountable odds. But that's never stopped me in the past.

Ealdorman Ælhun nods, the dome of his bald head shimmering beneath the sun that offers more light than heat.

"Aye, My Lord King. We will."

Tatberht accepts that he must remain behind in Northampton. Oda doesn't. That leaves me with a conundrum. I do consider asking my Aunt to give Oda some of her herbs to make him sleep so that we can go without him. But I'd kill anyone who did that to me. Oda will simply have to manage as best he can. And if he can't manage, then he'll be left behind in one of the settlements along the way. Hiltiberht looks at me in hope, but his smile quickly drops away, and he nods in understanding. I won't risk him.

And so we sleep. Well, my warriors' sleep, first I have to speak to my Aunt, and of course, Edmund hovers behind me.

I would pierce him with my gaze, but it wouldn't do any good. All I need now is for Rudolf to stick his beak in as well.

"I'll hold Northampton for you." Once more, I speak to someone forged from the same stuff as Ealdorman Ælhun and I. Although, she lacks the impurities that stain me and the ealdorman.

"Good, I assumed you would." Edmund's mouth is entirely open, shock written into his features. I quirk an eyebrow at him. I'm keen to see how this plays out. Did he genuinely expect me to gainsay my Aunt? He thinks I'm braver than I am. And equally, my Aunt is the right person to hold Northampton. She has the men who are mine to command, but who in reality, are loyal to her. She has the authority of being my Aunt, and she doesn't even need that.

As I've said before, if she'd been taught to fight with sword and seax, spear, axe and shield, the Raiders would have been felled years ago – no need for my involvement at all.

"I don't foresee the Grantabridge jarls moving from their shelter until the weather turns, but if they do, keep safe behind the rampart and walkway. Taunt them, but don't start an outright attack, not until I return from the north."

"And London?" Bloody London. I grit my teeth.

"If Bishop Smithwulf makes trouble, you have my authority to deal with him. I would like a messenger sent to Bishop Wærferth. He should be the one to reprimand him for such disloyalty, as you advised."

A gleam enters my Aunt's eyes – a threat she appreciates. I'm happy for Smithwulf to be handled with diplomacy. If that fails, I have no qualms about turning my weapons on him. I'll give him a chance because my gaze is directed northwards.

"And Edmund, you'll travel with me this time," I say it just to make sure he knows my expectations. He nods. At least he's been expecting that order.

I lay a kiss on my Aunt's cold cheek.

"Stay safe and stay well," I caution her. She grips my forearm.

"It's more imperative that you do the same," and I turn aside. She and Edmund have words to exchange, and I don't need to witness them.

Turhtredus and his men will escort me north. I would hope to be joined by others along the way, but with Kyred already north, and with my men and Turhtredus', with Ealdorman Ælhun ensuring the hinterland of Mercia is guarded, I feel as well prepared as possible.

I roll in my cloak, welcoming the thought of deep sleep, only to be roused by a commotion at the door when the grey light of night still covers the interior of the hall.

"My Lord," an arm on my shoulder, roughly shaking me, and I grip it fiercely, only releasing my hold on the yelp of pain.

"I'm awake," the two words are spoken slowly, my eyes open on the scene before me. "Who disturbs my sleep?"

"An urgent message from Bishop Burgheard of Lindsey."

"Fuck," I'm on my feet before the words have left the lips of the Mercian warrior's. Evidently, he was on guard duty.

I make my way through the sleeping forms, littered this way and that, and then out into the cool night air. The promise of a hard frost glitters in the area visible in the flames from the braziers.

The man waiting for me still holds his horse, although Hiltiberht hovers close by, waiting to take the animal. I can see why he doesn't. The man will fall without such support.

"My Lord King," his breath hitches, as though he's the one who's been galloping and not the horse.

"Tell me."

"Bishop Burgheard demands your assistance against the Raiders. The ealdorman does nothing to prevent the incursions."

"Incursions. I understood Jarl Halfdan remained on the far bank of the Humber."

But the man, chest still heaving, shakes his head.

"No more, My Lord King. They've been sighted on the Humber. At least ten ships, perhaps more."

I nod, my lips tight, my expression grim.

"We're leaving as soon as the sun gives us enough light," I confirm, hoping that it might bring the messenger some relief.

"You must travel with all haste. Bishop Burgheard has sent his warriors to the Trent, but they will be overpowered if it comes to a battle."

"Nothing like some confidence," I smirk, trying to take the edge of derision from my voice.

"So there are what, a thousand Raiders?"

"It would seem so, yes, My Lord King."

"Go inside, get some sleep. By the time you wake, we'll be gone. Where is Bishop Burgheard?"

"He remains in Lincoln."

"Return to him when you're able. Now, release your horse. The animal needs looking after, not leaning against." The messenger's eyes flash with surprise. Perhaps he's not even realised he hangs on his horse quite so tightly.

"My Lord King," he bows his head low, swaying, as Hiltiberht finally claims the animal.

"Thank you. One more thing. Is there snow on the ground?"

"No, the thaw has melted most of it. It's icy in some places, but the roads remain passable."

That will at least allow me to move with all haste. And it seems I must ride faster than the wind.

Fucking King Alfred. If not for him, I'd be in the north already. Jarl Halfdan skewered on the edge of my seax.

CHAPTER 16

I considered leaving Haden behind; only Hiltiberht has saddled him, made him ready for what can only be described as a sprint to the north. I eye the wound, noting that it seems much healed from whatever my Aunt has ministered to the horse.

I also note the stubborn stance Haden has adopted. Like my men, I get a distinct impression that he's coming whether I ride him or not.

So now, with some problems crossing the Nene without the aid of a bridge, I head north, the clatter of hooves the only sound to permeate my senses. Everything else is drowned out, even conversation, by the rush of icy wind through my hair and the sound of horses over the stone road. It's bastard cold, but my fury warms me.

I know we won't make the journey in one day, and yet, I'm determined to get as far as possible. In no time at all, we leave Watling Street behind us, a solitary rider peeling away to travel to Warwick with Ealdorman Ælhun's instructions to his men there. And then we reach the Foss Way. I spare a thought, reminded of my dash to Repton when the Raiders claimed it as their own. I hope Eowa's well. I'd have gladly welcomed him into my war band, but he's not a warrior and never will be. Perhaps he's lucky to have no greater concern than the forest he calls his home. Certainly, he doesn't have the weight of a kingdom to shoulder.

Ealdorman Ælhun and the remainder of his men leave us there, their destination Repton, along Watling Street, where Ælhun is to inform Bishop Deorlaf of what's happening. I know Deorlaf will send warriors, perhaps to Repton, but more likely, along the Trent. He's not one to shy away from any sort of altercation.

I look behind me. My warriors are close, the remainder of the Mercians under Turhtredus less tightly packed, their horses perhaps flagging from the unexpected speed after a winter spent indoors. I'm not surprised.

I only call a halt when an early sunset darkens the way ahead. I'll take many risks, but not at such speed with our mounts. And if we're not travelling at speed, we may as well stop for the night. I'd hoped to find the Trent before dark, but the sound of the wide river doesn't fill my ears.

"Set guards," I call to Edmund, dismounting from Haden, appreciating that my legs and arse don't ache as they did the day before. I inspect his wound, Rudolf beside me, squinting in the rapidly fading light.

"We need fires," I command over my shoulder as well. Some might say a fire will only allow our enemy to find us, but no fire will mean death for someone on a cold night like this. The heavy clouds are obscuring the moon and stars, promise rain, or worse. We need to keep warm. We require good food. We must be in as good condition as possible when we face Jarl Halfdan.

"It looks good," Rudolf speaks with amazement in his voice.

"What does she use?"

"I don't dare ask," I mutter. Rudolf vigorously nods.

"One day, she'll have to share, or we'll lose the knowledge."

"I imagine the monks know," I offer, not wanting to consider a life without my Aunt. She's my father's much younger sister, not quite my age, but certainly not as old as the title perhaps implies. I imagine I'll be dead long before her. Especially if I have to keep fighting the bastard Raiders with such regularity.

"Well, it looks really good, and I didn't notice him favouring his other leg, so there's no harm done." Haden turns his inquisitive nose at Rudolf's words. I notice the grin on the lad's face and suppress mine as Rudolf speaks to my horse. The pair of them are as daft as the other. It just shows how deceiving looks can be. To anyone watching the interplay, you could be forgiven for thinking Haden was a passive beast of burden, Rudolf no more than the ploughboy. I'll pity anyone who has to come up against them.

"Rudolf, we're on the first watch," Pybba's words cut through our conversation. Rudolf grins ever wider.

"Leave some food for me," he taunts, almost skipping away.

"I wish I had his damn energy," I complain to Haden, wiping the sweat from his withers with a strip of cloth, having removed his saddle.

"I'm glad you fucking don't," Wærwulf interjects. I'd not appreciated I was speaking aloud. "You'd still be on the road, despite the dark." He's removed his helm, his head gleaming in the reflected light from the fire being brought to life under the expert hands of Hereman.

"How's your nose?"

"Hurts like a bastard, but it's healing. Now all I've got to do is not pick the scab. That's more of a challenge."

"Well, it certainly, enhances your... looks," I try the word. It doesn't do justice to the angry slice that will forever mar my warrior.

"I'm not going to worry about it. I don't have to fucking look at it," and he moves aside, cackling, leaving Cinder to pick at the stray grasses poking through the flat patches of undergrowth. There's little else to show that winter could be on the way out. Certainly, the fields we've ridden by have been dark and uninviting, any crops well-hidden beneath the piles of mud and horse manure.

Without the aid of Rudolf, it takes me longer than I think to see to Haden's wound, following my Aunt's strict instructions regarding washing it and applying a fresh layer of herbs to the wound site. Not that Haden complains much beyond a nip on my hand. I'm just all fingers and thumbs. I'm not a natural nurse.

Eventually, Icel takes pity on me.

"A hand, My Lord?" His tone solemn.

I risk a glance at him.

"You alright about this, Icel?" I've noticed that Edmund is subdued as well.

I wish I'd killed Jarl Halfdan when I had the chance.

"Aye, My Lord. It'll be better when the fucker's dead." I hope we both speak of Jarl Halfdan. "I'd beg the boon of ending his life myself, but I appreciate that you'll want the honour."

For a moment, my movements still. Again, I've not considered that either.

"I can't swear I won't do it if I happen upon him." Icel nods, his hair shimmering with the dancing flames.

"I can't swear it either," and he chuckles, a rare sound these days.

"I imagine Edmund can't either."

"No, in fact, My Lord, you might find yourself doing more than trying to kill Jarl Halfdan. You might need to keep Edmund and me apart as well."

I grunt at the words, appreciating this is Icel's way of warning me.

"We'll just have to look after one another," I confirm, meeting Icel's hooded eyes in the semi-darkness. "There's no fucking point in injuring one another when we all want the same thing."

"Aye, My Lord, you have that right," Icel confirms. I wish I could see his face, but it's impossible.

I work in silence then, until the smell of the cookpot drives me to hurry.

"My thanks," I offer, tidying away the supplies into the saddlebags lying on the floor.

"And you have mine," Icel responds mercurially, walking away. I watch him, lips twisted. I'll seek out Hereman and perhaps Pybba. It comes to something when my warriors don't appreciate what's best for them, but then rage and a desire for revenge does that to even the most staid of warriors.

I take the last watch, having slept through much of the night.

It's bastard cold when Gardulf wakes me with a firm shake of my shoulder.

"Sorry, My Lord," he suppresses a yawn. "It's your watch."

"Aye lad, thanks for waking me." I stretch and move silently, well, as silently as I ever can, to the outer rim of our makeshift camp. I notice the frost on blankets and cloaks, the breath of the horses and shiver inside my cloak, stamping feeling back into my feet by stalking around the perimeter.

I pull ice crystals from my hair and rub my nose to remove the hard snot that's formed there while I've slept.

Damn the fuckers. It's too fucking cold for war, and yet, I've already killed men while the snow lay thigh high on the ground. I'll do it again if it brings me Jarl Halfdan's marbled body.

Revenge warms me. I should have been wary of that.

We find the Trent early that morning. It's not quite a raging torrent, but it's not far from being one.

I turn to assess my force. Without Ealdorman Ælhun and his warriors, it feels pitifully small, even with my Aunt's Mercians under Turhtredus. I know Bishop Deorlaf will send more men and that Kyred's already to the north. I hope Bishop Burgheard will have men ready and willing as well.

A thousand of the fuckers. From where does Jarl Halfdan get the men? What does he promise them in exchange for their services? Certainly, I don't appreciate the allure, far from it.

"I recognise this place," Edmund confirms, riding beside me, Jethson's coat flashing in the bright sunshine. It doesn't promise any heat. And I curse its deceitfulness.

"I do as well," I confirm. "We can't be far from Swarkeston. We can cross at Newark and avoid getting wet."

"Yes," is the only response I receive, my eyes seeking out Icel amongst my host of men. Some of them smile, others laugh, and a few look mournfully at the river. It seems we all have memories of this place. I curse then, for I've not had the opportunity to speak to Hereman or Pybba.

Icel is one of the few who looks unhappy. I should have left him in Northampton, I know it, but equally, I appreciate it would have been cruel. I would have felt uneasy with the decision, and sure as shit's shit, I know Icel would have followed my procession anyway. Easier to have him where I can keep an eye on him. I hope.

"From here on," I call to my warriors. "We need to be more alert. Our news is days old. I can't see that Jarl Halfdan will have made it down the Trent, not yet, but I can't be sure of that. Ride ready and armed."

Hereman nods to me as I speak, his hands reaching to ensure weapons are in easy reach. Gardulf, Leonath, Lyfing and Siric, those who were absent last time, eye the Trent with mild interest. They've heard the stories countless times, but that means nothing, and they know it. Their experiences of the river will be different and have yet to make themselves evident.

"There's a bridge at Newark," I reiterate so all can hear. "We'll cross there." I have no intention of splitting my small force. Not this time. I'll keep everyone where I can see them, and for as long as it's possible.

Splitting my force has done nothing but cause me problems in the past. Edmund has been wounded, Icel was lost. It's more down to luck than anything that they ride beside me now.

I pause to glare at Turhtredus. I don't doubt his loyalty, but last time I was at the Trent, Lord Osferth played me for a fool. The same won't happen this time. I'm convinced of that.

With a gentle knee to Haden's side, sparing my heels because I don't want to remind him of his hurt, I encourage the men to greater speed.

The winter hasn't been kind to the track that leads beside the Trent. I've pulled clear of the Foss Way. It's still there, almost shadowing my actions, but I want to be as close to the riverbank as possible. I'm searching, and so are my warriors.

I can see where trees have lost their footing on the riverbank, tumbling forward or held at odd angles, the flow of the water forcing leaves and then branches to part with the tree. I can also see where floodwaters have thundered far up the sides, the tell-tale marks of heavy stones and discarded jetsam and flotsam jarringly out of place.

But there are no bodies and no sign of the Raiders. That pleases me but not enough to ride carelessly.

I've sent no one ahead. We ride together, in tight formation, not one behind the other, but in some semblance of order, Pybba with Rudolf, Edmund beside me, Hereman with Gardulf. I'm not sure when that happened. Hereman has never been accepting of others too close to him, but his nephew doesn't seem to count.

Further back, Lyfing and Goda ride side by side, Ælfgar and Beornstan, Ingwald and Gyrth, Siric and Leonath. It's always struck me how my men had one ally they will trust to fight beside them above all others. I don't much mind, as long as someone has my back.

I need to commission some repairs to the riverbank and the Foss Way. The Foss Way hasn't endured by neglecting it. If the people of Mercia want me to ride to their assistance at great speed, I require decent roadways.

I must speak with Bishop Burgheard, ensure the Lincoln quarry can supply what's needed. If not, I'll seek elsewhere. I know fine stone isn't uncommon throughout Mercia. Some might think the best way to use it is to build with the stuff, but there's no fucking point in having fancy buildings if no one can travel to see them.

Haden flicks his ears beneath me, perhaps alert to my contrary mood. I'm tired and angry, and I know the only thanks I'll be getting at the end of this journey is a bloody great big battle. I smirk. I don't mind the battle. I just need it to put a stop to these Raider incursions. I can't fight everywhere at the same time. I'm just relieved that the fragile alliance with the Welsh Gwentmen seems to be holding.

Rudolf gradually moves Dever in front of me. I eye the horse critically. Rudolf needs a new mount, I've been thinking about it for a while now, but the pair are well suited. And Rudolf's light and agile. Dever probably doesn't even notice the weight of him. I don't look forward to the conversation. I can't put it off indefinitely.

Above my head, clouds move slowly and sullenly. The sun's there, but it's not offering heat or light. My breath plumes before me. It's getting colder. It smells like snow, and the further north we travel, the more convinced of that I become.

At Newark, startled eyes meet our approach until Denewulf and Eahlferth appear from across the bridge.

"My Lord King," Denewulf offers, eyes taking in my appearance and the strength of the force that follows behind.

"Jarl Halfdan threatens to return to Mercia," I inform everyone there, wishing I had better news to share with them. "You'll have seen some of my warriors come this way."

"Yes, My Lord King, we have. It's not news to us. We've prepared to meet the enemy, should they travel this far south. We have piles of stone to throw on their ships, and we'll destroy the bridge if such is required."

Prior knowledge accounts for the lack of shock at my announcement. I share a smile with those who'll meet my eyes.

"If the Raiders get this far, then I've failed. Send word to the bishop, to Repton and Northampton. There are more warriors who'll protect you."

"You won't fail, My Lord King," Eahlferth assures me, and I confess, such confidence bolsters me. I would never think I'd need it.

"Turhtredus," I beckon him close. He knows what's coming.

"We'll travel on this side of the river and then towards Torksey."

"Stay safe, and stay well," I instruct him. I'm splitting my force, yes, but I'm keeping my men at my side.

"Until we return then," and I encourage Haden across the long wooden bridge, being careful not to look down. I've never been good with being high up. I don't want to be mesmerised by the rush of the water down below. It's too fucking cold for a swim.

On the far side of the river, landmarks become more familiar to me, perhaps to Haden as well, as he increases his speed, wariness gone. Still, I search for the Raiders. Will they have made it this far? Have they already over-awed the strength of Ealdorman Aldred and Kyred? I hope not. Has Kyred already killed Jarl Halfdan? Equally, I hope he hasn't. I want that prize just as much as Edmund and Icel lust for it.

And then, between one heartbeat and the next, the sky turns a malevolent grey pink, and it starts to fucking snow.

"Marvellous," I growl, fat flakes landing on my cloak, turning Haden's neck all to white, the river, the track, the way ahead, obscured almost beyond all recognition.

CHAPTER 17

Not that I call a stop. No. I've seen what the weather can do. It will both be an advantage and a hindrance. Certainly, I doubt Jarl Halfdan will have such qualms.

But, my thoughts return to my young guide from my last journey to Torksey. I immediately regret his absence. He would have known where to go even as I find my view of the way ahead being obscured.

It's not yet night-time, and yet it might as well be.

"Fucking bastard weather," Wulfred's words echo to me through the strained silence that only snow can bring. Every hoofprint muffled, every laboured breath too loud. It's as though we walk beneath heavy boughs, the ground beneath our feet absorbing all sound, the sky above us out of sight, the light muted to frustratingly little. We might as well be blind.

"Well," and Rudolf's youthful voice follows Wulfred's, a direct counterpart to the other's boom, "this is marvellous," and he laughs. The sound soft, dampened. Yet, it brings a grin to my face as well.

"Wrap up warm, watch where your horse steps," I call the instruction back to my men and then face Edmund.

"Are you able to see?"

Edmund's incredulous expression tells me all I need to know about my solicitous request.

"I can see fucking better than you," he mutters, encouraging Jethson to lead the way. I allow it, forcing Haden to my wishes more easily than I might like, falling back to ensure others are in a better mood.

"These Raiders bring their bastard weather with them," Pybba complains. I can see he's flung another cloak over the one he already wears, his breath billows before his face; his handless arm smothered inside both cloaks.

"Does it hurt?" I ask him, thinking of the aching menace around my leg, the slice Hereman inflicted twinging in the cold.

"Aye, it does. The cold gets into it, saps my energy," and I watch him shiver. "Don't even suggest it, My Lord," are his next, strained words. I snap my mouth shut as Rudolf arches an eyebrow at me, his face appearing pale and wraith-like from beneath a cloak that's been made for a man twice his size.

"Make sure you don't get lost in there," I offer, attempting to make light of our unfortunate situation. At least in the south, it snowed after we'd killed most of the Raiders. Well, that's how I try to remember it.

"I can see why most people refuse to attack in the winter," Sæbald words drip with frustration. It's impossible to see where we're going. Without the river at our right side, we'd be lost already. I consider calling a halt, trying to find a building, or the treeline to shelter within. But speed's essential.

If the snow falls, and falls, lying thickly on the ground, it'll be difficult, but not impossible, to reach Gainsborough. In our absence, I can only imagine the damage that Jarl Halfdan could inflict. I can't allow him to gain admittance to the settlement, to potentially force up defences to ensure he remains safe inside.

The Grantabridge jarls are bad enough, and they're locked up tight on the very periphery of Mercia. Some might even argue they're truly in East Anglia. I'm not about to allow Jarl Halfdan to potentially reclaim Torksey.

"In the reign of King Wigstan, we fought the Gwent Welshmen while a winter storm ravaged in the hills. There were three hundred of them at the beginning. In the end, there were only three." Icel's words resonate around my warriors. Heads snap up at the words. Icel has a fucking funny way of raising morale.

"And who was that against?" Ah, Rudolf. He's as prepared to be distracted as Icel. It heartens me. It's cold, and it's only going to get colder. At least if the Raiders hear us and attack, it'll be a sure way of warming our bones.

"Some Welsh king," Hereman booms, but Icel ignores him, his words appearing out of the snow.

"Idwallon or Ithel, it's impossible to remember them all in the right order. They had as many kings as Mercia did at the time. Always killing each other, or dropping down dead in the heat of a battle."

"How old were you?" I grin at the persistent questioning.

"Old enough," Icel retorts, unperturbed by Rudolf's question.

Some of my men ride in silence as I direct Haden to walk amongst them, checking everyone to ensure they're well covered from the snow. Others mutter one to another while Gardulf moves forwards more quickly, his head up, his horse stepping smartly. It seems, like Rudolf, that he's not heard all of Icel's many, many, many stories.

Edmund, I notice, is suspiciously quiet. He leads from the front, or at least, that's where I left him.

"We met in a deep valley, the hills stretching to the sky, not that we could see them. Everywhere I looked, there was merely snow and then more snow. The clouds met the land, and the horses shivered despite being covered in blankets and riders. We lost men that day, and not because they died on the edge of a bloody blade."

Even I shudder at the words, almost opening my mouth to tell him to shut up. I don't need my warriors worrying about freezing to death. But there's no need.

"But I mean real snow and a wind that left you feeling naked and exposed as it funnelled between the two hills. Not like this," there's scorn in Icel's words, and I almost choke with outraged laughter.

Damn the bastard. His stories are always meant to inspire or frustrate. Frustrate most of the time. Today he's trying for scorn. Icel will get the men to Jarl Halfdan one way or another. He has revenge on his mind, just as much as I do. And, of course, there's Edmund as well.

I consider the last time I laid eyes on Jarl Halfdan, pleased to feel the familiar roar of outrage as then, tempered only by the knowledge that since our previous encounter, I've beaten back the three other jarls. Halfdan will be no match for my warriors and me. Doubt doesn't even enter my mind about that.

"It's impossible to see anything," Edmund's voice is edged with frustration as it floats back to me, his words reminding me of his uncharacteristic silence. In the short time since the storm began, the visibility has reduced to little more than above Haden's head. It's dangerous to be out here, or at least it would be, if not for the river and the horses own initiative.

"We need to find shelter," Edmund's words chill me more thoroughly than the storm, and yet, he's right.

"There should be trees to the north," Rudolf offers. I agree with him, but right now, north is merely a wall of driving snowflakes, so thick it should be possible to count the delicate pattern on every single one before they join their allies on the ground or on my cloak or in Haden's hair.

As quickly as I can, I make my way back to Edmund's side. He scowls at me, his eye fierce, his displeasure written into the lines of his rigid body.

"I didn't make it fucking snow," I feel stung into stating.

"Did I say you bloody did?" His tone could freeze me if the snow and the wind weren't already doing so.

"Right, we'll stretch out in a line, heading inland. If everyone keeps the person in front of them insight, we shouldn't lose one another while the lead horse seeks out shelter." It's the best I can offer, and my warriors know it.

"I'll go first," Rudolf calls, his cheery voice a counterpart to the grumbling of the older men. "I've been this way before."

"Go on then. Pybba, follow him. Icel, follow Pybba, Hereman follow Pybba."

"My Lord, with due respect, I think we can form a line without you ordering us to do so," Sæbald's words aren't quite the criticism they sound.

"Just don't get bloody lost," I caution, swallowing down my unease. The only advantage to our current predicament is that no one else can fight in this. They'll be sheltered beneath a roof and with a roaring fire in the hearth, or at least I hope they will be.

Oh, the life of the warrior king of Mercia. It's filled with comfort, fine wine, and thick furs—my arse.

Eventually, I direct Haden to follow the swaying backside of Cinder, aware that only Edmund lingers behind me, close to the river. We still walk northwards but in one single line, abreast, not one behind the other.

"I hate this fucking river," I hear Edmund whinge but don't reply. I understand why. I feel the same, but the Trent hasn't always been how the Raiders infiltrate Mercia. Once, long before my birth, it was merely a river, teeming with fish and offering the hazards of a flood to rejuvenate the over-worked fields close to the river, even if it's a disaster at the time.

I cower deep inside my cloak. I'm not one for misery, but my nose is aching from the cold, and I can feel my cheeks burning beneath the onslaught of the brisk wind and driving snow. Not even the thought of a cheery hearth can delude me into feeling warm.

Head down, we press on, Haden's gait steady and slow beneath me, as though he tries each step before allowing any weight to rest on his leg.

"You see, I bet you wish for a warm stable now," I mutter, thinking of his earlier fury at being caged. I'd welcome a stable now. I'd even welcome a drafty ruin if only it allowed me to kindle a fire and warm my aching hands.

"We've found the treeline," Wærwulf calls, turning Cinder, but waiting for me to follow him first.

"Excellent," I shiver, the word, only just making it through tight lips.

"Edmund, follow me. We've found the treeline," I lift my voice, pleased it sounds firm.

"About bloody time," ricochets back to me, and he's soon beside me, Jethson now a white horse, nose down. Everyone's exhausted, cold and frustrated. We're hardly the all-conquering force come to wreak havoc on Jarl Halfdan. I'll have to change that, but only when we're warm and safe, beneath the trees.

If we need to ride out again, it'll have to be when the storm has abated. Right now, we can ride through the Raiders without knowing they're there. Such a thought isn't reassuring.

It's an effort to force a path through the rapidly increasing snow. Even though the other horses have preceded us, the snow's falling so quickly, their hoof prints are quickly obscured.

And then I duck, beneath a low hanging branch, and the world changes from white to one of dulled browns and greys.

"Fucking bollocks," Wulfred grumbles, stamping his feet while moving to brush the settling snow from his cloak and Cuthbert. Cuthbert looks as disgusted by the turning weather as his rider. I almost smile at his attempt to dislodge the snow stuck in his mane by rubbing it against Wulfred's back in the places he's already cleared the snow from his cloak.

"Ah, you daft bastard. Wait," Wulfred cautions, noticing his intentions.

Haden noses his way into a space, Jethson behind him. Rudolf is grinning as he meets my gaze.

"Welcome to your residence for the night, My Lord King," he sweeps a bow, and even the grumpiest of my warriors barks with laughter. And by that, I mean Edmund.

It isn't dissimilar to where we've sheltered so many times before. The only real difference is that it's much lighter under the trees. That makes no sense to me, but I'm grateful all the same. Better to be able to see than to fall over one another before a fire can be started. It's also much, much warmer, the thick branches, heavy with pines, shielding us from the worst of the wind.

"Fuck, I hate the winter," Hereman grouches, rubbing his back even as he stretches it, arcing his body. "It makes every little injury, from a slice on a finger to a hoof in the back, ache like a bastard."

I'm not about to disagree with him, and neither are the remainder of the men.

"Watchmen?" Icel asks me, his deep rumble disguising his true feelings on the matter.

"Yes, but everyone needs to stay beneath the trees. I can't imagine anyone attacking us, but well, it pays to be vigilant." I think back to all the times, even the most recent when I thought we were safe but weren't.

How the night goes will depend on how far Jarl Halfdan has penetrated Mercia. I'm not convinced that Kyred and his men will have allowed him far, not if they can prevent it. The snow will stop further advances unless they come by river. I have high hopes that the crossing at Littleborough will have been suitably strewn with items to stop that happening. Certainly, I know such precautions will have to be taken at Swarkeston. But that's further south than we are.

It's a consolation that the inhabitants of Newark haven't seen the Raiders on the Trent. That means they must still be further north than we currently are. Unless, of course, they've simply ridden down Ermine Street. But that's not Jarl Halfdan's intention, I'm sure of it. He wants to be at Repton.

Repton calls to him in a way nowhere else within Mercia can. No doubt, the thought of controlling the royal mausoleum appeals to him. It doesn't appeal to me, but the dead have a power that evades the living. Of that, I'm convinced. Although, Mercia's dead include the usurper kings. I'd happily have them thrown out. Perhaps I might in the future when there's peace and not war.

"I'll take first watch," Icel announces, already striding back the way we've come, a lingering hand on Samson's back. The horse watches him go mournfully; no doubt reminded of their last journey along the Trent.

"I'll send Rudolf to relieve you," I call after the hulking shadow of Icel. No doubt he wants to be alone with his thoughts.

I remove Haden's saddle and tack, carefully checking his wound as I do so. His breath, and that of the other horses and my warriors, quickly warms the space we've sheltered within so that by the time I sit before one of the four small fires, I'm sweating.

"What are you doing?" I ask Rudolf, a foul stench in my nostrils. His good cheer is infectious.

"May as well toast it. It'll taste better, and it'll be warm. Here, I'll do yours if you want," I shake my head, listening to the sizzle of a piece of cheese as it falls into the fire off his piece of bread.

"Suit yourself," he shrugs, blowing on the toasted bread and bubbling cheese. My stomach growls at the same time.

"Fine, but I'll do it." We haven't travelled to cook meals each night. We have bread, cheese, and cold meat, but I confess, his idea appeals to me.

Edmund glowers at me as I bite into my slightly black bread. His expression only darkens as I bite into the too-hot cheese, reaching for my water bottle at the same time.

"Daft sod," Pybba offers mockingly. I find myself grinning as widely as Rudolf. Fuck, it feels good to annoy everyone else while enjoying myself.

"Good idea," I speak around my mouthful of melted cheese and warm bread.

"It's good when you can't be arsed to cook anything," Rudolf agrees, and by then, others are following his example. Rudolf, because sometimes he can do so, merely enjoys the spectacle without ridiculing the others. Not that everyone has the same success.

"Fuck," all eyes turn to Leonath. He's up on his knees, a thin twig in one hand, seax in the other, as he tries to scoop his rapidly burning bread from the heart of the fire he sits around.

"Bollocks," he further exclaims, a thoroughly blackened square of bread at his feet.

"I can't eat that," he complains, looking at Rudolf as though it's his fault, face set in a glower of frustration.

"Here, have some of mine," Siric offers, hastily dividing his food. I'm aware of Rudolf moving so that he isn't visible to Leonath and shake my head at his folly. Prepared to play with the big boys until one of them might want a piece of him.

"It's not going to stop snowing," Pybba's words are mournful, as he holds his handless arm as close to the fire as possible. His face is edged with pain, the leaping flames making him appear both white and shadowed, almost hallowed. I swallow at the sight of him. Am I seeing an image of the future at that moment? I cough, ground myself back in the immediacy of our situation.

"It hurts as though the hand is still there," he explains softly, and I nod in understanding. I look at my men. What scars we all carry. We're all battered and bruised, and not just physically.

We're all evil fuckers, when we need to be. It doesn't mean we take pleasure in it. Well, not all the time. Of course, it depends on who our enemy is.

We wear our actions in more than just the fine lines around our eyes, the plethora of long-healed cuts and nicks taken in battle or training, from the brawls that can happen when any man has drunk more than his fill.

And it's far from done.

And then Edmund begins to speak. His words somehow both mournful and prideful.

"*A man of the Hwicce,*
He gulped mead at midnight feasts.
Slew Raiders, night and day.
Brave Athelstan, long will his valour endure."

Silence greets the words, but not bitterness, my memories tumbling down paths I've not considered since Athelstan's death on the day the Raiders first tracked me down. It feels like years ago, but it isn't, not at all.

"*Beornberht, son of the Magonsæte.*
A proud man, a wise man, a strong man.
He fought and pierced with spears.
Above the blood, he slew with swords."

Beornberht had been one of my favoured comrades, just as Edmund and Icel, his voice a counter to their most virulent complaints.

"*A man fought for Mercia.*

Against Raiders and foes.
Shield flashing red,
Brave Oslac, slew Raiders each seven-day."

I know I'm not alone in gazing into the fire, in seeking out memories of my lost men. Only then Edmund offers new words, not those he composed for Icel, but fresh ones.

"Hereberht was at the forefront, brave in battle.
He stained his spear, and splashed with blood
A thousand and more before Halfdan's men
His bravery cut short his life."

Somehow, no matter how eloquent the scop had been, Edmund's words cut the deepest.

"A friend I have lost, faithful he was,
After joy, there was silence
Red his sword, let it never be cleansed
A friend I have lost, brave Eoppa."

Edmund speaks so coherently, more able to voice my thoughts than any other. But then, with a quirk of his head, a smile on his lips, he rouses us to greater cheer

"Sturdy and strong, it would be wrong not to praise them.
Amid blood-red blades, in black sockets.
The war-hounds fought fiercely, tight formation.
Of the war band of Coelwulf, I would think it a burden,
To leave any in the shape of man alive."

"We'll honour them all by killing Jarl Halfdan and the scum who flock to him," Icel's voice rumbles around the fire as he appears before us from his watch duty. He eyes Edmund thoughtfully, even as the rest of my warriors cheer, offering their promises to the dead. I watch my two warriors, aware Hereman does the same, Gardulf too. Two men, sizing one another up. They've made their peace, I thought, but perhaps not quite yet.

Icel nods, Edmund accepting whatever silent communication passes between them, and then the moment's broken, a snap of a dried twig, and we're all reaching for our weapons. It isn't as though we've made a secret of our hideaway, not with four fires, not with the number of men.

"Sorry," Lyfing calls, his voice high and edged with laughter. "I went to piss," he erupts into the firelight, his lips parted in laughter.

"Fucking branches," he objects, sagging down beside the fire, even as Rudolf explodes to his feet with no effort at all.

"I'll take next watch," Rudolf announces jauntily, while others, now the threat has gone, turn to roll themselves in cloaks and any other clothes they might have. It'll be a bitter night, the howling of the wind penetrating our warm space as though from far away.

"I'll relieve you," Lyfing calls, an apology in his words. I shake my head, my mind still on my lost men and the need for vengeance. I need to temper it or risk losing all because my rage is too great. I'm not going to allow that to happen. Angry warriors make mistakes, overreach themselves, think of vengeance before practicality.

I'll ensure Jarl Halfdan never returns to Mercia again if he even manages to fucking leave.

CHAPTER 18

We break into a world changed overnight.

The promise of the Trent is visible; how could it not be, but between us and it, lies a swathe of white more impassable than the river in flood.

"Fuck," I gaze at it in dismay. Yes, we walked through the blizzard close to London, but this is something else entirely. I want to turn northwards, to where I hope Jarl Halfdan and his cronies will be, but with the trees at my back, I just can't see far enough.

"Fucking wonderful," Pybba's words drip with scorn.

The path we've taken to the shelter of the trees is entirely obscured, not even a pattering of bird or animal prints visible in the thick snow that reaches well beyond my knees, and I'm a tall man.

"It's bloody impossible." Edmund, never slow to share his dire predictions.

"It can't be," I huff, his words more than anything, forcing me to admit that even if I wanted to shelter by the fire until the snow melted, I can't. Not with Mercia threatened.

"If we can't move, neither can fucking Halfdan," Edmund interjects. I don't turn to look at him, my eyes on the impossibility of yet another task that must be completed.

"The weather is doing us a favour. We can't not take the opportunity it offers." Icel speaks with resolution. Sometimes I believe he can make men stronger just with the right words offered at an opportune moment. He need not even heft his sword or war axe. Certainly, I stand taller.

"We need to get on as best we can," I confirm, not about to debate it, reaching to rub my hand along Haden's nose. I've checked his wound. It hasn't erupted after yesterday's excursions. I can hear the sound of my warriors preparing mounts and themselves for what will come. It's going to be another fucking hard day.

"The sky's clear. There'll be no more snow today," Pybba admits begrudgingly.

"And the wind's dropped," Rudolf adds helpfully. He looks altogether too fresh for someone who's spent a good portion of the night wide awake while the rest of us slept. At least Gardulf has the good graces to yawn. I notice Hereman ruffling his hair, but Edmund's still all but ignoring his son. Damn fool.

"We need to make our way to the riverbank," I decide, hoping it's the right decision. "There's more chance of the snow being swept into the river there. It should be easier going." Silence greets my words. I take it for agreement.

"Then, My Lord, I suggest you go first." Edmund holds out his hand, but I could happily punch him in the face. Sardonic bastard.

"We'll walk there," I determine, trying to convince myself, as I lead Haden beneath the heavily boughed branches. I can smell the cold, the bite clear and cold in my throat, my tongue throbbing with the sensation.

"Fuck," I settle my cloak closer, ensuring it completely covers my scar. It'll hurt like a bastard. I spare a thought for Pybba and his missing hand. At least my neck's still there, and I can massage it when it hurts too much. What can Pybba do to ease his pain?

After all of ten steps, my legs ache, my old wounds throbbing with the action. I grit my teeth. I don't risk looking back or even forwards more than I need to for assurance that I'm going the right way. It's going to take a long time to retrace the steps we took last night. And every single bastard step of it's going to ache.

And it does. Despite the jovial words of my warriors, that boom in the still air, the journey's torturous. The snow's uneven, one step up to my ankles, the next almost up to my waist. Haden's forced to step high or cleave a path with the front of his body.

I'm sweating, frustrated and aching from head to toe by the time the sound of the river becomes immediate. It isn't in flood, but I'm sure it's risen from the day before. I grunt, aware it could make it that little bit more difficult for ships to counter the currents.

Indeed, the elements are doing all they can to cast back the unwanted attentions of Jarl Halfdan. Pybba's right. We have to take advantage of every bit of help we're receiving. I'm relieved to see the snow lies less thickly on the river banks. The journey should be more manageable if my warriors ever join me.

Heaving cold air into my lungs, both enjoying and regretting the sharp sting and the feeling of my numb lips and thighs, I check on the progress of the others.

At least, I consider, everyone has left the shelter of the tree line, but it's a motley collection of warriors who come towards me. Rudolf, just behind me, is none the worse for wear, although he breaths deeply. Dever looks at me with resentment, his nostrils rimmed with pieces of ice. I feel a moment of pity for him, which he counters by neighing loudly, the sound causing Rudolf and me to swivel, hands on weapons, looking for the cause of his concern.

His nicker assures me that there's nothing. Damn the fucker, laughing at me like that. I cast aside all pity. He's a hardy horse. He might not be as fast anymore, but he makes up for it in sheer stubbornness.

Pybba's next, and I encourage Haden to walk along the river bank, mindful of the hidden pitfalls of clumps of dead grass hanging on until the warmer weather and holes left by burrowing animals. It won't do to make it this far and then twist an ankle. I don't mount up, not yet. I'm going to be waiting for a good long while yet.

"I'll ride on," Rudolf announces, hand above his eyes to shield them from the bright sun. "See what's what."

"Stay where we can see you," I caution, thinking it a good idea, all the same.

"I'll go with him," Pybba proclaims, mounting Brimman. "I'm not standing around getting cold all over again," he huffs. I arch an eyebrow, realising he speaks the truth. There's little or no wind. Yet, the sun offers no heat, only brightness. I'm already starting to lose the feeling in my feet.

"Fucking bollocks. Why can't the bastard have stayed by his hearth for the winter?" I carp, but my words are unanswered. We all know the reason. The Raiders are contrary fuckers. All of them.

The sooner they're as cold as the weather, we can sit by our hearths, sharing tales of how we killed them all or sent them tumbling back to their ships, like rats leaving a burning building. We'll grow bored with the telling.

My belly rumbles, and I snatch the cheese left in my saddlebags. It's the wrong time of year to have excess food to spare, but all the same, my Aunt has managed to cobble together enough for us all to be able to eat for at least seven days if it takes us that long to get to the north. At this rate, it might just do that.

I squint into the distance, aware that despite my words, Rudolf and Pybba are fast reaching the extent of how far I can see. Not that I can see anyone else about, not on a day like this.

And then I gasp, grateful that none of us is by nature skilled with a bow and arrow because before me, close enough that its inquisitive brown eyes are clearly visible, a stag appears, fleeing through the snow with an effortless I admire. It's alone and all the more majestic for that.

I point, words failing me as I absorb the magnificence of such a creature, my heart swelling to see something so beautiful when I'm so filled with rage and fury. I feel Haden raise his head only to dismiss the creature entirely. When I swivel my head, none of my comrades is looking.

"Oye," I call, aware my reaction will scare the animal away.

Rather than the eyes of Icel, or Hereman looking where I point, hands rush to weapons belt, and I sigh. Why have I even bothered?

"What?" Icel calls chin on his chest, hand fumbling.

"The stag," I retort, an edge of fury to my voice. "I'm trying to show you the damn stag," but of course, the animal is long gone. I can feel Icel's eyes on me.

"You call us to arms because of a stag?"

"I didn't call you to arms. I wanted to show you the animal."

"Well, you're shit out of luck," Edmund snarls, coming closer to me. "We're hunting Raiders, not fucking stags."

"I'm sure," I breathe slowly. "There must be time each day to appreciate the beauty of our surroundings, of what Mercia is?"

"There'll be time for that when the fuckers are all dead. Now, come on, those two are getting too far ahead. We need to catch them." Rushing beyond Haden and me, Edmund forces Jethson through the more thinly lying snow. I watch them, mouth twisted with fury.

"He's such an arsehole, sometimes," Hereman muses, no hint of apology in those words, even while Gardulf's young face flashes with fury. Edmund's making no friends today.

"I saw the stag," Gardulf mollifies as Hereman careers after his brother. "It was a beautiful creature. Surely a sign of our success in the coming days." The words startle me. I haven't realised that Gardulf was akin with the more archaic of Mercia's religions. Not that it concerns me. I'm surprised my Aunt allows such things, but then, she's learned her herb-craft from somewhere. Perhaps it was from those, like Eowa, who eschew the church, preferring to convene with nature instead.

Slightly placated, Haden picks a path behind Gardulf. In allowing the other horses to go first, it makes it easier for Haden. He doesn't need to lift his leg so high or push as much snow aside with each step. Not that he likes it, not at all. In no time at all, I find myself in the firing range of Kermit's constant farting. The smell ripples through the air, my nose turning upwards, as Haden endeavours to slide past him.

"What have you been feeding him?" I demand to know.

Gardulf meets my question with furrowed brows.

"Just the usual stuff, oats and grasses." But there's hesitation in the words.

"And perhaps some things he shouldn't have been eating," Gardulf admits reluctantly.

"It's not going to make you many friends," I admit, laughing now that I'm out of the firing line, a backwards look assuring me that Leonath had just got a whiff of the same. His eyes are crossed, and his mount looks anything but happy.

"It's always the same when he's trotting. It's better if we flat out gallop."

"That's not likely to happen today," I indicate the pile of snow.

"Then people are going to have to learn to enjoy the smell," Gardulf retorts, even as Leonath speeds in front of him.

I grin, moving on, ensuring that ahead Rudolf and Pybba stay within sight. The reflection from the snow is blinding, but there's no heat to it. I can feel the coldness of the water reaching me to add to my woes. All I need to see now is a Raider ship, and the day would be about fucking perfect.

I wanted to make it to Torksey at the minimum, but I don't think that will be possible, aware we still need to follow the river back on ourselves. It would have been easier to come by ship, I muse. But, with our skills, we'd have been more likely to end up in the Humber than Torksey. I smirk at the thought. We're horsemen, not shipmen.

We managed well enough last time, but that was in the heat of summer. A dunking might not have gone amiss. Now, it'll probably kill us.

Haden trots beyond the point where I've seen the stag, and I glance at the snow, hoping to see some hoof prints, but if they were there, I can't see them. But then, the animal leapt so high, perhaps it barely touched the snow. I shrug. I know what I've seen. Whether it's an omen or not, I don't know.

Others quickly follow Leonath, Gardulf struggling with his flatulent mount over the treacherous footing. I might have felt some commiseration for him, but the smell's terrible, like an overripe body left out in the summer sun. I'm not willingly going to endure that again.

And then, ahead, I see that Rudolf and Pybba considerably slow, and I urge Haden on. What have they seen in the rippling waters of the Trent?

Nothing in the water, so it seems. No, their eyes are lifted upwards, a pall of smoke darkening the horizon.

It seems we've found the Raiders.

"But what's burning?" It's not the first time Rudolf asks the question, and I still have no answer for him.

"Something," Pybba grumbles, perhaps in the hope Rudolf will be happy with that. But he's not.

"We won't know until we get there," I speak through thin lips, my heart steady in my chest, even while thoughts of revenge drive me onwards.

The smoke is coming from our side of the river. That's good. The rest of the Mercians under Turhtredus have travelled along Ermine Street and will meet us at Littleborough. And then our combined force can attack the Raiders. I can't see that any of the bishops will send men out in this weather. It's going to be Kyred's men, and mine, and those who serve Turhtredus. If there are ten ships worth of Raiders out there, it's not going to be enough. Only, I'll ensure it is enough.

But for all I want to rush, the day advances too quickly, the snow hazardous for the horses, and for me when I dismount and try and walk myself.

"We won't arrive before tomorrow," Edmund mutters gloomily.

Our long line of warriors is much tighter now, all of us ready for any unexpected attack. I keep searching the river, but there's no sign of detritus in it, and why would there be? It would flow the other way—frustration claws at me. I want to be where the fire burns. I need to know what's happening there.

And then, the Trent drives us back before allowing us forward again, and it feels as though half the day is spent merely repeating steps already made. With my eyes on the smoke, I've not noticed where we were, and neither have those of my men who've been this way before. The snow hasn't helped. Everything's obscured, apart from the river at our side. It's as persistent as the fucking Raiders.

At least I'm warm, the promise of yet another Raider attack driving me onwards.

Above my head, the sky darkens, a lack of clouds and a bright moon, making it possible to keep moving, even as the temperature drops lower and lower.

It's a good thing I have my wrath.

My world narrows to the white snow beneath Haden's hooves, the sound of men and horses laboured breathing and the crunch of hooves through snow that grows colder and colder. Can I be grateful that no more snow falls? Not at all. I need a thaw, and I need a thaw quickly, but that's not going to happen.

Eventually, Haden stumbles, his hoof slipping before him. I've been expecting it to happen for some time, my body tense on his back. Lithely, ignoring all the aches and pains of my wounds and muscles, I leap clear from him, landing with a crunch in the crystalline surface, just about managing to keep to my feet. A cry undulates through the air, and I quirk an eyebrow at Rudolf's horrified face, even as Haden regains his balance.

"Not quite as old as you think I am? Aye?" But I don't wait for an answer. I hurry to check on Haden, hands running along his flank, eyeing his wound, pleased it doesn't bleed afresh but is knitting tightly together.

That's when they fucking come.

CHAPTER 19

They erupt from the snow before us as though bears from hibernation smelling food for the first time in months. My hand is already on my seax, even though my vision realises what's happening after the rest of my senses.

How long have they been there? I hope they're cold and useless, even as heat burns through my body, all aches dispelled, all muscles working.

It's dark, but the moon is bright, and I detect no more than thirty Raiders. I understand who they are even before their leader shouts his instructions from somewhere amongst them.

"*Angreb*," his deep voice bellows. Followed by "*skjolde*" and "*våben*." We all recognise what that means, and I don't need to offer the same. My warriors know what to do, even though we're burdened by the narrow track and the presence of our horses.

Not that it hampers Hereman. He crashes through the snow, circumnavigating horses and comrades as he goes, spear already flying through the air, glinting with the promise of ice from the heavens. A heavily bearded man shrieks in terror, the cries choked off in a wet gargle, even as I smirk. They thought to have the element of surprise, but I have Hereman. He's a fucking surprise to me. Every single day.

Hereman is already raising his war axe to slash at the next warrior in his way. I hurry to follow him. I don't want him surrounded and cut off from the rest of us.

Only Gardulf is there, wildly following his uncle into the fray, leaping through the snow reminiscent of the stag earlier, and of course, Edmund has no choice but to follow his son and brother with a growl of frustration. At least he won't have to think about it, just act.

"Arseholes," Pybba huffs, dismounting with more care and ensuring Brimman can't trip on the reins by tying them up high in the event the horse has to flee.

I hurry to do the same with Haden, wishing there was more room between the river and the path, but there isn't. The horses will need to stay where they are. We'll have to take the attack to the enemy.

The slice of a spear falling through the snow informs me the animals are in danger. I risk glancing along the line to where Lyfing has realised the problem. He slaps a flank, his horse belatedly realising what needs to be done, turning to evade the Raiders.

While the rest of the men hasten to assist Hereman, Edmund and Gardulf, Lyfing rushes down the line of horses, a slap here, a quick turn there, and too slowly, the horses retrace their steps.

I hear the next spear before it impacts the snow, and thrust my shield upwards, my arm quivering with the impact, but Haden's safe. He nickers softly, perhaps in thanks, or a complaint that it was a bit of a close one. Then he reverses into the next horse, and those in front of him, alert to the danger, begin to do the same.

Hereman has been joined by ten of my warriors. They've quickly formed a shield wall, and the Raiders, spaced out while hiding beneath the snow, are already struggling.

I turn my shield with difficulty, tugging on the spear. It's well-wedged, falling from such a height. It refuses to release itself, and then I hear the sound of another missile fleeing through the air. I thrust my shield high once more, aware it's ungainly, but this spear clatters harmlessly to the floor.

I smirk, bend my knees, shield still raised, and retrieve it from the snowy ground. I lower my shield, aware that the presence of the horses behind me has gone. Not that I rush the throw. I'm not as talented as Hereman. Scratch that; I'm not as bloody lucky as Hereman. Not with a spear. A seax and sword are my weapons of choice; an elbow and a forehead, almost as effective.

I need to sight my target, and I do. A figure watches me, shadowed by the light of the moon so that I can see little but a shape. My heart thuds. Could this be Jarl Halfdan? But no, it can't be. The build is too slight, but he's the one giving the orders to the rest.

With half a smile, I aim and thrust the spear high into the air. My foe watches my movements, expression inscrutable at such a distance, as he turns to run away.

I don't need to watch the rest. His shriek of pain drives me to join my warriors.

The fucker is dead. I aimed for where he was going to go, not where he was—damn fool.

Without him there, I notice that another voice resumes instructing the Raiders from amongst those battling Hereman, Edmund, Pybba, Rudolf, Gardulf, Gyrth, Sæbald, Siric, Goda and Wærwulf.

I expect the snow to lie deeply here, but it doesn't. The enemy has done us all a favour by clearing much of it so that a crisp white hollow makes it easier to move without lifting legs high. At the same time, it's made the ground more treacherous. The ground is slippery, the ice far from inviting. Men might die here from a shard of ice just as easily as a sharp blade.

The shrieks of the Raiders fill the air, an unholy sound. Do they mean to wake their gods, or are they merely craven arseholes?

The rest of my warriors stand at the backs of their comrades, but a movement in the distance catches my eye. The horses are safe, I hope, but perhaps not.

"Lyfing, with me," I beckon him, and he glances at me in dismay, chest heaving, as I hurry to retrace the steps he's just taken.

"What?" But he must see it too because his steps are following mine, the crunch of boots in the semi-cleared area of the path, assuring me that I'm not alone. What is it with these bastards and my horses? Do they mean to repay me for all the ones I've taken from them? I merely reclaimed those mounts for Mercia.

Behind me, the shouts and bellows of men fighting to the death threatens to pull me away from my purpose, but even though my eyesight isn't as clear as Edmund's, I know what I saw.

This is about distraction, and I'm not one to be easily distracted.

"There," I huff, the air burning through my throat, already dry from the cold air.

"I see it," Lyfing wheezes. At least four shadows are converging on the horses. They can't have anything but malevolent intentions. I'm frustrated. I'd not felt as though we were being followed that day, but it seems it was worse than that. We were being hunted, and that boils me.

And then I misstep, sliding perilously towards the ground, only to collide with Billy. His backside arrests my fall, even as he surges forward.

"Steady boy," I gasp, Lyfing somehow gathering up Billy's reins, preventing him from fleeing in fear.

"Thanks," I exclaim, swallowing the words with a sharp inhalation.

Lyfing doesn't speak. He's scurrying onwards. I glance forwards. The shadows are closer now.

I slip between Billy and the river, a slap on his shoulder in apology and thanks, ducking low as I move more slowly. I have no idea if the Raiders have seen me or not. They're likely to catch sight of Lyfing as he continues to run, his crunching footsteps audible this far from the site of the attack. Well, I call it running, but it's more like flailing. If he's lucky, he'll keep upright. Fuck, it's impossible to hurry over snow.

I speed up a little, using the tall horses to shield my movements, fleeing towards Lyfing, passing Keira, Jethson, Haden, Magic, Kermit, Jaspar, Brimman, Dever and Cinder, before I need to move with more caution. I feel their interest, and Haden stamps a hoof as though trying to trip me, but it's more than that. I swear these horses are preparing to attack the attackers. I smirk at the thought. They've spent far too much time with their riders.

The clash of iron on iron assures that Lyfing has encountered the enemy. He'll need my help, but first, well, I've glimpsed one of the fuckers trying to slither his way down the line of horses. I stifle a bark of laughter as Lyfing's mount stamps heavily on the Raiders foot. His screech of outrage ensures that I take him through the neck as I dive over the horse's black back, seax held in front of me, piercing the man with all the force of my weight behind the blade.

He buckles to the floor, pulling me over with him.

"Fuck," I complain, arms wild, a face full of horse hair for my thanks, and no doubt, the stench of Lyfing's arse from the saddle as well.

I land with a clatter of leather and metal, impacting the still writhing body of the man I've killed. Immediately, the scent of shit and blood fills my nostrils, and with it, the even more unpleasant smell of Lyfing's mount taking an almighty piss on the floor.

"Fucking bollocks," I scamper to my feet, aware I'm making too much noise but desperate to be away from the horse's stream. Bad enough a man's piss, ten times worse, and ten times more, when a horse empties its bladder.

Leaping to my feet, I see many things at once, but none of them makes sense until I wrench my seax free and settle to my next kill.

White-eyes, white teeth and an even whiter neck greet me. I grin while the man shrieks, dropping the rein of the next horse and desperately trying to scamper away. He slips, either on the piss or the blood, I don't know, and as he thuds to the ground, I quickly reverse my grip and slice open his neck. Lyfing's horse stamps on the dying man for good measure, the body bucking upwards, only for a roll of green shit to land on the dying man's forehead.

I grin, enjoying the moment, even as I remember what I've

seen in the blink of an eye.

Lyfing is being overwhelmed, and so too are my warriors further away. There are more of the bastards than I thought, hiding beneath the drifts of snow. More of them than two against one, much more, and I'm here, watching men being attacked by horses.

And that gives me the impetus I need.

I can't hear the shrieks of the far distant battle, but I can see what's happening as the enemy attempt to encircle my warriors. Damn the fuckers.

Quickly, I slick the blood from my seax in a clean handful of snow, pulling my sword into my other hand. I tread as quickly as I can, mindful I don't want to impale myself, and then slide my blade beneath one of the warrior's byrnies before thrusting it deep into his chest. His slashing movements cease mid-air, a cry half-cut off, as Lyfing makes a wild strike with his seax, crunching the man's nose. Our foe drops to the floor. Now there are only three of the enemy. Lyfing battles the taller of the three, and I take the smaller. That leaves one man alone, and he turns, licking his lips, trying to decide what to do.

With a desultory swipe at my immediate opponent, I rear backwards, thrusting my arse into the other man's crotch, following up with an elbow swipe to his nose. And he staggers, one way and then the other, even as I counter the blows from the man who spits every time he breaths. Lyfing thrusts his seax into the man's underarm, and I take his neck.

One each. I grin, the delight of battle bubbling inside me. It's easy then to concentrate, find the rhythm of the final man's movements, and strike when he least expects it.

As he slithers off the end of my blade, a roar of sound reaches my ears.

"Hurry up, Lyfing," I call, eyeing the horses. They've turned as well, ears pricked. No doubt every one of them hears their masters cry.

I catch Haden's brown eyes. If he could nod in understanding, that's what he'd do.

Lyfing is beside me, chest heaving, war axe and seax held loosely in his bloodied hands.

"Bastards," he states, hawking to clear blood from his mouth. He looks hale. I'll have to accept that he is.

"The horses?" he demands to know.

"The horses," I confirm. We don't have a reserve force to assist us, but we do have our mounts.

Quickly, he jumps into the saddle. I rush to Haden, a word of instruction for the other beasts I pass on the way, an expectation that they'll follow us without too much difficulty.

The only problem is the path.

I slide towards Haden, entirely out of control, the surface too treacherous to risk.

"We'll have to do this the hard way," air explodes from my mouth as I hit Haden too fast. He stands steady, head turned to eye me with disgust.

"Sorry, lad," I offer, thrusting myself into the saddle, even though I've not managed to take a full breath yet.

I don't look at what's happening in front of us. My focus needs to be on getting there, not on feeling out of control.

"This way," and I encourage Haden into the pristine snow to the side of the slippery walkway, the moon as bright as day, lighting the path we need to take through the knee-high snow. Haden rears at my command, and then, just like the stag, he seems to skip through the snow, bounding from hoof to hoof, the other horses following him, Lyfing encouraging from the back. Not that they need the added incentive.

The moonlight flashes over blades and edges in the distance, my gaze focused on the immediate foreground, checking for any hidden dips and holes, perhaps highlighted by the snow, or revealed by the moon. I don't want to lose an animal.

I have my seax to hand. I don't trust that more of these fuckers aren't lurking beneath the snow. Mad bastards, all of them. It's so cold my breath freezes in my beard, my tongue threatening the same until I snap my mouth shut again.

I risk looking at my warriors. We're getting closer but not yet close enough to do more than witness what's coming.

The enemy outnumber my men, they will even with the addition of the horses, but if we're not quick, they'll be cut off from my assistance.

Hereman rears up from his place in the shield wall, all arms and legs, his rage doing more to terrify the enemy than his accuracy. Icel is beside him, his movements more constrained and twice as lethal. I can see a small knot protecting someone at the core, and I aim Haden that way. I'll rescue them, and then the horses can knock the others into the snow.

I lead on, mindful that this could all go wrong between one heartbeat and the next, feeling Haden tremble with effort beneath me. Will we make it in time? We better do because I fear to know who's so beleaguered. I won't lose another of my loyal warriors on a Raiders' blade. I fucking will not.

Haden crashes into the Raiders trying to attack my warriors from the rear. And he's not alone. Jethson, never one to be outdone, is beside him, and so too is Billy.

I've not fully appreciated the speed Haden has managed to attain, almost as though there's no snow and no one lying on the ground, dead or bleeding. A yell and I see wild eyes as a warrior rolls clear of the high hooves and the snapping teeth. Fuck, I recognise Rudolf in the centre of the circle, Pybba at his side.

Time seems to slow. I might be too late, even now.

The Raiders' voices surround me, ranging from outrage to delight, but it's the sound of the thunder I bring that drowns out all else. The horses are pissed, and I mean, pissed.

They don't slow enough to help my warriors, but they send the enemy running all over the place, hooves high in the air, teeth snapping with anger. They might delicately take an apple from their rider, but those teeth are nasty when riled.

I can hear my warriors calling to their mounts, and a shrill scream rents the air. Fuck. One of the horses.

With less control than I might like, I try and turn Haden, but he's as alert as I am. Between one heartbeat and the next, he's come to a complete stop, turning and rushing back the way we've come. He just misses Pybba and Rudolf, the pair emerging from their struggles, Rudolf's reactions keeping them both safe. Haden's focused on one thing and one thing only. Killing any Raider who gets in his way as he rushes to Dever's aid.

Dever might be old, but he fights with ferocity, black and white hooves high in the air, swinging his head, eager to dislodge the Raider who thinks to claim his back, a wicked-looking seax slowly working its way into the black horsehair close to his neck.

"No, you fucking don't," Rudolf's words reach me, but I'm already flinging myself from Haden's back, knocking the Raider to the floor in a tangle of limbs. I might hold my seax, but I'm punching him with my left hand, over and over again, the air driven from his body, as he looks at me in horror.

"You little shit," I spit into his face, only for Dever to intervene.

I swing my head aside, a thick globule of flesh landing on my chin, the crunch ringing in the air all I need to hear. The man is dead. His skull caved in. That'll teach the fucker.

"My thanks," Rudolf heaves air into his surging chest, stretching for his horse.

"We're not done yet," I grumble. My warriors were outnumbered two to one, perhaps three to one. With the horses, the odds have somewhat evened out, but the animals don't wear the protective equipment we do. And, these Raiders don't seem scared of trying to ride away.

I clasp his hand and lurch to my feet. The ground gleams wetly with blood and piss. Hereman continues to roar, Icel fights on, his movements lethal and measured. Edmund is hammering away at any who comes close to him. Blood shimmers on his byrnie and down his face. The rage has him, and it's not about to leave him—his missing eye glimmers with the intent of the seeing.

"Pybba, can you fight?" I demand to know.

"Yes, My Lord," he seeks out Brimman amongst the mass of churning horseflesh.

"Protect the horses," I bark at Pybba and Rudolf, Ordlaf and Leonath as well. "Use them if we need them."

Haden noses the body far from gently, only to glance at Dever, almost as though the pair of them converse about the kill, glib words light with the relief that the enemy is dead. I shake my head.

It's not fucking done yet, no matter what they think.

The Raiders who emerge from beneath the snow drip with living ice, faces blue in the moonlight. And it's made them all mean fucking bastards.

Their weapons gleam, expressions thirsting for their privations not to be a waste of time and effort, and my men and I are outnumbered.

"Gyrth, Wærwulf, assist Hereman," I snap. There's no oversight here, no plan to bring this battle to an end quickly. And why would there be? I thought we faced an equal number. I didn't realise we'd been tricked. I should have been more cautious.

"Beornstan, Wulfhere and Osbert, take the Raiders around Edmund."

Edmund fights as though he's alone in the world, with a thousand warriors to kill, but he doesn't need to do it single-handedly. Not when there are so many of us. And even if every single one of his offensives is successful, the maroon flying through the air speaking of terrible wounds being inflicted.

The rest of my warriors fight one on one. Gardulf remains close to his uncle and father but held back by the deadly enemy. Oda and Eadulf have three men trying to attack the two of them, fighting together, one drawing the Raiders aside so that the other can hack into exposed necks and arms. It won't be long until they're dead, especially with Jaspar and Simba nipping at the men and generally getting in the way of any attempt to escape. There's nothing like being trapped between two horses to make a man realise he's not the master after all. A horse allows you to ride it and direct its steps. That should never be forgotten.

"Lord Coelwulf," the taunting voice emerges from the snow

before me. He wasn't there a moment ago, but now he is, large hand on huge war axe, a knowing glint in his moon-darkened eye, the weapon's blade promising nothing but death. He could be dressed in glinting rings or merely the leather of a byrnie. It's impossible to make out the detail.

"So, you've come to save Mercia once more," I don't know the man, I'm sure of it. I note that he speaks my tongue. His conceit is misplaced, but then, one day, mine will be as well, and my overconfidence might be the death of me. But not today.

"No, I've come to end your life," I roar, running at my foe, placing my feet with care to avoid the slippery blood and shimmering ice. I could knock myself out just by landing heavily and be skewered through the heart before I even came round. I'm forced to leap as one of the Raiders crashes to the floor beneath me, slipping, and in mid-air, time seems to slow. I turn, seeking out my warriors, ensuring all is well, deciding where to strike the sneering bastard.

Ideally, I'd like to take him through the top of his head, but his helm looks sturdy in the flash of moonlight that reveals so much more to me. I don't want to dent my seax or injure my hand with the reverberation from such an impact. It still aches from the spear that impacted my shield.

No, I hang in the air, sucking my lower lip, considering the best way to kill my foe, and only when I land does time return to normal. By then, my blade is busy, cutting one way and then another, slicing across his belly with one hand, taking his neck with the other, my enemy, for all his cockiness and confidence, too slow to counter any of the strikes.

When he falls to the floor, warm breath leaving his body and washing me in the first bit of heat I've felt for some time. I shake my head a little. Why didn't he defend himself? Daft bastard.

But he's not alone.

Another stands to face me. The jeer on his face, long beard obscuring his neck, tells me that these men believe themselves invincible. Perhaps, I consider, they've never fought the Mercians before. Has Jarl Halfdan been forced to find new blood? Were the rest of his men too damn scared to face us? I fucking hope so.

"Bastard," I spit, pleased to get the gob of blood out of my mouth. It catches the moonbeam, flickering and flashing as it lands on the dead man, a loud fart filling the air, the smell of piss making me wrinkle my nose.

"Jarl Halfdan has offered a reward for you, dead or alive," the man cackles, his hands busy on his weapons belt. But my eyes are drawn behind him. How many are there? One on one, I can fight all night, all next day if I must. If they form a shield wall, I can still keep fighting, but I'll need my warriors, and we're spread out. Cries and shrieks fill the air, the huff of effort, the thuds of the dying and the dead.

My foe flicks his head back as though to show me his neck, to pretend to his superiority.

"What is the reward?" I ask just because I'm curious to know how much my death is valued. Before I was the king, they sent two thousand men to track me down. How many have Jarl Halfdan sent this time?

"As much gold and silver as will keep a man and his family an entire lifetime."

"Well, that really depends on the nature of the man, surely?" My tone is conversational. I refocus on my enemy. I'm content that my warriors are doing well without me. I'll learn what I can before this man is dead. I don't mind chatting before I kill him.

It seems my words are too complex. My enemy glares at me with incomprehension.

"A man who wants nothing more than to live in a hut all his life will need little. A man who thinks himself a king will want more. What, precisely, do you believe Jarl Halfdan will give you? What does he have in his power to gift? Mercia isn't his. And, I doubt he'd be in Mercia if he held great swathes of land else-where."

A rumble of fury begins somewhere deep in the man's chest. I roll my eyes. It seems this man is no great thinker. I'm not to question what his lord has offered. He's a damn fool not to have uncovered all the details before committing himself to the task.

"So, it seems you want to kill me for a pittance of silver and little else. I assure you, I'm worth fucking more than that."

I launch myself over the farting, dead man, aware his clothes will be the easier way of gaining a decent purchase for what I plan next. Seax in my right hand, my war axe in the left, I direct the one at his heart, the other at the top of his left arm. Either blow will work. But of course, I have the momentum, and I move far more quickly than he's expecting. When my forehead impacts his nose, I hear the satisfying crunch of breaking bone. It's almost disappointing to realise that my seax has pierced the man's heart. I aimed it upwards, not downwards, my impetus ensuring it penetrated what I now discover to be a leather byrnie.

"He'll hunt you down and kill you," my falling foe is all bluff and hot air.

"Well," and I stamp down, wrench my seax free. "He better find someone who can fucking fight," I offer, dismissing him and moving on, eyes keen to ensure my warriors aren't overwhelmed.

A dark pool of glowing fluid surrounds Edmund, the snow almost hissing as it melts beneath the hot mixture. And yet more come against him. I turn aside, checking the others. I believe all of the hidden men are now in full sight. I can count too many of them still, but I also think we're prevailing.

Beornstan moves to reinforce Edmund's back, the two working together, even though they can't see what the other does. While Edmund rears upwards, Beornstan is down low, and vice versa. I'm impressed, even as I seek out whichever horse shrieked in pain.

The moon reflects from the snow, almost blinding in its ferocity when I peer towards it. There are shadowy figures and shadowy horses, most of them easily identifiable if they're my men. I know the stance Lyfing prefers, the way Hereman stands before launching his spear, and the way that Berg holds his head. But my eyes alight on something amiss, and then the sound once more reaches my ears.

Cuthbert, Wulfred's mount has been set upon by not one but two of the Raiders. Pybba and Rudolf are unaware of the problem because they battle against five Raiders, all trying to get to the horses from the front of the group. Ordlaf and Leonath stand their ground to the rear, but Cuthbert is amongst the horses. He rears and kicks, his screams akin to murder, unsettling the rest of the mounts.

I see the glint of a blade, the threat of grinning white teeth. There's one of the bastards there, amongst my horses. Perhaps he was hiding beneath the snow in that spot. Maybe he's rushed into the horses, lucky to escape any injury, and now he's set his sights on Cuthbert.

I realise I'm not alone in my concern. Wulfred has heard the cries of his horse. He's torn, I can see, blade raised as he battles beside Goda.

I determine to go to Cuthbert's aid, only for a blade to flash before my eyes. An ouff of discomfort, and my seax slides into the belly of the dying man. Crouching low to the ground, I dart, first one way and then another, mindful of where I need to go and the slick ground beneath my feet. It's not just ice that threatens to trip me, not now.

I hear a cheer and imagine our foe think I'm trying to escape with my life. They couldn't be more wrong.

I crash into the mass of seething horses. Panicked eyes and shrill shrieks show me how unhappy the horses are. Berg nips my hand, Magic my ear, and I slap them both on their flank. Better to get them away from this mess before more than one of them is injured, even if by mistake.

Cuthbert, I imagine, hears my progress because it's not quiet. His eyes alight on me as I push through Simba and Chocolate and face the Raider who thinks to steal away another horse.

I pause, only momentarily, blade raised because the thief is little more than a child, certainly younger than Rudolf.

His face is devoid of a beard, eyes blazing with fear. I can see when he swallows the action far too prominent.

"What are you doing?" I ask, rather than slice through such an inviting proposition without thought.

He shakes his head, not understanding my words, and still, I refrain from attacking.

"Get off the horse," I command instead, miming that he should stand beside me.

He shakes his head, brown curls flying with the movement. He bites at his lower lip.

"Mercian or Dane?" I demand to know.

"Neither," his accent is different to mine, but the word means the same. I narrow my eyes, aware that the battle continues around me while I make polite conversation.

"Slave?" I demand to know.

Again he shakes his head.

"North," and he points in the direction he must think is north. I notice then that he wears good clothes, too good for a slave, his boots sturdy as he stumbles to the floor.

"From north of the Humber?" I persist. Why can he only offer me one-word answers? Do I scare him? I probably do. I stink of the slaughterhouse.

"Yes. Jarl Halfdan said my father must fight to keep his lands, but my father is ill. I came in his stead." His long sentence startles me.

"And where are you going?"

His wide-eyed stare assures me he has no idea other than to leave the battlefield. I make a snap decision, hoping I won't regret it.

"What's your name?"

"Magnus." He has weapons on his belt but hasn't even attempted to seek them out. It's not natural for him to fight. He doesn't have the skills for it.

"I take it this is your first battle?"

"Yes, yes, My Lord," he confirms, bowing and lowering his head at the same time so that I get an eyeful of dark brown hair.

"Stay here. Don't steal my horses. I'll protect you as best I can. Stay out of sight of the Raiders. They'll all be fucking dead soon enough."

A slow smile steals over his young face, and I nod and grunt my approval.

"Take this," and I tug a cord around my neck, on which sits one of my only items of nostalgia. "Show it to my men if they come upon you and I'm not here. And give it back to me at the end of the battle."

I can hear Wulfred over the press of horses. Not all of them have moved aside, and indeed, while Cuthbert has calmed, his eyes showing a hint of embarrassment now that I speak to the man he thought meant to steal him, there's no need for the others to move aside.

Wulfred's words are filled with fury for "that fucking bastard Raider stealing his beloved Cuthbert."

I aim towards the sound, hoping to intercept before he cuts without realising the boy is our ally, not our enemy. It's often the way. I'd sooner ally with the Welsh Gwentmen against the Raiders even though on another day, I'd happily slit their throats for even breathing wrong.

"He's well," I encounter a puffing Wulfred, waylaid by the helpful black and white arse of Haden.

"Come on, the horses are well, including Cuthbert. You have my word. Let's finish this."

There's more than our air rising into the clear sky. The scent of horse shit is rife, as are other, less pleasant odours.

"Aye, well, I hope you killed the fucker," Wulfred chunters, taking me at my word. I'll handle that matter of the thief's survival in good time.

The Raiders who attempted to steal the horses are dead or dying, Pybba and Rudolf both breathing heavily. Edmund and Beornstan are also panting, peering around as though amazed they yet live.

But the enemy is far from all dead. They've retreated, and I know that they'll come at us again.

"Rudolf, Pybba, get your arses here," I call to the pair of them. "All of you, come here, now." I don't feel exhausted, far from it, despite all the running and killing. My blood runs hot, warming even my hands and my feet.

Edmund glares at me as though he's forgotten who he is and what he does, chest heaving, so that's he's half obscured by his breath.

"Gardulf, get your father," I growl. I need them at my side, and fucking quickly. The Raiders aren't about to have a cheery ale before they resume the attack.

"Hereman, here, now," I bellow, pleased when Rudolf takes up my cries, realising far more quickly than the others what's about to happen. I spare a thought for my captured Northumbrian. If he means me harm, it'll come any moment now, but I don't believe he does. I've always been able to judge most men quickly, apart from the lying bastards.

Lyfing makes his way to his horse, Rudolf doing the same when he finally arrives. Of us all, only Icel remains out there, standing alone, daring the Raiders to come for him. His blood burns too hot. It's not like him, but I leave him well alone. I won't allow them to beat him, neither will I allow him to face the Raiders, even if he fancies it.

"Daft cunt," Wulfred comments, jerking his head towards the solitary figure. Icel looks menacing, and I can only see his back.

"Aye, well, we've all got our demons to exercise," I offer, not about to get into an argument about it.

"Him more than most," Wulfred confirms. "Cuthbert?"

"A young lad, forced here by Jarl Halfdan merely wanted to escape. I've left him in there. With the horses." A look of surprise touches the dips and hollows on the old bastard's face.

"Aye, My Lord. Well, I pity the poor bastard. Won't know his arse from his elbow, let alone his seax from his bloody shield. And Cuthbert is one for making a fuss about fuck all."

"My Lord," Sæbald issues the warning. The Raiders have made some decisions, and now they walk towards us in the moonlight, steps measured, shields, some of them already showing a fair amount of maroon, held in hand.

"Any wounded?" I demand first.

"Me, My Lord," the voice is surprisingly hale for someone who professes to be wounded. Although it's also a bit wet.

"Eahric, what the fuck happened?" He makes his way between the rest of my warriors, loosely grouped in a circle around me. His face is a welter of blood, dripping from between two broken teeth and onto his chest.

"Shield boss," he complains, and I nod, wincing as I see how much blood there is.

"Will the helm come off?" I ask. It's dented and caved in where his nose should be.

"No, it won't."

"Then, stay here, with the horses, and watch out for the Northumbrian lad amongst the horses. You can't fight like that."

"Sorry, My Lord."

"Not your fault, and you'll live with the pain," not the most sympathetic, but then, there are twenty-three or twenty-four Raiders coming ever closer. At least we're just about evenly matched now.

"Scare the horses away if the Raiders come for them," I instruct as an afterthought, the order closely followed by an outraged neigh from Haden.

"Or let them fight," I shrug a shoulder, swallowing my instruction. Cuthbert made so much fuss when he felt threatened, but they're not all like that. They're as blood-thirsty as the rest of us.

"Shield wall," I confirm, looking to Edmund and also Pybba. Pybba sighs while Rudolf moves quickly to ensure Pybba's shield is looped over the handless arm.

"We've nearly beaten them already," I confirm. "Now we just need to finish the fuckers off."

A bellowing clash fills the air, and I wince. One of the Raiders, a tall man, hair flashing white in the moonlight, has decided to take on Icel's provocation. His fellows cheer the endeavours, but it won't end well.

I watch, as do my warriors, slightly fascinated to see how the foe-man thinks to fell Icel. I consider that they know one another but dismiss it just as quickly. It's Jarl Halfdan's man, the jarl whose name I forget, that Icel wishes to kill above all others,

Edmund as well. This man isn't him, I'm sure of it.

The enemy fights with a war axe, the edges looking far from smooth even from this distance—a dirty bastard, eager to make death as painful as possible. A growl begins in my chest, reaching my mouth without me even realising. Icel better not fall to such a cocky bastard.

Icel counters the move easily, seemingly effortlessly. I hear the sound long before I've seen the responding thrust from Icel's sword. I smirk—Icel toys with the man. I know what he's doing. Not that I disapprove, but it would be nice if the fucker took my commands and didn't simply do as he wished.

"Come on, while the stupid gits focus on Icel."

We move forward with some care, the ground slimy and uninviting, the detritus of battle meaning we're right to be wary. I have Hereman to my left, Edmund at my right, although I appreciate that Gardulf has been shipped off far down the line. Goda has taken the far right, Sæbald the left. Seasoned men who know what tricks the enemy might try to play if they manage to overwhelm the centre or if they decide to attack one of the ends instead. We're only one man deep. It'll be more than enough.

Pybba and Rudolf are beside Hereman. Pybba would sooner be at my more immediate side but knows better than to jostle into place as Edmund has done. I notice the tense faces, the bruises starting to form, the blood that's stopped flowing, helms set straight, more than one man ducking low to run snow over the edges of their filthy weapons.

Fuck, they make me proud.

And still, the Raiders cheer their man, thinking perhaps that I'm Icel, that Icel is me, that they can finish this before it truly begins, that their losses will only be the men who are dead so far. My cheeks tighten, and it's not the cold this time. The Raiders need to know their enemy better than they do.

My steps are sure, the promise that the horses guard our backs, more than enough for me. There are no Raiders to the south of me, only to the north. I spare a thought for the lad and Eahric. But, Eahric is hardly incapacitated. I simply won't take the risk with him. And Magnus is no warrior. And still, the Raiders watch Icel.

The moonlight is so strong, it sends an image of the ensuing battle crawling towards us. I don't know whether to watch the actual fight or the one that's being played out in shadow form on the snow. The noise of the weapons clashing together seems to drown out all sound, even that of the gurgling river beside us. Even that of the horses and Eahric. I imagine he's found Magnus. I imagine he's already forced oaths to be sworn. Eahric won't take any chances, and I'm surprised that I have. I'm not one for taking kindly to those who battle us. But then, I don't think Magnus is our enemy, for all he has a Norse sounding name.

A thundering hum, iron on iron, and the Raiders cheer. I lift my head, take in the sight. Icel isn't weakening, but he pretends to an infirmity, encouraging the man closer. I shake my head. The poor fucker stands no chance. He might wear a byrnie that flashes blackly in the moonlight, greaves and even the hint of metal at shoulders and groin, but he simply doesn't have the skill, not against Icel.

We're closer now, almost close enough for Hereman to send a spear into the concaved shield wall. They can't keep a straight line, not even when that's their only purpose.

I think to shout to Hereman, but he nods when I meet his eyes over the iridescent snow. Hereman knows not to give the game away just yet.

The snow is deeper here but still glassy. It's a fucking effort to keep lifting my knees higher. I hazard we might be going slightly uphill. It might give the Raiders an advantage, but they'll need to be paying attention for that to happen.

"Attack," I roar, close enough to smell Icel. The white-haired man startles at the noise. He dies on Icel's blade with a soft whimper, mild surprise on his face. The Raiders cries of terror tell me they've miscalculated. A spear flies through the air, impaling the most alert of the men, running towards Icel, revenge written large on his broad face, no need to see his eyes clearly because it oozes from him.

"What took you?" Icel rumbles, focused on the skewered foe-man, even as we absorb him into our shield wall.

I don't respond. I'm focused on the two men before me. Edmund should take one of them, but for some reason, they're bunched too tightly here so that two men stand in the place of one. Edmund has his foe already, Hereman has his, and I, of course, have two. Fucking marvellous.

I slam my shield into that of the first of my enemy, an effort to hold him while I strike out with my seax against the other man. He labours to knock my weapon aside with his shield, and I'm forced to duck aside, rein in my seax so as not to lose it.

Not a successful attack. Far from it.

Hereman is busy with his opponent, the two of them trading blows with weapon and shield. I catch sight of Edmund, and he's fully engaged as well. Not that I mind facing two men. I shove my shield at the face of the first man again. He's probably expecting a new tactic, but sometimes repetitious is just as effective. My seax goes above the other man's shield. This time, I feel an impact. It's not the strongest of blows, but a cut on the chin, dark hair fluttering to the ground, gives my second opponent such a shock, he jerks backwards.

He overbalances with the force of the action, the ground polished. His shield rushes upwards, about to impact my face, as I rear backwards, ducking low, even as I thrust my shield upwards. The second enemy is slower with his weapon this time. By the time I see it with my peripheral sight, I'm stabbing down, finding a gap between byrnie and beard, drawing blood, but not enough because I have to thrust aside to avoid the war axe the other man flings at me.

My shield batters aside the war axe, my legs shaking beneath me. I can feel the slipperiness of the ground, the tension in my feet trying to keep me upright. The war axe is pushed away, the shield following the movement. Only then I reverse it and slam the shield boss into the face of the prone man. Eahric's wound gives me the idea, and the questing hand with his weapon, slumps to the ground, lifeless, for all, he's not dead.

My first enemy growls loudly, frustrated by the failure. Not that he has long to live to decry the second man's death. Hereman has killed his foe. Almost languidly, he slices a blade into the side of the war axe-wielding Raider. As he stills in death, I move my shield aside and cut down, slowly and with precision, to end the beating heart of the prone foe-man.

"My thanks," I call to Hereman. I get no response and blink away the sweat of my efforts to see he's now assisting Pybba. Edmund is close to finishing his enemy, face white with fury and rage. The man bleeds from a wound on his chin, his byrnie darkening as breath rattles through his throat. It's not going to be long.

It's not going to be protracted for any of these warriors. My men have made their kills or are close to it. Rudolf continues to battle. His opponent is a giant of a man, towering over my young one-time squire. I could interfere. I will intrude if needs be, but no man ever learnt to fight without fearing that each stroke might be the last he ever makes.

Pybba's enemy is down, and he stands much closer to Rudolf, war axe in hand. I know he mirrors my resolve.

Other than Rudolf, Goda and Sæbald are still fighting fiercely. Of course, the enemy they face is more than aware they're alone, and the chance to survive is much closer for them. If they can just make it to the horses, of course.

A cry rips through the air, and my gaze is drawn to the horses. Eahric stands there, chest heaving, and I'm moving without thinking.

"Fucking bastard. Never trust a man from the north of the Humber," I'm chuntering to myself, already preparing to sprint towards Eahric and whatever trouble Magnus is making, all thoughts of forgiveness and understanding fleeing my mind.

"My Lord," Hereman's bellowed words stop me, something in his voice drawing my attention away from Eahric. In a blur, I turn, appreciating that Eahric is alerting me to something behind me, not in front of me. And I peer into the distance, hand over my eyes. There's no fear in the men, or at least, I don't think there is, but by now, they perhaps welcome the fuckers dying on their blades and so don't feel any.

But that's not what it is, far from it.

The Mercians have arrived, Kyred leading his warriors towards me, and I grin, only for my joy to falter. Has he killed Jarl Halfdan already? I want that bastard for myself.

CHAPTER 20

N ot that Kyred and his warriors seem hale. The closer they come to us, the more my eyes pick out small details. One of the horses limps a little, breath blooming in the cold air with the effort, one of the warriors has a swollen eye, another a sodden linen around his face.

Fuck. They're not victorious. And Kyred's face, when he's before me, head bowed, tells me both too much and too little.

He wears no helm, his dark hair a matt of dried blood, his eyes haunted. He makes no effort to dismount. I appreciate that he can't, not without falling. A linen is wrapped around his upper thigh, his face sheeted in sweat, and yet he grins all the same—crazy bastard.

"It's good to see you," he huffs, Edmund and Icel moving to my side so that the four of us can speak in some privacy. Rudolf, showing his growing wisdom, moves among the dead enemy, his voice raised high as he and Pybba discuss their spoils for the day. Hereman joins in, although I feel his gaze on my back. He wants to know.

All of the men want to know.

I hear a roar of triumph, and Goda stands heaving, his opponent falling into the snow, the blood visible from here, as it drains into the churned white.

Kyred left Northampton with fifty men. I don't see that many now. But they aren't as diminished as they could be.

"And you," I offer. "But tell me, how bad is it?"

"It seems you've met some of Jarl Halfdan's warriors, but there are more, many more," his words are laced with fatigue, his face as white as snow, his gaze taking in Sæbald. He, too, has finished fighting, so all our enemy are dead. I can't see that they'll be the last we face.

"You've already fought them?"

"Yes, we fought through them to get to you, but it seems you've already met the advanced force."

I nod, refusing to glance around at the carnage.

"They tried to trick us by hiding beneath the snow."

"They'll try fucking anything," his words ripple with scorn.

"Are you all wounded?" I ask, noting that one of the warriors has slipped forward, threatening to tumble into the snow. Hereman has moved quickly to his side, two hands holding him upwards. Rudolf has scampered beside him as well, although he and Pybba still offer an overly loud running commentary.

"Tie him in the saddle," Edmund calls, not that they weren't already doing so.

"He can't fight tied in his saddle," Kyred complains.

"There's no more fighting for you. Not like this," I acknowledge, knowing the words will be hard to hear. "Retreat to Newark. It's not far from here, but first, tell me what you can."

For a moment, I think Kyred will argue with me, but then his face scrunches with pain, and he nods, words beyond him for the moment, hand resting on his thigh.

"Jarl Halfdan doesn't have as many ship men as we feared, but they're trying to take Gainsborough. The ealdorman is inside, we couldn't get to him to reinforce him before Halfdan, and his men moved into place. I believe they mean to take it and buttress it; hold it as a kingdom inside Mercia."

The words infuriate me but are far from unexpected.

"How many?"

"More than you, a thousand, maybe, but no more than that. Not that it's a small number. We encountered a more elite band of warriors when we tried to gain entry last night, but some of them just seem to be sitting around trying not to freeze their arses off in the fucking cold. We'd been with Bishop Burgheard in Lincoln, but I thought to sneak into Gainsborough." Kyred shivers as he speaks, and I nod, absorbing the news.

"Then we'll warm them up a bit before sending them into a fiery hell for all time." There's bluff in my words, but also a promise. A thousand men is not an insurmountable obstacle, not in weather like this, but it must be done. There's no choice.

Kyred smiles, a weak thing, and I appreciate that he's in far more pain than he's allowing me to see.

"How far is it from here?"

"Half a day, no more. You'll be on them soon enough, but you'll have to cross at Littleborough to be on the correct side of the river. We only crossed in an effort to cut off the advanced party, but I see you've managed well enough."

"Go, all of you. Protect Newark and seek assistance there. When you can, travel onwards. Get to Northampton."

"Aye, My Lord. We will, and My Lord, kill 'em all. All of them. I've had enough of the fuckers." Kyred holds me with his hollowed-out eyes, and I feel my throat grow tight.

I reach up, grip his arm, far more gently than usual, but firmly all the same.

"You have my oath on that," I assure him, and then I raise my voice a little.

"We'll kill all the bastards, I assure you. Now, my brave Mercian warriors travel safely and well. Live to fight another day." The cheer is ragged, gaunt faces seeking me out, and I grin, stretching my mouth wide, ignoring the chill that's seeped into my heart and my beard. No man who doubted himself ever won. I banish the worry. I have Raiders to kill.

I allow Magnus to leave with Kyred. He doesn't know the area, he doesn't know Jarl Halfdan, and it's just reassuring that one amongst that number will keep conscious while they travel. I'm not sure how many of the men will make it to Newark alive. I hope they all do, but whether they die or live, I'll avenge them. I'll wreak my revenge.

"Leave them," I call gruffly when Kyred and his men have trundled through the carnage of our brief skirmish, and some of my warriors are still picking over the dead. Jarl Halfdan hoped to catch me unawares. It's not going to happen. "We need to get on, not worry about the trinkets from these fuckers." My warriors are grim-faced, the exertion of this battle etched into cold faces, and yet they don't complain.

They never do.

Eahric refused to leave with Kyred, but between him Icel and Pybba, they've managed to remove his helm without damaging him further.

"Fucking hell," the oath explodes from my mouth, unbidden. "You'll scare the bastards half to death," I exclaim, catching sight of his squashed nose and bloody cheek. It looks like it should be hurting a lot, but Eahric has half a smile on his face. Where there's no sense, there's no feeling.

"Pity it's not entirely to death," Eahric complains, his voice nasally.

"Doesn't it hurt?" Rudolf asks. We're supposed to be riding one behind the other, through the path left by the Raiders and Kyred and his men. But we're not. Obviously.

"Aye, young man, it does hurt. But, it's bearable."

I roll my eyes at the words. The camaraderie of my warriors leads them to say and do all sorts of ridiculous things. I should have sent him with Kyred. I really should, but I didn't want to waste my time arguing with the stubborn fool.

I've inspected my warriors. There are more cuts and knocks, a nasty bruise blooming on Sæbald's left eye, an ugly slice across Lyfing's nose, and Hereman is wincing, clearly having aggravated his wounds taken close to Northampton, but overall, I believe my warriors are at full strength. Even Ælfgar, who insisted on coming north, is in good spirits even with his deep cut. I think he should have stayed at Northampton with Tatberht, but what do I know?

Edmund has determined on leading the group beneath the moonlight. I'm correct that there's a slight incline which the

Raiders came down. From the top of it, it's possible to see the flickering lights of what must be the camp around Gainsborough. This must be from where the smoke has been coming.

From this distance, it looks small, as though I could crush it beneath my boots. I wish I could. We've tried and been largely successful, with all kinds of misdirection when fighting the Raiders. But, the attack from beneath the snow shows me that they're learning. Have they always fought in such a way, or am I forcing the actions upon them? I should like to know, and yet it makes very little difference.

Now, I need to determine how to undermine Jarl Halfdan's efforts to bring his new attack to a premature end. And that means that there's only one actual course of action to take. No one's going to like it. Even I don't like it.

"I know what you're considering," Pybba's words are softly spoken as Brimman comes close to Haden. "It's madness, and I won't allow it."

"How will you fucking stop me?" I could curse Pybba for reading my mind.

"That doesn't matter. What matters is that I will stop you. And you know it. We don't even know where Jarl Halfdan is. How then, will you take him in man to man combat?"

"There'll be a way," I reply stubbornly. I keep looking towards the lights of Gainsborough and the camp that surrounds some of it.

"It'll be a sure way of dying," Pybba announces. I can tell he's not going to debate it with me.

"Then what would you suggest?"

"Fuck knows, but your plan won't work. Think of something else," and he turns Brimman aside. I growl beneath my breath. Bastard. Telling me my plan won't work and having nothing else to offer.

I glance at the sky, a flash of movement allowing my eyes to alight on an owl outlined against the black of the sweeping expanse of crystalline stars. I wish I could fucking fly. I'd hunt him down and land on Jarl Halfdan from behind. He'd not expect that. Not at all.

"I'll do it," Hereman brings Billy close to me. Billy's black coat shimmers as though the liquid night.

"Do what?" My tone is far from friendly, as I note the wince of pain again even while he speaks.

"Take Jarl Halfdan in one to one combat. I'll hunt him down and find him. It'll be my fucking pleasure."

"How would you do that?" I demand to know. "You're a big man, Hereman. It's not as though you can hide behind others. And, you're quite unmistakable." Hereman shrugs, reaching his hand towards his beard to crack an icicle from amongst the mass, lips tight with pain.

"I can do it," he merely repeats, his stubbornness making me smile, despite it all.

"I don't doubt that. The question isn't if you can, but how you can. We don't even know where Jarl Halfdan is. He might be surrounded by a hundred of his thousand warriors. How would you get through them?"

"Well, that would be for you to organise. I only promised to kill the fucker." Hereman's voice holds no humour, even though I turn aside, a grin on my tight lips.

"I thank you for your offer," I bow my head before him when I'm confident of not laughing. Hereman would do it. I know he would. Equally, I can't think of a single one of my warriors who wouldn't offer to do the same. We all want Jarl Halfdan dead, some more than others, admittedly, but all of us, all the same.

We just need to find a way to do it.

I consider Jarl Halfdan then. So far, he's not struck me as a charming man, not that anyone needs to be nice to bring warriors to their side. But there should be something about a war leader, some charisma that makes it impossible not to fall under his spell, to believe the outrageous claims that tumble from his lips. He has a lot of men. I can't deny that. He had many at Repton. He's recruited yet more to replace the number that died.

Some even risked their lives to rescue him from Littleborough. But why still evades me.

Is it merely the allure of his brother? I doubt anyone within Mercia, Wessex, East Anglia or Northumbria is ignorant of who Ivarr was. But Ivarr is dead, and Jarl Halfdan isn't living up to his brother's reputation. Far from it. Yet, the jarls Anwend, Oscetel and Guthrum joined with him. And now, he has the men of Northumbria sending their sons to fight in their place.

There's something about Jarl Halfdan that I fail to understand but which others notice, until, of course, they no longer do.

"What's at Gainsborough?" Rudolf asks the question. Dever's eyes are busy on the ground beneath his feet. It's getting colder, not warmer, as the night drags on. The patches that have been cleared are both easier going than virgin snow but also more dangerous.

In the places where man or beast have relieved themselves, the water has long since frozen, and who wants to slip on someone's piss? The steaming heaps of horse shit are more welcome. They're easier to see and easier to avoid, the smell overwhelming the sharp scent of winter.

"Fuck all," Edmund has brought his sourness back to my side, leaving the leading of our group to Goda. I nod in greeting, noting that Edmund hasn't removed the slashes of blood that cover his exposed skin. They flash darkly against the blue pallor of the cold. It's not an appealing look. His old eye wound is starkly illuminated, his rage evident in his posture. Jethson snorts at Haden, not an unwelcoming sound but hardly friendly. His head hangs low. Jethson has grown tired of forging a path through the snow.

"Have you been to Gainsborough?" I ask him, surprise in my voice.

"No, but I know Mercia. Gainsborough is smaller than Northampton, smaller than Grantabridge. It's hardly somewhere for which I'm keen to die." His words drip with disdain.

"Jarl Halfdan has a thing for small places," I muse. Repton might be a Mercian mausoleum, but it's tiny. Torksey was little more than a temporary camp, and now he's set his sights on Gainsborough. The only thing these places have in common is that they're all on the Trent. It's the Trent that gives Jarl Halfdan his opening into Mercia, as though the kingdom wants to be invaded.

Without his ships, Jarl Halfdan would be nothing. But of course, it's ships that Mercia doesn't have, not in great numbers, only for trading. What Mercia has is oak for building boats and horses to race to counter the Raiders.

"Jarl Halfdan is a small thing," Edmund all but spits. I hold my tongue. Edmund is entitled to his hatred. I just need to hope that he puts it aside when we face the enemy in battle. An angry Edmund might make mistakes.

"I don't think so," I eventually counter. "Without Jarl Halfdan, Mercia wouldn't be endangered. The Raiders to the south only came because King Alfred enticed them from Wessex. The Grantabridge jarls, equally, are only in Mercia because of Halfdan."

"Then," and Edmund's single eye blazes so bright I think I might burn, "we must kill Jarl Halfdan."

"I agree."

"I imagine you mean to do it?" Edmund's scorn is more potent than Pybba's prohibition.

"I do, yes."

"Then you'll die a fool, and Mercia will be broken apart, split between Jarl Halfdan and whomsoever his new allies are."

"Without Jarl Halfdan, his alliances will crumble, at least, splinter, as happened after Repton."

"Yes, they will, but how do you mean to reach a man who will stand at the back of a thousand warriors, watching and never taking part? He won't stand forward, as you would, My Lord King." Again, disparagement, but Edmund has given me an idea, and so I grin, allowing it to roll around my head while my men pass ideas back and forth, far from quiet, far from cowed by Halfdan's persistence.

I have my warriors and those that have followed me from Northampton.

Jarl Halfdan has ten times that number.

It was never going to be a fair fight, but then, I'm not known for being fucking fair.

CHAPTER 21

I'm not happy about it, but there's someone amongst our number who can and will be able to make his way to Jarl Halfdan's side without being noticed. Rudolf.

My heart almost quails when the realisation hits me as we make our way over the ford at Littleborough. The place is heavy with memories; this is where I discovered Edmund's injury and where I believed Icel dead. Even though Icel now rides in front, and Edmund is none the worse for his loss of sight, the recollections are strong. Not that the conditions could be any more different.

It's cold enough for my beard to be filled with particles of ice, for the same to have formed in Haden's tail, and for the comfort of my warm boots to be wanting.

We rode for much of the night, but I did call a halt, allowing men and beast to sleep where they could, the dubious shelter of a long-abandoned building ensuring some protection from the cold, even if it lacked a roof. I allowed fires to be lit. It's not, after all, a secret that I hunt Jarl Halfdan. He knew enough to send warriors to try and kill us on the other side of the Trent. It might surprise him that I yet live, although probably not. We've circled one another before. We both survived that.

And now, almost within sight of Gainsborough, I pull Rudolf to my side. Pybba is incandescent with rage, and others in the group are complaining as well. Why they ask, would I send the newest recruit? It seems none of them can appreciate that sending a sprightly lad, with no visible wounds to his face, hands, or body, will attract no suspicion at all. Or at least, much less than sending a one-eyed, one-handed, or giant of a monster to infiltrate Halfdan and his warriors. Not to mention those missing fingers, pieces of an ear or just those plain hobbled by old wounds that I see when I look at them, but which they've forgotten about because that's what we do.

We take our wounds, we learn from them, we heal, and then they become so much a part of us, we don't consider them anymore. We don't see them. Not unless the cold reminds us.

"You know what to do?" My voice is harsh, and he winces before swallowing heavily and then nodding.

"You know to be careful, to keep yourself safe and to come back alive?" These words are softer, as Rudolf pats Dever. "Dever won't move without you," I caution, hoping that such a check on his ambitions will stop Rudolf from being overly foolish.

"Stop worrying," but his words are pitched too high. He clears his throat, begins again, a hint of surprise in his eyes at such a reaction.

"I know what to do, and I know what not to do. I know when to take a risk and when to realise it's all pointless. But I won't let you down. You have my oath." His words are filled with conviction by the time he finishes, eyes blazing, chest heaving. He's unrecognisable from the youth he was less than half a year ago. Well, apart from his continued tendency to too many elbows and knees.

"Then you need to go," I state firmly, trying to deny my desire to hold him back, to cancel my instructions to him, to tell him it was all a big fat fucking mistake.

We've lingered during the day, although it's been painful, the combined problems of too little sleep and too much cold weighing on us all. But Rudolf needs the cover of darkness to make his way into Jarl Halfdan's camp, and my warriors need the distraction of dawn to assist them when our attack finally comes.

"Aye, My Lord," Rudolf is already standing in the snow, Dever watching him with sleepy interest. Rudolf stifles a yawn, and I'm about to open my mouth, call him back when he grins and turns to scamper away.

The snow here is well-trodden, the path to Gainsborough easy to see. Horses have passed this way, many of them, the brown hue speaking of old blood. I don't know whose. Neither can I tell how many went south and how many north. My fellow Mercians under Turhtredus haven't yet joined me, a cause for concern, but we can't wait, not because I'm impatient, but because it's too fucking cold.

The river has been sluggish, ice threatening to coat it, even where it runs high and low, the far distant pull of the Humber tugging at it, or letting it go, with little or no rhythm. Any ships' commander would know the answers to the Trent's contrary ways, but I don't. I know horses and weapons. I know the fucking Raiders. They're welcome to the perverseness of the sea, and the river, and the complications of sails and oars and other such things.

Rudolf quickly disappears inland, reminding me of his agility and youth. I turn to face Edmund, Pybba and Hereman, Icel as well. Pybba's furious, Edmund's face downturned, Hereman's faintly smiling, the promise of what's to come making him forget that I turned down his offer of assistance. Icel. Well, Icel is Icel. He's about as easy to disentangle as a ball of twine stretched and rerolled so many times it's impossible to know which end is the beginning and which the end.

"This is a fucking stupid idea," Pybba rages, turning Brimman aside, and taking Dever with him. I nod. I'm not disagreeing. Edmund grunts, returning to our small camp. There's a campfire, warm meat cooking, the hare taken by surprise and easily caught. It might only be a mouthful each, but warm food in the belly can get a man through the coldest and darkest of nights, especially with the promise of a bloody battle with the sunrise.

Icel begins to speak.

"In the reign of Wiglaf, I was no older than Rudolf. I didn't have his bravery, but I had his need to impress. I lived through it. So will he." The words are meant to sound reassuring, and they both do and don't accomplish that. I remain where I am, aware that the rest of my warriors stream away, keen to eat and sleep, to allow the horses some rest, to think their dark thoughts, to wonder at my decisions.

I thought Jarl Halfdan would send more warriors to hunt me down, but the non-appearance of the rest of the Mercians leads me to believe that he did and that they stayed to the east of the river, not the west.

I spare a thought for my missing men, hoping that Kyred has made it to Newark, that the bishops are even now sending more men, especially Burgheard of Lincoln. Soon, soon, I'll need everything to fall into place. Soon, soon, I'll leave my warriors to carry out my instructions in my absence. I know they won't let me down, even if they spit and rant while doing so.

I've sent Rudolf inland, but I scamper along the riverbank. It's bastard cold, the lure of the water almost enough to send me into its reaches. But I have things to do.

My warriors sleep, all apart from Goda, and I forced him to allow me beyond his guard and into the wilderness. He'll face the wrath of his comrades in the morning. There's nothing I can do about it. They'll realise that they would have done the same.

My Aunt would curse me for my actions, but Rudolf can't do this alone. I need to assist him, even if he doesn't know I'm there.

Haden is with the rest of the horses, Dever as well. I move on foot, the ground threatening to trip me with every step I take. It's frozen solid, even the swirls of the soil, which might typically yield beneath my boots, failing to do that. It only makes it even more difficult.

Night has long since fallen, the moon obliterated by passing clouds, only a slither showing in defiance of the ease with which it lit our path two nights since. In the distance, there's a haze over Gainsborough, flickering flames reaching into the sky, but it's the river that guides me. If I had to rely on the fires, I'd not find it. The river ensures that I do.

Rudolf's task is to infiltrate the Raiders. I could have sent

Wærwulf, but Magnus has alerted me to the very simple fact that Jarl Halfdan's force doesn't entirely comprise Raiders. There are boys, or rather young men, from north of the Humber, and Rudolf is confident and cheeky enough to pretend to what he isn't.

And my task? It's simply to ensure that Rudolf lives through this. I know Pybba, Hereman, and Icel would more than willingly have performed my self-imposed task had I asked them, but I can't risk it. No. I've sent Rudolf to do this, and it falls to me to ensure he survives.

I can hear my Aunt in my head, cursing me for my misplaced sense of honour. Our imaginary conversation keeps me alert as I scamper along the river. There are ominous sounds of ice fracturing and water gurgling. Such gives me hope that there'll be no ships on the river. I can't imagine Jarl Halfdan wanting to risk his vessels with the obstinate nature of the frozen water. It would be altogether too easy for the ships to rupture. Then, he'd have no means of escape and no means of getting deeper into Mercia unless he took horses or retreated north of the Humber.

I don't think he'll do that, not a second time.

Jarl Halfdan has returned to Mercia, and his ambitions are as rampant as last time, and more, they're riddled with the knowledge that last time, he failed when he thought to win. If he loses again, I can't see that he'll keep the loyalty of his warriors. After all, he'll have nothing with which to buy their loyalty. No leader can send men to their death when there's no treasure involved. Well. Most men can't. Again, I think of my warriors. They fight for Mercia, not for wealth and gold.

Fuck knows what motivates the Raiders if it's not pure greed.

"Fuck," I slip on the river bank, the word escaping my mouth even though I've vowed to silence. I'm too close to Gainsborough to be making such mistakes. I can't risk being discovered. Not now. Rudolf's life depends on my survival.

I run all the arguments through my head, the ones about wounds and being instantly recognisable, and appreciate my recklessness. I right myself, hesitate to ensure no one has heard me and then continue along the uneven path I'm fashioning. Perhaps, I should just walk upright, straight into the enemy camp, all this scrabbling in the dirt and ice, the snow turning to water and freezing once more, making it even more lethal, but no. Jarl Halfdan would know who I was. He wouldn't make the same mistakes again. I'm sure of it.

Eventually, I begin to hear the rumble of conversation, the dull murmur of voices trying to keep one another awake on watch duty. I pause, strain to listen to all I can. The glow of flames illuminates the space before me, but I don't want to look at it. My eyes are accustomed to the dark. I'll blind myself if I stare directly at the campfires.

Instead, I look along the stretch of the river. It runs remarkably straight here. In the distance, just about illuminated by the slither of moonlight, I can see some ships, but only one of them lies in the water. The others have been brought ashore. I try and count them. Only it's too dark until I work my way beyond them. Jarl Halfdan is very confident of his success if he's raised the ships from the water. Although, well, that single ship assures me that he'll run if needs be. It shouldn't surprise me that he's a craven bastard.

On my front, I work my way up the riverbank, eyes low, the sharp scent of cold in my nostrils. It's cold, on the ground, the snow all but ice, but at least it's not damp and sodden. That would be worse, sinking into my byrnie, trews and threatening rust for my weapons.

I've moved away from the voices. When I risk looking, the view before me is dark and uninviting. There are some shelters before me, and I have to assume that this is Gainsborough itself. Not that I can see much, but it looks to be little bigger than Repton, the promise of a deep ditch and a half-finished rampart just about visible, for all the Raiders surround it.

But, with the snow and ice, the rampart, half-built or not, is enough of a deterrent, for now. The very thing that has hampered my progress assists those inside. I imagine that Jarl Halfdan will assault the settlement as soon as the weather clears. For now, as far as I can see, he's set a camp to the north and the south of Gainsborough. I don't know if it extends to the east, but there's not one by the riverbank, other than the two voices I heard earlier, close to the ships.

Once more, I'm surprised that the Raiders are so callous of their ships. I would expect them to mount a much heavier presence there, but no doubt, they don't expect the Mercians. Not yet. If at all. Not when they've sent Kyred running.

Fuckers.

I continue my journey, boots pressed into the snow at an angle, feet flat, to drive me forward, my face barely above the covered ground. And then I reach my destination and sink into the ditch.

It's deeper than I expected, the snow reaching to the top of my thighs. In no time at all, my feet will be as cold as my face, but I pull my cloak over my head and stand, forcing my way through the snow. If someone were to come and look, it would be easy to see that something passed this way, but I'm counting on the arrogance of the Raiders. They've proved themselves remarkably bad at understanding what their eyes tell them.

And, it's not the Raiders that I want, but the Mercians.

My breathing labours, the passage through the snow even more difficult than when the Raiders stole our horses, but ahead, I can see what I want. There has to be an entrance to Gainsborough, and I need to get inside, tell Ealdorman Aldred my intentions and have him ready to assist my warriors. We're a small force, but that shouldn't stop us.

The snow in front of me abruptly shimmers, and my hand is on my frozen seax, even as I hear the huff of another's breath.

"Mercian," I hiss, my words only just visible.

"Wha?" the voice cuts off halfway through the word, a pale face emerging before me, eyes gleaming brighter than the moon.

"Fuck, get inside, quickly," I'm relieved the man recognises me, even though I don't know who he is. I follow in his wake, not that his breaking of the deep snow makes all that much difference to my labours.

"Help me," and two sets of hands reach down from the gloom to grip his arms, held above his head. He slips from the snow, and I can hear a heated debate before the same is offered to me. I emerge with a soft popping sound, face down, on ice and mud strewn ground. The idea of warmth is close by, but I'm not led to the brazier. Instead, I push back onto my knees and meet the fascinated gaze of four men.

"My Lord King?" the first stutters, horror on his face with the recognition.

"Aye, if you like. Where's the ealdorman?"

"He's, well, he's sleeping," the second offers, a cloak covering most of his face. I look around me. There's an opening between the rampart, and I'm just to the side of it. In the distance, it's as though a thousand fires blaze, a threat, not a comfort, and I swallow down my unease at what I've done.

I'm in the heart of the enemy, and I don't even have Edmund or Icel at my back.

"Wake him, and take me to him," I command, rising swiftly, although the movement costs me dear. I'm too old for this shit.

"My Lord King," the voice is filled with trepidation. I allow the man. He's shorter than I first took him to be, to lead the way. I tower over him, eyes trying to see as much as possible.

It's a small settlement, Edmund was right, but I can see that the ealdorman has plans for it. A half-built barn is covered in snow, it lacks a roof and most of two walls, but it's large, bigger than anything at Northampton. There's also a stable, fully enclosed, and from within, the usual sounds emanate, even the loud fart of one of the sleeping horses. I grin. It's good to be reminded of the mundane when all around has fallen to shit.

The building I'm taken to is about half the length of the half-built hall, but it's too dark to see a great deal. The door is opened after a hurried conversation. I feel the first blast of hot air for many days. Immediately, my skin starts to ache. Too hot, too cold. My body isn't happy either way.

The man, casting his cloak over one shoulder, rushes to a door and enters with only a cursory knock. An outraged voice greets the action, and I turn aside, smile at the door warden as we all try not to hear the altercation. There are about fifty men, and women bedded down around the heaped hearth. Some of them stir at the noise, others startle awake, hands reaching for weapons that aren't there while they sleep. I nod at them, pleased to see the number of warriors.

Ealdorman Aldred stumbles from the room, pulling his arms into a tunic. I turn and glare at him. His eyes boggle from his thin face.

"I would expect a man under siege to be more alert," I comment, ice in my voice.

"My Lord, My Lord King, what are you doing here?"

"I've come for the good company and ale," I retort, my skin crawling with frustration. He opens and closes his mouth, entirely lost for words.

"Have your warriors made ready. We've come to relieve you, and drive Jarl Halfdan back across the Humber, if not to his grave."

"How many are there, My Lord King?"

"Enough," is all I say, hoping I'm right, my thoughts with Rudolf, not with the ealdorman.

"Of course," and he bows, but I don't miss his gulp of unease. The fucker better not have done anything stupid such as forge an alliance with Jarl Halfdan, in the same vein as King Burgred, because if he has, I'm going to have to cut him down, and in the not too distant future.

It's still dark when I return to the watch post. It's been reinforced by a further five men. They bristle with weapons and the cold. There's been a swell of anticipation within the hall. The warriors there are keen to fight, far more eager than the ealdorman who's been directing them for the last few weeks. That's changed because I've arrived. I don't sit on my arse thinking about the battle. What would be the fucking point in that?

I've made it clear what I want them to do. Now it just remains to be done, as I slip back into the ditch, shivering at the touch of the snow on my body.

I know where Jarl Halfdan sleeps, thanks to the observations of the gate wardens inside Gainsborough. Now I just need to make my way to his side. And then, at my command, the warriors inside Gainsborough will surge out, just as my warriors surge inside. Provided Jarl Halfdan is dead by then, we'll win.

I know that Halfdan isn't dead yet. I don't know if that means that Rudolf is close or if he's been captured. But I'm not about to second guess myself. I have a plan in mind. I just hope it works.

I continue to follow the ditch, cloak over my head, an attempt to ensure no flame reflects from my weapons or my helm. It's even more challenging going, my limbs aching, my body cold before I even start the attempt.

I listen keenly, expecting an eruption of outrage, but nothing comes, not yet. Rudolf hasn't succeeded. But neither has he been caught. That cheers me. My thoughts turn to Edmund and Icel and the rest of my warriors. By now, my deceit will have been noticed. If I'm lucky, and my men remain loyal, they'll come all the same. If not, it must just be Rudolf and me who face the Raiders, alongside the Mercians from inside Gainsborough.

When I deem it safe enough, I slither from the ditch, more like a snake than a man. The continuing darkness should cover my movements. I hope it does. I don't wish to be skewered to the floor.

Snores fill the air, most of the warriors fast asleep, unaware that soon they'll be roused from their sleep, forced to fight in whatever they have to hand. I grin, desperate to rekindle my enjoyment in this venture, even though my neck aches with the cold, and I can feel where every stitch was written into the skin down my back. I'm too fucking old for this. I'm the king of Mercia. I should be sending men to do this. But, who am I trying to fool? I'd not let them have all the fun to themselves.

Beyond the first line of canvasses, the fabric rigid with ice, I slowly rise, first to my knees, and then to my feet, my head the last thing to come upright, allowing me to cast eyes on the Raiders finally.

I shudder. They're here with little more than fabric above their heads, the base of the tents hidden beneath the dirty snow they've traipsed through, pissed into as well if the dark hue of some of the snow is indicative. Dirty bastards.

I take one step and then another, trying to move silently, even though I can't, not with the weapons on my belt and the helm over my head. It fits perfectly, and still, it makes a noise. My cloak covers it, but that might not be enough.

"For fuck's sake," I grin then, turning to meet Icel's eyes. Damn the bastard. He wasn't supposed to follow me, but he rears up from behind me, rage on his face, fury in his tight movements. He worries I'll kill Jarl Halfdan before he gets the opportunity.

And then another head appears, and this one isn't quite as furious. In fact, a flicker of relief shows in the hollows beneath his eyes.

"Coelwulf, what are you doing here?" Rudolf emerges from behind one of the canvasses, his face so blue with cold, it's visible despite the darkness, the vestiges of dawn still some time away. The fact he calls me by my name attests to his surprise and relief.

"I," but I don't get time to answer.

"He thought to do it himself, damn bastard," Icel huffs, striding beyond me as though the need for quiet and gentle steps is long gone, as though there aren't a thousand warriors all thirsting for our blood snoring around us.

"But, I'm here," Rudolf sounds a little bereft but then brightens, coming to my side, as Icel continues onwards, his focus on the structure beneath which Halfdan must shelter. It's the largest of them, and once more, as at Torksey, benefits from being made of wood, not material.

A warrior stands on watch duty by the door, but he sways on his feet. Hardly alert.

"I was about to go in," Rudolf states, even though he's standing a step or two behind me.

"I know lad, I know. But, just on the off chance that you needed a hand, I decided to join you. The others will begin the attack soon, and the warriors from inside Gainsborough will do the same."

"And what of Icel?"

"He does what the fuck he wants, it seems." I'm keen to follow on, but even I'm aware that the three of us are making far too much noise, although Rudolf and I whisper, one to another.

"He's going the wrong way," Rudolf comments, and I don't immediately catch his words because I'm biting my lip, trying not to tackle Icel so that I can get to Jarl Halfdan first.

"What do you mean?" I turn to glare at Rudolf as his words finally register.

"Halfdan isn't in there. He's over here, in one of the other canvasses."

"Really?"

"No, My Lord, I've been lying beside it all night just for the hell of it."

"Show me," I demand, and Rudolf nods and then moves so quickly, I almost lose sight of him amongst the maze of canvasses. About now, I could do with some more light, the grey promise of dawn to streak the distant horizon, but it seems that dawn is to be delayed, today of all days.

With a glance to ensure Icel is stalking the guard ahead, I can hardly recall him to me, not with the distance so great, I follow Rudolf, sliding beneath two canvasses, gritting my teeth with the hope I won't trip over something forgotten about in the snow.

I become aware of the dull sounds of a man and a woman coupling, and I roll my eyes. If I'm going to kill a man, I'd sooner it wasn't because he'd been caught with trews around his ankles. But Rudolf stops beside the tent, a flush of heat to his pale cheeks visible in the glow from a smouldering fire in front of the shelter.

A man grunts, a woman encourages him onwards, or at least, that's what it sounds like, and then Rudolf is slipping between the two pieces of fabric, held taut over the wooden structure and before I can stop him, he's inside.

"Fuck," I didn't want him to go before me, but evidently, Rudolf has been considering how to kill Halfdan, and he's chosen to do it now. I expect there to be a roar of outrage, but there's nothing, if anything, the woman's cries grow shriller, a little more desperate. I consider that Rudolf is standing, goggle-eyed, at whatever's happening in there.

And then I hear a cry of disbelief from the wooden building, quickly followed by the unmistakable sound of two weapons clashing. Icel has begun his gruesome work, even if his intended target isn't there. It won't be long until Jarl Halfdan hears it as well.

"Hurry the fuck up," I whisper, wishing Rudolf could hear me, but of course, he can't.

I wince, listening to the growing sound of the attack, aware that Icel stands alone, that the men of Gainsborough won't join the battle, not yet, because I've not given my signal, and I don't want to, not until Halfdan's dead.

And then there's a shriek. It's worse than iron over scraping over stone, even more distressing than a pig forced to slaughter.

"*Skiderik.*" From inside the tent, there's an upwelling of activity, no doubt Halfdan staggering from whatever position he was in to his knees. I track the movement, thrust my sword through the winter-hard fabric.

"Fuck," the blade takes more effort than I'd like, the sound of ripping too loud for my ears, and yet I skewer something, the blade slipping into flesh, just as another screech of fury erupts from the wooden building. The canvass tumbles to the ground, a familiar hand reaching for the slit doorway as I reclaim my sword. I tug on Rudolf, but he holds firm as the material defies its hardness and billows and buckles.

Rudolf erupts from the doorway, blood on his face, a grin on his cold cheeks, and I'd like to think that Halfdan is dead, but I know better.

"I took the woman," Rudolf explodes, "and you killed her with your blade. She's skewered, right through her breasts, and out her back." He mimes the act as he speaks. I didn't want her dead, but it seems I miscalculated about who rode who.

254

"Hum," I didn't want her. I wanted Halfdan.

"And Halfdan?"

"Lives, for now." Rudolf indicates the canvas, but I'm aware of an upwelling of noise from all around me. We've been discovered while Halfdan still lives.

"Set something ablaze," I instruct Rudolf. "Make it big, and make it quick, or the others won't come."

He pauses, and I shove him away because something is emerging from the doorway, and that something is mine to fucking kill.

CHAPTER 22

I give him time to get to his feet from the ground but not time to pull his trews up, and his manhood stands proud and unsatisfied. It's too much of a target, as his naked flesh ripples with the etchings that mark him as the wolf-lord.

With ease, I rush him, giving him no time to realise the enemy isn't the same one who just interrupted his fun. But somehow, he has a blade to hand, an evil glint in his eye, as he counters my downward thrust, even if he's forced to jump back onto the fallen tent to do so.

"Fucker," I expel, aware that someone is loudly thumping a shield with a war axe, and the groans of sleeping men and women mean they won't be for much longer.

I need Halfdan dead and quickly.

"Who are you?" Jarl Halfdan grumbles, thrusting forward with his seax in an effort to draw blood while I'm assessing my next attack.

"Your death," I offer, admitting it sounds dramatic. Behind me, flames leap high into the greying horizon, and I hear, from far away, the answering call of my warriors. I know it can't be the Raiders because they're still not fully alert to what's happening.

I also sight the Mercian warriors emerging from Gainsborough in the growing light. Perhaps, this will work, after all.

I sidestep the feeble attack, slashing high with my seax, distracting Halfdan so that it's almost too easy to reverse my grip, stab downwards and sever half of his cock.

His shriek of agony sounds from far away as I watch his flesh tumble to the floor, immediately lost amongst the mess of the canvass and the discarded items that spill from inside to outside.

Halfdan thunders to his knees, hand around his bleeding loss. I aim for his neck, eager to have this over and done. The movement is quick, slick, and he follows his knees to the floor, pale flesh outlined by the growing pool of red.

"We need to get to Icel," I order Rudolf, even as he looks over my shoulder and down at the mess of the man.

"Is he dead?" Rudolf asks breathlessly, and I nod.

"He's not going to live through that," I point down at the wounds and growing pool of blood.

Surveying the scene, I appreciate that even with Halfdan dead, these warriors won't know that, not while the light remains so poor. Even if we thrust his weeping body at them, they'll not know who it was.

But, it's not easy to get to Icel. Not now some of the Raiders are alert to the infestation. The yells coming from Gainsborough and my warriors are hardly quiet, and indeed, Rudolf isn't alone in forcing the sporadic fires into greater life. Flashes of flame roar upwards, making it hard to see, the light blinding after so much darkness.

A hand grabs my boot, and I stab down without a thought, a bellow of agony assuring me that I've hit my target. In front of me, Rudolf stumbles and goes down with his seax in one hand, war axe in the other, chunks of flesh flying through the air.

A man runs screaming at me, shield in one hand, war axe in the other, although he wears no boots even though the ground is frozen rigid. Rudolf quickly moves to stab down, skewering his foot so that when the warrior runs on, unable to stop his momentum, he leaves behind more of his foot than can keep him upright. Rudolf grimaces, accepting his seax is gone, for now, as he leaps high and lands on the falling man's back.

Rudolf hacks down into his chest, yet more blood and clots of flesh flying through the air, landing in a sick mockery of heavy snow around us, staining the already polluted crispness. War is a fucking dirty business.

More and more of the Raiders are advancing, attempting to surround us, even as the thunder of shields on shields assures me that the Gainsborough warriors are quick to erupt from behind the makeshift ditch and rampart. I must assume my men will be doing the same from the other side of the camp. They've never let me down before. They sure as fuck better not start now.

I take my next foe across his exposed middle, the flesh ripping open with the lightest of touches. He screams his rage, square face furious and bulbous, as his war axe thinks to take my right ear. I duck aside, miss the weapon, forcing my seax deeper and deeper into his slit belly. He shudders to a stop, and I spit aside gore that bubbles from his mouth. I dispassionately note that it lands on his slackening face.

Rudolf is batting aside the next to come at us. His movements are so fast, it's a blur. The only way I can follow his blades is to witness the wounds appearing on those he fights. A thin man tumbles aside, an axe cleaved between his legs, a smaller man ducks low but still rears up with a seax thrust through his nose.

I punch a warrior aside who thinks to take Rudolf from behind, bringing an end to his heroics. I thump into his back, stunning his actions, and he turns, breath rattling, and it's almost too easy to slit his throat.

Rudolf fights on, but his actions are earning him more and more attention. I rush in close, keen to ensure no one else tries to interrupt him by attacking from the back.

"Behind you," I huff, aware my words are laboured. It's hard work over the slippery surface. It's fucking deadly, having roused a swarm of bees from their slumbers.

"Aye, My Lord, I won't slice you," Rudolf offers. His voice is suddenly deeper, and I smirk. Damn the bastard. He's enjoying this.

Turning so that we fight back to back, I thrust aside both a sword with my seax and a shield with my war axe. The shield overbalances the man, and just to finish him off, I apply a firm kick to his backside. He lands on the ice, hands put down to prevent his face from crashing into the ground, slipping to either side. Blood erupts, and I quirk an eyebrow.

"It's fucking easier when you do it to yourself," I comment, elbow high to fend off the next foe-man. He ducks aside from the movement, a spear in his hand, allowing him to keep his distance. The sword wielder comes in close. I eye him, time the action, and bend to steal the discarded shield from the man still floundering on the floor. It counters the sword, and then the spear, and then I use it as well, aiming for another nose, but instead crashing into a neck, or so the gasping sounds alerts me.

Another one down, but behind, there are more and more rampaging bastards, and there's only Rudolf and me.

I take a steadying breath, steal my resolve for what's going to be a long and bloody battle. There's no easy way out of this.

I could berate myself for being a fool, but that would be a waste of my thought process.

Instead, I stab outwards with my seax, thrusting it up into an armpit, the scent of an overripe body making my head swim.

"Filthy bastard," and I finish the job with the shield. I feel him fall, but I don't see it because the man with the spear is back. Damn bastard is persistent, but then, men with a long piece of wood between them and a seax tend to be.

Next time it comes close, I slice upwards, trying to sever the spearhead from the piece of wood and almost succeeding. It dangles, half attached, and with my shield, I punch the rest aside.

"Now, let's see what you can do with that," I eye the spearless spear. "I might get a nasty splinter," I allow, moving my neck from side to side, eager to dispel some of the tightness there, ignoring the sharp scratch of my old wound. It's been too cold for too long, and my muscles remain cool and not blazing hot. I'm going to hurt tomorrow. That's a certainty.

But, the man is mown down before my eyes, another warrior using him as a means of gaining greater height, his sword dangling in his hands.

"Move forward," I roar at Rudolf, stepping backwards and hoping he has the wits about him to understand my instruction. The

Raider misses me, his blond hair hallowed in red from the fire, so it appears he emerges from hell. He lands so heavily on the hard ground, I hear his bones creak, and then, he slips, sprawled out on the ground beneath me. I sigh, reaching for the spear-less spear. I'm not wasting good metal on this daft fucker. Even without the shaft, the wood easily pierces below his ear, and another one is dead.

I cast my eyes around. Rudolf and I are gathering quite the horde of the dead, and I've also caught sight of the Gainsborough Mercians battling through the fray. I hope they've left enough to ensure Gainsborough remains intact. I wouldn't want to win the battle just to find the Raiders have succeeded where they've failed so far.

I don't want to have to fight my way in when it should be easy to keep the bastards out.

But, I don't see Icel, and neither do I see the rest of my warriors.

"We need to get to the building," I call to Rudolf.

"What do you think I'm trying to do," he explodes, his words more powerful than some of the attacks being made against us.

The Raiders are sleep-addled, some half-naked, although why they'd strip off in this bastard weather, I've no idea. If my muscles are frozen, then theirs are unresponsive. Time and time again, I thrust into a weak attack, noting the surprise on the face of the dying man.

Jarl Halfdan, damn the bastard, has brought men to their deaths. He's forced a battle in the depths of winter, with snow lying thickly on the ground and his men too cold to fight for their lives.

"My Lord?"

"What?" I huff, forcing another seax aside with the borrowed shield.

"I can see Icel." I lick my lips, tasting the salt of my exertions and only the hint of ice. I test the two Raiders considering attacking me and deciding there's time yet, turn to see what Rudolf has seen.

Icel has been set upon by just as many Raiders as Rudolf and me. He stands with his back to the half-destroyed building, his war axe in one hand, shield in the other, and he simply scythes down those who think to attack him. He looks to be in no danger, none at all, but no man can keep up such an attack. Sooner or later, he'll lose all power in his arms, and then he'll be easy picking.

"Lead us there," I order, meeting the thrust of a sword by moving aside, knocking the Raiders arm downwards so that the sword does nothing but bounce off the frozen ground. Not even the amount of blood, sweat and piss can thaw the bastard snow.

"What do you think I'm fucking doing," Rudolf roars once more, and I chuckle, meeting the second foe's attack with the force of my helmed skull against the softness of his face. I don't quite get his nose, but blood pools from where teeth used to be.

He howls, there's no other word for it, and comes at me quicker this time, colossal war axe in hand, swinging it from side to side as though that's the way to tackle me. He broadcasts his attack so clearly that I almost grow tired, waiting for the eventual slash. I cut down, sever his forearm, thrust him aside. I feel the space behind me and step back into it. Rudolf and I can't become separated, not now we have so many of the Raiders trying to kill us.

I'm busy with the shield. The weapon of choice might be one that cuts and slices, but there's nothing like a shield for sheer brutality. I lose count of the number of faces I thrust the shield boss into, the number of men who stagger away, unable to see, tears in their eyes, teetering into their comrades, slipping on the ice, so that both go down for every single one of my strikes.

Sweat pools down my back, drips into my eyes from my drenched hair, but my breathing stays even, my movements effortless, and for the first time all day, my feet feel fucking warm.

Rudolf moves slowly but surely towards Icel, cleaving a path through abandoned canvasses and the rapidly growing pile of bodies. Not that it stops the Raiders. They're no better than cows maddened by the summer flies. They come at us both, thinking only of our deaths, but it's they that end up cut and bleeding, breaths rasping through chests scoured with blades.

And then, almost within touching sight of Icel, I finally face a foe who's taken the time to dress and arm himself.

The man is tall but not as tall as I am, his face elongated beneath the blackened helm that covers his head. No hair shows beneath it, and I think him bald or shaved, no hint of a beard on a pointy chin. Damn, he could cut without the need for a blade.

His eyes are cold and flat beneath the nose guard and the rest of the helm, and he doesn't play with his weapons, testing them for balance or weight. This man is a true warrior.

Arms flashing in the growing grey light of dawn, he comes at me with two seaxs, one held in either hand. They look deadly, sharpened to a slim point. I don't think I've ever seen anything like them before. The fact that those Raiders thinking of attacking me step aside to allow this man to come at me, tells me the others respect him.

A man with a reputation. I might allow Edmund to add a verse to his scop's song when I kill this one.

I spit the taste of blood and sweat from my mouth, eyes narrowing as I consider my next move. Rudolf moves in behind me, and I step back, the feeling of his absence telling me all I need to know.

The Raider nods at me, almost as though two equals meeting. Is he a man of honour? I doubt it. None of the Raiders is honourable. They're all just hungry and desperate to win battle renown. I'm not about to add to this warrior's reputation, but he might add to mine.

And still, he doesn't attack. I notice his boots are layered with fur, a man who like to keep his feet warm, and then I menace forwards. He wants to lead the altercation. That much is clear. He wants to be the one to decide when our weapons will clash first and where they might clash.

Fuck that.

Reaching for my weapons belt, I flick a small eating knife

into my hand, throwing it directly at his face. I know it won't cause an injury, but the warrior steps back, avoiding the missile. Fury kindles in his cold eyes. I've got him. He approaches me then, and that's good. I can't rush him; that would leave Rudolf exposed.

Both seaxs flash, but I don't even watch them, focusing only on the man. His eyes tell me where he means to attack. I duck aside from his two-handed attack; shield raised high to ensure the blades don't take Rudolf in the back.

I expect to hear the jingle of iron falling to the hard earth, but I don't. I lower the shield just enough and meet his expectant eyes. They're even warmer now, his lips held tightly together. But, still, he thinks to beat me.

"Fuck this," I explode, the space between us so small that I can smell whatever he ate last and its rank, like the breath of a boar. My seax stabs upwards, aiming for his chin. Still, he moves aside, feet lithe over the ground, and he stays upright by resting on one of the groaning bodies, a loud fart filling the air as the stomach empties with a foul aroma, another shade of brown appearing on the churned snow.

I'm careful where I step, aware that there are bodies and abandoned weapons all over the place. But, just on the off-chance, I fake a loss of balance, and the Raider is on me immediately, left hand, right hand, left hand, both seaxs trying to batter aside my shield and byrnie.

I feel the coldness of the weapons, but nothing more, because they might look sharp and deadly, but they're weaker because of that. No weapon so slim is good for anything but piercing, and he's not about to pierce me.

The shield crashes with his hand, the left hand fumbling the blade so that it falls to the floor. Not that it concerns him, he reaches for another from his weapons belt. There's at least four of them on there—a strange weapon of choice. Perhaps the man is an assassin, more used to killing his foe when he sleeps than when raging against him.

Those Raiders who've stepped back, keen to see what the man

can do, share uneasy glances, and I consider whether this is all some sort of trick. Do they hope to distract me with the sharpened seaxs and then attack me with a spear or war axe?

The shield is before me, protecting as much of my body as possible, but my eyes are cast downwards, looking at my boots. The sharpened seax has landed not far from my right foot. I lift my foot, grip the weapon beneath it, and pull it closer, an idea forming in my mind, even as I have to counter another flashing attack with seax and shield.

The rush of air from my enemy's weapons conveys his intentions to me, and when Rudolf steps forward once more, I risk bending low, knowing that the bastard won't get lucky and skewer Rudolf instead of me. Then the sharp blade is in my hand, and flying through the air, a projectile, just like a spear, only much smaller, and it easily pierces his chin, holding him there, while blood pools and drips to the floor, sizzling when it hits the ice-hardened ground.

"Stupid bastard," I complain, surveying my work, meeting the Raiders eyes. They still blaze, only now with confusion. I move into the space Rudolf's created, almost slipping on someone's entrails, and the two seax wielding warrior falls to the ground, headlong, body extended, as though he's been felled from behind.

I shake my head, turn to the next warrior, but they're backing away, the three men, eyes wild with whatever's happening behind me, and I shrug. It can only mean one thing.

Icel is now part of our attacking force.

I'd not want to face the bastard in a battle, and I'm Coelwulf, King of Mercia, and quite handy with seax and sword, even if I do say so myself.

CHAPTER 23

"**F**ucking bollocks," Rudolf's words assure me that I'm right. They're edged with amazement, and from someone who's just fought as he has, it reinforces the fact that Icel is a monster with a sword and seax.

I've been worried that some part of him is missing, but not anymore. I risk turning my back on the enemy, allow myself to take in the scene.

Icel, decorated with the blood of his enemy, is dealing death as though he were merely counting sheep into the pen.

His endeavours are effortless. For all I think he moves more slowly than in the past; it's still too quickly for the enemy to correctly interpret what he's going to do. Screams and shrieks fill the air from those unfortunate enough not to have backed away. Space opens up behind Rudolf and me, the Raiders taking slow and careful steps before racing away. They run in all directions, left, right, towards the river, towards Gainsborough, and more than half of them slip and slide on the ice and blood already showing our path to this moment.

With the dawn a myriad hue of violet and mauve, it's becoming easier to see, which accounts for the fuckers who run away. I watch and then hear the renewed sound of clashes. Good, the Gainsborough Mercians are not shy in ending the battle.

Not that everyone runs.

"Watch your back," I instruct Rudolf, and he twists, weapon already raised, edge glinting with more than just the threat of death, tufts of hair and chunks of blood marring it. His foe is an older man, heavier, taller, slower. He'll inevitably crumble to the floor.

But Icel is still battling, and he might become overwhelmed, and so, with Rudolf at my back this time, I join the fray. The Raiders who face Icel are armed and protected, byrnies and boots on their feet. I take them to be Jarl Halfdan's special guards. I wish I could parade the dead body before them, but they believe their lord is inside the wooden structure, and between it and them is Icel.

I use my seax differently now, slicing, not stabbing, opening up byrnies where I can and where I can't, aiming for unprotected lower legs. A man who can't stand, can't fight. Not well, he can't.

I don't kill all of the Raiders. There's not the time. Better to hamper them now and get to Icel's side so that we can despatch them once we're together. I can't see beyond the structure, so I don't yet know if my warriors fight to get to me, but I assume they do.

"I can't find him," Icel calls to me, his words barely spoken above his normal voice, even as he beats aside one warrior with his war axe and then another with his seax, leaving them both mewing like babies.

"He's dead," I reply, reaching down to slice open the inviting skin above a booted foot. The man howls, and I mean howls, before rearing up at me, fury in his eyes. I shrug my shoulders, and he screams, finding strength from somewhere to lunge at me, full-bodied. It must hurt like fuck, but all he accomplishes is to impale himself on my seax, the blade visible through his neck.

"Fuck," I complain, the weight dragging at my arm until I lower my hand, and the body slips to the ground.

"How do you know?" Icel isn't happy.

"Rudolf found him fucking in one of the tents. We killed him there." Silence greets my words for all of the time it takes to swallow, but then the Raiders must realise what we say, and a voice rumbles from behind us.

"That wasn't me," and I face my enemy, Jarl Halfdan, as he

appears from out of the gloom, byrnie gleaming, hair slick, the wolf tattoos visible on his arms. He looks shockingly familiar to the man that Rudolf and I just cut down, but this is the man who's evaded me so many times in the past.

Halfdan calls something in Danish, and a wave of warriors appear from behind him. These men are armed to the teeth. Byrnies flash as though polished, helms are blackened, and well-fitting and they all have no problem traversing over the snow.

"You killed my brother's men, but they were hardly warriors of great renown." Jarl Halfdan speaks my tongue, and that infuriates, even as I accept he's not dead, and I still have to kill him.

He has at least sixty warriors surrounding us, while the Gainsborough Mercians are busy with the enemy that try to flee. My warriors are still not in sight, and this can only mean that Rudolf, Icel and myself must kill twenty men each before we even get to Jarl Halfdan.

I've faced worse odds. The challenge doesn't dismay me. How can it when Halfdan smirks at me, his face wrinkled and cold, as though he's won already? Will the bastard never learn?

"Well, if you've got some warriors that might be worth our efforts, bring them on," I retort, heart steady in my chest. Rudolf nods along, Icel steadying his posture, just waiting for one of the men to launch themselves at us.

Halfdan joins them, stepping into the group as they make way for him. He's dressed for battle, his black helm firmly wedged on his head, his hands resting lightly on his weapons belt.

"I'll kill you and take Mercia," Jarl Halfdan vows menacingly, his eyes holding mine.

"You can fucking try, but you've not had the most success, now, have you?" I taunt, enjoying the ripple of fury over his face, hoping the jibe will infuriate, make him keen to prove his worth, and that I'll be able to face him before the rest of his men.

I'll kill twenty Raiders to get to him, but it'll be just as sweet to end his life now.

Beside me, Icel stands firm, his still body belying the lethal nature of his attack when it comes.

"Come now, King Coelwulf, isn't it? You can hardly think to ridicule a man such as I into battle. Why would I fight when I have all these to do it for me?" Only his words are cut off by a black spear, landing just in front of him, so tight to his face that the end twangs into his nose as he moves forward.

I know what that means, and Halfdan glances at the missile as though disbelieving it's truly there. My cheeks lift in half a smile.

"Come, Jarl Halfdan, fight me now, and your men can leave here when you're dead and return to whatever god-forsaken hole from which they crawled."

Halfdan's moves to wrench the spear from the ground, but it's held tight, and he's forced to abandon the attempt, kicking it as he stands so that it only fucking hits him in the face again.

He steps back, his men doing the same, their faces perplexed. Behind the black helms, the nose guards splitting a man's face so that it's hard to focus on the pair of eyes, I see some unease. These men don't want to die, not today. Some of them would happily allow their leader to take a chance instead of themselves.

Another spear lands in front of Halfdan, the sound almost a shriek as it thuds into the ground. Fury coalesces on Halfdan's face, and I know what he's going to do, even before he raises his hand.

"*Angreb,*" he calls, as he merges once more into the row of men, disappearing before I can rush at him.

"Gutless bastard," Icel rumbles, and then another spear hits its target. The man looks from the wood sticking from his chest to his hands, suddenly covered in blood, horror on his round face, blood dripping into his black beard. Poor bastard. At least it'll be over quickly for him.

I can hear the disorderly arrival of my warriors from behind, and I quirk an eyebrow, lick my lips.

"Which one of you bastards wants to go first?" I call, and then as one, Icel, Rudolf, and the remainder of my men, crash into Jarl Halfdan's elite warriors.

We meet as though two waves vying for the same space, some tumbling over the top of others, others being entirely engulfed.

The first warrior I face carries a shield and seax, but he has no time to aim a strike before I barrel into him, and he lands heavily on the floor, both falling from hands as his elbows jar on the hard surface.

I stand over him, giving him half a chance, but when acceptance enters his eyes, I stab down through his heart, feeling it judder and halt.

"Where the fuck have you been?" Edmund is beside me, his white face twisted with rage. No doubt he's seen that Jarl Halfdan has left his warriors to fight.

"Fighting," I exhale, turning my back on him to shove my shield into the next warrior. The man is squat, reaching only just above my waist, and that makes it more challenging to unsettle his balance with the shield wedged against him.

His weapon, black-tipped, seeks out my seax arm, and I turn aside, allowing Edmund to stab into his chest before he can have more success.

Edmund's chest hardly rises and falls, as though he does this more easily than simply breath.

"My thanks," I call, but he's not listening. I can tell just from his stance that his thoughts are far away. Edmund wants to kill Jarl Halfdan, as do I. As does Icel. We might come to blows yet about who gets to make the killing blow. I thought I'd done it. Damn that fucker who looked so like Halfdan. Damn him to wherever the Raiders go after death.

Hereman fights beside me. He jabs with another spear, I think perhaps the one he's retrieved from the ground, and with the extra reach, the Raider he faces stands no chance. None at all.

"*Skiderik*," is spat into my face, and I rear backwards, the stench of bad teeth and rotten ale too much for me to take.

"Fuck off," I reply, shield in his face, knocking the blackened stumps of his teeth to the ground. The bastard doesn't even notice. No sense, no pain.

I thrust the shield again, this time aiming for his neck, but he's a clever fuck, and skips beneath the sharp movement, coming up, seax aimed at my stabbing arm. His eyes glint, the growing light making it appear as though he burns from within.

And he's good. I feel the sharp sting of the blow.

"Bastard," and I swivel, shove my arse into his groin and rear back with my head. This time I get his nose, and he staggers. Allowing my momentum to take me, the shield impacts his chest, and now he can't breathe even though he still stands, a look of triumph in his eyes for drawing my blood.

"Tell whoever the fuck needs to know when you're dead," I call, slicing into the area beneath his shoulder, the rapid stream of blood assuring me that he'll be dead soon enough. "Let's hope they have songs of who killed you where you're going," I finish, dismissing him even though he still stands.

The Raiders who faced us are better at this task than the initial group of warriors, but still, we're cleaving through them easily enough, so where the fuck is Jarl Halfdan? Has the bastard run, tail between his legs again, hoping for a ship to save him? He better not have done. I'll not miss the chance to kill him this time.

But I don't have time to look. Not yet. I eye the next target. He's been standing just to the rear of the rest of the men, perhaps uncertain about what to do, but more than likely, just too fucking scared to do anything.

There's a world of difference between sparing and facing twenty raging Mercians in full flow. I doubt he's ever seen the like.

It could be easy to kill him, but suddenly he straightens, as though someone else has pulled him tight, elongating every muscle, and he meets my eyes. Fuck me. It's as though I face death itself. I've fought dead eyes, black eyes, lifeless eyes, but these seem to absorb what little sun there is, and he growls at me, one cheek raised, teeth on display. Is he a man or a beast? Have the Raiders forged the skill to turn wolves into men, and vice versa.

I acknowledge the intent in that look, and he runs at me.

His steps are light, his knees almost hitting his elbows, bent upwards, weapon in hand, and I imagine he'll slip any moment now. I don't know if I want him to or not. I might like to kill such as him.

And of course, he doesn't slip, instead jumping from prone body to prone body, finding height with every leap. I know what he plans. I've done it myself. It's not a terrible tactic. Well, it wouldn't be if he faced anyone other than me.

I hold my ground; easier to make him think he's got a chance than have him veer aside. At the last possible moment, I sprint sideways, feet firmly planted so that I don't fall, and the Raider sails overhead, my body held low, too far for his weapons to make any impact.

The passage of his air ruffles my beard, the scent of him making me wrinkle my nose, and he lands, or rather tumbles. By mischance, he misses the seeping body waiting for his feet and instead, his eyes spiral widely, trying to stay upright, and I hear Hereman chuckle.

He looks funny as fuck; that can't be denied.

"You showed such promise," I offer, moving almost languidly to slice across his exposed back. Sometimes they make it too easy.

Rudolf will enjoy pilfering his wealth, that's for sure.

With Hereman watching me, I appraise the battle. My warriors hold the upper hand, but something's not quite right.

"What's Icel doing?" I ask, expecting no response. Icel is engaged in a fierce attack. I'd expect him to win easily, his movements so fast, but no matter how often he jabs and thrusts with his seax and war axe, his enemy isn't giving any ground. I'm not the only one to notice.

"Who is it?" I furrow my brow, moving around Edmund so that I can get a better look. Rudolf is already standing there, mouth open as he watches, running his fingers over his seax blade and removing clumps of hair and flesh without seeming to notice.

"Who's that?" but suddenly, I know.

"Damn the fucker," Jarl Halfdan hasn't run. Far from it, in fact. No, he's decided to counter my attack with one of his own, against Icel. Icel, usually so cool and calm, fights with barely suppressed rage. He hungers for Halfdan's death. How Halfdan knows that I have no idea, but it's a powerful weapon.

And now, as I watch, and more and more of my warriors cease their endeavours to do the same, I finally understand why Jarl Halfdan can bring such men to his side.

"He fights like you," Rudolf breaths, the words escaping his mouth unbidden.

"Aye lad, he does," Pybba agrees reluctantly.

"Then I must be the one to counter him," I assert, pleased to have that as my excuse for interfering. If you can call it interfering when I intend to save Icel, because one's things for sure, he's failing, growing tired. While Jarl Halfdan has a rapidly shrinking group of warriors as his comrades, they're still there, determined to take advantage of Mercia's weakness, but today, Mercia can't be fucking weak.

CHAPTER 24

Icel is forced down on one knee when he overextends his right arm, almost losing his balance on the slick surface. Grounded, Jarl Halfdan darts forward, stabbing ferociously. I expect Icel to counter it, but he must carry a wound because his movements are too slow. Halfdan lifts a bloodied blade, a smile of pleasure on his ugly face.

"Don't you fucking dare," I bellow, my voice so loud it resounds like thunder, distracting Halfdan, my intention all along.

Icel has the time to recover himself, staggering upwards, while Halfdan faces me, a look of displeasure on his face. I can see his tactic now. He means to deprive me of my warriors, one by one, isolating me, making me weak. It's good he started with Icel. Only, it seems he hasn't.

Inserting myself between Icel and Jarl Halfdan, I realise that another warrior is sprawled on the floor, the back of his head far too familiar to me. He better live; that's all I have the time to think before Halfdan begins his attack.

I thought him too spineless to face me one to one. That's not the case.

Halfdan's movements are supple and fluid. He moves with the ease of a much younger man, but one assured of success.

He carries a seax and a war axe, although there's a sword available to him as well, the handle visible above his black helm, held tightly to his back. I thought my last kill had the eyes of death. Halfdan has the eyes of a confident warrior, knowing, watchful, eager. They promise death, and that's an entirely different proposition.

Icel has been helped by Hereman to one side, Sæbald to the other, but he's not happy about it.

"He's mine, My Lord. He's fucking mine," he rants. It's not like Icel to be so bloody stubborn.

Halfdan and I both menace with our seaxs. I feel the double eagle-head against the hardness of my gloves. His seax, I note, carries the emblem of the wolf, cold blue eyes peering from the handle.

And then we spring at one another, his seax goes high, mine low, and yet we both move aside, avoiding the cuts for now.

I follow up with a similar swipe low, and he goes low as well this time. Our seaxs clash, shimmering sunlight striking at just the right moment to make it appear that sparks fly. I smell his sweat, as close as we are, and I feel his strength. It matches mine for now.

Face to face, I trace the line of his jaw, just visible beneath a beard adorned with trinkets, so many of them they clack together as his head shudders with the effort of keeping me at bay.

In my other hand, I hold my war axe, and I'd like nothing more than to swing it at his head, but all of my strength is centred on my seax. Whoever gives first will be the weaker of us. It's not going to be me.

He's muttering to himself, his words unknown to me, either a chant or something else. Perhaps he calls on something other than himself in assistance. I wouldn't be surprised. I trust in my skill, my strength, my ability, and if that's ever failed me, which it hasn't, I know my warriors will step in. They rescued me when I was outside Northampton. They saved me from the woodlands. They will always rescue me. I doubt Jarl Halfdan has the same assurance.

The fighting all around us has ground to a stop, an uneasy truce. After all, why would men risk their lives when there might be no need to in but a few moments?

I eye his sword, peering at me from over his shoulder. The

mocking wolf face earns a wry smirk from my straining face. I could take it right now. I could kill the fucker with his blade.

I feel his stance start to falter, the strain on his face causing spittle to fly with his chanting, and I hold, pressing that little bit harder, aware I've not given everything, not yet.

And he breaks aside, panting heavily, his eyes showing fury as he skips backwards. I don't give him the time he needs to recover. He wouldn't offer me the same.

I launch myself at him, only realising by the flash of relief on his face that this is what he wants me to do. My war axe swings wide. I thrust it to clash against his right side. His byrnie holds, for now, but he loses balance. Halfdan might think to play with me, pretending to weakness when he's strong, but a particular blow will always show the truth of the matter.

Now that I've considered his sword, I want it. I want to feel the weight in my hand and delight in slicing through his chest with it, or across his throat, or preferably, right through the fucker's skull.

His seax stabs out at me. I force it aside with my war axe, swiping it across my body to do so. At the same time, I slash with my seax, first blood welling on a section of his beard shorn away by the stroke. A yelp of outrage disturbs his chanting, and again, he darts away from me, feet light, even if he's using up all of his resources to stay alive.

Icel seethes from behind me.

"Take him, take him now, kill the fucker, use your seax, across his neck, don't just give the bastard a shave," and I roll my eyes.

"Shut the fuck up," Edmund menaces, but actually, Icel is doing some of my work for me, even while he struggles to catch his breath and regain his equilibrium. I can tell that Halfdan expects me to carry out Icel's instructions. So, all I need to do is the opposite.

"His belly, slice open his belly." So I aim for his seax arm, again, a welter of blood showing where he thinks to wear no protection but his wolf tattoos. I blind the animal.

"His thigh, stab into it." So I jab upwards, aiming for the area below his armpit. I miss it, but a flicker of consternation passes Halfdan's face. Will he be warier now?

"His neck."

I slash down with my seax, cutting through the thick leather that protects his calves, leaving part of it flapping as he dances from my path.

The Raiders are sullen in their encouragement to their jarl. Again, the words rumble from them, perhaps a battle incantation, and I appreciate that they're creating a rhythm to guide Halfdan's blows.

He aims for my face, no doubt keen to repay the assault on his chin. I swerve the attack, offering my elbow as payment.

Halfdan's face is growing steadily pinker, finally warming up after days of cold temperatures. His body is growing more limber, his actions more fluid. Yet, blood drips from his chin, landing on the churned snow, our passage spreading it far and wide.

It looks as though I've slaughtered a pig and not just given someone an overly close shave.

"Take his right hand," Icel instructs, the fury still in his voice at being withheld from the attack, but I appreciate the lessening of tension. He exactly knows what's happening.

I slash at Halfdan's left leg, opening up a lesion above his knee. The blow doesn't quite strike true, or he'd be fighting with a broken knee.

Fuck.

While I'm low, his war axe passes over my head, a soft ding showing his aim was almost accurate, although my helm stays firm. I need to be careful. He might be growing weaker, but Halfdan is also starting to read my intentions better.

I rush into him, war axe angled at his chest, his eyes reflecting rage, his chest rising and falling. He attempts to evade the action but tangles his legs before slipping in the growing mass of blood on the ground. He bleeds from two places now. Neither a mortal wound, but I'm just beginning.

And then his seax slicks into my lower arm, just above where I hold my war axe, and a hot spike surges up my arm. He's drawn blood, although he doesn't know that because my glove absorbs the tell-tale sign, and I don't react, even though a lesser man might.

But, he does sense something because he comes at me, seax flashing, war axe looming, a flurry of strikes against me, although not one of them makes it beyond my guard.

Damn the fucker. He has the upper hand. For now.

I dodge and slash, turning, swirling, ducking low, rearing back, mindful of my steps on the slick ground, aware that Icel still hollers but that I can't hear his words, not while my ears rush with the thrill of trying to elude Halfdan.

Seax arm up, war axe arm low, I keep up with his speeding attack, and then I get lucky, another slick on his chin, and more of his trinkets tumble to the ground, crushed beneath my feet. He bleeds more; this cut deeper, revealing the promise of bone. I sense his wrath and annoyance, but most of all, his pain.

I follow up with a mighty blow against his right side with the war axe, but it only skitters over his byrnie. I'm forced to tense my arm to bring the action back under my control.

Halfdan senses an opening, and he shoves his war axe against my seax arm, and the handle hits home, my hand fleeing open because he's managed to hit, somehow, that part of my arm that tingles, that brings about an uncontrollable response. My seax thumps to the floor, and I finally hear Icel's words instead of just his noise.

"Shoulder, back, shoulder, neck," Icel's not the only one to be shouting. I detect Rudolf's higher tones, and I slash downwards, aiming for ankle and foot. Only Halfdan is too fast, and he jumps clear, turning the movement into an advance, his seax running down my bent back, even though it doesn't pierce the leather.

Instead of rushing to stand upright, I swing my war axe again, eyes focused on where my seax has surely tumbled, but I don't see it, although my weapon digs into Halfdan's flesh once more. But it's still a glancing blow. I'm starting to think he wears some sort of protective equipment designed to evade all but the most direct of impacts.

When I stand upright, his seax is almost on my nose. He's standing too close as well. I'm thankful for my helm, then. I twist my neck, bring up my seaxless hand, and bang the seax aside. The weapon cuts deeper this time, forcing the earlier cut deeper and wider, but the blood still doesn't show.

"Bastard," I offer. He has two weapons, and I only have one.

"Hold," Icel calls, and I take his advice, rushing Halfdan, war axe swirling, fist punching, landing on his chin wound, so that my hand comes away bloodied this time, but at least it covers my blood.

He howls, eyes glazed with pain, and I continue. Slashing, punching, threatening to head butt, and Halfdan steps back, once, twice, and then more and more, so that his warriors are forced to part ways to allow him through as he almost runs away. He's nearly back inside the ruin of the steading he sheltered within.

The chanting of his warriors intensifies, and while I think I've done a good job of revealing his weaknesses, he's suddenly running at me, weapons out of control. Slashing, hacking, and now I'm the one moving back to avoid the attack.

And my foot catches on something, and my arms spiral around me. The air leaves my body, and I'm down on the floor, the wet snow and warm blood seeping into my clothes as my chin bounces on my chest. For a frantic moment, I can see two of everything.

I hear a collective gasp from my warriors, well, all apart from Icel.

"Get up, get up," he rails, and I think he's crazy this time, but I stay low, listening to Halfdan's cackle as he threatens me with seax and war axe. He thinks his actions keep me on the ground, but they don't. I've seen what tripped me—my damn seax. I reach for it, eyes on Halfdan, not my blade, and I crush it, unheeding that it's landed upside down and blood pools between my fingers.

Halfdan aims a swipe at my head. I duck even lower, scurrying forwards in the snow so that I rear up behind him, fully armed once more, despite the two injuries I now carry.

I jump high, reach for his sword with my seax hand, and just about get my fingers to it before he turns, anger on his face. The sword is loose, though, and it tumbles to the floor, out of my reach, and more importantly, out of his.

His war axe looms at me, coming for my throat, my chest, my belly, each swipe just about missing me as I dodge every attack, trying to insert my war axe between his and mine. I thrust it in the air, catch it lower down the wide wooden handle, forcing the bottom of the war axe into his face.

Halfdan's eyes blank, just for a moment. I'm rushing around him, eyes keen for the prize of his sword, half-buried in the snow, but before I can get my hand to it, I feel the unmissable ache of cold iron at my throat, and I still, hand reaching, war axe facing down.

The bite of the iron comes ever closer, the reminder of my last injury making it difficult to swallow or breathe or consider moving.

Fuck, the bastard has me. He'll kill me, here and now, even though I'm fully armed, and his sword is within reach.

Silence reverberates, not even Icel offering his advice. I close my eyes, picture my Aunt's look of horror, the anger on Edmund's face, and the dismay that Pybba will wear.

This is it.

I thought to die before, protecting my warriors, protecting Mercia. But now it seems Jarl Halfdan is to have the last bastard word after all.

CHAPTER 25

"**G**et low," Icel's voice is louder than thunder, my limbs almost doing as he demands.

Only then I don't. Instead, I press on that fucking blade, hands questing for the sword. I know what it feels like to have my neck ripped open. But I know something else as well, and I doubt many do. Whether Icel does or not, I'll have to ask him later.

For now, I press on the seax, Halfdan's hand shaking with the effort. I meet his eyes evenly, no hint of fear in mine, while his glow with triumph. Daft cunt.

I feel the skin start to give, but still, he makes no motion to cut me or to move it aside, and my hand, slick though it is, is almost on the hilt.

Jarl Halfdan's warriors' jeer and catcall, the air rife with the cries of triumph, of the promise of death for my small force.

Stupid bastards.

My fingers reach the hilt, but slick from it, my glove saturated with blood. I growl, the sound bringing my throat even closer to Jarl Halfdan's blade.

He crows. I can't call it anything else. Rather than finishing the job, he shrieks with triumph, and I finally make a firm connection, hold the hilt tight. It lifts from the ground without so much as a slither of sound. I force it behind my back, even though my arm protests at the unfamiliar action. I close my eyes, consider Halfdan's posture. Only then do I jab the sword across my back, giving it an extra stabbing action as it pierces byrnie and then flesh.

And then I force it even deeper, the satisfaction of knowing it's another man's blood that streams over my back, another man's piss that pollutes the snow, allowing me to enjoy the moment.

His seax hand falters, coming closer, the grip tighter and tighter. I'm wedged between seax and blade, but Halfdan is cut and bleeding. I'm not wounded anywhere near as badly as he is.

The jeering falters once more, falling away, silence filling the air again, all apart from Edmund.

"Get the fuck on with it," he rants, and I smirk. He has no patience. None at all.

I wrap my remaining hand around my enemy's leg, able to grip the seax Jarl Halfdan holds at my throat, overlaying his hold with my hand. I can feel the shaking in his hand coursing through his body. I can feel it down his legs as well.

But I'm still trapped. For now.

I thrust my elbow upwards, but there's not enough room to land the blow on his stones.

"My Lord King," Edmund's voice once more. "We haven't got all fucking day."

If he means to anger me, he's going about it the wrong way.

I try and reverse my grip on the sword, thinking to pull it clear to enable me to stand, but my hand won't cooperate. It's weak from being in that position for too long. And the seax blade wavers once more.

I don't think Edmund truly appreciates my predicament. The damn bastard. I can hear something tapping with impatience, no doubt his seax on his war axe. I close my eyes, try and see my position as though I'm a bird far overhead. But it's no help. All I can see is the sword over my back, not the problem at my throat.

Only Jarl Halfdan staggers, the leg I encircle with my arm remaining firm, but the other one moves away from me. Finally, I have some room with which to play.

I force his hand away from my throat, even though he still holds the seax. I stab into his thigh, feeling the bones in his wrist crack at the unnatural movement. I'm finally able to duck low beneath the sword that sticks from his belly, the seax now in his thigh. I stand, note his face is bleached of all colour, lips faintly blue.

I nod at him, one warrior to another, sucking in a breath.

"You fucking lose, Jarl Halfdan. You fucking lose," and my warriors rush the Raiders, and Jarl Halfdan is immobile. He can do nothing but watch, and bleed, and fucking die.

Icel, Hereman, Edmund, Rudolf, Pybba, Sæbald and Lyfing, reach the enemy first. They kill without thought, without anger, with just the right amount of detachment to ensure everyone is fucking dead.

I nod at the rest of my warriors, the Mercians from inside Gainsborough included, as I feel my throat, aware of the trickle of blood, of the healed wound, forced opened at the right side of my neck. I remove my glove, the hand appearing reddened and not white, the stickiness of the blood making me wish I'd kept the covering on and not forced it clear.

My legs shake, my arms as well. I glance at Halfdan once more. His sword still protrudes from his belly, but at an angle, the hilt too heavy to stay upright, pulling at him, making the cut an agony.

"That's got to hurt like a bastard," I offer, but I'm reaching for my seax, now I can see it, my focus on the Raiders. I bend to check on Wærwulf, pleased to feel his chest rising and falling beneath my whole hand, even if he's unconscious. I turn his head, make sure he can breathe while I'm away.

These Raider bastards should never have followed Jarl Halfdan. And I'm about to show them just how deeply they're going to regret their actions.

"For Mercia," I roar, pleased my voice is firm.

"For Mercia," echoes back to me, and I confess, a grin touches my cheeks as I dance into the Raiders still determined to fight.

They really should have fucking run away.

Historical Notes

The Anglo-Saxon Chronicle makes no mention of affairs in Mercia in AD875. It mentions only what is happening in Wessex, with a passing reference to Northumbria. This is to be expected. The Anglo-Saxon Chronicle was a Wessex invention, under King Alfred, begun in the 890s. Whether it was intended to whitewash events in Mercia or not, must be debated. Certainly, it had a Wessex bias, and this needs to be remembered when considering the value of it for events throughout all of England.

Still, this silence speaks more loudly than any information offered. Something was afoot, and this is my attempt to offer some sort of accounting for Mercia. It is entirely fictional.

My decision to take the Raiders to Gainsborough is based on the fact that King Swein of Denmark made it his base when attacking England in the early 1000's and that King Cnut, his son, also used Gainsborough in the same way.

As I've said elsewhere, I've not been able to determine where the ealdormen mentioned in the charters that King Coelwulf witnessed were based in Mercia. I have simply guessed, and it is probably wrong, but there's not enough information to say either way. I would rather use the proper names, and get the places wrong, than make it entirely fictitious.

I wrote this book during the snow storms in early 2021, when

I went out walking every day, no matter the weather. A stag did erupt from the woodlands to startle me.

The story of Coelwulf and his warriors is far from done.

CAST OF CHARACTERS

Coelwulf's Warriors

Ælfgar – one of the older members of the warband
Athelstan – killed in the first battle in The Last King
Beornberht – killed in the first battle in The Last King
Beornstan
Coelwulf – King of Mercia, rides **Haden**
Edmund – rides **Jethson**, was Coelwulf's brother's man until his death. Brother is Hereman.
Eadberht
Eadulf
Eahric
Eoppa – rides **Poppy**, dies in The Last Horse
Gardulf – first appears in The Last Horse – Edmund's son
Goda
Gyrth
Hereman – brother of Edmund, rides **Billy**
Hereberht – dies at Torksey, in The Last Warrior.
Hiltiberht - squire
Ingwald
Icel – rides **Samson**
Leonath – first appears in The Last Horse
Lyfing – wounded in The Last King
Oda
Ordheah
Ordlaf
Oslac
Penda – first appears in The Last Horse – Pybba's grandson

Pybba – loses his hand in battle, rides **Brimman** (Sailor in Old English)

Rudolf – youngest warrior, was a squire at the beginning of The Last King, rides **Dever**

Siric – first appears in The Last Horse

Sæbald – injured in The Last King, but returns to action in The Last Horse

Tatberht – first appears in The Last Horse, normally remains at Kingsholm. Rides **Wombel**

Wærwulf – speaks Danish, rides **Cinder**

Wulfstan

Wulfhere – a squire, grandson of Tatberht, rides **Stilton**

Wulfred – rides **Cuthbert**

The Mercians

Bishop Wærferth of Worcester

Bishop Deorlaf of Hereford

Bishop Eadberht of Lichfield

Bishop Smithwulf of London

Bishop Ceobred of Leicester

Bishop Burgheard of Lindsey

Ealdorman Beorhtnoth – of western Mercia

Ealdorman Ælhun – of area around Warwick

Ealdorman Alhferht - of western Mercia

Ealdorman Æthelwold – his father Ealdorman Æthelwulf dies at the Battle of Berkshire in AD871

Ealdorman Wulfstan – dies in The Last King

      His son – (fictional) dies in The Last King

      Werburg – his daughter

Ealdorman Beornheard – of eastern Mercia

Ealdorman Aldred – of eastern Mercia

Lady Cyneswith – Coelwulf's (fictional)Aunt

Raiders

Ivarr – dies in AD870

Halfdan – brother of Ivarr, may take his place after his death
Guthrum - one of the three leaders at Repton with Halfdan
      His sister
Oscetel - one of the three leaders at Repton with Halfdan
Anwend – one of the three leaders at Repton with Halfdan
      Anwend Anwendsson – his fictional son
Sigurd (fictional
Olafr (fictional)
Estrith (fictional)

The royal family of Mercia

King Burgred of Mercia
    m. **Lady Æthelswith** in AD853 (the sister of King Alfred)
    they had no children
Beornwald – a fictional nephew for King Burgred
King Wiglaf – ninth century ruler of Mercia
King Wigstan- ninth century ruler of Mercia
King Beorhtwulf – ninth century ruler of Mercia

Misc

Cadell ap Merfyn – fictional brother of Rhodri Mawr, King of Gwynedd (one of the Welsh kingdoms)
Coenwulf – Coelwulf's dead (older) brother
Wiglaf and Berhtwulf – the names of Coelwulf's aunt's dogs, Lady Cyneswith
Wulfsige – commander of Ealdorman Ælhun's warriors
Kyred – oathsworn man of Bishop Wærferth of Worcester
Turhtredus – Mercian warrior
Eanulf – Mercian warrior
Beornfyhrt - Mercian warrior
Heahstan - Mercian warrior
Denewulf and Eahlferth – inhabitants of Newark

Places Mentioned

London – more strictly Lundenwic and Londinium at this

time
    Gainsborough, in north-east Mercia.

    Northampton, on the River Nene in Mercia.

    Grantabridge/Cambridge, in eastern Mercia/East Anglia

    Gloucester, on the River Severn, in western Mercia.

    Worcester, on the River Severn, in western Mercia.

    Hereford, close to the border with Wales

    Lichfield, an ancient diocese of Mercia. Now in Staffordshire.

    Tamworth, an ancient capital of Mercia. Now in Staffordshire.

    Repton, an ancient capital of Mercia. St Wystan's was a royal mausoleum.

    Gwent, one of the Welsh kingdoms at this period.

    Warwick, in Mercia.

Torksey, in the ancient kingdom of Lindsey, which became part of Northern Mercia

Passenham, in Mercia

River Severn, in the west of England

River Trent, runs through Staffordshire, Derbyshire, Nottingham and Lincolnshire and joins the Humber

River Avon, in Warwickshire

River Thames, runs through London and into Oxfordshir

River Stour, runs from Stourport to Wolverhampton

River Ouse, leads into the Cam/Granta, runs through Bedford (Bed's Ford)

River Nene, runs from Northampton to the Wash

River Welland, runs from Northamptonshire to the Was

River Granta/Cam, runs from Cambridge to King's Lynn (East Anglia)

River Great Ouse, running from South Northamptonshire to East Anglia

Kingsholm, close to Gloucester, an ancient royal site

The Foss Way, ancient roadway running from Lincoln to Exeter

Watling Street, ancient roadway running from Chester to London

Icknield Way, ancient roadway running from Norfolk to Wilt-

shire
Ermine Street, ancient roadway running from London to Lincoln, and York.

MEET THE AUTHOR

I'm an author of fantasy (viking age/dragon themed) and historical fiction (Early English, Vikings and the British Isles as a whole before the Norman Conquest), born in the old Mercian kingdom at some point since AD1066. I write A LOT. You've been warned! Find me at mjporterauthor.com, mjporterauthor.blog and @coloursofunison on twitter. I have a newsletter, which can be joined via my website.

Books by M J Porter (in chronological order)

Gods and Kings Series (seventh century Britain)
Pagan Warrior (audio book coming soon)
Pagan King
Warrior King

The Ninth Century
The Last King (audio book now available)
The Last Warrior (audio book coming soon)
The Last Horse
The Last Enemy
The Last Sword

The Tenth Century
The Lady of Mercia's Daughter
A Conspiracy of Kings (the sequel to The Lady of Mercia's Daughter)

Kingmaker
The King's Daughter

Chronicles of the English (tenth century Britain)
Brunanburh
Of Kings and Half-Kings
The Second English King

The Mercian Brexit (can be read as a prequel to The First Queen of England)

The First Queen of England (The story of Lady Elfrida) (tenth century England)
The First Queen of England Part 2
The First Queen of England Part 3

The King's Mother (The continuing story of Lady Elfrida)
The Queen Dowager
Once A Queen

The Earls of Mercia
The Earl of Mercia's Father
The Danish King's Enemy
Swein: The Danish King (side story)
Northman Part 1
Northman Part 2
Cnut: The Conqueror (full length side story)
Wulfstan: An Anglo-Saxon Thegn (side story)
The King's Earl
The Earl of Mercia
The English Earl
The Earl's King
Viking King
The English King

Lady Estrid (a novel of eleventh century Denmark)

Fantasy

<u>The Dragon of Unison</u>
Hidden Dragon
Dragon Gone
Dragon Alone
Dragon Ally
Dragon Lost
Dragon Bond

Throne of Ash (coming soon)

As JE Porter

The Innkeeper

Mystery

The Custard Corpses – a delicious 1940s mystery

Printed in Great Britain
by Amazon

41081908R00165